FLYING WITH THE ANGELS

FLYING WITH THE ANGELS

by

Victor Pemberton

Magna Large Print Books
Long Preston, North Yorkshire,
BD23 4ND, England.

British Library Cataloguing in Publication Data.

Pemberton, Victor
Flying with the Angels.

A catalogue record of this book is
available from the British Library

ISBN 0-7505-2117-1

First published in Great Britain 2003 by Headline Book Publishing

Copyright © 2003 Victor Pemberton

Cover illustration © Mark Vinney by arrangement with
P.W.A. International

The right of Victor Pemberton to be identified as the author of this work has been asserted by him in accordance with the Copyright, Designs and Patents Act, 1988

Published in Large Print 2003 by arrangement with
Headline Book Publishing Ltd.

Magna Large Print is an imprint of Library Magna Books Ltd.

Printed and bound in Great Britain by
T.J. (International) Ltd., Cornwall, PL28 8RW

For the Roberts family
Julia, Mike, Josh and Zach

who flew with the angels
and made a happy landing

Prologue

1982

Toowoomba was a long way from Islington. Nobody was more constantly aware of that than Lizzie. Although she loved her adopted home, she so often felt a yearning for the old country on the other side of the world, and especially for the family she had left behind there such a long time ago. Oh, she loved Rob. He was probably the kindest person she had ever known in her entire life, and she was the luckiest woman alive to be married to him. And she loved her kids too – though they were no longer kids but young adults who had drifted off and done well for themselves. But deep down inside, Lizzie was still very much an Angel – one of the much-loved family. She always had been, and always would be.

Lizzie was up early that morning. In fact, she hadn't really slept much the previous night; too much on her mind, too much to look forward to. Not so with Rob. He had snored his head off from the moment it touched the pillow. He hadn't even woken at the first rays of the sun, which had burst through the partly drawn curtains and flooded the bedroom with a triumphant riot of gold. But then, the poor man was whacked out; helping Lizzie get the place ready for their special visitor had taken its toll on him. After all, he was only a few years off

11

retirement, and despite the fact that he looked much younger than his age, his days of playing cricket for the Toowoomba eleven were now well and truly in the past.

'If you think you're going to lie there all day like a ruddy duke, Mr Thompson,' Lizzie said, in a mock Australian accent, which had significantly failed to smother her native north London upbringing, 'you've got another think coming!'

Rob only stirred when Lizzie leaned down and kissed him gently on his gradually balding pate, which she found so sensual.

'What's all the rush?' he said, straining to open his eyes in the piercing sun, his rasping accent completely betraying his own middle-class Islington origins after nearly thirty-five years away from 'the old country'. 'Fer Chrissake, Liz, she's not due till two o'clock this afternoon.'

'Even so,' insisted Lizzie, nestling down beside him, 'it could take us up to two hours to get to Brisbane. The last thing I want is for her to arrive and find us not there waiting for her.'

'We *won't* be late, Liz,' he sighed. 'I know it's your mum, but you mustn't get so worked up. Everything'll be fine. We'll give her a great time.' Rob pulled gently away and collected the remains of a cigarette he'd abandoned in an ashtray the evening before. 'Y'know, Liz,' he said, shaking his head, 'as long as I live, I'll never understand you and your ma. You used to be such good mates and then – wham! Suddenly it's as though you've never known each other. I mean, you've only ever written to each other a dozen times or so since we came out here.'

12

'Oh Rob,' said Lizzie, in an attempt to justify the rift, 'you know what it was like before we left. Mum never wanted me to come out here, you know she didn't. She did everything in her power to stop me. It was terrible.'

'Then why now?' asked Rob, persisting. 'If you still feel that way, why ask her out here now after all these years?'

'Don't be so stupid, Rob,' she said. 'It's only in the last few years that we've had any money to live like we do now. It was a struggle from the moment we got out here, you know it was. We could never have afforded to bring Mum out here before now.'

Rob smiled knowingly at her. 'Come off it, Liz,' he said, affectionately. 'That's not entirely true, is it? If you'd wanted to see her, you could have brought her over any time. For that matter, we could've gone over there on a visit ourselves. But every time I've mentioned it, you've always found a reason why it wouldn't be a good idea.'

Lizzie found it difficult to find an answer. It was true that she had avoided going back home and she had resisted the urge to bring her mum over to Australia before now, even though during the past ten years or so they could have afforded to do so. But why? Surely her mum had shown that she had forgiven her for leaving the family during that bleak winter in 1947 and had written Lizzie a touching farewell note.

Theirs had always been such a close and loving relationship. During those early years at home, Harriet Angel had come to rely so much on her eldest daughter. Lizzie was the one she could

13

trust, could really confide in. If ever there was a crisis that she couldn't resolve herself, it was always Lizzie she turned to and not her husband Frank. She absolutely idolised Lizzie, and Lizzie loved her too, loved the thought that her mum was someone she could talk to or turn to when she had a problem of her own. So what *was* it that had kept Lizzie and her mother apart for so long? Whose fault was it? Who was to blame? After all, she had never meant to hurt her mum, never meant to break her heart. But at the time, leaving home, leaving loved ones behind, seemed to be the most sensible thing in the world to do. Her dad, Frank, had known that; he had agreed wholeheartedly with Lizzie's decision. In fact, if he had had his way, he would have taken his entire family away from that hellish winter and all the misery of life in post-war England.

Lizzie had never regretted her decision to come out to Australia with Rob. He was her man, and she had always loved him. If he had asked her to follow him to the ends of the earth, she would have done so. No, life during these past thirty-four years had been good for the Thompson family. They all had good jobs, there were no queues for everything you wanted to buy, no dull grey skies day in and day out, no hollow calls from politicians to endure endless days of hardship and austerity. Despite the difficulties of starting a new life in a foreign land, it had all been worthwhile. No. The reason the two women had made an unconscious decision to keep apart all those years was because of Frank, because in the few letters that Harriet had written, she had

14

never told Lizzie the truth about what had really happened to him after she left and why he had died so prematurely. She had never answered any of the questions that Lizzie had asked repeatedly. In fact, it seemed as though the entire family had been keeping something from her, as though there was something they didn't want her to know. And she resented it.

'At least you've seen Susan and Don,' Rob called from the bathroom. 'They didn't seem to resent the fact that we've made a go of it out here.'

Lizzie ignored Rob's remark. She was still bitter that when her younger sister and her husband had come out on a visit a few years back, they too had skilfully avoided answering any of her questions about her dad. 'Susan was always out for a good time,' she called back. 'She only came here because she and Don didn't have to pay for anything more than their fare.'

'That's not a very nice thing to say about your sister,' suggested Rob, peering briefly round the bathroom door, his face covered in shaving foam. 'I thought you were supposed to love your family?'

'I do love them,' insisted Lizzie. 'I've always loved them – Susan, James, Benjamin, Cissie – all of them. But they've never really made much of an effort to keep in touch with me, neither them nor their kids.'

Razor in hand, Rob came out to her. 'You mustn't blame 'em too much, Liz,' he said, smiling, and stroking her hair affectionately. 'We live in a completely different world to what we

15

came from. Take my own lot. If it wasn't for Dad's letters, I'd hardly know that any of them still exist. Time changes people, Liz. They have to live for themselves, for the world they live in – not for strangers on the other side of the world.'

'Strangers?' Lizzie looked at him, puzzled. 'My own family?'

'All I'm saying,' said Rob, 'is that you should never expect too much from your own flesh and blood. That way you don't get disappointed.'

She squealed and pushed him away as he suddenly kissed her on the lips, leaving a large patch of white shaving cream on her face. She chased after him as he made a quick dash back to the bathroom and locked himself in. 'I'll get you for that!' she yelled, wiping the shaving cream off with the back of her hand. She loved her relationship with Rob, the way he teased her, the way he always made her see clearly in difficult situations. She'd had no idea he was going to be such a tower of strength and support to her when she first met him back home in Islington. In fact, it was hard to believe that he was once responsible for nearly killing her. Did it really happen, or was it all a dream? A lifetime away, and yet, it was as though it had happened only yesterday.

As she pulled back the sheets to let the bed air, her eyes fell on the collection of framed photographs on the wall above her. Most of them were of her own kids, Betty and Lou, and their kids, Lizzie's grandchildren. But amongst them was a fading, blown-up snapshot photo of the family she had left behind. Rob was right. As

16

Lizzie looked at them, they *could* almost be strangers. Apart from Susan and Don, she would hardly know what any of them even looked like now – especially her mum. She climbed up on to the bed, and took a closer look. They were all there, the whole Angel family: her mum and dad, Susan, James, Benjamin, and her mum holding baby Cissie. She peered even closer. Her dad had that perpetual, reassuring smile on his face, as if to say, 'Nothing's as bad as you think, Lizzie.' In complete contrast, her mum's face looked pale and drawn, fraught with anxiety. But it was a young, pretty face, steel hard with obstinacy and determination. Is that how she'll look now? Lizzie asked herself. Will I still be able to look her straight in the eyes and say, 'I'm sorry, Mum. I'm sorry for letting you down. I'm sorry for not being there with you when Dad died. I'm sorry not to have been the daughter you trusted so much.'

In just a few hours, Lizzie would know the answer to the question that had troubled her for so many years.

Harriet Angel was wide awake. Despite the endless hours cooped up in an airliner as it made its laborious way across the skies of the world, she had hardly slept at all. Part of the reason for this was, of course, the sheer terror of having her feet off the ground for the first time in her life, an ominous feeling that it was impossible for those massive wings to keep such a giant machine up in the air for so long. But there was another reason, and it had been consuming her mind ever since

17

Sue, Jimmy, and Ben had seen her off at Heathrow Airport what now seemed like an eternity ago. Her thoughts were not on how she was ever going to know how to change planes at Sydney, or why she had refused to allow Lizzie and Rob to come down all the way from Brisbane to meet her, but how she would react when she saw her eldest daughter for the first time in thirty-four years.

'Can yer see Oz yet?'

The strong Australian accent coming from the young teenage girl in the seat next to her, jolted her from her thoughts.

'No,' said Harriet. 'It's too dark.'

'Won't be fer much longer,' said the girl, who was so lithe she was able to sit cross-legged on her seat. 'Sun'll be comin' up any minute. Then yer'll get a great glimpse of some of the best beaches in the whole damned world! Provided there're no clouds around, of course!'

Harriet smiled back at her. She was a pleasant enough girl, but ever since she'd woken up after sleeping all the way from Singapore, she had been a real fidget. By the time they had even crossed the English Channel, Harriet had heard the girl's entire life story.

'Are you looking forward to seeing your parents again?' she asked.

'Me?' replied the girl. She was clearly not prepared to be asked such a question. 'In a way, I guess,' she said. 'I probably won't even know them. An' they sure won't know me.'

'But you said you've only been away from home for a year.'

18

The girl slumped her head back in her seat. 'A year's a long time,' she said, with a sigh. 'Well, in my books it is.' She turned to look at Harriet. 'I left home and went to England when I was seventeen. I was underage, of course, but I told my mum and dad that if they tried to stop me, I'd find a way of going and never come back. In the end, they let me do what I wanted. It was a smart thing to do.'

Even in the dim cabin light, Harriet could see the girl had a pretty, elfin-like face, but a jaw that was set and determined.

'Don't you *like* your parents?' Harriet asked tentatively.

'Like them?' the girl replied. 'No, I don't like them. But I do love them. Trouble was, they always wanted me to see things the way they saw them. There were times when I felt so hemmed in, I just couldn't breathe. I told them that I had to find out about life for myself, and I could only do that if I didn't have them holding on to my pigtails all the time.'

As she listened to the girl, Harriet couldn't help but notice the cropped blonde hair, far removed from the pigtails. 'What did they say to that?' she asked.

'Oh, they cried,' said the girl. 'Well, Mum did. Mum always cries. You only have to say "no" and she's off!'

'It can't have been easy for them?' suggested Harriet.

'No,' answered the girl. 'But it wasn't easy for me either. I was shit scared going all that way on my own, arriving in a country that was freezin' cold in every sense of the word. Lucky I soon teamed up with some mates from back home, otherwise I'd probably've ended up on the streets. Thing is, though, I had to prove something – not only ter Mum an' Dad, but ter me too. Of course they don't know yet that I'm only comin' home for a holiday – so it's not going ter be easy. But I've made a good life for myself now in England. After all, everyone has the right to search fer a better life fer themselves if they can. Don't you agree?'

Harriet smiled and nodded awkwardly.

A few minutes later the girl uncurled her feet from her seat. Then she got up, and, immediately waking up the poor man on the other side of her, scuttled off to the toilet at the rear of the cabin for the umpteenth time.

Harriet turned, and tried to peer out through the small cabin window into the strange darkness of the night. Why did it all look so different from back home, she asked herself. After all, dark was dark; every night was much the same as another, unless you could see the stars or the moon or the clouds or whatever was around at the time. But what *was* different about this particular night, was that she was flying through it, high above she knew not where, heading towards a reunion with a daughter and son-in-law that she hadn't seen for what seemed like a lifetime. And as she stared up at the moon, a great full and incandescent white in the night sky, so close that she felt she could almost reach out and touch it, the only words ringing in her ears were of a tearaway Australian teenage girl who, in her own simplistic

20

but endearing way, had given her the confidence to put right what she should have done years ago: '*After all, everyone has the right to search fer a better life fer themselves if they can. Don't you agree?*'

By the time Harriet had nodded off and woken up again, blinding sunlight was streaming through the cabin windows, and down below there were the first clear signs of that vast expanse of land that her daughter loved so much. Quite suddenly, the years seemed to have rolled by.

She and Lizzie had come a long way since that sombre, merciless English winter of 1947.

Chapter 1

It was so cold in London that the River Thames was in danger of freezing over again. No one in their right mind ventured out without being firmly wrapped up against the biting December wind, the ice-cold drizzle, and the relentless early morning frost. The first signs of snow had appeared no more than three weeks after thousands of people had crowded the streets of central London to watch the royal wedding procession of Princess Elizabeth, and although just a light, temporary cover at first, the early snowflakes had given notice of something much more ominous. The winter of 1947 was already showing signs that it was going to be as bad as the previous winter, which had been the worst in living memory and, despite the fact that the war had been over for more than two years, waiting in long queues at shops was still a daily chore – for food, clothes, fuel, and even the smallest luxury, such as pencils and writing pads, which had become almost impossible to obtain. Ration coupons were reviled; they had been in circulation for long enough, and nearly everyone was fed up to the teeth with them, so much so that many people began to wonder why the hell they had fought a war in the first place if victory meant such hardship.

Lizzie tugged at the long thick icicle that, with a

dozen or so more, had formed from the overflow of the gutter along the flat roof of the Angel family's prefab in Andover Road. Her young brothers and sisters squealed with delight as the icicle came away almost immediately in Lizzie's hands, and the younger boy, Benjamin, who was eleven years old, grabbed it from her and brandished it as though it was a sword. His older brother, James, who was fifteen, got the next icicle from his older sister Susan, and he immediately challenged Benjamin to a duel with it.

'Zorro! Zorro!' proclaimed Benjamin, and roared with laughter as they clashed 'swords', breaking them into pieces. Susan glared at them both as though they were nothing more than stupid little boys.

Lizzie cleared the rest of the icicles, then rubbed her hands together to try to get some warmth back into them. 'I bet there'll be just as many tomorrow morning,' she said, shivering with the cold.

'I hope so!' howled Cissie, who was eight, and the youngest of the family. 'I hope there are lots and lots of them!'

'Oh, don't be so silly, Priscilla!' rebuked Susan, who always tried to give the impression that she was older and more sophisticated than her eighteen years. 'If it gets any colder, we'll all freeze to death in this stupid house. We're never going to get any more coal for the fire, never!'

'I'm sure Dad will bring some home with him when he comes,' said Lizzie reassuringly. 'He said he was going to try and get a bag from that coal merchants up Hornsey Road. I just hope he'll be able to carry it all that way.'

'He said exactly the same thing last week,' replied Susan snootily. 'And what happened? He came home empty-handed – as usual. He's absolutely useless.'

Lizzie didn't like to hear her sister talking about their father in such a dismissive way. Lizzie was twenty years old, the eldest child in the family, and she loved both her father and mother very much. It annoyed her to hear them run down by her younger sister, who would never think of soiling her own precious hands to help out with some of the housework. 'You shouldn't talk about Dad like that, Susie,' she said firmly. 'He does his best, walking the streets day after day looking for fuel to heat the house. But if there isn't any, what can he do about it?'

Susan sniffed haughtily, and pulled her coat collar up around her neck. 'My friend Jane Hetherington's house has always got a huge fire burning in their living room,' she said grandly. '*Her* father and mother would never let their family go cold.'

'Jane Hetherington's a stuffy old cow!' barked James provocatively. 'She used to smoke Craven A fags in the girls' lav at school.'

Lizzie stifled a laugh, but the others didn't.

Susan was outraged. 'Don't you dare talk about my friends like that!' she snapped, eyes blazing. 'Jane Hetherington has more manners than all the lot of you put together!'

'She's an ugly old cow!' insisted Benjamin, whose favourite hobby was to mock his snooty sister.

24

This was more than Susan could take. Shooting her brother an icy glare, she took a swipe at him with her right hand. But Benjamin was too quick for her, ducked, and rushed off round the back of the house. To gales of laughter from the others, Susan chased after him, followed by Cissie.

Thoroughly amused, Lizzie watched them go, and for a moment or so she just stood there listening to the squeals and shouts as Susan ran out on to the nearby bomb site in hot pursuit of Benjamin.

Once they were out of earshot, Lizzie ambled across to the front gate. It was only a small garden, and now it was barren and bleak, with the dead blooms of some of the summer roses lying withered and frozen on the rock-hard soil of the narrow garden beds. Nevertheless, Lizzie loved the place because it was home to her and all the Angel family. She stopped at the gate, and turned to look back at the small prefabricated house. Her face broke into a faint, affectionate smile. They were lucky to live there, she told herself, her eyes scanning the bungalow-style building, which was virtually no more than a large metal hut, with most of the panels made from asbestos. It wasn't much, but at least the family didn't have to live in squalor like so many other people who had been bombed out of their homes during the war. They had somewhere dry to sleep and eat, and if it wasn't for the acute shortage of fuel, the house would also be snug and warm.

Then she thought about her mum and dad, and how they had struggled to bring up their family on what was little more than a pittance. Lizzie knew only too well how defeated her dad felt about not being able to provide for the family in the way he had always done before he was called up. But it wasn't *his* fault that his well-paid job as a department manager at the North London Drapery Stores wasn't waiting for him when he got back home from the war. It wasn't *his* fault that, while his family were taking cover in a public air-raid shelter towards the end of the war, their home had been demolished by a flying bomb. Over the past few years, life had been cruel to so many people like her dad, and there was no doubt that the tragic turn of events had crushed Frank Angel's pride in his ability to provide for the family he loved so much. But Lizzie was proud of the way her dad had accepted fate, and no matter how much he hated the job he had had to take as a fish-gutter in Billingsgate Market, he was at least bringing home a few pounds a week to keep the family going.

Lizzie sighed. Thank God for Mum, she thought, the way she supported her husband, making him feel that everything he did was special and important. Harriet really was an Angel, in every sense of the word.

All around Lizzie church bells began the call to Sunday morning service. Her face lit up as she listened; it was so uplifting to hear those beautiful sounds again that had been so sadly missing from life during the war years.

'Reckon a gel like you oughta be in church on a Sunday mornin'.'

Lizzie swung round to find Andy Willets talking to her from the other side of the gate. 'You can talk!' she returned light-heartedly, but quick as a flash. 'If anyone needs to go to church it's you!'

Andy grinned. Despite the fact that the Angel family were a cut above his own station in life, he liked Lizzie. He liked her a lot. She had a strong sense of humour, and was always good for a laugh. He also fancied her like mad, but he knew that was a lost cause, for he was not only a couple of years younger, and shorter in height than she, but he had red hair, and Lizzie didn't like redheads: he could tell.

'I don't like Sundays,' he said. 'Never 'ave. People eivver sit round reading newspapers, or listen ter the wireless all day. Once yer've 'eard *Family Favourites* from nine ter twelve, 'alf the ruddy day's gone.'

Lizzie did have quite a soft spot for Andy. He always had a cheeky expression on that round face of his, and she knew how shy he was about his red hair and freckles. 'You could always go for a walk in the park,' she said. 'It's lovely there on Sunday mornings.'

'I would – if you'd come wiv me,' replied Andy quite shamelessly.

Lizzie grinned. 'Don't be so silly, Andy,' she said, self-consciously tucking her long brown hair beneath the hood of her coat. 'You're very popular with the girls. I know plenty who'd love to go for a walk with you.'

'Yer don't 'ave ter make excuses ter me, Liz Angel,' replied Andy, taking a puff of the fag end he had lit earlier. 'I know your bloke'd bash the daylights out er me if I tried ter muscle in on 'is gel.'

'Now you *are* being silly, Andy,' said Lizzie. 'Rob isn't like that. He's decent, and – well-mannered.'

'An' I'm not. Is that it?'

Andy's response disturbed Lizzie. Despite his rough exterior, Andy had a soft centre, and she would never do anything to hurt him. 'You're not only decent, Andy,' she said, 'you're a diamond.'

He came straight back at her. 'Diamonds cost money,' he said. 'I come cheap.'

She gave him an affectionate smile. 'I've got to go and help Mum get lunch.' She turned to go.

'I don't blame yer,' said Andy. 'I mean, people 'ave ter stick ter their own kind. It's only right.'

Lizzie threw him a passing farewell smile as she moved off.

'Mind you,' continued Andy, calling after her, 'if anyfin' should 'appen to 'im, fings could change – couldn't they?'

Lizzie came to a halt and swung him an irritated look. 'If anything should happen to him?' she asked. 'What exactly do you mean by that, Andy?'

Andy took a quick pull on his fag. 'Well, let's face it, the way fings are these days, it ain't always easy ter 'ang on ter yer job – is it?'

Lizzie stared at him for a moment. She couldn't make out whether he was being mischievous, or trying to tell her something. 'Andy,' she said, her friendly smile gone, 'do you know something I don't?'

Andy shook his head vigorously. 'Nah, nuffin'

like that.'

'Then why did you say it?' insisted Lizzie. Staring directly at Andy, she could see the tip of his nose was now a bright red in the biting cold, and the dog-end between his lips was already so small that it was in danger of burning him. 'Rob has a good job in that car salesroom up in the New North Road. He says that when things get better in the country, cars are going to be the thing of the future.'

Andy was sceptical. 'Cars are a luxury, Liz,' he said with a grin. He took the dog-end out of his mouth and threw it down on to the pavement. 'People spend cash on food – when they can get it – not on cars.'

'Look, Andy,' said Lizzie, 'I don't know what you're trying to say, but–'

'I'm not trying ter say *anyfin*', Liz,' insisted Andy, shrugging his shoulders innocently. 'All I'm sayin' is that fings don't always go the way yer want 'em. I mean, look at me. I've bin 'angin' round that Labour Exchange every day since the end er the war, an' the only job I've ever got is cleanin' windows two or free days er week. The only reason I brought up the subject was 'cos I've seen Rob 'angin' round the Lane so many times when I've been up there.'

Lizzie did a double take. 'The Lane?' she asked tentatively.

'Petticoat Lane,' said Andy. 'I sometimes get some work from Micky Fitch's jumble stall.'

Lizzie was now beginning to feel not only curious, but also anxious. 'And you've seen Rob up there – during the week?'

'Loads er times,' said Andy. 'I don't s'ppose there's anyfin' to it. 'E probably 'as some business up there in that car showroom.' He now felt guilty. 'Nah – nuffin' to it,' he said. 'Just tell me ter mind me own bleedin' business. There's nuffin' wrong with yer Rob. I'm just jealous, that's all. I should be so lucky ter get a gel like you. See yer then.' He turned up the collar of his jacket, put his hands under his arms to warm them up, and disappeared down the road.

Lizzie turned from the gate and made her way back into the house. But she stopped briefly to take a look over her shoulder at Andy, who was now no more than a distant figure at the end of Andover Road. As she went into the house, she took a swipe at the last remaining icicle clinging to the roof gutter. It came down with a crash, and broke into pieces on the frozen concrete path.

Sunday lunch was a pretty meagre affair. Although there were two wage earners in the family, their combined pay was so modest it was scarcely enough to cover the rent and daily meals for the family. Without Lizzie's job at Woolworths in Holloway Road, things would be worse, but it was a source of constant despair to Frank Angel that his daughter was earning more than he in his fish-gutter's job at Billingsgate Market. None the less, Lizzie's mum, Harriet, always made the most out of what money was coming in, and, like today, she made sure that she kept the best until Sunday, when she was able to splash out on a bit of scrag end of lamb, which she had roasted, some dried garden peas, and a few of the carrots and onions she had grown in the back garden during the summer months, and bottled in preserving jars. There was also some shredded white cabbage, which Harriet had steamed and then fried in some of the fat from the lamb. Unfortunately, there was none of the family's favourite, roast potatoes, this week, for there was now an acute shortage of potatoes everywhere, with people queuing each day at greengrocers' shops all over London. The Angel children's greatest quality was that they never complained about their hardships, for they knew that their mother did her best to keep their stomachs full, and always managed to make the most basic of food look as if it was a banquet fit for the King and Queen.

The one thing that no one could do anything about, however, was the cold, and, as usual, Susan had no hesitation in her own mind about who was to blame for that.

'I don't understand it,' she said, her mouth full of cabbage. 'Some people must have coal. I mean, when I walk home from the polytechnic in the evenings, there's smoke coming out of chimneys all the way.'

Frank shook his head glumly. 'They're lucky people,' he said. 'I've walked the streets trying to find where they get it from. And even when I do, they've sold out even before I get there.'

'You can get it on the black market,' insisted Susan.

'You need money for that, Susan,' said Lizzie, sitting opposite her sister at the dining table. 'They charge three times the cost of everything.'

'Well, it's worth it to keep warm!' replied Susan quite shamelessly.

'Since you've decided to go on to the polytechnic,' said Lizzie, acutely aware how tired her dad was looking after his early morning shift, 'I don't think you can talk about using up the little bit of money that Dad and I have to work hard for.'

Susan glared back at her. 'Oh, I'm *so* sorry,' she said cuttingly. 'I was forgetting how much we all rely on your vast wage packet from Woolworths!'

Harriet was proud of her eldest daughter for resisting the temptation to snap back at Susan. But as she looked at her family sitting around the table in the middle of the prefabricated living room, she knew how they were suffering. A few pieces of wood in the small fireplace from the bomb site at the back of the house were hardly enough to keep the place warm, and it broke her heart to see them all sitting around the table wrapped up in their scarves, woollen hats, school caps, and overcoats, eating the sparse Sunday lunch.

It was easy to see that Lizzie had inherited her looks from her mother, for Harriet had the same shape of face, and wavy auburn-coloured hair as her daughter. The only difference was that Harriet's once pretty looks had weathered with time and the constant worry of looking after her family. She was a softly spoken woman, who concealed her strong will and self-determination.

'I think the best thing we can do is to try and get some paraffin from Stone's,' she said. 'At least we can keep your two bedrooms warm during the night.'

Lizzie was having none of it. As it was, her mum and dad were sleeping in a bedroom that was so small, there was hardly room for them to get out of bed in the mornings. 'I think you and Dad should have one of the paraffin stoves,' she said firmly. 'Why should you be the ones to sleep in the freezing cold?'

'We're not cold at night, are we, dear?' replied Harriet, addressing her comment across the table to Frank.

Frank mustered a laboured smile. ''Course not,' he said, not very reassuringly.

'Once we snuggle up under the bedclothes,' continued Harriet, 'we don't notice how cold it is, do we, dear?'

Frank nodded.

Lizzie didn't believe a word her mum had said. All their lives Harriet and Frank had made the most tremendous sacrifices for their kids, and this was clearly no exception.

'What difference does it make?' said Susan. 'You won't get any paraffin out of that old skinflint Stone. There's always a queue outside his shop, and even when he gets some in, he charges over the top for it.'

'I don't think that's fair, Susan,' said Harriet. 'Like everyone else, Mr Stone must find it terribly difficult to cope with shortages of just about everything.'

Susan sniffed dismissively, and continued idly chasing a piece of carrot around her plate.

'Anyway,' said Harriet, quickly changing the

subject, 'what's on the programme tonight?'

Benjamin was the first to speak up. 'I'm doing Al Jolson,' he announced jubilantly. 'And James's doing Bing Crosby.'

'Twerp!' snapped James, slapping his brother on the back of his head. 'You weren't s'pposed to say!'

'What does it matter?' complained Benjamin angrily, giving his big brother a dig in his ribs. 'It's not *Variety Bandbox!*'

'We never tell what we're going to do in our Sunday shows till we do it!' growled James, who immediately engaged in a wresting match at the table with his brother.

Harriet leaned over and tried to separate the two of them. 'That's enough now!'

Across the table, young Cissie was jumping up and down in her seat, laughing excitedly, clapping her hands, and thoroughly enjoying her two brothers going at each other hammer and tongs.

'Frank!' begged Harriet. 'Talk to them.'

Frank put down his knife and fork. 'James! Benjamin!'

The moment they heard their father's voice, the boys separated. One word or look from Frank was enough to tell them that the longer they fooled around at the table, the more they were playing with fire. Frank was no disciplinarian, but despite his feelings of incompetence, he was determined that his children would grow up to treat both him and their mother with respect. 'I don't want to hear another word,' he said firmly. 'Now get on with your lunch.'

James and Benjamin duly obeyed. They knew only too well how unwise it would be to push their luck too far.

Harriet waited briefly for the boys to settle down, and then turned to Lizzie. 'What about you, darling?' she asked. 'Who are *you* going to be tonight?'

Lizzie slowly put down her knife and fork, and wiped her lips on her handkerchief. She knew this question would be coming up sooner or later, and she was dreading it. The 'show' the family put on every Sunday evening had been going on since the kids were little. She knew only too well how her parents looked forward to it. What made matters worse was that she, Lizzie, was always the 'star' attraction, doing impersonations of film stars, and singers, and all sorts of people who made the news. Harriet, in particular, always looked to Lizzie to be the life and soul of the party, and it was a hard expectation for her to live up to.

'If you don't mind, Mum,' she said hesitatingly, 'I won't do anything tonight.'

There were groans from everyone around the table, as Harriet swung a worried look first at Frank, then back to Lizzie. 'Lizzie!' she said incredulously. 'What's wrong? Don't you feel well?'

Lizzie smiled back bravely. 'No,' she said, trying to make light of it, 'I'm perfectly well. It's just that I don't really feel up to it.'

Again Harriet exchanged a quick look with Frank. 'But – you always do the "show" on Sunday evenings,' she said, turning back to

Lizzie. 'It wouldn't be the same without you.'

'Oh, don't keep going on, Mother!' sighed Susan, thoroughly bored with the conversation. 'What does it matter if we don't have a "show"? I've always found them very childish, anyway.'

'Nobody cares what *you* think!' snapped Benjamin. 'You never take part.'

'Thank goodness!' agreed James.

'I'll do it next week,' said Lizzie. 'But not tonight.' She got up from her seat, picked up her plate, and took it out into the kitchen.

Harriet watched her go, then flicked Frank another anxious look.

Lizzie took her empty plate into the kitchen, and left it on the draining board whilst she filled a kettle of water, and took it to the gas stove. As there was a shortage of every type of fuel, the gas supply was only sufficient to produce half-power, and so she knew it would be some time before the kettle boiled for the washing-up. Like everything else in the prefab, the kitchen was small and only just functional. When the family had first moved in, the official excuse for the sparse accommodation provided was that it would only be 'temporary', and that as soon as the situation in the country had improved, the family would be offered something 'more suitable'. But more than two years had passed, and still they had to live in a place where they had nowhere to bath, and with a lavatory that was built in a shed outside in the back garden. She stood at the sink, looked out aimlessly through the small kitchen window, and sighed. What a miserable existence for a family that had known such a better life, she told herself.

'This is not like you, Lizzie.' Her mother, carrying a pile of plates, had come into the room. 'No show on a Sunday evening? What's this all about?'

Lizzie stood to one side to let her mother put down the plates. 'I just don't feel like it tonight,' she said. 'In any case, I haven't thought of anything to do.'

'You wouldn't have to do anything special,' replied Harriet. 'We could all have a singsong. We've got the gramophone.'

For some reason, this brought the first smile to Lizzie's face. 'If I hear Bing Crosby and The Andrews Sisters singing "Don't Fence Me In" once more,' she said, 'I'll go round the bend!'

Harriet put her arm around Lizzie's waist, and gently asked, 'What's it all about, darling?'

Lizzie hesitated for a moment. 'Rob hasn't been going to work,' she said. 'He's been spending a lot of his time up Petticoat Lane.'

Harriet was puzzled. 'Petticoat Lane?'

'Andy Willets says he's seen him up there during the week. There must be something wrong if Rob's not going to work.'

'But I thought Rob had a good job.'

'So did I until this morning. But the more I think about it, the more I remember how these days he never wants to talk about what he does at work, who the people are he works with. He's been in such a funny mood. I mean, you know Rob. He's usually such good fun, always good for a laugh.'

Harriet thought about this. Yes, Rob Thompson

was indeed a lovely boy, happy-go-lucky, just like Lizzie. And she knew only too well how, ever since Rob had come back from his call-up at the end of the war, the two of them had grown closer and closer. There was no doubt about it, Lizzie was in love with the boy, and every time Harriet had seen them together, it looked as though Rob felt the same way about Lizzie. And yet it was a strange feeling for Harriet to know that her eldest daughter had discovered a kind of love that was different from what she had known within her own family. This was Lizzie's first and only boyfriend; she had never had a serious relationship with anyone before, and she had much to learn, much to experience. She had to learn about trust, about being able to trust the man she loved. Not that Harriet had any real concerns about Rob Thompson for, like Lizzie, he came from a good family, whose values were based on trying hard to earn an honest living, and live a decent, respectable life. Harriet had no reason to doubt that he also valued all those things. But what was going on? From what Harriet knew about the boy, he was not one to keep secrets.

'Have you spoken to him about it?' she asked.

'I will do,' said Lizzie. 'He's supposed to be taking me to the pictures tomorrow evening.'

'If you're worried,' suggested Harriet, 'why don't you go round and see him this afternoon? There's no time like the present.'

Lizzie shook her head. 'I don't want him to think that I'm trying to find out everything he does. In any case, there's probably some perfectly good reason why he's not been going in to work.'

Harriet smiled affectionately at her. 'You're probably right,' she said. 'But you might just as well set your mind at ease – don't you think?'

The Thompsons' terraced house in Arthur Road couldn't have been more different from the Angel family's prefab in Andover Road. Set on three floors just a few doors away from Dr Fitzgerald's surgery, like all the other houses in the road it looked as though it had once been part of an elegant Edwardian community, which had been home to the comfortable, but hard-working lower middle class. However, although the road had survived relatively intact during the war years, bomb blast had taken its toll on windows, roof tiles, and exterior stucco, and, with the post-war shortage of paint and building materials, the outward appearance was decidedly shabby.

By the time Lizzie got there, it was already getting dark, and the pavements were icing over again rapidly. Just above her, hundreds of long pointed icicles had formed along the gutter pipes of every house in the terrace, making a glistening fringe. The Thompsons' front garden gate was frozen shut, and it took all of Lizzie's strength to prise it open, but as she looked at the path leading to the front door, it was clear that the few steps she needed to get there were going to be quite perilous, for it was nothing more than a sheet of solid ice. With some trepidation, she approached the front doorstep. Although she thought Rob's parents were absolutely lovely people, she always felt a bit nervous in their company, mainly because she was never sure whether they really approved of her relationship with their son, or whether the warm and friendly welcome they always gave her was only because they didn't want to upset Rob. After all, Rob had only been demobbed from the army for the best part of a year, and the gruelling last year of the war, fighting in France and Germany, had taken its toll on him. As the doorbell hadn't worked since the start of the war, she used the heavy iron door knocker.

As usual, Rob's mother, Sheila Thompson, came to the door and met Lizzie with a huge smile.

'Lizzie, my dear!' she called. 'What a lovely surprise!' She was a large woman, who had a mass of brown curls, and always dressed for comfort, with her heavy woollen cardigan she had knitted herself, and her bright blue carpet slippers, which by her own admittance she had worn since the year dot. 'Come on in, dear!'

Lizzie stepped into the hall. Although the house was cold, it was certainly warmer than the Angels' prefab.

'Can't stay long, Mrs Thompson,' she said. 'Mum wants me back before dark. I just wondered if I could have a few words with Rob.'

'I'm sorry, my dear,' said Mrs Thompson, looking surprised. 'Rob's not at home. I thought he said he was going to see you tonight.'

Lizzie was taken aback. 'To see *me?*'

'Why yes,' replied Mrs Thompson. 'As far as I know, he was going to call on you. I think he's been feeling a bit fed up with himself. He's been mooning around the house all day.' She peered quickly over her shoulder to make sure that her

40

husband couldn't hear her through the half-open door of the living room. 'I don't want to seem nosy, my dear,' she said, lowering her voice, 'but is everything all right between you and Rob?'

Again, Lizzie was taken aback and, for once, was tongue-tied. 'I – I don't know what–'

Mrs Thompson leaned close, and gave Lizzie an affectionate smile. 'It's just that, well, both his dad and I know Rob thinks the world of you. His face only lights up when he's talking about you. But he's – I don't quite know how to say it – unsettled. Yes, that's it. Ever since he got demobbed, he hasn't been able to settle down. Unfortunately, Rob isn't the kind of boy you can offer advice to, or even talk things over with, otherwise we could try to help him. It's a pity, because you and he are so good with each other: you're so alike, so outgoing and happy-go-lucky. But something needs sorting out, and I just hope that you can be the one he'll listen to.'

After Lizzie had left the Thompsons' house, she quickly made her way home down Arthur Road. The journey would take no more than ten minutes or so, for once she had crossed the main Seven Sisters Road, it was a fairly direct route up Hornsey Road. But as she went, the short journey seemed interminable. She was convinced that Rob was in some kind of trouble.

She pulled the hood of her coat over her head, and tied the drawstring tight beneath her chin. What sight there had been of the sun all day was now nothing more than a ribbon of golden glow behind a dark, menacing evening cloud. It was

41

bitterly cold, and her face felt flushed red against the freezing breeze. She moved as fast as her legs would carry her, but the pavements were treacherous, and one false step meant that she would be sprawled out on her face. Mercifully, the street gaslights had already been lit, which helped to lighten a prematurely early evening dark, especially as most shops were unable to afford to keep their lights on in the windows, owing to the high cost and shortage of power. In an attempt to avoid the chilly wind, she kept her head bent firmly down towards the pavement, but no sooner had she reached Hornsey Road Baths when she suddenly came into collision with someone who had been approaching from the opposite direction.

She looked up with a start to find herself immediately engulfed in someone's arms. 'Rob!'

Rob didn't wait a minute. He hugged her, then kissed her firmly on the lips.

'Where've you been?' Lizzie asked, as she pulled away.

'I might ask you the same question,' he replied, his face barely visible under the hood of a navy-blue three-quarter-length duffel coat. 'I went up to your place. Your mum said you'd gone down to Arthur Road to see me.'

'*Your* mum said you'd gone to see *me*.'

Rob smiled mischievously. 'Looks like we can't do without each other.' He kissed her again.

'What's going on, Rob?' Lizzie asked. 'What's the matter?'

Rob's expression changed immediately. He looked quite shifty. 'Wrong?' he asked. 'Because I couldn't wait to see you?'

'We arranged to meet tomorrow night. You know I always stay home on Sunday nights for the family show.'

'Well,' he replied, 'since I happen to love you, and since we're going to be married one of these days, I don't see why you shouldn't miss the odd performance or so. Right?'

Lizzie chuckled back at him, and smiled. 'Right!'

Rob slipped his arm around her waist. 'Let's walk,' he said.

Lizzie shivered. 'But I'm frozen!'

Rob wrapped his arm around her tightly, then hugged her close to keep her warm.

Without asking where they were going, he allowed her to lead them off. They turned round and wandered aimlessly back down Hornsey Road. For several minutes they said nothing. Lizzie leaned her head against his shoulder, and she could feel the warmth of his body. She didn't have to look up at his face to recall what he looked like, for she could see it in her mind's eye, those strong, perfectly formed features, well-defined eyebrows and long eyelashes, and a thick flock of naturally curly brown hair, which looked wonderful even when it wasn't combed, which was fairly frequently. Rob was the sort of boy she felt safe and secure with. Although he had the body of an athlete, he also had a nature that was kind and considerate.

'Something has to be done, Liz.' Rob's words came without prompt. They continued to stroll, but Liz looked up at him. 'Things are going to

43

get worse before they get better.' He looked down at her. It was so cold, condensation was filtering from his mouth like small puffs of cloud. 'I'm sick to death of trying to be someone, when all I get is one job after another that pays a pittance.'

'But you don't have to be anyone other than what you are,' said Lizzie, leaning her head back on his shoulder. Fortunately he was much the same height as herself, and so there was no need for her to stretch. 'I like you the way you are.'

'That's not what I mean,' he replied, with just a touch of irritation. 'I mean, what's the use of trying to earn a decent living, when you can't even afford to ask the girl you love to marry you?'

'Marry?' Lizzie brought them to an abrupt halt. 'Are you asking me to marry you?'

'Of course I am,' he retorted. 'Not now. Not this minute. But eventually. But I just don't know how I'm ever going to be able to afford to ask you.'

'Oh – Rob!' Lizzie slipped her arms around his waist, completely oblivious to the elderly couple who were just passing them, attempting to pick their way nervously along the perilously frozen pavement. 'Is that all? I thought it was something serious.'

Rob was puzzled. 'Serious?' he asked. 'You think I'm not serious about us? You and I have been together since we left school. I've never been with another girl; I've never wanted to.'

'No,' replied Lizzie, moving them on again, and trying to explain. 'What I meant was, is that the reason you've been so down? Because you don't

44

have enough money to ask me to marry you?'

'No,' replied Rob firmly, bringing them to a halt again. 'What I'm saying is that there's no hope in this country – not for anyone. You can't live without money. Without money, there's no future. I don't see the point of working at a job with no prospects.'

Lizzie hesitated. 'Is that why you haven't been going to work?' she asked carefully.

Rob's whole attitude seemed to change. He pulled away, and quickly fumbled around in his duffel-coat pocket for his packet of cigarettes. When he found it, it proved difficult for him to take out a cigarette because his fingers were so cold they just couldn't hold it, but when he finally succeeded, he slipped it between his lips without lighting it. Lizzie watched him anxiously as he took out a box of matches. 'How did you know?' he asked, after he had struggled to light up.

'Andy Willets told me he'd seen you a couple of times – up Petticoat Lane.'

Rob was visibly angry, and for a moment he just looked at the ground and pulled on his cigarette. 'Andy Willets should mind his own bloody business!' he said eventually. With that, he moved on, Lizzie at his side.

'Don't be angry, Rob,' she pleaded, clearly aware that she had hit a raw spot with him. 'I was just worried that something might have happened at work to upset you.'

'You're right,' he said. 'Something *had* upset me. The job, the paltry one pound ten bob a week they paid me for it, and the people who

45

think I owe them something.'

'You owe nobody *anything*, Rob,' insisted Lizzie, sliding her arm through his as they walked. 'After all you did when you were in the army, it's all of us who owe *you*.'

A few minutes later, they reached Seven Sisters Road, where they turned up towards the direction of Finsbury Park. As they went, a freezing drizzle fluttered down on to them, covering their coats with damp that would soon turn to ice, so Rob led them hurriedly into the front doorway of the Gas, Light, and Coke Company, with its gas fires and gas cookers in the window, which, considering the acute shortage of every type of fuel, seemed to be something of an irony.

'Don't get me wrong, Liz,' said Rob, undoing his duffel coat and draping half of it round Lizzie's shoulders to keep her warm. 'I didn't give in my notice because I didn't like the job. I *did* like the job – in a matter of speaking. But I just wasn't prepared to go on working from nine to six each day in a car salesroom office for the rest of my life. And for *what*, Liz – *what?* Drudgery, that's all it was – drudgery! And then I look round and see how people are trying to survive on practically nothing – queues everywhere, tension, no fun, no prospects, people bored out of their minds with austerity – and here we are two years *after* the war! Believe me, Liz, it's never going to get any better. As long as we sit back and let it all happen, there's no hope for any of us. If we're going to survive, we're going to need money – lots of it!'

For a brief moment, Lizzie thought about what

he had said. Then she asked, 'Is that why you've been going up to Petticoat Lane each day, Rob? Because of money?'

Chapter 2

In the 'threepenny and sixpenny' store in Holloway Road, it was hard to believe that in less than a week it would be Christmas Day. Like all the other shops and stores, poor old Woolworths was doing its best to put on a brave show, but as there had been a shortage of Christmas decorations, even they had to be rationed to first come first served. Do-it-yourself paper chains, popular with the kids for generations, had sold out, and most families either had to make do with the leftovers from the previous Christmas season, or use cutup strips of newspaper to hang across the ceilings of their 'front rooms'. However, despite all the gloom and despondency, the 'Woolies girls', as they were affectionately known, did their best to keep up the spirits of their customers, and all the counter assistants, including Lizzie on gramophone records, were doing what they could to make Christmas shopping a joyous occasion.

''Ave yer got the new Vera Lynn yet?'

Lizzie, about to put on a record of the current Ink Spots favourite, looked up to find an adolescent schoolboy calling to her from the small crowd who were gathered around her counter. 'Sorry,' she called back. '"No Regrets" is sold out. We're waiting for a new supply.'

'Will yer 'ave it in before Chrissmas?'

'Can't promise,' apologised Lizzie. 'We've only got five more shopping days to go.'

'Not much good *after* Chrissmas, is it?' growled the boy cheekily. 'I wanna give it ter me mum fer a present.'

'Tell your mum to come in,' Lizzie called back, quick as a flash. 'I'll sing it to her!'

To the delight of the crowd, she launched into an impersonation of Vera Lynn singing the song in question.

Irritated, the boy gave up, and pushed his way out through the crowd.

Lizzie finished the first verse, and put on the Ink Spots record. As the mellow strains of 'Whispering Grass' floated out across the store, Lizzie found herself besieged by customers who were buying up every gramophone record they could lay their hands on. As always, Bing Crosby seemed to be the number-one favourite, and 'White Christmas' was still selling like hot cakes, but today he was being run a close second by the smooth voice of female crooner Anne Shelton with an old favourite, 'Always'.

'I'll be glad when bleedin' Chrissmas is over!' groaned Potto, the other girl working with Lizzie on the records counter, and whose real name was Edith Potts. 'This job's enough ter put yer off songs fer life!'

Lizzie laughed out loud as she struggled to serve the demanding hands that were stretching-out at her with sixpenny bits and shilling pieces, desperately trying to buy their 'popular hits of

48

the week'.

'Stop complaining, Potto!' she called back over the store's general hubbub. 'Just think of all that lovely roast turkey and gin and tonics you'll be getting on Christmas Day.'

'Huh!' came Potto's wry retort. 'I doubt my mum'll 'ave enough coupons ter buy a string er sausages an' a glass er Tizer!'

Lizzie laughed again. But with the general panic to buy something – *anything* – for Christmas gifts, by the time the relief staff arrived to take over at the lunch time break, she was dead on her feet.

The staff canteen was thick with smoke. Everyone, except Lizzie, seemed to have a fag dangling from his or her mouth, and the combination of the smell of cottage pie, boiled cabbage and Woodbines was not exactly conducive to a healthy atmosphere. But, although exhausted from the Christmas rush, most of the staff were in high spirits. It was hard to say whether this was because of the rumour that the 'threepenny and sixpenny store' was going to provide a special roast turkey meal for lunch time break on Christmas Eve, or because they would soon all be getting a two-day break.

The close friendships amongst the female staff was very evident, for there were small groups of them eating together at tables all around the canteen.

'That's the trouble with you English,' said Mabel Gosling, as she joined Lizzie and Potto at their table. Mabel's nickname was 'Maple', because she'd just recently returned from Canada after being evacuated there as a kid during the war. 'You're too afraid to stand up for your rights.'

'So wot's that s'pposed ter mean?' asked Potto, who, like the other girls, couldn't bear the way Maple put on a phoney Canadian accent.

'It means,' replied Maple, 'that everyone should stand up and be counted. This country is in a hell of a state – no food, no decent clothes, freezing cold. Just look at the shops. This is supposed to be Christmas and there's nothing to buy. I say that if you don't tell the politicians what you think, then you might just as well jump in the river.'

'Be a bit difficult,' said Storky, the other girl at the table. 'They say if it gets much colder the Thames could freeze over.'

'What a country!' growled Maple.

'Oh, I don't think it's all that bad,' said Lizzie, trying to lighten the conversation. 'We're just going through a bad time, that's all. After all, we came through the war, so why shouldn't we get through the peace?'

'I don't know what you're talking about,' retorted Maple sulkily, whilst lighting up a fag. 'This is a terrible country. Nobody in their right mind would want to live in a place like this.'

This remark infuriated Potto. 'Well, if yer don't like it,' she snapped, 'why don't yer go back where yer come from?'

'Don't worry, that's exactly what I intend doing,' insisted Maple haughtily, puffing on her fag. 'I only came back to see Mum and Dad, but as soon as I've saved up enough money for the fare, I shall go back to Canada. There are good jobs for people like me there.'

'Oh?' quipped Potto sarcastically. ''Ave they got threepenny an' sixpenny stores over there too?'

Before Maple had a chance to retaliate, Lizzie chimed in quickly with a hilarious melodramatic impression of what seemed to be every Bette Davis movie. 'Oh my God!' she howled, clutching her head as if in mental anguish. 'I can't go on like this – I just can't go on!'

All heads turned to look at her from the other tables, and everyone burst into laughter. 'Attagel, Bette!' yelled one of the girls. 'You tell 'em!'

'I can't go on!' insisted Lizzie, in her mock Bette Davis voice and expression.

The others laughed and applauded, all except Maple, who was definitely not amused. 'Very funny,' she rasped in her phoney Canadian accent. 'But I bet *you* wouldn't say no if you got the chance to emigrate.'

There was a sudden silence from Lizzie and the other girls.

Maple gradually became aware that all eyes were turned towards her. 'Well,' she said, a bit concerned that she had jarred a few nerves, 'everyone's doing it. Canada, Australia, South Africa. I've heard that some people are even going out to live in India.'

'India!' Storky nearly choked on the fag that she had just lit up. 'Who wants ter go an' live wiv ol' Gandhi!'

This broke the ice, and the girls laughed again.

'In any case,' added Potto, 'India don't belong to us no more.'

'Neither do Canada and Australia,' said Maple, 'but at least they don't have ration coupons and queues for everything.'

'Well, yer wouldn't get me goin' out ter live in some foreign country,' insisted Potto defiantly, screwing up her blood-red features as though she had just swallowed a lump of sour rhubarb.

'Nor me,' agreed Storky, disdainfully throwing back her head of tight brown curls.

'Canada is *not* a foreign country,' said Maple, as though giving them a history lesson.

'And neither are Australia and South Africa. They're all part of the British Empire.'

'Ha!' snorted Potto. 'Not much longer, the way fings're goin'!' She turned to Lizzie. 'Wot about you, Liz?' she asked. 'Would *you* go an' live abroad?'

Liz hadn't really heard Potto's question. For a few seconds it seemed as though she was sitting all alone, miles away from the canteen, with her workmates bickering amongst themselves, and the sound of Billy Cotton and his band and singers belting out 'Jingle Bells' on the Tannoy system throughout the store. But it was no longer Bette Davis that was cascading through her mind, but the sudden thought that if she were to marry Rob, it would mean that she would be leaving home, leaving her mum and dad and her brothers and sisters, and what would she do if she didn't have them around to talk to? What would she do without being able to turn to her mum for advice on practically everything she ever did in life? But then she chuckled to herself inside; even if she left home, her mum and dad wouldn't be all that far away, and they would always be around for her. And then her mood changed again. But what would she do if her family *weren't* around? A cold chill went up her spine.

'Liz?'

Lizzie came out of her daydream to find Potto, Maple, and Storky waiting for her comment. 'Oh – I'm sorry,' she said. 'What did you say?'

'I asked if you'd ever go to live abroad,' Potto said.

'Abroad? Me?' Lizzie's reaction was swift. 'Oh no – not me – never!'

'Why not?' asked Maple. 'Everybody's doing it.'

'If *everybody's* doing it,' quipped Potto caustically, 'then there won't be anyone left! Anyway,' she used her empty plate to flick some ash off her fag, 'why should someone like Liz want ter leave the country? Her feller's got a good job, an' 'e'll take good care of 'er. Ain't that right, Liz?'

Lizzie thought about that for a moment. 'Oh – er – yes,' she said, careful to conceal her uncertainty.

Maple shrugged. 'Well,' she said, twisting the remains of her fag on to Potto's plate. 'It's everyone for themselves, of course. But I just hope this guy of yours has prospects. Make no mistake about it – this country's going downhill fast.'

This hit a raw note with Lizzie. 'You're wrong, Maple,' she said firmly. 'This is a wonderful country, and I, for one, would never leave it.'

'Hear! Hear!' said Potto and Storky in unison, at the same time applauding her.

Lizzie was heartened by the support she was

getting from her two workmates, but as the sound of Bing Crosby singing 'White Christmas' echoed from the Tannoy speakers, she wasn't quite sure whether she really believed what she had just said.

Frank Angel hated working at Billingsgate Market. It was not that he had anything against the place – after all, it was the only job he had managed to get when he came out of the army – but the fact was it just wasn't right for *him*, and in more ways than one. The market itself, situated on the banks of the River Thames near London Bridge, was once a landing-stage for provisions, but since the late seventeenth century it had been used exclusively for the sale of freshly caught fish, which was a godsend to London's wholesalers and restaurant owners, who flocked there early every morning to snap up everything from North Sea cod to bloaters, mullet, plaice, skate, shrimps, eels, crabs, and fresh cockles and mussels. As fish was practically the only food that was not on ration, the place had been popular all through the war years, despite being blasted many times by enemy bombs.

No, Frank's real problem was with the men he worked with. Billingsgate porters had a reputation for being foul-mouthed, which in many ways was distinctly unfair, for most of them, like Frank himself, had wives and families of their own to whom they showed appropriate respect and respectability, and he had no doubt in his mind that many of the men, who came from both the north and south of the river, had hearts of gold. The real trouble was simply because Frank stood out from them like a sore thumb. Whereas they fantasised a good deal of the day about women, and what they'd like to do with them, Frank found their repartee a little young for him. It wasn't that he was a prude, but because he loved and respected his wife, he didn't like to hear women talked of as though they were merely sex objects. In many ways, Frank blamed himself for the fact that he didn't get on well with many of his colleagues. He never joined in with their banter, never went drinking with them in the pubs at lunch time or after work, and always rushed off every evening to catch the bus back home to Harriet and the kids. Frank was a cultured man who loved to read books, which more often than not irritated his workmates, who found it impossible to believe that he was incapable of joining in their endless discussions about football and dog-racing, and they therefore called him 'Toff'.

Frank also hated the actual work he had to do, gutting the fish and cutting off the heads, packing the cleaned fish in cratesful of ice, and if that wasn't bad enough, the winter was already turning out to be particularly gruelling, with temperatures dropping to below zero even during the day.

However, he did have one mate who didn't mind his company – Dodger, who got his name because he would do anything to avoid work, a young bloke who was a real wide boy, pure Mile End, right down to his winkle-picker shoes, flat cap, and Woodbine fag that was always drooping from his lips. 'I say, bring back Winnie!' he would say most mornings, arriving late for work, eyes half closed after a night out on the tiles. ''E's the only bloke who can pull this country tergevver!' The fact that Dodger was a self-declared working-class Tory impressed none of his workmates, for they knew only too well that he would vote for any party that would give him the freedom to flog his fags, booze, and nylon stockings on the black market.

But at least Dodger's good humour always managed to bring a smile to Frank's face, for despite the drabness of the times, Dodger was a survivor, and knew how to take care of himself.

'Even if he got back into power,' said Frank this morning, gutting a haddock and wiping his hands down his apron, 'I doubt he'd do much to improve things. This country's a lost cause.'

'Don't you believe it, mate!' insisted Dodger, waving his knife as though he was going to use it for more than just gutting a fish. 'Ol' Churchill's got it up 'ere...' He pointed to his own forehead. 'Savvy. That's wot 'e's got. That's 'ow 'e got us ter win the war.'

Frank was only half listening.

Dodger moved closer towards Frank along the well-used wooden bench. ''E told us 'ow ter do fings – wivout makin' a song an' dance about it.'

Frank was puzzled.

Dodger qualified what he was saying. 'Let's face it,' he said, after a quick check over his shoulder to make sure that no one could overhear him, 'who wants ter stand in this freezin' cold dump, crack er dawn, day after day, knackers frozen to the core. I tell yer, Frank, this is no job for the likes er you an' me. Not fer wot this bloody lot pay us!'

Frank carried on with his gutting. 'Not much we can do about it, Dodger,' he replied. 'The alternative is to spend the rest of our lives in the dole queue.'

'Ah now,' insisted Dodger, who was practically whispering into Frank's ear, 'that's where yer wrong. There are *uvver* ways, yer know.'

After a moment's hesitation, Frank looked up at him. 'If you're thinking what I think you're thinking...'

'Come off it, Frank,' said Dodger. 'Yer've got a wife and kids ter fork up fer – right?'

Frank nodded.

'Then yer've got ter see that they get wot they need? Right?'

'Dodger–'

Dodger was impatient with Frank's protest. 'A few extra bob a week could take care of that all right, Frank,' he said, again flicking a quick look over his shoulder to make sure that the other men couldn't overhear him. 'In fact, if yer play yer cards right an' go along wiv me, yer could be rakin' in more than a few bob.'

Frank didn't know what to say, and tried to pretend that he hadn't been listening to a word Dodger had been saying. He had heard all this before – time and time again. Nearly every bloke in the market knew about Dodger's devious activities, and although Frank liked the young bloke, he had no intention of getting himself associated with a spiv handling stolen goods. And yet the more Dodger talked, the more Frank had grave misgivings about himself, about his own reluctance to do something positive for his family. Times were harder than anyone could remember, so why shouldn't he get in on a lucrative business that would at least help him and his family survive the winter? Every time Dodger had approached him on the matter, every time he, Frank, had said 'no', he'd thought about how cold his hands were, chopping off the heads of ice-cold fish on a well-worn timber cutting-board; he thought about him and Harriet and the rest of his family all wearing overcoats to go to bed, with not enough sixpenny or shilling pieces to put in the gas meter. Was this the way to live? Was this the way for civilised human beings to survive? Was this the way the country repaid the men who fought for it during the war – by treating them as though they were nothing better than cattle? He looked around the market and saw all the other men toiling away in the freezing cold, all of them earning no more than a quid or so a week, with mouths to feed at home, and not enough money to buy a half-bag of coal – even if they could get such a thing.

Dodger leaned close again. 'I know a bloke–'

'Oh, shut up, Dodger!' snapped Frank, slamming down his gutting knife. 'You *always* know a bloke.'

Dodger ignored Frank's irritation, and continued, 'I know a bloke who needs – an "in between".'

Frank, exasperated, tried to move away, but Dodger grabbed his arm and held on to him. 'All 'e needs is fer someone ter – flog a few fings fer 'im. You know – a few fags, coupla bottles er gin, some nylon stockings and gels' dresses–'

'I don't know anything about women's clothes,' replied Frank irritably.

Dodger grinned. Despite his protests, Frank was showing a subconscious interest. 'Nuffin' ter know, mate,' he said, voice low. 'Just show the customer, an' let them do the rest.'

'Come on, you two!'

Both men turned round to find Bert Spinks, their foreman boss, breathing down their necks. 'What's this then – a muvvers' meetin' or somefin'?'

'Sorry, Bert!' replied Dodger, as he and Frank went back to work. 'Me an' Frank was just discussin' the diff'rent types er fish we get down 'ere in the market.'

'Is that so?' replied Spinks, in a mock toff's voice. 'Well, may I suggest that you an' Mr Angel 'ere get on wiv cuttin' up the fish instead of chin-waggin' about 'em all day!'

'Yes, Bert! Right yer are, Bert!' Dodger's return carried more than a hint of sarcasm. 'So wot d'yer say?' he said, turning to Frank again once Spinks had moved on. 'Are we on, mate – or ain't we?'

Frank hesitated, then turned to him. 'I'm sorry, Dodger,' he said. 'I'm not your man.'

Even as he spoke, however, deep down inside he felt a sense of real uncertainty.

It was dark when Lizzie left work. It was usually no more than ten minutes' walk home from the

Woolworths store in Holloway Road, but tonight the weather was foul, with a high wind and ice-cold squally showers, which were gradually turning to sleet and seeping through her fawn-coloured topcoat and hood, which had been one of the few things that had survived the bombing of the Angels' house at the end of the war. She walked with Potto for part of the way, but it was so cold they could hardly say much to each other, and by the time Potto had turned off along Seven Sisters Road towards her own home near Finsbury Park, the only thing Lizzie wanted to do was to get home as fast as she could. Although there was an acute shortage of power, a few shops had managed to light up Christmas trees in their front windows, which, after the bleak war years, did cheer up the dark night atmosphere, and give some impression that Christmas itself was only a few days away.

Lizzie was glad the war was over. There were times when she'd thought it never would be, and even now, well over two years since VE Day, she found it hard to believe that she could actually look up into the sky without feeling threatened. The sad thing was, however, that the hard times were continuing, and everyone inevitably had a long face. There was also so much anxiety and concern around. People were so desperate for food and some decent clothes that they seemed prepared to go to any lengths to get what they wanted. It scared her.

It scared her especially when she thought about Rob, and what he had been doing with his time since he gave up his job. Was he involved in some crooked business, like the black market or something? It sent a cold shiver up her spine even to think about it. Rob was such a good person, so kind and considerate. It horrified her to think that he might be involved in something that broke the law. She knew for a fact that the police were on the look-out for people who did such things. She had read it in the newspapers, and heard it on the wireless. But then she thought that whatever her doubts, she knew that Rob would never do anything stupid. He wasn't a hot-head. He was a lovely person, so kind, so protective, and so good-looking. Even as she pushed hard against the force of the gale, she could see him in her mind's eye, with that mischievous twinkle in his eye, teasing her about the way she did impressions of people, and constantly kissing her on her lips every time she laughed. Oh God – how she loved him! And he loved her. Everyone knew it, and so did she. Rob had been the only boy she had ever been out with, and, as far as she knew, she was the only girl Rob had been out with. Both sets of parents had often said that the two of them were a 'match made in Heaven'. Well of course they were: Lizzie *was* an Angel.

Just as she had turned into Andover Road, head bent down against the wind, she bumped into someone in the dark who was just coming out of the newspaper shop on the corner.

'You got eyes in the back of yer bleedin' 'ead or somefin'?'

Lizzie immediately recognised the ancient female voice that was scolding her. It was old Lil

Beasley, who was eighty-five if she was a day, and who swore the word 'bleeding' in conversation almost as many times as she broke wind in public.

'Sorry, Mrs Beasley,' said Lizzie, trying to steady the crotchety old girl. 'It's such a dark night, I didn't see you.'

Lil Beasley stood her ground, and flashed her torchlight into Lizzie's face. 'Oh, it's you, is it?' she rasped, blowing her nose without wiping it. 'Should've known it was one of you Angels.'

Without another word, she started to move off. Lizzie went with her, but hardly had to slow her pace at all for the old girl was still pretty nimble on her feet. Lil lived in nearby Bedford Terrace, and was one of a breed of old ladies who seemed to have been widowed during the Great War, and who fate had decided to isolate in small terraces in backstreets all over the borough.

'This bleedin' wevver's gettin' on me nerves,' she grumbled as she went. 'I wouldn't've come out if it wasn't fer me *Evenin' News*. My neighbour's son used ter pick it up fer me, but 'e went an' got 'imself a bleedin' gel of 'is own an' moved off ter 'Arringay – bleedin' stupid goon!'

Lizzie felt her heart bleed for the poor old thing. 'If you need anything any time, Mrs Beasley,' she said, having to raise her voice above the wind, '*please* let us know. I could always drop off your newspaper on the way home from work, and even if I'm not around, I could get one of my brothers to–'

'Stop talkin' to me as though I'm an ol' woman!' snapped Lil. 'I'm not in me box yet, although the way I'm goin' wiv my bleedin' landlord, I soon will be!'

Lizzie turned with a start. 'What do you mean?' she asked anxiously.

'Wot d'yer fink I bleedin' mean?' replied Lil. ''E's freatened ter chuck me out on the streets. Says 'e can't afford ter let people like me 'ang on in 'igh-class property like mine. 'Igh class! Wallpaper hangin' off the bleedin' walls, plaster comin' down off the bleedin' ceilin', I 'ave ter go up an' down the bleedin' stairs ter the outside lav, *an*' I've got cockroaches in me bleedin' bed. 'Igh class – ha!'

Lizzie saw Lil to the end of the road, but as the old girl was as defiantly independent as ever, Lizzie was not allowed to accompany her any further. But as she turned to go home, Lizzie couldn't help pondering on what Lil had been saying about the threat of being thrown out of her home after living there for more than thirty years. Where was the local borough council to allow such a thing? Was there no one who could speak up for people in such a predicament? Since the end of the war, ruthless landlords had become ten a penny. Everyone seemed to be out to make money in one way or another. In some respects, of course, it was only natural for, after all, these were hard times, when so many people didn't know where the next meal was coming from – or even if there was going to be a next meal...

But then, a terrible thought occurred to her. Suppose the local borough council decided to do the same thing to them? Would it be possible for them to throw the Angel family out on to the streets because they needed to raise more cash from the homes they owned? Another cold chill went down her spine, and by the time she had reached home and gone into the prefab, she was consumed with foreboding.

''Bout time you got home!' The first voice Lizzie was greeted with came from young Benjamin, who was hunched over his stamp collection at the sitting-room table. 'Mum says she's left some stuffed marrow in the oven. But the gas has gone out, and we don't have any tanners to put in the meter.'

'Don't worry,' said Lizzie, quickly taking off her hat and coat and leaving them in the bedroom she shared with her brothers and sisters. 'I'll warm it up by the fire.' This was clearly not going to be an easy task, for the place was, as usual, ice cold, with nothing more than a glow from burned timber in the fireplace.

'Is that all there is again?' called Susan from the washroom. 'Stuffed marrow! Can't we ever have any meat in this house?'

'I *hate* stuffed marrow!' groaned James, who was doing his homework at the same table as his brother.

'We have to make do!' called Lizzie, who had now moved off into the kitchen. 'The way things are, we're lucky to have anything to eat at all.' When she came into the sitting room carrying a metal baking dish containing the stuffed marrows, she saw the uphill challenge she faced at the fireplace. 'Ah well,' she sighed. 'Let me see if I've got a coin.' She quickly returned to the

64

kitchen with the stuffed marrows, put them on the small worktop there, and hurried into the bedroom to retrieve her purse from her coat pocket. Luckily, she found a shilling piece there amongst the halfpennies and farthings, so she quickly returned to the kitchen with it, climbed up on to a chair and slipped the coin into the gas meter above the door. Then she went to the stove, collected the box of matches there, and lit the oven. 'Success!' she proclaimed.

Even though the gas flame was no more than a flicker, she soon had the baking tin of stuffed marrows back on the middle shelf of the oven.

Back in the sitting room, Lizzie found Susan flopped out on the utility settee, towel around her head, and wearing her topcoat, which her mother had managed to buy on ration coupons for Susan's birthday the year before.

'As a matter of fact,' said Susan, aimlessly filing her fingernails, 'I think it's very inconsiderate of Mum and Dad to go visiting Gran on a night like this.'

'Gran is an old lady now, Susan,' replied Lizzie. 'She's Mum's mother, and she cares for her, especially when she lives all on her own with no one to take care of her.'

'I wasn't talking about her,' said Susan airily. 'I was talking about us. When we have to go out and work all day, you expect to have something decent to eat when you get home.'

'You don't *go* to work!' snapped James, who had never got on with his sister. 'You only go to the polytechnic so that you can get out of going to work and earning some money.'

Susan sat up with an angry start. 'That's not true!' she barked. 'When I start earning *my* living, I want to *do* something with my future. I don't want to spend the rest of my life working behind a counter in a department store.'

Lizzie refused to be put down by her younger sister's unpleasant jibes. She had gone through all this before, and had learned how to ignore it. 'Of course you don't, Susan,' she said sweetly, whilst trying to poke some life back into the dying embers of the fire. 'I'm sure you'll be a great success in life.'

'Do Mrs Mop for me, Lizzie.' Young Cissie's request was a sure sign that she was bored with watching Benjamin sort through his stamp collection.

'Don't be silly, Cissie,' said Lizzie. 'I haven't got time to do impersonations. I'm trying to get our supper ready.'

'Oh come on!' groaned Cissie. 'Just a quick one. Mrs Mop's my favourite of all the ones you do.'

Much as she loved her little sister, Lizzie hated it whenever she had to stop everything she was doing just to act the clown. It was also hard for her to explain to her family that doing impersonations of people was a way of showing her own true feelings. Being someone else was in some strange way an attempt to disguise the fact that she had very little confidence in herself. 'Can I do yer now, sir?'

Lizzie's sudden belting out of the famous *ITMA* character's catch phrase sent young Cissie into shrieks of hysterical laughter. 'Again! Again!'

she roared, clapping her hands together wildly.

'Can I do yer now, sir?' repeated Lizzie, rolling up her sleeves as though she was about to char for the popular radio show's leading character, 'Mayor' Tommy Handley.

Even James joined in with the laughter, but Susan, bored with the same old nonsense, got up from the settee, and swept off into the bedroom, slamming the door behind her. As she did so, however, James's laughter turned into a bout of coughing.

Lizzie rushed across to him. 'James?' she asked anxiously. 'Are you all right?'

James stopped coughing immediately. ''Course I'm all right!' he replied tetchily. 'I just got a tickle in my throat. I wish people wouldn't keep fussin' about me. People are always fussin' about me!'

Whilst he was speaking, their mum and dad arrived home.

'I've got potatoes for us!' exclaimed Harriet triumphantly, holding up a string bag full of potatoes that were becoming as hard to get as gold nuggets. 'Gran sent them to you. I think her greengrocer must be in love with her!'

A short time later, the whole family were sitting down to a meal of small marrows stuffed with celery and carrots, and dried peas, and Gran's boiled potatoes. During the meal, Lizzie was pleasantly surprised to see how sprightly and buoyant her mother was, but it wasn't until later in the evening, when the rest of the family had gone to bed, that she found out why.

'Everything's going to be all right,' said Harriet

enthusiastically, crouched on the rug with Lizzie in front of what had, until an hour before, been a few pieces of burning, crackling wood. 'Your dad says he's got the prospect of some extra special work with a lot of money and potential. He says things are going to be different from now on – that we won't have to stay in this place much beyond the winter.'

Lizzie's eyes lit up with excitement. 'Oh, Mum!' she gasped, taking her mother's hands and squeezing them. 'That's wonderful, absolutely wonderful! What sort of work is it?'

'I don't really know,' replied Harriet, less enthusiastically. 'He says it's too hush-hush to talk about just at the minute. But if your father says it's something worth doing, I'm sure it must be. He's such a good man. He does love us so much – especially you.'

Lizzie was puzzled. 'What d'you mean, especially me?'

'Oh, come on now, Lizzie,' said Harriet. 'You must have known all these years that you're his favourite. You always have been. He says you're the one that helps to keep this family together.'

Lizzie felt awkward. 'I don't think that's true,' she replied.

'Oh, yes it is,' said Harriet, moving close to Lizzie, and putting her arm around the girl's shoulders. 'It's not that we don't love the others, but you're such a good girl. You keep our spirits up, especially when we're down.'

'Oh, Mum, that's ridiculous! Just because I do a few impersonations for the family on Sunday evenings.'

Harriet hugged her close. 'It's not just the impersonations, darling,' she said. 'You see, your dad and I know how you hate doing them. But you do it because you want to distract our attention from all the hell we're going through. You were the same during the war, when the house was bombed and we lost everything. If it hadn't been for you, I don't know how we'd have survived. *I* know that, and so does your dad. That's why we both love you so much.'

Lizzie didn't know what to say. The one thing that was certainly true was that she did love her family, and would do anything she could to keep up their morale. But it took more than one person to keep a family together.

Harriet turned to face Lizzie. 'I also think your dad knows just how much he owes to you for helping him to see straight. Many a time he's been beside himself with worry about work and money and God knows what, but you've always been the one who's just sat down and talked to him, and made him see that things are never as bad as they seem. Unfortunately *I've* never been the one who could do that. And as for Susan...' She sighed. 'Well, the only person *she's* ever been able to help is herself. I blame myself for that. I should never have let her think that she was any better than the rest of us – but she does.'

'And neither am I, Mum,' said Lizzie. 'I'm no different from Susan. I'm no different from any of the Angels.'

'Oh, yes you are, my darling,' Harriet said, gently kissing Lizzie on her forehead. 'There's no one quite like you. If your dad does get this extra work, it'll be thanks to you for giving him the will to go on.'

That night, Frank Angel got very little sleep. Lying alongside Harriet in a bed that was hardly big enough to hold two people, wearing their topcoats to keep warm on a particularly freezing cold night, the sound of heavy rain pelting down on to the flat metal roof of their prefab, one of many buildings that surveyors had predicted would last for no more than a couple of years at the most, Frank felt as though he was a million miles away from reality, the reality of a place that he had once been proud to call the home of the Angel family. By his side he could hear Harriet's gentle breathing as she drifted into dreams of a better life, a life he had promised her and their children so many times, a promise that had remained unfulfilled for so long.

He turned on his side, so that he could face her. It was pitch-dark, so he couldn't see her, but in his mind's eye he could see that face, that same sweet, loving, caring face that he had cherished since the day they had met, and which was now so racked with pain and anxiety. But as he lay there, he came to a decision, right there and then, a decision that would change things once and for all. No longer would he allow his family to suffer. No longer would he be ashamed to face them when he came home each evening. From now on things *were* going to be different, on that he was determined. And if it meant becoming the sort of person he had never wanted to be – then so be it.

Chapter 3

Despite the shortage of practically everything in the shops, the barrow boys in Petticoat Lane were doing a roaring trade. Every day leading up to Christmas, the crowds had been packing into the famous East End market, desperate to buy up whatever bargain they could lay their hands on, but now, with only two days to go, the scramble for last-minute shopping had turned into a frenzy.

One of the busiest stalls was Charlie Feather's bric-a-brac – which is what he called it, but in fact it was nothing more than a glorified mobile junk shop. However, from time to time he did pick up something quite interesting, such as the floral patterned po, which a toff from the West End took a shine to and gave him five bob for the asking. In fact, the thing was worth no more than a tanner at the most. It had come from a bombed-out house in Brick Lane up in Mile End. Over the past few years, Charlie, with the help of his missus, Doris, had worked up quite a good business, clearing out houses when somebody died, and making a small profit from the sale after doing a deal with the deceased's relatives. It was hard work, of course, sorting through the rubbish and cleaning up what was left, especially when the only form of transport they had for moving the stuff was a horse and cart, which Charlie hired from the local brewery. Not an easy job for Charlie in his advancing years, he with no kids of his own to help out.

That's why he was grateful for young Rob Thompson. Rob was a tough young man, plenty of brawn as well as brain, and he was someone Charlie could trust. In fact, in many ways, Charlie knew only too well that if it wasn't for Rob, the future of his hard-earned business would be decidedly shaky. Trouble was, though, it was unlikely that Rob would stay on board for long. He was an ambitious young bloke, someone with plans of his own.

'Charlie,' called Rob, who was helping out on the stall nearby, 'I've just sold that Coronation serving plate.'

'Due what?' asked Charlie, whose ears were so large they looked as though they were flapping. '*Wot* plate?'

Rob leaned close, and turned his face away from the customers. 'The one you've been trying to get rid of for months.'

A look of sheer astonishment came over Charlie's ruddy, frozen complexion. 'Blimey!' was all he could say. This young bloke sure had the gift of the gab!

Hands from the crowd of shoppers were now reaching out, sifting through the carefully arranged display of brooches, 'fine bone' tea sets, pots and pans, second-hand books, linen tablecloths, every type of glassware imaginable, and an array of small porcelain figures that had once adorned the mantelpieces of many of the late departed.

'Somebody wants ter buy Mrs Simmons' easy chair!' called Doris from the pavement behind the stall, where all the second-hand furniture was being inspected by prospective customers. ''Ow much?'

'Six bob!' yelled Charlie, wiping a perpetual dewdrop from the tip of his nose.

'This bloke says it's got woodworm!' called Doris, who was so wrapped up against the cold you could hardly see her well-worn features and the fag balanced in between her lips.

'Then charge 'im anuvver tanner!' quipped Charlie. 'We charge extra fer worms!'

This brought a roar of laughter from the crowd, who were used to Charlie's good-natured banter with his customers.

The crowd started to thin when the intense cold became even more cruel as a light fall of snow began to settle on the stall awning.

Doris came forward, and poured all three of them behind the stall cups of tea from a vacuum flask. 'Who was it who said we 'ad the 'ottest summer on record this year? Must've bin a bleedin' Eskimo!'

Rob took his cup and wrapped his hands around it to warm them.

While this was going on, Charlie was keeping his beady eyes on two small boys who were standing on tiptoe fingering some of the collection of small pill boxes on display.

''Ow much, mate?' said one of them cheekily, as though he was about to produce a fat wallet from his pocket.

'Why?' asked Charlie tersely. 'Wot d'yer want a

73

pill box for? Comin' on poorly, are yer? Sod off!'

The two boys did two fingers to him, and rushed off to yells of 'Silly ol' bugger!'

Rob laughed as they went. 'Remind me never to have kids when I marry!' he joked.

'That's a good point,' retorted Charlie. 'In't it about time yer made an honest woman of that gel er yours?'

'That'll be the day,' replied Rob gloomily. 'Not on what I earn.'

For a split second, Charlie looked quite hurt. 'Come off it, son,' he said. 'I know I don't pay yer a fortune, but it gives yer a leg up.'

Rob suddenly realised that Charlie had misinterpreted what he had meant to say. 'No, it's not what *you* pay me, Charlie,' Rob said. 'It's the fact that there doesn't seem to be a way in hell that you can get on in this damned country. It's worse than during the war.'

'That's not wot yer mean at all, is it, son?'

Rob turned to look at him.

'Yer 'aven't told 'er yet, 'ave yer? Yer 'aven't told that gel er yours 'bout this job, 'bout workin' fer me an' Doris up 'ere?'

The snow was now coming down thick and fast, and what was left of the shoppers had quickly retreated to take cover beneath nearby shop awnings. It wasn't exactly a blizzard, but the wind that came with it was enough to blow flakes of snow on to the bric-a-brac displays, which Doris had very quickly covered over with several sheets of cardboard.

'Don't worry,' said Charlie, sipping his tea. 'I'd feel the same if I was you. Young bloke wiv your savvy. This is no place for someone like you wiv *your* brainbox.'

'That's not what I meant, Charlie – honest it isn't.'

'Oh, don't worry,' said Charlie, quite un-fettered. 'If *I* was just started out, *I* wouldn't want ter spend me time tryin' ter make a few bob by clearin' out people's 'ouses. I tell yer, if *I'd* 'ad me time all over again, I'd definitely do somefin' else.'

'If *I'd* 'ad me time all over again,' chirped in Doris, 'and I 'adn't met Charlie, I wouldn't've bin 'angin' around this bleedin' dump. I'd've bin off wiv my sister Elsie down under.'

Rob was puzzled. 'Down under?'

'Australia!' snorted Doris, who pulled back her hood to reveal a face that was so lined, it looked as though the number 38 tram had done several return journeys across it. 'If I'd 'ad any sense, I'd've gorn off wiv 'er an' 'er Ted when they emigrated there before the war. They wanted me ter go too, but in those days I could never've afforded the fare.'

'Bit diff'rent now,' said Charlie. 'Now yer can go fer ten quid.'

Rob turned with a start. 'Ten quid?'

'Assisted passage scheme,' said Doris. 'Appar-ently the Aussies're desperate ter get people ter go an' live over there. All yer 'ave ter pay is ten quid, an' they pay the rest. I tell yer, if *I* was a young bloke just startin' out, yer wouldn't catch me stayin' on in *this* country. I know where I'd be 'eadin' off to!'

By the time James and Benjamin came out of Hornsey Road School, it was already dark. As this was the last day of school until the New Year, they were later coming out than usual, but for once they didn't mind one bit, mainly because they had enjoyed themselves thoroughly at the school Christmas party all afternoon. In fact, it was a bit of an anticlimax when they found their mum and dad waiting for them with the other parents outside, which meant that they had to calm down, something Benjamin in particular found difficult when he was excited. It had also not escaped Benjamin's attention that his mum and dad were carrying several shopping bags and a large wrapped parcel, which he was convinced was his very own Christmas present.

A few minutes later, they crossed Seven Sisters Road and made their way to Hicks the greengrocer. As to be expected with a shortage of vegetables, there was a slow-moving queue stretching right back to The Eaglet pub at the corner of Hornsey Road. As the earlier light fall of snow had now started to freeze, the pavements were quite treacherous, with icy patches glistening beneath the dazzling light coming from the street lamps. Fortunately, Harriet Angel had already done her vegetable queuing earlier in the day, which meant that she and Frank could go straight to the assistant who was selling what they had come for, their Christmas tree, of which there was still a reasonable selection.

Whilst they were waiting to be served, however, Harriet got into conversation with Martha Cutting, her neighbour, who lived in one of the houses that had survived the bombing at the far end of Andover Road.

'Bet you're none too pleased about gettin' the push, are yer?' said Martha, whose gaunt, thin features stuck on top of a painfully thin body made her look like one more change of knickers and she was ready for her box.

Harriet turned to look at her with a start. 'Due what, Martha?' she asked. 'Getting the push?'

'Ain't yer read this week's *NLP?*' asked Martha. 'It's all in there – in the *North London Press* – about pullin' down the prefabs up our road.'

Harriet froze. She felt as though all the life had been sucked out of her. 'They're going to pull down the prefabs – *our* prefabs?'

'That's wot it says.' There was just a hint of smugness about the way Martha was breaking the news, as though it gave her some kind of satisfaction, for despite the fact that she got on with the Angel family, she didn't really consider them to be part of the 'real' residents of the road. 'They say the borough council always said the prefabs were only temporary. They was only put up by the Yanks to help put a roof over people's 'eads.'

'People who were bombed out, Martha!' snapped Harriet rather sharply. 'People like us who had no choice, who through no fault of their own lost everything they had in the world!'

'Are you sure about this, Martha?' asked Frank, sharing Harriet's obvious concern. 'They actually say that they're going to pull down the prefabs, without consulting any of the people who live in them?'

'It's true, mate,' said a middle-aged man stand-ing amongst the cluster of people waiting to buy a Christmas tree. 'Not only in Andover Road, but all the uvvers as well. I saw it meself in the paper this mornin'.'

'Well, did they mention where they're going to put us all?' asked Frank, as angry as Harriet.

'Ha!' replied the man. 'D'yer fink they'd bovver over a little matter like that?'

Everyone now seemed to be joining in the discussion, and showing their contempt for the way people were being treated by the authorities.

'Those prefabs,' growled Harriet, 'were sup-posed to stay for as long as people had nowhere else to go! There's a housing shortage all over London. Even if we *could* afford to move, where the hell do they think we're going to find a place to go *to?*'

With the exception of Martha, there were murmurs of agreement from everyone in the shop.

'The way fings're goin',' called a rather cross elderly woman from the queue nearby, 'we'll 'ave a bleedin' revolution in this country! 'Ow much more do they fink we can take?'

More murmurs of agreement.

James and Benjamin were getting thoroughly bored hanging around listening to a whole lot of grown-ups miffing on about things that didn't concern them.

'Mum,' moaned Benjamin, 'can I have a coupon to buy some sweets round at Pop's?'

'Oh, shut up, Benjamin!' growled Harriet, too beset with her own anxiety. But she quickly realised that she shouldn't be taking it out on the boys. 'I'm sorry, son,' she said guiltily. 'Of course you can.'

'You won't get any sweets,' insisted James to his young brother. 'Pop never has sweets, only liquorice rolls.'

'Well, you can try,' said Harriet, sorting through her handbag for one of the family's food ration books.

Frank sifted through his trousers pocket and came up with a handful of coins. 'Here's a bob, son,' he said, handing James a shilling coin. 'And get a copy of the *NLP* while you're there.'

As the two boys rushed off, Harriet swung an anxious look at Frank. All her fears, all the things she had been dreading, seemed to be coming true. And as she and Frank moved to the front of the cluster of people buying Christmas trees, the festive season seemed to be the very last thing on her mind.

On the stroke of six o'clock that evening, all the shops in Holloway Road closed their doors for the day, leaving hordes of Christmas shoppers to struggle their way home in the biting cold. Fortunately, the long nights of blackout from the war were now a thing of the past, and at least there were street lamps to brighten their way home. The 'Woolies girls' left by the staff entrance behind the store in Enkel Street. Among them were Lizzie and Potto, who were both making their way as fast as they could towards Seven Sisters Road where Potto was going to catch her bus home.

'As long as I live I'll never get used ter the cold,' said Potto, who was wrapped up in a warm coat, woollen scarf over her head, and galoshes, but was still frozen to the core. 'I'm a hot-blooded girl. I deserve to live like Dorothy Lamour on a nice sandy beach in Tahiti.'

'Don't see you in a grass skirt, though, Potto,' replied Lizzie, rushing along breathlessly at her friend's side. 'You might be attacked by some feller with a lawn mower!'

'Some 'opes!' snorted Potto, as both girls roared with laughter.

'Well, at least we know one person who doesn't mind the cold,' said Lizzie. 'Our Maple must feel completely at home in this weather.'

'Don't yer believe it!' retorted Potto. 'I'll bet she knows no more about Canada than I do.'

'How come?' asked Lizzie, hurrying to keep up.

'Never you mind,' replied Potto. 'Don't you worry, I've got my spies who know a thing or two about our 'igh-flyin' mate.'

Before Lizzie had a chance to ask her what she was talking about, Potto suddenly made a quick dash across Holloway Road to catch her bus. 'Tell yer more termorrow!' she called as she disappeared into the crowd of home-going shoppers.

Lizzie was too cold to watch her go. All she wanted to do was to get home, for the temperatures were dropping fast, and all the signs were that it was going to get even colder.

She hadn't got very far before she suddenly heard her sister Susan's voice calling to her. 'Wait for me. What's all the rush? These pavements are like ice.'

'They say there might be a heavy fall of snow

tonight,' said Lizzie, refusing to slow her pace. 'I certainly don't want to be out in it.'

'Well, you won't find it much better at home,' replied Susan, who was wearing a totally impractical pair of half-heel shoes. 'Sometimes I feel warmer outside in the street.'

'Stop complaining, Susan,' said Lizzie, hurrying on. 'We're lucky to have a roof over our heads.'

'Ha!' scoffed Susan. 'Not for much longer, by the sound of things.'

Lizzie came to an abrupt halt. 'What's *that* supposed to mean?' she asked.

Despite shivering from the cold, Susan delivered her reply with an almost triumphant smirk. 'They're pulling us down,' she said. 'Haven't you heard?'

'Pulling us down?'

'The prefab, stupid! Somebody at the borough council said the prefabs have outlived their use. Don't tell me you haven't heard? It's all in the local rag.'

Lizzie felt her blood turn to ice. Although shoppers were rushing home all around her, she felt totally alone, as though she was marooned in the middle of an island in the middle of the Arctic Ocean. 'They've actually said that they're going to pull our place down?' she asked, in a daze. 'All the prefabs in Andover Road?'

'Not only in our road, but all the others as well. Personally, I don't believe a word of it. I'm frozen!' Susan pulled the collar of her coat tightly around her neck, and walked on. 'In any case, it was only one person at the town hall who said it.

81

It's not official – or so they say. Anyway, as far as I'm concerned, they can pull the place down tomorrow.'

Lizzie grabbed hold of Susan's arm and pulled her to a halt again. 'Don't say things like that, Susan!' she snapped. 'Don't ever let me hear you say things like that, do you hear?'

'Well, it's true!' growled Susan defiantly. 'I hate the place. I've always hated the place. It's not a home, it's a tin hut. It's cold, and it's not got nearly enough room for a family of seven.' She pulled away again, and strode off.

Lizzie went with her.

'I hate the way we have to listen to those – those *sounds* night after night. It's disgusting! It's inconsiderate.'

Lizzie was now getting irritated with her. 'What are you talking about now, Susan?'

Susan stopped again. 'What do you *think* I'm talking about? Those sounds. Those terrible moans and groans from Mum and Dad's room. They seem to forget there's only a thin wall between us and them. Sometimes I lie there at night listening to it, trying my best to cover my ears and pretend it isn't happening. I tell you – it's disgusting!'

If anyone was disgusted now, it was Lizzie – disgusted that she had a sister who could think in such a way; disgusted that she couldn't accept that their own mother and father had a right to make love to each other. Ever since Susan was little, Lizzie had known that she was the odd one out amongst the family. Lizzie could never remember a time when Susan hadn't had delusions of her own self-importance, refusing to accept that she was anything other than a cut above her own stratum of society. Worst of all was the fact that Susan didn't know how to love herself. In fact, Lizzie doubted whether her sister had one scrap of love in her entire body.

'In case you've forgotten, Susan,' she said, their faces bathed in white light from a nearby overhead street gaslamp, 'Mum and Dad are married people. They love each other. That's why we're here – you, me, James, Benjamin and Cissie.'

Susan looked embarrassed as people turned passing glances at them as they hurried by. 'And what happens if Mum has another baby?' she demanded petulantly.

'Don't be ridiculous, Susan!' sighed Lizzie. 'Mum's forty-one years old. She's too old to have any more babies.'

'Just as well!' said Susan. 'They can't afford to look after one child, let alone the five of us. Everyone knows it. Everyone says so.'

'*Who* says so, Susan?' asked Lizzie, now totally annoyed by her sister's biting remarks. 'Your worldly friend Jane Hetherington?'

Susan took an angry breath, and glared at Lizzie. Even though she was aware that her older sister was working so hard to help support the family, Susan still resented the fact that Lizzie was always considered by them all to be such a 'goody-goody'. 'You can say what you like,' she said. 'You can insult me as much as you like. But I'm telling you, I don't like my own mother and father making those sounds in the next room to me every night. So the sooner they pull down that prefab, the better I'll like it!'

Lizzie watched her go in disbelief. This time she didn't try to follow her.

No matter how hard she tried, Lizzie couldn't bear Mike Dunhill. He was a real know-all, a kind of middle-class wide boy, the son of a well-to-do self-made man and a mother whose only interest in life seemed to be in agreeing with everything her husband said. Lizzie also resented the fact that, unlike Rob, Mike had never been called up or had to do any National Service, which was obviously because his father had 'contacts'. Oh God, she thought, why was life always about who you knew, and not about your own true worth? But Mike was Rob's best friend; they had known each other since they were at school, and as Rob always tolerated Lizzie's friends with such patience and thoughtfulness, she had little choice but to put up with Mike's bombast and constant boasts that he had more than enough money to give him a good life. And yet, as Lizzie and Rob stood amongst the small group of young people who had gathered together in Dick's Wine Bar in the Holloway Road the following evening, she wondered why it was that, if Mike didn't have to worry about money, he was throwing this farewell party after giving up a lucrative job as an assistant manager in insurance, and heading off to the wilds of some distant African jungle. It sounded like the ultimate economy.

'Utter boredom,' said Mike, downing his fourth

glass of red wine since Lizzie and Rob had arrived. 'I can put up with a mediocre job, but I can't put up with a mediocre country.'

'And you think things are going to be better in Rhodesia, Mike?' asked Lizzie, who wasn't in the least interested in his reply, for it was entirely predictable.

Mike, his neck bursting out of his white collar and blue striped shirt, replied with some disbelief, 'Do I *think* it's going to be better? I *know* it is!'

'But do people in a place like that *really* buy insurance?' asked Lizzie mischievously.

The others in the group laughed.

'Mike's not going to work in insurance out there,' explained Rob, who slid his arm protectively around Lizzie's waist. 'He's going to do something completely different.'

'Farming!' proclaimed Mike triumphantly.

Lizzie screwed up her face. 'Farming?' she asked incredulously.

'It's the thing of the future, Liz,' Mike replied proudly. 'As soon as I get out there, I'm going to buy a hundred acres, settle down, find myself a nice little woman, and grow as much maize as I can. You know – sweet corn. The natives love the stuff.'

Lizzie was genuinely puzzled. 'Seems such a jump from sitting in an office to working in a field all day,' she said. 'I mean, what do you know about farming, Mike?'

It was Rob who answered her question. 'Mike's been on an evening course,' he said. 'He's got it all worked out.'

'In any case,' said Mike, running his hands through his bush of long blond hair, and then lighting a cigarette with an expensive-looking lighter, 'I'm not afraid of hard work. All I can do is to try.'

'But won't it be lonely out there?' asked Lizzie, intrigued. 'I mean, not knowing anyone?'

'Oh, there are plenty of our own kind out there,' said Mike, puffing on his cigarette and blowing out smoke rings.

'There are loads of expats,' said Rob. It was as though he was trying to impress Lizzie with what Mike was doing. 'Quite a lot of people emigrated before the war. From what I hear, though, they work jolly hard. It's not all fun and games.'

'The gin and tonics are not bad, though!' insisted Mike, laughing at his own joke.

Some of the others laughed with him, but, to Rob's embarrassment, Lizzie remained stubbornly unsmiling.

'Come on now, you lot!' called Mike to his mates, moving off amongst them. 'Drink up! It's the last chance you'll get to have one on me!'

The wine bar was now thick with palls of blue cigarette smoke, and despite the glass of white wine that Lizzie was trying hard to swallow, she found it difficult not to choke in the stifling atmosphere. The barman was run off his feet, and the dozens of old empty wine bottles that adorned the ledge above the counter were rattling amidst the raising of voices in the crowded bar.

'Can we go outside for a few minutes, Rob?' Lizzie asked, reaching forward to put her empty glass down on the bar counter. 'I can hardly breathe in here.'

A few minutes later the two of them were standing outside in the doorway of the bar. In front of them the pavements were glistening with the evening freeze-up, and they were grateful they had kept their warm topcoats on. Inside, they could hear the sound of Mike and his mates getting higher and higher, louder and louder. Lizzie turned away and tried to pretend that she couldn't hear it all.

'You don't like Mike, do you?' asked Rob, sliding his arm around Lizzie's waist to keep her warm.

Lizzie suddenly felt guilty at the high-handed way she had behaved. 'Oh, Rob,' she said, biting her lip. 'I didn't mean to–'

'It's OK,' Rob assured her. 'I don't mind, really I don't. I know Mike can be a bit much at times.'

'But he's your best friend. I shouldn't have been so condescending.'

'Oh, yes,' replied Rob softly, placing his hand beneath her chin, and gently tilting her face up to look at him. 'Mike's my best friend all right, and I'll miss him. But, you might like to know, Lizzie Angel, I don't *love* him like I love you.' He leaned forward and kissed her tenderly on her lips.

Lizzie closed her eyes, and responded. But while their lips were pressed together, her mind was ill at ease, and when they parted, she couldn't help asking what she had been straining to ask. 'Is that something *you'd* want to do, Rob?'

Rob looked at her. He knew at once what she was getting at but played for time. 'What d'you mean?' he asked. 'Do *what?*'

'Farming – in Rhodesia?'

Rob stared at her for a moment, then burst out laughing. 'Me?' he spluttered. 'A farmer in Rhodesia? I couldn't even afford the fare.'

'But if you could?'

This was the sort of question that Rob had been dreading, but although he had been expecting it, he just didn't know how to answer. So he just tried to bluff his way through. 'If you're asking if I'd ever leave you,' he said evasively, 'the answer's no.'

Lizzie persisted. 'No, Rob,' she said. 'That's not what I'm asking. Everyone keeps talking about emigrating here, there and everywhere. Everyone keeps talking about how terrible this country is. I'm confused. I don't know what to think any more. But I honestly don't think things are as bad as they seem.' She looked up, and could just make out the outline of his face silhouetted in the dim light from the bar window. 'Are they, Rob?'

Rob was silent for a moment. Then he suddenly broke away, drifted out on to the pavement, and slid his way towards the road.

Lizzie was taken completely by surprise, and when she saw him leaving the kerb and sprinting out into the middle of the main Holloway Road, she started to panic. 'Rob!' she yelled. 'What are you doing?'

Fortunately, because it was so late in the evening and it was now unbearably cold, the road was completely deserted. So Rob made his way straight to one of the two tram lines that was glistening with ice right down the middle of the road. 'I love an Angel!' he yelled, arms out-stretched, as he delicately picked one foot in front of the other, as though he was walking on a tightrope. Then he looked up at the dark, evening sky, and yelled again, 'Can you hear me? I love an Angel!'

'Rob!' Lizzie ran out to him. 'Get out of the road, Rob. It's dangerous!'

'No one can touch us, Liz,' he said, grabbing hold of her, and hugging her in his arms. 'As long as we're together, where does it matter *where* we are?'

'Please, Rob!' begged Lizzie. 'Please, darling!' At that moment she heard the clatter of a tram approaching down the hill from Archway Junction. 'Oh my God! Rob! A tram!' She tried to tug him away. 'Please, Rob! *Please!*'

Oblivious to the danger, Rob held on to her, and carried on talking. 'Try to remember that, Liz,' he said, resisting her attempts to pull him away. 'When two people love each other, it doesn't matter which part of the world they go to. As long as they're together, Liz. As long as they're together...'

The tram, with all its interior and exterior lights blazing, was approaching at speed.

'For God's sake, Rob!'

Rob held on to her, and hugged her closer. Then he turned them round to face the oncoming tram, still treading, balancing on the slippery tramline. 'Promise me, Liz!' he insisted.

Within an unsafe stopping distance, the tram's driver applied the vehicle's brakes, flashed his headlights, and clanged the tram bell.

'Rob...!' Lizzie's urgent pleas were going unanswered.

'Promise me, Liz,' persisted Rob. 'Promise me that you'll always trust me, that you'll always be with me – wherever we go, whatever we do...'

The tram's brakes were desperately screeching to a halt.

'Rob...!'

Finally, Rob pulled her out of the path of the oncoming tram, and rushed her back on to the safety of the pavement.

The tram continued on its way, sliding past them, down towards the Nag's Head.

'Bloody maniacs!' yelled the conductor from his platform. 'They should lock up nutcases like you!'

Chapter 4

Bing Crosby was singing 'White Christmas' yet again. Lizzie couldn't remember how many times she'd played it on the gramophone counter in Woolworths over the past six weeks or so, but now that young Benjamin was playing it on their own gramophone in the prefab, it was driving her right round the bend. It was also totally inappropriate, for, despite it being one of the coldest Christmases they had ever known, the one thing they hadn't had on this particular day was snow. But at least for the first time since the winter began, the place was warm, cosy and snug, due to a roaring coal fire, which was burning in the grate, thanks to one of Frank Angel's friends at work, who knew someone who knew someone who knew someone who knew where Frank could lay his hands on the odd hundredweight or so of coal on what promised to be a 'regular basis'.

'Well,' said Lizzie, helping her mum to lay the table for Christmas Day lunch, 'I think we're the luckiest people in the world to have such a warm house. I think this friend of Dad's must be a very nice person. Who is he, anyway?'

Harriet's reply was vague. 'No idea,' she said. 'Just someone who gets on well with your dad.'

Even though her question was still milling around in her mind, Lizzie let it pass. But there were other things she wanted to bring up with her mum, and as her two brothers were in their bedroom, she went across to the bedroom door, and closed it. Bing Crosby's lush crooning was immediately relegated to a distant sound.

'Have you and Dad talked any more about what you're going to do?' she asked. 'About this place?'

Until now, Harriet had tried to avoid any talk about the report in the local rag, which had tried to suggest that the borough council were about to kick out all the residents of the prefabs. Especially now. Especially when the Angels were about to sit down to Christmas Day lunch. 'I don't think we *have* to talk about it,' she replied lightly. 'If you ask me it's just some idiot who's trying to dig up a story to scare the life out of us.'

'Whoever he is,' said Lizzie, 'he's succeeding.'

Harriet didn't reply. She just carried on setting

91

the table, and trying to look absorbed in what she was doing.

'Mind you,' said Lizzie, refusing to drop the subject, 'it wouldn't be such a bad thing if they *did* kick us out of here. I mean, the council are bound to find us a new place, aren't they? I've heard they're building a new block of flats down the bottom end of Hornsey Road somewhere. At least they'd feel like a real home.'

Hardly had Lizzie got the words out of her mouth when her mother looked up at her and snapped back angrily, 'I don't *want* to be put in a block of flats with a whole lot of people I don't know! I want my *own* home, like we used to have when we lived like civilised people! What's the matter with you, Lizzie? Don't you care what happens to the family? D'you want to be stuck in a council place for the rest of your life?'

Lizzie was a bit surprised by her mother's outburst. Although she remembered how much her mother had loved the big house the family had lived in before it was bombed, it worried her that snobbery was a part of the reason why Harriet was so intent on not living amongst other people.

'But at least we'd have neighbours,' said Lizzie, 'people we could talk to. Hardly anyone talks to us in this road. They still think of us as intruders.'

Harriet knew there was truth in what Lizzie was saying. But she still had a horror of living so close amongst a whole lot of people who were so different, not only in class, but in manner, from those of her own upbringing in middle-class Crouch End. Realising she had somewhat overreacted to what Lizzie was trying to say, she looked up from what she was doing, and tried to soften her stance.

'It's no use, darling,' she said, with a sweet, reasoning smile. 'I'm not cut out to live with the smell of other people's cooking day in and day out.'

In many ways, what her mother had just said explained an awful lot to Lizzie about Harriet's whole attitude to life. When the family had lived in the big house in Upper Holloway, Harriet's home was her castle, and when she lost it, it was like a part of her own body had been torn away from her. The house was not only detached, but it was spacious, on three floors, and Harriet often liked to talk of it really being in Highgate, because that's where most of the better off lived. It was all nonsense for, with five kids to bring up, Harriet and Frank rarely had enough money to live in the style that Harriet would have liked, despite the fact that Frank's father had left him a small amount of money when he had died before the war. So the loss of her 'real' home had been a great shock to Harriet – in more ways than one. Lizzie knew that her mother would never change her ways, so she decided not to pursue the matter any further. Even if she had, she knew it wouldn't get her anywhere, for despite the fact that her father was the main breadwinner of the family, Harriet Angel was always the decision maker.

A little later, the family opened their Christmas presents, which had been placed, as they always were, under the sparsely decorated Christmas tree in front of the sitting-room window. The

93

presents were fairly modest. Benjamin was absolutely tickled pink to get a Hornby toy train engine, which was going to be the beginning of a new collection to replace the one he lost when the old house was bombed. James loved the football annual he got, for it was a game he was passionate about, and even Susan had a smile on her face when she found that her main present was a brown leather purse she had seen in Selby's department store when she had been out shopping with her mother. Lizzie didn't know how to react when she got her mother and father's present to her, for it turned out to be something for her wedding trousseau, which seemed an odd choice considering that Rob had not yet even formally asked her to marry him, although secretly, she hoped it wouldn't be too long before he did. Naturally enough, Frank and Harriet's presents for each other were also modest – that is, until Harriet discovered that she had an extra present, a small horseshoe-shaped pin brooch, which was totally unexpected, and, to her mind under the circumstances, an extravagant and unnecessary thing. As soon as the present opening had finished, Lizzie went round and collected all the wrapping paper, making quite sure that what was left after Benjamin and James had finished with it would be stored and used again the following year.

Later that morning, Lizzie, James, Benjamin and Cissie went to collect their grandmother, who lived alone in a ground-floor flat just up the road in Tollington Park. Although Gran was only in her late sixties, during the past few years she had gradually been losing the sight in both her eyes, caused by some kind of degenerative disease that had come without warning. But, for her age, she was quite sprightly, and, unlike her daughter, Harriet, was considered to be something of a tomboy and a mimic – and it was probably her that Lizzie took after.

'Now don't you two go pulling me over!' said Gran, as her two young grandsons each held on to one of her hands as they supported her along the treacherously icy pavements. 'Because if you do, you won't get your Christmas presents!'

Benjamin was too excited to take any notice of what his gran was saying, for he was trying to slide on the ice as he walked.

After a moment, the two boys decided to rush off ahead, leaving Gran to cling on to Lizzie's arm and Cissie tagging along behind.

'We should have got you a taxi or something, Gran,' said Lizzie, with her grandmother on one arm, and Gran's shopping bag of Christmas presents in her other hand. 'It's far too dangerous for you to walk out in this weather.'

'Poppycock!' insisted Gran. 'I'm not made of jelly. I may not be able to see so well, but I've still got all me marbles – *and* two good feet!'

It was true. Gran had never given in to her disabilities, and carried on as though life was the same as it had always been.

As they picked their way precariously along the slippery pavements of Tollington Park, their faces cherry red in the cold, from a distance both Lizzie and her grandmother could almost have been taken as sisters, for they were the same medium height, thin and wiry. The two boys were now well out of sight, sliding their way along the pavement as though it were an ice-skating rink, laughing and yelling back to their sister and grandmother to come and join them.

Only when they reached the corner of Hornsey Road did Gran suddenly remember that perhaps she wasn't quite as young as she used to be. 'If ever you need any money,' she said, pausing to catch her breath, and quite out of the blue, 'you only have to ask. You know that, don't you?'

Lizzie was taken aback by her grandmother's sudden gesture. 'Thank you, Gran,' she said, clinging firmly to her grandmother's arm. 'It's sweet of you to offer, but I can manage, really I can.'

'That's not what I'm saying!' grunted Gran irritably. 'That's the trouble with you Angels. Far too proud. Always pretending that things are perfectly all right, and that you don't need help from anyone. Well, let me tell you something, my girl. This country is going to the dogs, and it's every man and woman for themselves. D'you hear what I say?'

'Yes, Gran,' replied Lizzie obediently. When her grandmother was in this kind of mood, she always knew it was quite useless to argue.

'I don't have much,' continued Gran, 'but I've got a little something locked up in my Post Office savings. There's a bit for all of you, but you're the eldest. You're going to be the first that needs to get out of all this mess.' She looked up at the dark grey sky as though she wanted to scold it for not allowing the sun to get through. 'Your grandfather always said that there's no place like dear old England. But sometimes I wonder. Especially with these damned winters that go on for ever.' She started to move on again. 'If I'd had my way, I'd have got us both to go and live in the south of France. At least we'd have seen the sun there.'

'Just as well you didn't,' said Lizzie. 'The Germans would have probably locked you up in a concentration camp.'

'Oh, that was later,' said Gran. 'I'm talking about *before* the war, twenty years ago. Life was so much better than all the rubbish we've got now. Just look at it. This is supposed to be Christmas Day and there's not even any snow!'

Lizzie laughed. 'We can't blame anyone for that, Gran!'

'D'you know what I'd have liked to have been?' Gran asked, now striding out faster than Lizzie. 'I'd have liked to have been a Bluebell Girl.'

'A what?'

'A Bluebell Girl! A dancer at the *Folies Bergère* in Paris.'

'Gran!' Lizzie was shocked. 'They're the ones who take off their clothes in front of all those men.'

'I know,' said Gran, with a mischievous twinkle in her eye. 'Just think of all the fun I could have had.'

'I don't think Grandfather would have approved.'

Gran snorted dismissively. 'Oh, *he* wouldn't've cared,' she said. 'In his young days, Albert was quite a gadabout himself. He always said, "If you don't make the most of life while you can, one

97

day it becomes too late." That was always my trouble. I missed out so much in life. When you get to my age, you look back and think of all the things you'd have liked to have done, but never got round to.' She squeezed Lizzie's arm, and flashed her a quick, knowing look. 'I'm telling you, child, if you don't take the opportunities when they come, they may never come again.'

Lizzie sort of knew what her grandmother meant, but she didn't really take it in. Not just yet, anyway.

Rob Thompson was spending Christmas Day with his own family. When it came to this time of the year, Sheila and Graham Thompson always made an effort to ensure that as many of their family as possible should have Christmas lunch under the same roof in Arthur Road, and this year was no exception. As usual, the place looked a picture, for Sheila was quite a creative woman, who, even during the most austere days of the war, had managed to make the most of very little. The Christmas tree in the front bay window of the sitting room was over five feet tall, and covered from top to bottom with baubles that had been accumulated over the years and carefully stored away in boxes in the attic. This year, she even had a few candles on the tips of the branches, which terrified her family, who all expected the place to go up in flames the moment she lit them. But the best part of the Christmas festivities for both Sheila and her husband was having their children all together at the same time. They were all there: Rob's older brother, Joe, together with his grans and grand-dads from both his mother and father's sides. Then there was Uncle Louis and Aunt Gladys, who came down all the way from Sunderland every Christmas, and cousins Eunice, Pat and Roger, who all seemed to get on well with Rob, despite the fact that whenever they met, which was not very often, they usually bored the pants off him. So the Thompsons were a close-knit family except, of course, when it came to politics.

'I still say it's all Attlee's fault,' said Graham, Rob's father. 'Call himself a Prime Minister?' he scoffed derisively, nearly choking on a mouthful of the turkey that his brother, Louis, had brought down from a farm near where he lived. 'I mean, you've only got to look at him. A puff of wind and he'd blow over! Weak as they come.'

'He can't be all that weak,' said Aunt Gladys, who had a northern accent, and had no time for the constant harping that was going on in the south about people she herself had voted for. 'After all, he did get rid of Hugh Dalton.'

'Dalton!' Graham nearly had a fit. 'The worst Chancellor of the Exchequer this country has ever known. He's practically brought this country to its knees.'

'If you think _he_ was bad,' said Rob's cousin Roger, who had an irritating habit of scraping his empty plate with his knife and fork, 'just wait till you see Stafford Cripps.'

'Frankenstein's monster!' quipped Rob's elder brother, Joe.

Most of those eating at the dining table laughed. But not Aunt Gladys, who glared at her plate without comment.

'I don't see that we should blame someone just because of the way they look,' suggested Uncle Louis. 'Let's face it, Churchill's no oil painting.'

'The country's in a mess, Lou,' insisted Graham. 'And it's all thanks to your lot!'

'As a matter of fact, I don't think the problems we have now are anyone's fault,' said Sheila tactfully. She was sitting at the far end of the table and glaring reproachfully at her husband, who was sitting opposite her at the other end. 'It's the fault of the war. It's left this country bankrupt.'

'You're right,' said Aunt Gladys, using her sister-in-law as her only ally in the room. 'It's going to take a long time to get on our feet again.'

'Rubbish!' blasted Graham, slamming down his knife and fork. 'Look at Hitler's lot. Even Germany's doing better than *this* country, and we're supposed to have won the ruddy war!'

'And in any case,' said Aunt Gladys, 'I think it's very stupid of people who are desperate to leave the country. Did you see what it said in the *Daily Herald* yesterday? Apparently, there are hundreds of people queuing up to go to Australia. Talk about deserting the sinking ship.'

'I don't blame them.' Rob's only comment guaranteed a surprised look from everyone around the table.

'You don't mean *you'd* do such a thing?' asked Uncle Louis. 'Would you, Rob?'

Rob downed the last of the beer in his glass. 'I didn't say I'd do it,' he said provocatively. 'I said, I wouldn't blame anyone if *they* did.'

Uncle Louis and Aunt Gladys exchanged a look of sheer disbelief. 'But don't you think this country is worth fighting for?' asked Louis.

Rob swung him an angry glance. 'I *have* fought for my country, Uncle Louis,' he snapped. 'In case you've forgotten, I nearly gave my life for it. But I don't see anyone in this government queuing up to thank me for it. The young people of this country deserve something better. And if we have to go elsewhere to find it, then that's the way it has to be.'

You could have heard a pin drop in the room. Rob suddenly looked around the table and found that all eyes were turned towards him. The only person who couldn't bear to do so, however, was his mother. But although her eyes were staring down aimlessly at her plate, an awful lot was churning around her mind.

The Marx Brothers were in the middle of their routine. Lizzie was quite convincing as Groucho, complete with a moustache painted on with soot from the fireplace, a cigar made out of newspaper, and her father's raincoat, which stretched down to her ankles. James was also good as Chico, with his hair combed into a fringe beneath his school cap, which was turned back to front, and the dining table a good prop for the piano. And it has to be said that young Benjamin made an interesting Harpo, with an old feather duster substituting for the long blond wig, and his mum's top coat trailing beneath his knees on the floor. In other words, the Angel family's Christmas evening entertainment was in full swing, with the Marx Brothers performing one of the many crazy acts they were famous for from one of their films, together with more vocal impersonations of well-known radio stars from Lizzie, a duet of 'When You Wore a Tulip', from Harriet and Frank, little Cissie attempting a Shirley Temple song and tap dance, and even Gran giving an unaccompanied rendering of 'I Love You Truly'. It was, as usual, a happy and raucous occasion, far removed from the trials and tribulations of the world outside.

During the interval, it was the tradition for Frank to go out into the kitchen to make the Spam sandwiches, but as Lizzie always considered that men were quite useless at doing such things, she went out to help him, leaving the others to listen to Gran telling one of her Christmas ghost stories, which, much to Susan's disbelief, she always insisted were true.

Lizzie loved being with her dad. He was such a warm-hearted man, who cared so passionately for his wife and family, and agonised constantly about not being able to care for them as much as he wanted to. Lizzie also considered him to be a really good-looking man, and had often imagined that in his younger days he must have had quite a few girls hankering after him. As she watched him wrestling with the almost impossible task of opening the tin of Spam, she slid her arms around his waist from behind, and hugged him tight.

'Don't come too close,' he joked: 'I still smell of fish!'

'I don't care,' said Lizzie. 'Billingsgate are lucky

having someone like you working for them.' She turned him round to face her. 'And in any case, fish or no fish, I wouldn't swap you for a million pounds.'

Frank grinned. 'You're only saying that because I'm the champion Spam sandwich maker!'

They chuckled together.

'Seriously, though, Dad,' said Lizzie, 'thank you for making this such a wonderful Christmas for us all.'

'Me?' said Frank. 'I haven't done anything. It's your mum that's done all the hard work.'

'I know,' said Lizzie, 'but you've encouraged her, and us. And what about all this coal? It's only thanks to you we've got such a lovely warm house for Christmas.'

Frank's expression changed, and he turned back to the kitchen table to prise the Spam out of the tin with a knife on to a plate.

At the same table, Lizzie started slicing the bread. 'He must be a wonderful man.'

Frank flicked her a puzzled look. 'Who?'

'The chap who got you the coal.'

Frank's expression didn't change, and he continued with what he was doing.

'Who is he?' asked Lizzie quite casually. 'Is he someone you work with?'

'Oh, for goodness' sake, Liz!' replied Frank, suddenly quite irritable. 'Who does it matter who it is? We got the coal, and that's all that counts.'

Lizzie looked up at him with a start, concerned that she had offended him. 'I'm sorry, Dad,' she said, her face crumpled up with anxiety. 'I wasn't trying to pry. I was only thinking how wonderful he must be – whoever he is...'

Frank tensed, and wished he could have bitten off his tongue. The last person in the world he would ever want to upset was Liz, *his* Liz, his eldest child, who had always been the apple of his eye, and the only one amongst his children with whom he could really have a down-to-earth conversation. 'I'm sorry, my girl,' he said, addressing her in the affectionate way he always used when he wanted to let her know how fond of her he was. 'It's just that, well – these days you have to be careful about where you get things from. It's a case of the survival of the fittest, I'm afraid.' He gave her a reassuring smile.

Lizzie smiled back at him, but she was uneasy. She didn't know why, but she was. 'I'm sorry, Dad,' she said.

Frank returned to his sandwich making, and started scraping each slice of the bread Lizzie had cut with a morsel of margarine. 'Anyway,' he said, carefully changing the subject, 'how's Rob these days? You haven't brought him round to see us lately.'

Lizzie shrugged. 'He's all right, I suppose,' she replied, somewhat half-heartedly.

Frank threw a quick look up at her. 'Only "all right"?'

Lizzie thought hard before she answered him. 'I just get a bit worried about him at times,' she said. 'He seems so muddled these days, so restless.'

'In what way?'

'I'm not sure,' said Lizzie. 'But he *is* very upset about the way things are going, about having no prospects for a really good job.'

Frank shook his head despondently. 'I know how he feels,' he said.

'What worries me,' said Lizzie, stacking a slice of Spam on to the bread her father had just scraped with margarine, 'is that there are times when he gets so worked up, he does things that are really – quite reckless.'

Frank was puzzled. 'Reckless?'

'Well,' continued Lizzie, 'last night, he rushed out into the road right on to the tram lines. Then he dragged me out there too. There was a tram coming too. It only just missed us.'

Frank was staring at her in horror. 'What!' he gasped.

Lizzie quickly qualified what she was trying to say. 'Oh, I'm not saying he was *really* trying to put me in any danger,' she said. 'It's just that he seemed to be trying to tell me something, trying to explain how he felt.'

'You don't have to kill someone to do that!' insisted Frank, who was really quite annoyed by the things Lizzie was telling him.

'No,' said Lizzie, deep in thought. 'It's not as simple as that. In a funny sort of way, it's a kind of cry for help. He's so frustrated about everything. There are times he won't even talk about things. He just seizes up inside. And then he takes risks – like the other evening. I think it's his way of getting something out of his system.' For a brief moment, she stopped what she was doing, and looked up at Frank. 'You know, Dad, I've often thought about this, but soon after Rob was demobbed, I met one of his mates he'd served with in France. His name was Geoff – a really nice chap. He turned up quite by accident when we were having a drink in Rob's local. But for some reason, Rob was furious, and he went all – funny. We got up and left, and when I asked Rob why, he just said that he didn't want to carry on a friendship with people he didn't want to see any more. He said that he just wanted to forget the war.'

Frank took this in. He understood only too well how the despair of post-war frustration was eating into people's attempts to improve their lives.

'But what worries me most,' continued Lizzie, 'is that he never stops talking about emigration.'

'Emigration?'

'Time and time again he goes on about leaving the country, and getting a job and a place of his own overseas.'

Frank should have felt anxious about what Lizzie was telling him, but he wasn't, for it was clear that Rob was feeling exactly the same as himself. Several times over the past few months, Frank had thought about doing exactly the same thing, applying for emigration for himself and his entire family, moving them to a place where they could breathe the fresh air of progress. But each time he had allowed the thought to shift further and further to the back of his mind, mainly because he could never bring himself even to suggest such a thing to Harriet, whom he knew would be totally opposed to such an idea.

'Is Rob really serious about emigrating?' he asked. 'Or is it just wishful thinking?'

'That's the trouble,' replied Lizzie. 'I think he *is* serious.'

'And would you go with him?'

'*Me?*' she gasped in horror. 'You must be mad! You don't think I would ever desert my own country – do you?'

'Why not?'

Lizzie was truly shocked to hear her father ask such a question. Wasn't it obvious that she was as English as they came, that to leave everything she had known and loved since the day she was born would be little more than an act of betrayal? 'I would never leave you and Mum, Dad,' she replied calmly. 'Surely you must know that.'

'You wouldn't *be* leaving us, Liz,' he retorted. 'It's not as though we'd never see you again.'

'How d'you know that?' asked Lizzie, disconcerted by her father's attitude. 'Suppose Rob wanted to go to Australia? It's on the other side of the world. Even if we could afford the fare to go there, we'd never be able to afford to come back home for a trip.'

Frank stopped what he was doing, looked up at her, and placed both hands on her arms. 'Listen to me, Liz,' he said earnestly. 'You and Rob are two young people. You have a future of your own together. If I had half the chance, I wouldn't hesitate. I'd take this family away from all this misery at the drop of a hat.'

Lizzie couldn't believe what she was hearing. Although she knew how depressed her father had been since losing his job at the North London Drapery Stores, she had never even considered the possibility that he would want to up his roots and take all his family off to a totally foreign environment.

'Has Rob asked you to go with him?'

'We haven't even discussed it.'

'But if he *does* ask you to go?'

Lizzie shook her head forcefully.

'You'd let him go alone?'

Lizzie froze. Until that moment, she hadn't considered such a possibility. 'If that's what he wanted,' she said tersely, 'I couldn't stop him.'

'I thought you loved him. Do you?'

'Of course I do. But it's my life as well as his.' She moved away from the table, and went to the kitchen window where she stared aimlessly out into the dark, crisp evening. 'I could never leave you and Mum, and Susan and James and Benjamin and Cissie and Gran. I could never leave all the things that mean so much to me.'

Frank went across to join her. 'Let me tell you something, my girl,' he said, at her side, hugging her affectionately around her waist. 'This is your family, and I know they love you as much as you love them. But we won't always be here. Your mum and I are not getting any younger, and as for the others – well, one day they'll all be going their own separate ways – that's how life is.' He turned her round to face him. 'You're not a child any more, Liz. You're grown up, and you know how to take care of yourself. If you have the chance to find a new life with someone you love, then, as much as we'd all miss you, you *have* to take that chance.'

Lizzie shook her head again. This was one occasion when she was not prepared to listen to her father's advice.

Frank smiled affectionately at her. 'You'll know,' he said, 'when the time comes, you'll know what the right thing is to do.'

He had hardly finished speaking when they were distracted by a loud banging sound on the front door. When they hurried out to see what all the noise was, James had already opened the door, where the young Jones kid from across the road was yelling out a message.

'There's someone on the phone for yer over our place,' he barked. 'Mum says you're ter 'urry up over, or she'll cut off.'

'Who is it?' asked Harriet.

''Ow should *I* know?' called the boy. 'All 'e said was could 'e talk ter Mr Angel.'

Harriet and Lizzie immediately turned to look at Frank, who was already making his way out the front door. 'What is it, Frank?' Harriet asked, anxiously.

'It's nothing,' Frank called, as he followed the Jones boy to the front garden gate. 'Close the door and keep the heat in. I'll be back in a minute.'

Before anyone could say another word, he and the Jones boy had disappeared into the dark, leaving Harriet to close the front door calmly. As she turned round, she found Lizzie giving her an anxious, questioning look. Without a word passing between them, they quietly went back to join the others in the sitting room.

Chapter 5

Most of the traders in Petticoat Lane treated Norman as though he was a bit of a joke. Although he'd had his own picture frame stall in the market for several years, no one really knew anything about him; they didn't even know his surname – or if they did, then they hadn't taken it in. But Norman was a hard worker, and despite the fact that he was well into his fifties, of slight build, and standing only five foot four inches in height, he was always the first trader to open up his stall early every morning, and more often than not, he could be seen lugging around heavy wooden crates for some of his fellow stallholders. Unfortunately, however, although he was accepted in the market, none of the traders wanted to become too friendly with him. His appearance and manner were considered by most of the blokes to be a little too effeminate, in particular, his voice, which was very light and sibilant. The stuff he sold on his stall also gave the impression that he was a bit 'arty' for the rough and tumble of an East End street market.

The only person who really got on well with Norman was Rob, who always defended him when some of the traders referred to him as 'the nancy boy on the pitture stall'. But during these dark and grim times, when Rob was desperately trying to plan a future for himself and Lizzie, Norman was quite unexpectedly turning out to be someone he could turn to for friendly advice. They really became acquainted just before Christmas, when Rob had stopped at Norman's stall to watch him making a picture frame for one of his customers, but by the New Year Rob found himself talking openly to Norman about his relationship with Lizzie, and his fears for the future.

'Never keep things to yourself,' Norman told him, as the two of them sat together in Joe's café just down the road at the far end of the market. 'That way they become a secret, and that's when girls really get annoyed.'

Rob sighed, and took a gulp from his mug of tea. 'But I could never tell Liz that I work for Charlie,' he said. 'The idea that I'd given up an office job to help clear out dead people's houses would knock her for six.'

Norman looked up with a start. His eyes were so dark, his eyelashes so long, and his complexion so olive-coloured that he could almost have been a native of a Mediterranean country. 'Are you tellin' me,' he said, the tip of his rolled-up fag just holding on to some drooping ash, 'that you haven't even told that girl what kind of work you're doin'?'

Rob pulled on his Player's Weight cigarette, and waited far too long before exhaling the residue of the smoke from his lungs. 'I just don't see the point,' he replied with a shrug. 'She knows I come up to the market every day, but that's about it. In any case, it's none of her business really. I'm the one doing the job, not her.'

'None of her business!' Norman's ash finally

floated down on to the table as he nearly choked on Rob's words. 'I thought you said Liz was your steady?'

'She is.'

'The idol of your life? The only girl you've ever loved?' Rob tried to answer, but Norman wouldn't let him. 'Rob Thompson,' he spluttered, as he removed the remains of his fag from his lips and twisted it into the tin lid ashtray, 'I'm ashamed of you! Two young people who are going to spend the rest of their lives together should never keep secrets from each other. If they have worries, they should sit down together and talk about them.'

'But Liz is a girl, Norman,' said Rob defensively. 'She wouldn't understand *why* I'm doing this job. She wouldn't understand that I'd sooner be doing a menial job with people I know and trust than sitting trussed up in an office all day. I need time to breathe, Norman. I need space to find a way of getting us out of this bloody country.'

Norman stared at him in disbelief. 'I must say,' he said, leaning back in his chair, 'you're going about it in a very strange way. Because Liz is a girl doesn't mean that she's a fool. A girl is just as capable of working things out as us blokes.'

Rob sat back in his chair, unaware that some of the traders at a nearby table were smirking at him. 'Norman,' he said impulsively, 'I want to emigrate.'

'So I gather,' replied Norman, who was already taking out another of his own rolled-up fags from a tobacco tin in his coat pocket.

Rob leaned forward in his chair again, and lowered his voice. 'No, I'm serious. The Aussies are offering a ten-pound assisted passage scheme. I've already made enquiries.'

Norman lit his fag, and inhaled. He smiled mischievously at the other traders nearby, who quickly looked away. 'Have you discussed this yet with your girl?' he asked.

Rob shook his head.

'Why not?'

'She wouldn't understand.'

Norman gave an exasperated sigh. 'There you go again!' he said. 'In your eyes, a girl never seems to understand about anything.'

Rob immediately tried to explain what he was saying, but was again prevented from doing so.

'What you're really saying,' said Norman, fag dangling from lips, leaning forward in his chair and squaring up to Rob, 'is that you're afraid of rejection.'

Rob did a double take. 'I'm what?'

'You don't want to discuss your plans with Liz, because you're afraid she'll say no.'

'Don't be stupid, Norman,' said Rob, with a dismissive grin. 'I'm not afraid of anything. Before I say anything to anyone, I want to make sure I've got everything set up. I love Liz. I want to give her a better life than what she or I have here.'

Norman shook his head. 'Then tell her so,' he replied, the sibilance more pronounced as he talked.

Most of the traders had now left the café, and Rob and Norman were now virtually alone. Joe, the owner, a heavy-looking man in his sixties, looked at his watch and hoped it wouldn't be too long before he could close up for the day. And so he dropped a few hints by wiping the table tops, then piling chairs up on to them.

'Let me give you a word of advice, Rob,' said Norman.

Rob felt a bit uncomfortable when Norman covered his hand on the table with his own, but he tried not to show it.

'No matter how much a girl loves her feller,' said Norman, fag still dangling from his lips, 'it's a big thing to ask any girl to give up her family, and then be dragged off to the other side of the world – no friends, no familiar things, no one to turn to in the case of a crisis. A relationship between two people is not one-sided, Rob. Important decisions have to be discussed, and then taken by *both* sides. I only wish I'd realised that a long time ago when I was married.'

'*You?*' Rob asked. 'You were married?'

Norman grinned. 'Don't look so surprised,' he said. 'It does happen, you know, even though in my case it was a big mistake. Unfortunately my other half could never accept me for what I am.'

Rob was intrigued, but did not pursue the subject.

Joe called across to them: 'Come on now, Norman ol' gel! Party's over!'

Norman threw a passing scowl at him, but refused to respond to his jibe. 'Just remember, Rob,' he continued, pressing closer across the table. 'Don't make the same mistake. If you love someone enough – *really* love them – then treat

114

them as your equal. 'Cos if you don't, there'll never ever be any respect between you.'

It was snowing when Lizzie trudged her way to work along Lower Hornsey Road. By the time she had made her usual short cut via Mayton Street, Pakeman Street and Roden Street, her top coat was covered with a thin layer of white, and if it hadn't been for the brown woollen stockings her mother had knitted for her, her legs would have been frozen. As it was, her ears were so cold they felt as though they were about to fall off, and no matter how hard she tried to keep the snow from leaping up into her galoshes, her feet still felt wet. How she hated the winter, especially *this* winter, which was turning out to be a real pig. However, she had heard on the radio that only a few days before, New York had had over two feet of snow in just a few hours, so she was very glad she didn't live in a place like that. In fact, despite all the problems with the country at the moment, she was glad that she didn't live in *any* other place. But she did resent having to work on New Year's Day, which seemed to be a stupid tradition, especially when most people had sat up to see in the New Year the night before.

Woolworths store was doing far less business now that the Christmas rush was over. Most of the department stores such as Jones Brothers, James Selby and the North London Drapery Stores had already started their traditional winter sales, but Woolworths and Marks and Spencer were busy replenishing their stocks, and tidying

115

up after several weeks of manic buying.

Lizzie was relieved that most of the rush for gramophone records had subsided, so she spent the morning of New Year's Day tidying her counter and getting the remaining stock into some kind of order. The fact that there were few customers around also gave her and Potto a chance to compare notes about their Christmas break. But today, Potto was brimming with excitement, for she had a bit of gossip that was to prove very revealing.

'I tell yer it's true,' she said, after checking that no one could overhear her. 'Maple's got a shiner!'

'Shiner?' asked Lizzie, puzzled.

'A black eye,' replied Potto, with relish. 'A real number one.' With that, she nodded across to the other side of the store where Mabel Gosling was serving on the electrical goods counter.

From that distance, however, much as she tried, Lizzie couldn't see Maple very clearly.

'I'd be *very* interested ter know where she got *that* from?' said Potto, beaming smugly. 'P'raps she tried it on wiv some feller who don't like maple syrup!' she said, digging Lizzie in the ribs with a dirty chuckle.

Lizzie was not amused. In fact, she felt quite sorry for Maple, for despite the fact that Maple was a boaster, it was terrible if some bloke *had* beaten her up. A few minutes later, Lizzie sorted out a small pile of unsold gramophone records, and told Potto to hold the fort whilst she returned them to the stockroom at the back of the store. After she had done so, however, she made a detour, which took her past the electrical

116

goods counter where Maple, her right eye swollen and blue, was sitting forlornly on a stool waiting for customers. However, as soon as Maple saw Lizzie approaching the counter, she quickly tried to duck out of sight. But Lizzie was not to be deterred.

'Happy New Year, Maple,' she said, peering over the top of the counter.

Reluctantly, Maple slowly sat up. 'What's 'appy about it?' she asked mournfully, her assumed Canadian accent now reverting decidedly back to north London.

'Oh, Maple!' cried Lizzie, who was shocked by the bruises on Maple's face. 'What happened?'

'I walked into a door, din't I?' she replied, trying hard to cover her 'shiner' as she talked. 'It was an accident. These fings 'appen.'

Lizzie didn't believe a word Maple had said. Apart from the 'shiner', Maple's cheek was not only blue, but had a small abrasion, which had a plaster on it. 'I'm so sorry for you, Maple,' said Lizzie. 'What a rotten thing to happen at Christmas.'

'Wot diff'rence does it make?' replied Maple. 'In my 'ouse, Chrissmas is the same as any uvver time. I 'ate it!' She sighed. 'I can't wait till I can get back ter Toronto. At least out there they know 'ow ter celebrate.'

'Oh, Maple,' said Lizzie, who felt genuinely sorry for her. 'If only you'd told me, you could have come over to my place for Christmas. We don't exactly overeat, but we have a really lovely time. My brothers, sisters and I always put on a show for my mum and dad.'

Maple looked at Lizzie in absolute bewilderment. She couldn't believe what she had just heard, so she dismissed it. 'Oh, yes,' she replied cynically.

'I mean it!' insisted Lizzie. 'We love company, especially at Christmas. And, in any case, just think what you're missing – not only my mum's Christmas pudding, but my impersonations. I can do Winston Churchill now – without the cigar, of course!'

Without realising it, Maple smiled. But as her face was smarting, it hurt. Her eyes flicked up, and for a brief moment, she found herself looking into Lizzie's eyes. She had never noticed them before, mainly because she had never taken the trouble to look. They were not only dark and mischievous, but they were also kind. In those few seconds, the quiet shuffling sound of customers moving around the store seemed to fade away, and the only face Maple could see was Lizzie's. Kindness was something Maple was not used to. She wasn't a particularly kind person herself, so she never expected it in return. But to be asked by someone to actually go and spend Christmas with them – this was new, especially by someone whom she had always thought to be just like anyone else.

Lizzie waited for a browsing customer to move on, then leaned across the counter. 'Mums and dads *can* be a bit of a problem at times,' she said, 'so I suppose I'm lucky. My family are one in a million.'

Maple lowered her eyes.

'If you don't mind my saying, Maple,' said

118

Lizzie, 'you should mix more with the other girls. I know they tease a bit from time to time, but they don't mean it.' She looked over her shoulder to make sure that Betty Walker, their shop supervisor, wasn't around, and also to check that Potto was dealing with a customer. Then she leaned across Maple's counter as far as she could. 'Tell you what,' she said, voice lowered, 'why don't you and me go out one evening? We could go to the pictures or something. Or we could go ice-skating up at Harringay Arena. I bet you're a wonderful ice-skater. You must have done lots of it in Canada.'

Still clutching her 'shiner', Maple stared in astonishment with one eye at Lizzie. It couldn't be true. It couldn't be true what she had just been asked. Go out? Spend the evening with someone? Someone actually *wanted* to spend an evening with her?

'Come on, Maple!' said Lizzie, urging her on. 'We'd have a lovely time. If you like, I'll introduce you to my boyfriend. His name's Rob. He's really nice. You and he would get on so well together, I know you would. If you want, you could bring a boyfriend along too. You do have a boyfriend, don't you?'

Maple hesitated, then slowly shook her head.

Lizzie replied without hesitation, 'Well, it doesn't matter. We'll just have to find you one. There's some lucky person out there just waiting to meet up with you.'

Out of the corner of her eye, she suddenly caught sight of Miss Walker doing her rounds of the store, so she made her parting from Maple

119

brief, but warm. 'Don't worry, we'll fix something, Maple,' she said. 'I'll speak to you later.' With that, she rushed off back to her counter.

Maple watched her go, then lowered her hand from her 'shiner'. For a moment or so, she just stood there, scanning the store with her one good eye and squinting with the other. The Christmas decorations draped overhead were already taking on a faded look, and the Christmas trees by the entrance doors were shedding their needles. There were now more customers browsing around the counters, but Maple hardly noticed them. Her good eye was too firmly fixed on one of the large tinsel decorations hanging across the ceiling from her counter to the children's book counter opposite. On the decoration were huge printed words which read: 'HAPPY NEW YEAR TO ALL OUR CUSTOMERS'. Maple found it hard to read the words, for both her eyes were far too full of tears.

Although Frank Angel was born and brought up in London, Rotherhithe was one part of the great city that he didn't know. Situated close to the River Thames, the area, particularly the Surrey Docks, had been badly damaged by enemy air raids during the war, and the numerous warehouses were in need of rebuilding. The surrounding residential area had also been badly bomb-blasted, and many of the rows of terraced houses in the streets Frank had passed through had completely disappeared. His journey was made even grimmer by the weather, for visibility across the river was so bad that it was almost impossible to see the other side. A thick blanket of ice-cold mist was clinging to the surface of the river, and although it was only two o'clock in the afternoon, it was clear that the long winter evening would soon overwhelm whatever daylight still remained.

Even before the war, Sidley Street had been a bit of a dump. These days it was positively run-down, for most of the houses were uninhabitable and deserted. It was a pity, for when they were first built, during the latter part of the Victorian period, they were considered to be very desirable middle-class properties, which only fell to the working-class dockers and their families when the docks themselves became more and more an essential part of Thames commerce. When Frank reached the house he was looking for, he found that it was a three-storey building, and just as dilapidated as all the others in the terrace, but, interestingly enough, none of the houses had front gardens, not even small ones, which meant that the front doors led out straight on to the street, and, for obvious reasons, every window in the house he was about to enter was boarded up.

'Ah, Frank!' said his young mate, Dodger, who greeted him at the front door. 'So yer found yer way all right?'

'It took me long enough,' replied Frank dourly, hurrying straight in out of the cold.

'Anyway, mate,' said Dodger cheerily, closing the door and bolting it behind them, ''appy New Year!'

Frank saw no need to respond to such unwarranted optimism.

As the power had been cut off long ago, the hall was lit by a solitary oil lamp, which not only threw long, eerie shadows on to the crumbling plaster walls, but also made the place reek of paraffin.

'Look, Frank,' said Dodger, voice low but echoing in the empty stairwell, 'before I take yer up ter meet the boys, I fink there's somefin' yer oughta know.'

The boys? Frank didn't like the sound of it. Who were these 'boys'? A bunch of spivs, hardened criminals, all ex-convicts who would slit his throat if he made a wrong move? As Dodger moved up closer to talk to him, Frank was already beginning to wish that he hadn't got himself involved.

'They pay 'alf up front,' whispered Dodger, flicking a quick eye up the stairs to the door of a first-floor landing room, 'an' 'alf when the job's bin carried out. But they don't like any slip-ups. If there are – yer out, an' there's no two ways about it. Savvy?'

What Frank suspected then was true. If he slipped up doing a 'job', they'd probably cut him up and throw the pieces into the river. It wasn't only the weather outside that was now sending a chill down his spine, but the dangerous atmosphere inside the house.

'OK,' he replied, though it wasn't OK at all.

He followed Dodger up the stairs, but before they reached the first-floor landing, the door Dodger had been looking at suddenly opened, and a beam of light from inside the room not only flooded the staircase and glared straight into

Frank and Dodger's eyes, but also created a menacing silhouette of the figure standing in the open doorway.

'Ah!' called the middle-aged man, whose voice sounded breathless, as though it was coming through a gas mask. 'Got here at last. Good man!'

Frank's knees almost gave way beneath him, and for one fleeting moment he wished he had Harriet at his side to support him. But as the man stepped back into the room to allow him to enter, Frank was surprised to see that he was not only white-haired, but that he was well turned out in a thick woollen crew-neck pullover, a fawn duffel coat and a brown trilby hat.

'Mr Parfitt,' said Dodger. 'This is Frank. Frank, this is Mr Parfitt.'

The man, who was really quite handsome, smiled, and offered his hand. 'I hasten to add that it's not my real name,' he joked.

Frank shook hands with him, then heard Dodger close the door behind them. The room he was in was predictably bare, with little more than a table and chairs, a couple of oil lamps, and another smaller table by the boarded-up window that was piled up with files and paperwork. But at least there was a paraffin lamp in the grate where a fire had not been lit since the war, and Frank could at last feel some warmth flowing back into his body.

'I'm glad you were able to come,' said Parfitt, retrieving his pipe, which was smoking in an ashtray on the table. 'Dodger told me you were on an early shift at Billingsgate today. Why the

123

English insist on working on New Year's Day is a mystery to me. We should all go to Scotland and eat haggis!'

Frank tried hard to smile at the man's light-hearted remark, but it wasn't easy.

'Anyway,' continued Parfitt, 'how d'you feel about joining our little enterprise?'

'Depends,' replied Frank, his hands in his pocket.

'On what?' asked Parfitt, who had quite a cultured voice.

'On what I'm expected to do,' said Frank. 'I don't want to end up in prison.'

'Quite,' said Parfitt, taking a puff from his pipe. 'Neither do any of us. But Arthur here has told you something about our "work", I presume?'

It was the first time Frank had heard Dodger referred to by his Christian name, if that was his real name. 'You want me to sell a few goods?' he said, casting a quick look at Dodger, and then back to Parfitt.

'Absolutely.'

'The black market is quite a dangerous game,' said Frank.

'Indeed,' said Parfitt, pipe in mouth, moving to the fireplace to warm his hands. 'But an essential way of life, thanks to the mess this country has got itself into. You know, I fought in the first war. But I never expected that my wife and family would be rewarded by one day having to queue up for potatoes, and God knows what else.'

Frank listened, and in his heart of hearts, he agreed. After all, he had said the same thing himself many a time.

'That's why we all have to pull our weight, and do something about it.' Parfitt took his pipe out of his mouth, and tapped some of the burned tobacco into the grate.

While he was doing so, Frank just had time to notice a mouse scurrying across towards another door in the room, from beneath which he could see light filtering.

'We're not criminals, you know,' continued Parfitt, digging into the bowl of his pipe with a used matchstick. 'At least, *we* don't think we are.' He looked across at Dodger. 'We're not – are we, Arthur?'

'Right, sir!' replied Dodger obediently. 'I mean, no, sir!'

'We're just ordinary people,' continued Parfitt. 'Ordinary people trying to help other ordinary people. The stuff we sell is not stolen – well, not in the true sense of the word. It's – "acquired".'

Frank knew exactly what he meant, for there had long been tales of goods of all sorts supposedly falling off the backs of lorries on their way to the shops, and so-called discarded, unusable items such as clothes and rotting meat. But his was not to question where the merchandise came from, only what part he had to play, and how much it would help him to support his family. 'What exactly is it you would expect me to do?' he asked.

Parfitt smiled, and tapped more stale tobacco out of the bowl of his pipe. 'I think the best thing we can do,' he said, 'is to introduce you to the other members of the team. That way you'll get some idea what we're all about.' He walked across the room to the other door, and opened it. Immediately, the room they were in was flooded with light. 'Please...?' He stood back to let Frank enter the room.

When Frank looked in, he was absolutely staggered. Not only was the far room stacked to the ceiling with wooden crates and cardboard boxes, but Parfitt's 'team' who were gathered there included one well-dressed elderly woman amongst a mixture of several young and middle-aged men.

'Now we can get down to some real business,' said Parfitt.

Chapter 6

Post-war Britain was now in the grip of another great freeze-up, not as bad as the previous winter, but enough. Trains on all railway lines, antiquated and unheated, were constantly being stuck in deep snowdrifts, buses were skidding all over the icy roads, domestic plumbing was a nightmare, with pipes frozen solid, and people yet again having to collect buckets of water from public standpipes out in the street, ponds and lakes frozen over, and wild bird life everywhere desperate for any scraps of food they could retrieve from the barren wastes of metropolitan and rural landscapes. To make things worse, on 1 January 1948, the price of coal – when it could be obtained – had risen by two shillings and sixpence a hundredweight.

Like everyone else, the Angel family did their best to cope with the trials and tribulations of trying to keep warm. But, despite the fact that Frank had somehow managed to provide the family with enough coal to keep the prefab from freezing up entirely, the place was still ice-cold, prompting Susan Angel to complain bitterly that it was like living in an igloo. James and Benjamin loved it all, especially when the ink in their inkwells at school froze up, and after the first heavy snowfalls arrived, Benjamin loved nothing more than to hide out in the garden and pelt his brothers and sisters whenever they came out.

Harriet was as stoic as usual, joining the queue at the standpipe in the street each day, struggling home on treacherous pavements with the water, and rationing it as carefully as she possibly could with such a large family. But at least it gave her the chance to talk to some of the neighbours, which was something she hadn't really done since the family had lived in the old house up near the Archway Junction.

'They say we're goin' er get a National 'Ealth Service this year,' said Martha Cutting, waiting in the queue with Harriet and some of the other residents of Andover Road. 'It means we won't 'ave ter pay every time we go ter the doctor's.'

'Oh, yes?' sneered old Lil Beasley, holding on for dear life to her precious chipped china jug. 'And who's bin pullin' *your* bleedin' leg then?'

'It's true!' insisted Martha, so thin and gaunt she looked like a walking skeleton filling up her bucket at the tap. 'Me an' Alf 'eard it in The

127

Eaglet the uvver evenin'. They say Aneurin Bevan's definitely goin' ter bring it in this year.'

'Aneurin!' grunted Lil. 'Yer expect someone wiv a name like that ter do *anyfin'* fer the workin' classes? Bleedin' foreigner!'

'Stupid cow!' retorted Martha. 'Bevan's not a foreigner. 'E's a Welshman. Anyway, 'e's a good man. I believe in 'im *and* this government. I voted for 'em at the election.'

'I know,' snorted Lil, determined to have the last word. 'No wonder we're in the mess we're in!'

'You know, Lil, I think it's probably a good idea,' said Harriet, trying to inject a little sanity into the banter. 'Let's face it, it doesn't really matter who's in power, as long as they can help make life easier for us all. Doctors' bills are a nightmare.'

'Not if yer took out insurance,' said Lil. 'I've bin payin' a bit into the Prudential each week fer years.'

It took a moment or so for Harriet to respond to the old girl's reprimand. Of course, she knew Lil was right: the only way to deal with the doctor's bills was to pay for them through one of the many insurance schemes, but ever since the Angel family had been bombed out, and Frank had come home to no decent job, sacrifices had had to be made, and she had long ago had to abandon the weekly payments she and Frank had made for years. 'You're quite right, Lil,' she said, doing her best to cover up. 'I don't know what we'd all do without insurance.'

On her way home, Harriet thought a lot about

128

what old Lil had said, and about how she would cope if any of the children were taken seriously ill. But it wasn't only doctors' bills that were worrying her, it was the fact that unless something happened soon, the Angel family were going to have to face a real crisis. Fortunately, the local borough council had denied reports that they intended to scrap the prefabs in Andover Road, but even so, the Angels were a large family, and they needed space; they needed privacy. Harriet blamed herself. She blamed Frank. They should never have had so many children. In their circumstances, even before the war, it was a reckless thing to do.

To make matters worse, they had hardly seen Frank since the New Year. All Harriet knew was that he went off to work at Billingsgate early in the morning, and he had not been returning home until late in the evening. She had decided not to question him too closely about where he was going, for he had assured her that his extra job was soon going to prove lucrative. That was all very well, thought Harriet, but here they were, halfway through January, heavy falls of snow each day, frozen pipes at home and in danger of bursting whenever the thaw eventually came, and still she had seen no sign of this so-called extra cash that Frank had promised would help lift them out of their predicament. As she struggled back home with her bucket filled with water, along snow frozen hard by the below-zero temperatures, past houses with windows frosted over and huge icicles dangling down from the roof gutters, hemming in the top-floor occupants in their rooms as though they were locked in prison cells, she was plagued with thoughts about Frank's 'extra' job, and what he was really up to.

'Mum! What d'you think you're up to?'

Harriet was taken by surprise when she suddenly saw Lizzie calling to her from the gate of their prefab. 'Lizzie?'

'You shouldn't be doing this job on your own!' said Lizzie, scolding her, and taking the bucket from her. 'It's far too heavy for you. Why can't you leave it till Dad gets home?'

Harriet decided not to answer that. 'What are you doing home so early?' she asked, holding the gate back to let Lizzie pass. 'It's only one o'clock.'

'I told you,' said Lizzie, struggling to carry the bucket, 'I've got a half-day off to make up for the overtime I worked before Christmas. I'm going up to the Lane to see Rob.'

'The Lane?'

'Petticoat Lane.' As she finally reached the front door, Lizzie was huffing and puffing. 'He's got a job up there. It's only temporary, until he's found something better. But he wants to introduce me to his new boss.'

Harriet didn't really take in what Lizzie was telling her. She just opened the front door for her.

'Anyway,' said Lizzie, once she had put the bucket down in the kitchen, 'Benji's home from school.'

Harriet turned with a start. 'What!'

'There's no need to panic,' said Lizzie. 'He said his teacher sent him home because he's got a bit

130

of a temperature. I packed him straight off to bed.'

Harriet immediately panicked, and rushed straight into the children's bedroom.

'Mum, there's no need to panic!' called Lizzie, as she quickly followed her mother. 'He's perfectly all right.'

In the bedroom, Benjamin was tucked up in bed, looking thoroughly sorry for himself.

'Benjamin!' said Harriet, going straight to him. 'What is it, darling?'

Benjamin groaned. 'I don't feel very well,' he replied. 'I'm sweating all over.'

Harriet felt the boy's forehead, which was bathed in perspiration. 'Oh, darling,' she said, gently stroking his forehead, 'you are, aren't you? It's all right. I'll make you a nice cup of Ovaltine. You'll feel better by this evening.'

'But I've got a pimple on my bum,' said Benjamin mournfully.

'A pimple?' Harriet quickly pulled the bedclothes down. 'Let me see.'

Benjamin glared at Lizzie, and refused to turn over until she had left the room. Lizzie grinned, and duly obliged.

The stall traders in Petticoat Lane market were doing their best to dig themselves out of a heavy fall of snow. It had come quite unexpectedly in the early afternoon, just as Lizzie was trying to make her way there by bus to meet up with Rob. By the time she arrived, however, business was gradually getting back to as near to normal as was possible under such severe weather conditions, even though the customers wandering in and out of the stalls were somewhat sparse. When she eventually found her way to Charlie Feather's second-hand stall, Rob was waiting for her. He was clearly on edge.

'Didn't expect you,' he said, giving her a quick hug. 'Not in this weather.'

'I got held up, mainly at home,' Lizzie replied. 'Benjamin came back early from school. He's got a bit of a temperature. Mum's decided to keep him in bed.'

'Poor old Benj,' said Rob, blowing warm breath on to his fingers to try to warm them into life. 'Sounds like he's in the best place. At least he's warm. Thanks for coming, Liz.' He smiled, and gave her a quick, intimate kiss. 'I've been longing to see you.'

Every time they met Lizzie felt all warm inside. Rob always had such a way of making her feel wanted, and she loved it.

'Oi, oi!' called Charlie, as he approached from the yard at the back of the stall. 'This'd better be the little lady yer've been goin' on about fer so long,' he grinned, 'or you'll be in real trouble!'

Lizzie and Rob laughed.

'Charlie,' said Rob, with just a tinge of nervousness, 'I want you to meet Liz. Liz, this is Charlie.'

'I've heard a lot about you, Mr Feather,' said Lizzie, with a huge friendly smile, while shaking hands with him.

'Not all of it good, I'll bet!' joked Charlie. 'I must say, our Rob 'ere's a good picker. Lucky sod. No wonder 'e wants ter whisk yer off away from us all.'

Rob immediately panicked that Liz had twigged something, so he quickly searched for a way out. 'What Charlie means,' he joked, 'is that he wants me to hang around this stall for the rest of my life, doing all the work, while he goes off for a fag and a bitter down the Queens Arms!'

Both Charlie and Lizzie chuckled. A difficult moment for Rob had been avoided. Or at least, he thought it had.

'Where d'you get all the stuff from?' asked Lizzie, her eyes scanning the wealth of goods on show.

Charlie was about to answer, but Rob cut in pretty sharply. 'Oh, from all sorts of places. Isn't that right, Charlie?'

Unfortunately, Rob had not taken Charlie into his confidence as to why he hadn't told Lizzie too much about the work he was doing, and where the stuff they were selling came from. 'Other people's places more like!' he retorted, with a chuckle.

Lizzie was a bit confused, but again she let it pass.

'Come on, Liz,' Rob said quickly, slipping his arm around her waist. 'Let me show you around Charlie's cave.'

Again Lizzie was puzzled, but after bidding farewell to Charlie, she soon understood what Rob had meant when he led her inside what was in effect a veritable Aladdin's cave, a large room in a small warehouse just behind the market. Here, old furniture was piled high alongside trays of jewellery, most of it junk, but some of it really

133

quite charming, together with household goods of every description – towels, linen, blankets, old hats of every shape and size for both men and women, and there was even a man's rather moth-eaten astrakhan topcoat, which positively reeked of dust and tobacco smoke. Once they were inside and Rob had closed the door, the place was pretty dark, so he turned on a solitary overhead light, which made everything look even more gloomy. 'This is where we all end up sooner or later,' Charlie had mused to Rob on many an occasion. 'Stripped of everyfin' we've ever worked for.' But for Rob, clearing out the homes of dead people was just another job that somebody had to do.

'What an incredible place,' said Lizzie, scanning what to her looked like one big junk shop. 'Where does he get all this stuff from?'

'Oh, Charlie buys and sells,' replied Rob evasively.

'Yes,' said Lizzie, looking through the piles of household utensils stacked up in the corner. 'But he has to get it from somewhere in the first place.'

Rob was at a loss for words. As he watched Lizzie pick up and inspect a large enamel saucepan that had clearly been well used, he knew that he couldn't keep things from her much longer. Norman had already told him that if he wanted to retain Lizzie's respect for the rest of their lives then he was going to have to be truthful with her.

'It all comes from dead people, Liz,' he said.

Liz swung him a startled look. *'Dead* people?'

Rob tried to explain. 'When someone dies,' he said, 'the relatives ask Charlie to clear the house of anything they don't want themselves.'

Lizzie was shocked. She looked back at the saucepan she was holding, and quickly replaced it in the box she had taken it from. Unconsciously she wiped her hand on her coat.

'Mind you,' continued Rob, moving across to the trays of personal possessions laid out on one of several trestle tables, 'by the time they've all had their pick, there's rarely anything of value left over. Some people are like vultures. They wait for someone to die, then pounce before anyone else can get a look in. There are times when I despair of the human race. They have no principles, no shame.'

Lizzie looked as though she had seen a ghost. With her eyes taking in what to her were the gruesome contents all around her, she suddenly felt as though she was standing in a graveyard. 'You mean,' she stuttered, 'that all this stuff once belonged to people – who've died?'

Rob nodded uneasily. 'Yes,' he replied. 'When Charlie gets the call, I go out with him, and help him clear out. After we've sorted through everything and got rid of the rubbish, we bring the rest of the stuff up here. Charlie gets a commission on anything he sells. The rest goes to the relatives.' He looked at Lizzie, who had a pained expression. 'It's not as bad as it sounds,' he said. 'When you're clearing out some of the things, you try to imagine the kind of people they belonged to. One way and another, there must be hundreds of stories amongst all this stuff. Take this, for example.' He sorted out an old pocket watch and chain from one of the trays of brooches, hair combs, dress buckles, cufflinks, fountain pens, keyrings, propelling pencils, pill boxes, bead necklaces and cheap jewellery of every description. 'This,' he said, holding up the watch by its chain and looking at it, 'belonged to some old boy who lived on his own in Mayton Street. Didn't have a penny to his name, or so they thought. But when he died, his relatives found over a hundred quid stashed away in notes under the floorboards in his bedroom. That's all they wanted, all they'd been waiting for. Cash, Liz. That's all people ever *really* want. They couldn't care less about personal possessions like old family photographs, or books, or things that could carry memories. All they're interested in is what's in it for them. But then, you can't blame them, I suppose. After all, it's only human nature. But *this*...' He opened the cover of the watch to reveal its yellowing face. 'This old boy's neighbours said they'd never seen him without it, always tucked up safely in his waistcoat pocket as though it was the most precious thing in his life, even though it's made of tin and only worth a few bob at the most. Apparently it was a present from his wife who died just a few years before him. They'd been married for over fifty years.' He replaced the watch in the tray.

But when he turned to look back at Lizzie, he found her making for the door. 'Liz!' he called.

Outside, it was snowing again, and as it was now the middle of the afternoon, the market traders were beginning to give up hope of seeing many more customers that day. As she came out of Charlie's 'cave', Lizzie turned up her collar, and waited for Rob to join her.

'Liz,' said Rob, after he'd closed the door behind him, 'what's the matter?'

'How *could* you, Rob?' she said, her face racked with anguish. 'How could you do such a terrible, such an awful job? It's like working in an undertaker's shop or a graveyard – involving yourself in other people's misery. It's nothing more than blood money.'

Rob was shocked by her attitude. 'Blood money!' he retorted. 'Liz, somebody has to do the lousy jobs in life.'

'Yes,' she said, 'but why does it have to be you?'

Rob was stung. 'You mean, because once people are dead they can just be dismissed as though they never even existed?'

Lizzie shook her head vigorously. 'I mean,' she said, 'that you're worth so much more, Rob, so much better. You're young, you have a brain, you shouldn't be wasting your life doing such menial things.'

Rob was now angry with her. 'For Christsake, Liz!' he snapped. 'Stop being such a bloody snob!'

This hurt Lizzie, and suddenly she turned and walked off.

'Liz!' Rob hurried after her, and brought her to a halt. 'Liz, I'm sorry,' he said. 'I shouldn't've said that. But I've got to do the things that I want. If we're ever going to have a chance in this world, I've got to find a way of earning a decent living.'

Lizzie shook her head. 'This is not the way, Rob,' she insisted calmly. 'I just don't understand why you had to give up such a good job in that office.'

Rob felt as though he was going mad. 'How many times do I have to tell you, Liz?' he said, with a deep sigh. 'I don't *want* to work in an office. I want time to think, to plan our future together.'

'By clearing out dead people's homes?'

As they stood there, staring at each other as though they were suddenly no longer two young people who had loved no one else since the day they first met, snow was drifting against them in a bitterly cold wind, leaving them both covered from head to foot in a thin, layer of white, whilst behind them, a family of spaniel puppies, waiting to be sold from cardboard boxes and blankets in the back of one of the trader's vans, were whining and barking, straining to get out into the great big unknown world that was waiting for them.

'I want us to go to Australia, Liz.'

Lizzie had been dreading this moment. Somehow she had always known that it would come sooner or later.

Rob had done what Norman had asked him to do. He had come out with the truth at last. This is what he had been planning to do. This is what he wanted, and this is what he had to have. But now he had taken the plunge, and could see the blank expression on Lizzie's face, he was beginning to have his doubts. 'What I'm doing now may not be earning very much,' he said, 'but it's given me time to work things out. We can have a better life in Australia, Liz. The sooner we get away from all this misery, the sooner we can build a future together.' Disturbed that there was no response from her, he gently took hold of her hands. 'What d'you say, Liz?' he asked. 'Shall we try and make a go of it?'

'I don't want to go to Australia, Rob,' she replied, her expression pained but firm. *'This* is my country. I don't want to leave it.'

'Can't we even discuss it?' he pleaded.

Lizzie couldn't meet his eyes. She merely shook her head, and lowered it.

'We *have* to, Liz,' Rob insisted. 'Because if we don't, this thing is going to come between us. And in any case, I've already started to make enquiries.'

Lizzie's eyes shot up. For one brief moment, she stared him out. Then she turned, and walked off into the snow.

Benjamin was now feeling really sorry for himself. Not only was the pimple on his bottom itching like hell, but it had also been joined by others, and within a couple of hours, he had already developed an uncomfortable rash on his chest. By the time Lizzie got home just after five in the evening, both Benjamin and his young sister, Cissie, had been packed off to bed with spots, which were also now appearing on their faces.

'Chickenpox?' cried Lizzie in disbelief, as she heard the news.

'The doctor says there's no doubt about it at all,' said Harriet. 'There was nothing I could do.

I had to call him in. You should just see them, poor little mites – covered all over in spots. I'm having a devil's own job to stop them from scratching themselves.'

Lizzie quickly took off her coat, and threw it on to the nearest chair. 'But what's going to happen?' she asked anxiously. 'They can't go out like that. They can't go to school.'

'Of course they can't,' replied Harriet. 'In fact the doctor says they've got to stay in their bedroom and not see anybody for at least two weeks. You know how infectious chickenpox can be.'

'But what are we going to do about James and Susan?' asked Lizzie. 'If it's infectious, they can't sleep in the same room.'

'I've already packed them off to your grandmother's,' said Harriet calmly and practically. 'Susan was so hysterical when she knew what was going on, I thought it was the best thing to do. Gran wanted to give up her own bedroom for them, but I told her it wasn't necessary. Susan can sleep on the Put-u-up in the sitting room, and Gran's making up a bed for James on the floor. I think you should go too to help out.'

'Don't be silly, Mum,' Lizzie said immediately. 'I had chickenpox years ago. You can't catch it twice. And, in any case, I want to stay here and help you.'

'I can manage perfectly well on my own,' insisted Harriet. 'Your father'll be home soon. We'll take turns at keeping an eye on Benjamin and Cissie during the night.'

Lizzie wasn't at all happy with the arrangement. But what her mother was saying made sense, for she knew only too well how infectious the wretched disease could be. When she was Cissie's age, she'd fallen victim to the fierce rash all over her body, and the constant itching that came with it, so much so that she ended up with two small scars at the top of her leg where the unbearable discomfort had almost driven her mad throughout what seemed to be several endless nights. But if she left her mother to look after Benjamin and Cissie, who would help her? Where was her father? Why had he taken to being out so much in the evenings?

There was a ring at the front door. Lizzie went to see who was there.

''Ere yer are then.' Old Lil Beasley looked like Nanook of the North, standing there on the doorstep, covered from head to foot in snow, clutching a bottle of something or other. 'Lemon an' barley!' she said, handing over the bottle to Lizzie. 'I give it ter my youngest when she come down wiv the itch. If they burn up wiv the fever, give 'em a glass er this. It'll keep 'em from dryin' up wiv first fer a bit.' With that, she turned, and started to leave.

Utterly bewildered, Lizzie called to her, 'Come in, Mrs Beasley! Please, come in!'

Lil didn't even turn. She called back, 'I ain't comin' in! D'yer fink I want ter stay out on a night like this?' Before Lizzie could say another word, using her torch to light her path, the old girl waddled off through the day's fall of snow, which had now turned to ice, and disappeared into the dark of the street outside.

'Thank you, Mrs Beasley!' Lizzie called.

141

'Thank you so much!' She closed the door, and found her mum watching from the kitchen. 'She's incredible!' she said. 'She's got to be in her eighties, and just look at her. How did she know?'

'She saw me in the street when I went round to get the doctor,' said Harriet. 'I suppose she must have just put two and two together. They don't make them like Lil any more.' She took the bottle of lemon barley from Lizzie, and disappeared into the kitchen.

'Why don't you go and get your things together?' she called. 'Your dad will be home soon. There's no point in your hanging around here. Grandmother's going to need some help to look after James and Susan.'

Lizzie did what her mother asked, and went into her bedroom to see the young patients. The room was in darkness, so she turned on the light. Both Benjamin and Cissie ducked under the bedclothes, and only then did Lizzie remember how, when she had come down with the disease, the light irritated her eyes.

'Are you all right, you two?' she called quietly.

'Don't be stupid!' snapped Benjamin from beneath the heavy patchwork eiderdown. 'Of course we're not all right. We're dying!'

Despite the awful situation she knew her young brother and sister were in, Benjamin's characteristic return couldn't help bringing a smile to Lizzie's face. 'I'm sorry, Benji,' she said. 'Is it really awful?'

'Go away!' was all he would say.

'Is there anything I can get you?' Lizzie asked.

142

'Go away!' he repeated, more angrily.

'What about you, Cissie dear?' she asked, standing at the side of her young sister's fold-up bed. 'Would you like a drink or something?'

For a moment, there was no reply from Cissie, but gradually, Lizzie could hear the poor little thing sobbing beneath her eiderdown. 'Don't worry, Cissie,' she said gently, affectionately, perching on the side of the small fold-up bed. 'It'll all be over soon.'

Cissie's head slowly appeared above the bedclothes. Her face was covered in bright red spots. 'Will it really?' she asked in a tiny, sobbing voice, her eyes squinting in the bright light. 'Will it really be over soon?'

Lizzie wanted to hug and kiss her, but common sense prevailed. 'Of course it will,' she said, reassuringly. 'Just be a brave girl, and all the Angels will soon be back together again.'

As she said it, Benjamin's head suddenly popped up from beneath his bedclothes. His face was absolutely covered in a vivid scarlet rash. 'Why don't you go away and leave us alone!' he growled.

A short while later, Lizzie was making her way along the frozen wastes of Hornsey Road to spend the night with her grandmother in Tollington Park. For most of the time, her eyes were pinned to the treacherous path beneath her, but just occasionally she would look up at the clear night sky, where the moon was ringed with a dazzling white halo, and the stars were crowding each other out, twinkling bright, and singing their praises loud about the long, hard

143

winter they were presiding over.

For Lizzie, however, it was not only another miserable winter, but the day now coming to an end had been cruel and harsh. Her mind was absolutely awash with anxiety, about her angry young brother and her tearful sister, and about the difficult time her mother was facing without her father's shoulder to lean on. But most of all, she was thinking about Rob, and how foolish she had been to walk out on him up there in the market. The guilt she felt was now taking hold, and every moment she thought about it, the more she felt her stomach contracting. How could she have reacted to the man she loved in such a way? Rob was a dear, kind person, who would never even harm a flea, so why – *how* – could she dismiss him in such a way? But then she thought about what he wanted her to do. How *could* she leave her home, her family, her country, and all the things she loved most, to start a new life in a land that she knew nothing about – a land that, to her, seemed as remote as another planet? No, it would be wrong to split the family. The Angels were not only a family, they were a team. She had a duty to protect them, to be with them whenever they needed her.

But at that moment, she was suddenly haunted by another thought. Duty? Were the family the only ones she had a duty to consider? Surely, one day each and every one of her brothers and sisters would go his and her own separate way – birds deserting their nest. Would she really be willing to stay behind, to remain with her mother and father for the rest of their lives? She sighed, and thought of her father. Oh, if only he could guide her, if only he could tell her what to do. He had always been such an influence on her life, had always given her the advice she needed. But where was he now? Why wasn't he there when she needed him most, when the family needed him most? She came to a halt. The string of the paper carrier bag containing some of her belongings was cutting into her frozen fingers, so she unhooked it, and transferred the bag to the other hand.

She looked up, and was about to go on her way again when she suddenly saw a distant figure making its way down Hornsey Road towards her. As it approached, she could just make out the face of the man who was bathed in the bright fluorescent glow of the winter moon.

It was her father.

Chapter 7

Lizzie hadn't slept properly for almost a week. It wasn't because she had to share the Put-u-up in her grandmother's sitting room with Susan, but because as each day passed without seeing Rob, she was consumed with guilt about the way she had talked to him the last time they had met at the market in Petticoat Lane. As she lay awake night after night, trying to blot out the sounds of James snoring on a mattress on the floor on the other side of the room, she kept churning over in her mind all the things she wished she had said to Rob, but more particularly, all the things she wished she *hadn't* said.

Most of all, and after a great deal of thought, she had come to the conclusion how silly and childish she had been about the work Rob was doing. He was quite right, of course: when people died, their homes had to be cleared out. And if it was something Rob had decided to do, then she should have at least had the grace to support him. Yes. As most people would agree, it *was* a gruesome job, but, as Rob had said, somebody had to do it, so why not him?

However, the one thing that had really stuck in her mind was the fact that Rob had called her a snob. For some reason, that had hurt her more than anything else. Lizzie had never considered herself to be a snob. She was too outgoing, too fond of people to be like that, and in any case, how could anyone be a snob when they worked for a few bob behind a counter in Woolworths? No. Time and time again over the past week, she had refused to believe that she was such a thing. She was no Mabel Gosling. She wasn't trying to be something she could never be. And yet ... and yet there *was* a grain of truth in what Rob had accused her of. It wasn't the fact that she found clearing out dead people's homes to be a distasteful way to earn money, but that Rob had taken a job that had, in her mind, lowered his station in life. The more she thought about it, the more she cringed at her stupidity. If she loved Rob, then surely she should love him for what he was, and not what job he did.

But as she tossed and turned under her eiderdown, trying desperately hard not to wake up her tetchy sister, she knew the main problem – the *real* one – was not about dead people's homes or being a snob, but about being asked to leave her home and family to go and live on the other side of the world. Was she right to have reacted in such a way, she kept asking herself. Was she right to be so adamant, so dogmatic? After all, Rob had a perfect right to decide what he wanted to do with his life, and if he wanted Lizzie to be at his side, then shouldn't she feel warm and grateful that someone loved her enough to want to plan their future together? No. There were two sides to every argument, she told herself. As much as she loved Rob, he should at least have had the decency to talk the matter over with her before going off to find out about how the two of them could start a new life in Australia. Even though she had suspected what he had in mind, he should have told her. But the more she thought about it, the more she realised how Rob had always been like that – always assuming that anyone would automatically go along with what he wanted, always taking people for granted. Nonetheless, she *did* love him, and if she loved him enough, then she would have to make an effort to compromise. Silence between two people who cared for each other was so pointless, such a waste of time and energy.

It was still dark when she got to work that morning. She hated the dark winter mornings, which seemed to go on for ever, and it was worse when the weather was as cruel and ruthless as it had been over the past few weeks. Although the doors of Woolworths store were not yet open to the public, some of the staff were already busy doing their respective jobs, counter girls tidying up, dusting their stock, and collecting change for their individual cash tills, superintendents scurrying around checking that there were no problems, and juggling with display boards, and male staff replenishing some of the heavier stock from the rear stockrooms. As usual at this time of morning, there were plenty of yawns, and after the dark outside, it took everyone a long time to adjust their eyes to the bright overhead lights.

When Lizzie arrived, she found a group of her workmates gathered around the gramophone counter. 'What's all this then?' she quipped. 'A mothers' meeting?'

'It's not funny,' said Potto, whose eyes early every morning had so many bags under them she looked as though she'd been up all night. 'I mean, I don't like Maple, but I don't believe fer a minute she's a crook.'

The other girls agreed.

Lizzie was shocked. 'Maple?' she asked. 'A crook?'

'Ol' Muvver Walker's suspended 'er,' said Storky angrily, her head of tight brown curls quivering with indignation.

'Cow!' said one of the other girls.

'Would somebody please tell me what this is all about?' demanded Lizzie impatiently.

Potto drew close to her, looked around carefully, and lowered her voice. 'Miss Walker reported Maple because 'er takings on electrics last night

148

didn't match up wiv wot she'd sold. She 'ad ter go an' see Personnel, an' they've suspended 'er pendin' a so-called investigation.'

'What!' cried Lizzie, in disbelief. 'But Maple would never steal anything.'

'That's wot *I* said!' insisted one of the other girls, glaring over her shoulder as though the dreaded Miss Walker was anywhere near, which she wasn't. 'It's just that bleedin' woman. She's got it in fer all of us!'

'Where is Maple now?' asked Lizzie. 'Did she go home?'

'She's upstairs in Admin,' replied Storky, still seething with anger, 'waitin' ter be interviewed by some high-an'-mighty collar-an'-tie bozo!'

Lizzie quickly looked up at the overhead store clock above the clocks and watches counter. There was still ten minutes to opening time. 'Cover for me until I get back,' she said to Potto. 'If Walker wants to know where I am, tell her I've got an upset stomach and have gone to the toilet.'

Billingsgate Market was a hive of activity. The morning's catch from Lowestoft had arrived earlier than expected, and it was a good one. Today there was an abundance of bloaters, kippers, eels and sprats, which were always snapped up by retailers very quickly, and together with the usual haul of crabs and shrimps from Cromer, there was a lot of frenzied work ahead for everybody. To add to that, the early morning North Sea catch from Hull was expected at any moment, and the place would

149

soon be overflowing with the public's favourite cod, haddock and skate. There was also a modest supply of exotic fish such as mullet and octopus, which was usually favoured by the continentals and the local toffs, together with their lobsters and imported caviar.

Frank and Dodger had got into work at six o'clock in the morning, when it was pitch-dark and freezing cold. By the time they had their first break at nine o'clock, their hands were as frozen as the fish they were packing into ice in the wooden crates. Working in such conditions had always come hard to Frank, and he was always depressed that even when he had left the market at the end of the day and stopped off at Hornsey Road Baths, the smell of fish still seemed to pervade every part of his body. The first fags of the day that he and Dodger shared at Fred's nearby tea stall came as a real life-saver, despite the fact that the smoke had to compete with the pungent smell of sprats and kippers. With the façade of the old Victorian building behind them, the street outside bristling with Billingsgate porters in white overall jackets, trilbies and flat caps, Frank and Dodger smoked their fags and warmed their hands on the enamel tea mugs.

'Congratulations, mate!' said Dodger, making sure he was not overheard. 'The Guvnor's real pleased wiv you. 'E said yer did a good job wiv all them fags the uvver night. Made a mint by the sounds er fings.'

'Well, I wish the same could be said for me,' said Frank, condensation from the cold darting from his mouth as he spoke. 'I'm still waiting for somebody to pay me for the work I've done so far.'

A wide grin engulfed Dodger's face, making him look like the Cheshire cat. 'I'm glad yer've brought that up, ol' mate,' he replied. He nodded to Frank to follow him away from the stall to a more secluded place nearby. 'Got a little somefin' for yer,' he said, reaching into his coat pocket and producing an envelope. 'The Guvnor told me ter tell yer that when yer ready fer the next job, there's more where that come from.' He grinned as he discreetly handed over the envelope. 'Don't spend it all at once, old son!'

Frank looked at the envelope as though it was alive. Then he started to open it.

Dodger immediately stopped him from doing so. 'Not 'ere, yer berk!' he whispered, looking round to see if anyone was watching.

'How do I know if it's what I agreed?' Frank asked stubbornly.

Dodger stiffened, and looked quite put out. 'Wot d'yer fink the Guvnor is – a crook?'

Reluctantly, Frank slipped the envelope into his pocket.

Dodger waited for him to do so, then again took a quick look over his shoulder. 'Know anyfin' about Peckham?' he asked.

'Peckham? South London, you mean?' Frank shook his head. 'I've never been there,' he replied.

'Good!' said Dodger. ''Cos that's yer next job. All next week. Guvnor's givin' yer the van again. The hard stuff.'

'You mean spirits?'

Dodger grinned and nodded. 'Got five contacts

down there. Mostly pubs, but one or two, shall we say, "private regulars". The law ain't too worried down here. Some of the flatfoots don't care about what we're doin', as long as we keep them well supplied. The Guvnor always knows 'ow ter play 'is cards.'

'This Parfitt seems to know a lot of things,' replied Frank, sipping his tea again. 'How come someone like him got involved in all this?'

'You 'eard wot 'e said,' said Dodger. ''E's as fed up about the state of this country as the rest of us. Just 'cos 'e's a toff don't mean 'e don't care. Same goes fer 'is missus. Daisy's a real lady. Did 'er bit drivin' an ambulance durin' the war. They're a great couple. Salt er the earth!'

Frank wasn't sure about Dodger's estimation of Parfitt and his wife, for whatever picture he tried to paint of them, they were still criminals, who, if caught, could go to prison for quite a long time. Come to that, so could he. He shivered, but not from the cold. At that moment, Harriet's face came to mind, and Lizzie, and the rest of the Angel family. What would happen if their so-called breadwinner was suddenly thrown into prison? How would they face up to their neighbours, relations and friends if they discovered he was a criminal? It didn't bear thinking about. But he couldn't go on the way he had been going since he got out of the army. He had mouths to feed, and it was his duty to do so in any way that he could. Desperate times called for desperate measures.

'When will I get instructions?' he asked.

Dodger broke into another of his grins. 'I'll see

yer ternight,' he said. 'I should 'ave some news by then.' He winked, returned his mug to Fred's tea stall, and made his way back to work.

Frank waited for him to do so, then did the same, but before going back to work, he found his way to the nearby public lavatories, which were reached by going down a flight of steps underground. Fortunately, there was nobody at the urine stalls, so he was able to go into one of the WCs unnoticed. Once he had locked the door behind him, he first of all tried to breathe some warmth into his frozen hands.

Then he reached into his coat pocket and took out the envelope Dodger had passed on to him. He was too nervous to open it right away, and for a brief moment or so, he just stood there staring at it, his stomach turning over at the thought that the reward he was getting for putting his liberty at risk was not going to be worth it. His first concern was that there was no bulk in the envelope, which worried him because he was expecting at least a few one-pound notes. Unable to hold back any more, he suddenly ripped open the envelope, and took out the contents. His hands shook. Inside were six crisp five-pound notes. It took him a moment to catch his breath. It was more than he expected, much more. He closed his eyes in ecstasy. When he opened them again, his entire body felt as though it was on fire. There were tears in his eyes as he again thought of Harriet, Lizzie, and the rest of the Angels. Suddenly, at last, the world seemed a far better place.

Lizzie found Maple sitting forlornly on a bench in the corridor outside the admin office. It was a bleak sort of a place, which still carried posters on the wall from the war warning that 'CARELESS TALK COSTS LIVES'. Maple was sitting drooped forward in her seat, head lowered, elbows resting on her knees. She was wearing a plain apricot-coloured woollen cardigan, and as she had on no make-up at all, her face looked pale and wan.

Lizzie quietly sat down beside her. 'Maple?'

Maple looked up.

'What's this all about?'

Maple shook her head. Her eyes were red and sore; she had clearly been rubbing them to hold back the tears. 'It's not fair,' she said timidly, and with no trace of her Canadian accent. 'It's just not fair. I didn't take *anything*,' she said. 'I've *never* stolen anything in my whole life.'

'I know you haven't, Maple,' said Lizzie, putting her arm around Maple's shoulders, and keeping her voice low. 'But what happened?'

It took Maple a moment or so to compose herself enough to answer. She was not a particularly attractive-looking girl, but she had lovely violet-coloured eyes, a clear, faultless, milky white complexion, and a perfectly formed mouth. Unfortunately, her mousy-coloured hair looked in a bit of a mess, mainly Lizzie supposed, because the poor girl hadn't slept much the night before. 'It was the Tuesday woman,' Maple replied.

Lizzie was puzzled. 'The Tuesday woman?'

'That same woman who comes in on Tuesdays,'

said Maple. 'She's always there. I try to keep my eyes on her, but I can't always, especially if I've got a crowd at the counter. The trouble is, she looks so nice. I mean, for someone who's as well-dressed as that, it doesn't make sense.'

Lizzie pressed closer. 'Maple,' she asked, flicking one eye to the office door, which she expected to open at any moment, 'what are you talking about?'

'It's this customer,' replied Maple. 'Well, she's not really a customer, 'cos she never pays for anything. She always comes in on a Tuesday – don't ask me why. But I've seen her many a time wandering round the store. She goes round all the counters, but as far as I can tell, she never attempts to get away with things elsewhere. Trouble is, I'm easy. I let her get away with it.'

Lizzie found it difficult to understand what Maple was telling her. 'Maple,' she asked, 'are you saying that this woman is a shoplifter – and you let her get away with things on your counter?'

'It's not that I let her get away with it,' sighed Maple, 'it's just that I'm too nervous to stop her. I couldn't bear it if there was a row right there in the middle of the store. I wouldn't know how to cope with it.'

Lizzie clutched her head in disbelief. 'Maple!' she cried, aghast. 'Do you realise that by letting this woman steal things, you're being accused of doing it yourself?'

'I know,' replied Maple. 'But I just can't help it. She has such a kind face, and she's got a lovely voice – just like you.'

155

'To hell with her face and her voice!' Lizzie said angrily. 'This woman's a crook! She's got you in big trouble. Do you realise they could sack you, and then hand you over to the police?'

'Well, it's not my fault, is it?' insisted Maple defensively. 'I haven't got eyes in the back of my head, and even if I did, it's up to the store to make sure there's someone to check people's bags when they leave.'

There was some truth in what Maple said, for, as far as Lizzie knew, there seemed to be no such thing as a plainclothes store detective to keep an eye on shoplifters. Even so, Maple had behaved very stupidly, and at the moment, Lizzie couldn't see how the girl was going to be able to save her job. 'There's only one thing for it,' said Lizzie objectively. 'If they don't believe your story, then we'll have to catch this woman ourselves!'

Maple was taken aback. '*Us* catch her?' she asked. 'How?'

'It won't be you, Maple,' said Lizzie, 'because you'll probably be the number-one suspect and won't be allowed back into the store. But if all the girls and I keep a look out for her, then maybe the management will have second thoughts about you. Although I'm bound to say, Maple, you have been very foolish. You know that, don't you?'

Maple nodded reluctantly.

Only too aware that the poor girl had suffered enough already, Lizzie put her hand under Maple's chin, and gently raised it. 'We'll sort it out, don't worry,' she said with a sweet, sympathetic smile. She wasn't exactly confident that what she'd said was true, and only hoped that they would be able to catch up with the 'Tuesday lady'. 'Now, tell me exactly what she looks like…'

The public telephone box in Bovay Place was just a stone's throw from Woolworths store in Holloway Road. Unfortunately, as it was the only one in the immediate vicinity, by the time Lizzie got there when she left work, she found two people standing outside in the cold, waiting to use it. The old lady inside was chattering away nine to the dozen, and as the instrument was clearly still a novelty to her, she was shouting into the receiver as though it was the only way the person at the other end could hear her.

Once she had finished, a young bloke in a motor-cycle jacket went in, and he stayed there for the best part of fifteen minutes, chatting up his girlfriend about knowing someone who knew someone who could get him a pair of nylons for her with clothing coupons.

After he'd succeeded in fixing up a date with her, he finally replaced the receiver, and held the door open for a young woman who hadn't taken the trouble to sort out a few penny coins for her call, and spent several minutes rummaging through her purse. With the task eventually accomplished, she put in her first penny coin and waited for the ringing tone. It was so loud, Lizzie could hear it outside. Eventually someone answered, and the girl pressed Button 'A' to begin her conversation. To Lizzie's surprise, however, the conversation lasted no more than thirty seconds, for the person she was wanting to talk to appeared not to have been at home.

Lizzie was only too relieved to get out of the biting cold wind for a few minutes, and she had her penny coins ready and waiting. She had only telephoned the Thompsons' house once before, and that was when she had to call off a date with Rob when her mother had the flu. The Thompsons were lucky to have a telephone at all, for very few people in the neighbourhood could either afford one, or were suspicious of having a new-fangled contraption in their own home. Of course, the easiest thing for Lizzie to do would have been just to stop off at the Thompsons' house in Arthur Road on the way home, but as she had been so awful to Rob the last time she had seen him, *if* he still wanted to see her again, she wanted to try to put things right between them before they actually met.

'North five-two-oh-eight.' Mrs Thompson's voice was clear and crisp at the other end, and even more so because she spoke in what Rob called his mother's 'special' telephone voice.

'Hello, Mrs Thompson. This is Lizzie.'

The 'special' telephone voice was delighted. 'Lizzie, my dear!' she purred. 'How lovely to hear you. What a beastly evening. You must be so cold.'

'I am, Mrs Thompson,' said Lizzie, dropping more than a broad hint that she didn't want to stand talking. 'D'you think I could speak to Rob, please?'

'Of course, dear,' replied Mrs Thompson. 'He's upstairs in his room. I'll go and call him.'

'Thank you.'

There followed what seemed to be an interminable wait, during which Lizzie could hear the sound of the nightly radio thriller serial *Dick Barton – Special Agent* booming through the telephone from the Thompsons' radio set in the living room. Although she had rehearsed what she had intended to say to Rob, she knew only too well that the words would not come easily. Would she apologise for the way she had spoken to him the last time they met? Or would she say all that when they got together again? But in one fleeting moment of panic, she tried to imagine what she would say if Rob told her he never wanted to see her again. Should she appear angry, hurt, indifferent? Or should she just take it all in her stride, and accept that there were more fish in the sea? At the other end of the telephone, she could hear Rob's footsteps as he hurried down the stairs. Her heart was racing faster and faster.

'Hello? Liz?'

The moment she heard his voice again, she wanted to cry. She hadn't seen him for over two weeks, but all of a sudden it seemed like a lifetime. 'Hello, Rob,' she said, after running her tongue over her frozen lips. 'How are you?' She awaited his reply anxiously, praying that he would sound pleased to hear her. She wasn't disappointed.

'I'm fine,' he said, careful not to show that he was so relieved to hear her voice again. 'Where've you been?'

A short time later, they were in each other's

arms, hugging and kissing, and behaving as though they hadn't seen each other for months. Neither had taken the dramatic step of apologising to the other, even though they wanted to. But as they stood there in the ice-cold dark of Bovay Place, with the sound of trains and trolleybuses rumbling down Holloway Road at the end of the street, their bodies pressed close together was proof enough that they had both been distressed not to be in each other's company for so long.

'I'm sorry, Rob.' There. She had finally said it. She never thought she would, but now that she had, she felt much better. 'It was a stupid way to behave.'

'I'm the one who's sorry, Liz,' said Rob. 'I was like a bull in a china shop. It took all my courage to tell you what I wanted to do, and then when I finally did, I just took you for granted.' He went silent for a moment. 'I missed you,' he said softly.

'I missed you too.'

'Cor! Ain't love grand!'

As the corner street gaslight wasn't working, Liz couldn't see who had been taking the mickey out of them. But by the sound of the voice, and the laughter that followed, they guessed that it was two clever young dicks, who had been loitering in the shadows nearby, listening to everything they had said.

Rob pulled Lizzie further into the dark behind a huge empty skip that had been filled with sand during the war, and used to smother small incendiary bombs. 'Liz,' he said, their faces almost touching, 'we've got to get something

160

settled. Do you want me to give up my job with Charlie Feather?'

Lizzie answered immediately, 'No, Rob! Of course I don't! It was stupid the way I reacted. You have every right to do any job you want.'

'Even if it includes clearing out dead people's houses?'

There was a momentary silence from Lizzie. 'If that's what you want, Rob,' she replied. She had to force out the words.

Rob now had her back pinned against a high garden wall. 'I want to tell you something, Liz,' he said. 'I've got a bit of money stashed away. I've been adding to it ever since I got demobbed. It's not very much, but there's enough there now for both of us.'

Lizzie was astonished. 'Rob!' she asked. 'What do you mean?'

'I mean,' he said, 'that I want to use it for you and me to get married, to set up home together. I think we should do it as soon as possible. Not too much fuss – just family and a few friends. Beales do catering for weddings. I'm sure my old man would cough up a bit extra to help us out.'

Lizzie was breathless with the speed at which Rob was telling her all this. 'But we can't,' she said. 'It's just not possible. Not now. Not just yet.'

'Why not?' asked Rob impatiently. 'What's the point of waiting? We love each other, don't we? And you've said plenty of times that you can't wait till we get married and have kids of our own.'

'I know,' said Lizzie, with obvious anguish, 'but

it's not as easy as that. You see, if we got married now, my father couldn't... Well, you know what I mean. My parents are supposed to pay for the bulk of the expenses.'

'Liz, I know that!' replied Rob. 'I know the circumstances your family are in, and there's absolutely no need for them to go to any expense. I've got enough money to see us through, Liz. We can stand on our own two feet.'

Although he couldn't really see her in the dark, he knew she was slowly shaking her head.

'Dad's a proud man, Rob,' she said. 'He'd never agree to let you and your family pay for his own daughter to get married.'

'I'm not asking for *anyone* to pay for us, Liz,' said Rob. 'All I'm saying is that it's quite pointless to wait until we've got enough money to spend the rest of our lives together. If we do that, we'll probably stay single for ever. Come on, Liz, let's give it a try. We've been together a long time now. We know each other, how the other feels and thinks.' He waited for a reply. But there was only silence from Lizzie. 'I tell you what,' he said, quite suddenly. 'Would you like me to talk it over with your dad? After all, you're under twenty-one and officially I should ask his permission. Oh, come on, Liz! What d'you say? For once, why don't we do something positive in our lives?'

Lizzie hesitated, then said, 'I *do* want to marry you, Rob. You know I do.'

'Then that's settled!' said Rob without waiting for Lizzie to say another word. 'I'll come round and see your mum and dad when I get back from

162

the Lane tomorrow evening. But I'm telling you,' he leaned close, and kissed her ice-cold lips, 'I still want us to go to Australia.'

Chapter 8

Susan Angel didn't take too kindly to the news that her elder sister was going to get married. Although it wasn't yet official that it was going ahead, the moment Lizzie had confided in her, she dismissed the idea as 'silly'. She had never really liked Rob Thompson, or that was the impression she had always tried to give: he was too full of himself, too forward. But she did find him handsome, in a rough, rugged sort of way, and so different from the bright young 'chaps', the stock market types she usually met up with, most of them introduced to her by her friend, Jane Hetherington.

For Susan, Jane was her perfect role model, who knew just about everything about everything and everybody. What's more, Jane was well read, and was always passing on to Susan her old copies of fascinating magazines like *Picture Post* and *Woman's Own*. Jane also knew how to dress, and to make the most out of her clothing coupons, and as her parents let her have anything she wanted, despite the shortage of practically everything, she seemed to have an endless wardrobe of pretty clothes.

Susan wasn't exactly ashamed of the fact that

her family were not well off, but she did yearn for the good things in life, and she blamed her father for not making more of an effort to improve his position. However, Susan wasn't all that bad. When she was young, she had sometimes shown surprising consideration for her mother, especially during those times in the war when her father was away in the army, and Harriet had been worried stiff after reading in the newspaper about all the horrors the British soldiers were having to face up to on the battlefields of France after D-Day. There was another side to Susan, a side she rarely allowed anyone to see, and deep down inside, despite all her grand ways and prejudices, she loved her parents. She was also the most beautiful of the three sisters, with a lovely rosy complexion, brown eyes, and long auburn hair that was tied in a bow behind, and even though there was hardly ever the chance to have new clothes, what she did have she used with great panache, such as a small cotton scarf thrown recklessly around her neck, or a pair of tiny clip earrings used to set off a brooch her mother had given her years before. No, Susan's main problem was jealousy, and it didn't help that she was a secret admirer of the man her sister was going to marry.

The following Sunday afternoon, Lizzie brought Rob home to tea. As her young brother and sister were now clear of the infectious stage of their chickenpox, Susan made quite sure she was there, and that she was looking as glamorous as she could possibly be. Since the end of the war, hard times had forced the Angels into giving up their ritual Sunday afternoon tea, with

Harriet's favourite cucumber sandwiches, and home-made cakes, but today there seemed to be an abundance of practically everything, including a jam sponge cake, which Harriet had made with dried egg powder, and which young James had every intention of finishing off the moment the present company had left him in peace to do so. Susan made sure she sat right opposite Rob at the tea table, and on more than one occasion did her best to catch his eye, much to the amusement of Lizzie, who knew exactly what her sister was up to.

However, Susan was not at all happy when, as soon as the meal had finished, she and James were shuffled off to the bedrooms, giving Harriet and Lizzie the excuse to clear the plates and do the washing-up in the kitchen, whilst Frank and Rob were left alone to have their little pre-arranged chat.

'I take it you've finally fixed up the day?' asked Frank, offering Rob one of his cigarettes.

'Not the exact day,' replied Rob, lighting up for both Frank and himself. 'But we thought some time in the spring.'

Frank raised his eyebrows. 'As soon as that?'

'If that's all right with you, Mr Angel?'

Frank grinned. 'With me? Of course it is, son,' he said. 'Lizzie's a lucky girl.'

'I reckon I'm the lucky one,' replied Rob. 'That's why I don't want to wait any longer. I've got so many plans for us, so many things I want us to do – that is, if I can persuade Lizzie to trust me.'

Again, Frank was puzzled. 'What d'you mean?'

165

he asked.

'Just that she's got a mind of her own,' replied Rob. 'You can never get Lizzie to do anything unless she thinks about the family first. I know her family's important to her – so is mine to me – but when it comes to our own future, I think you'd agree that we have to put ourselves first.'

Frank nodded. He knew exactly what Rob meant. Lizzie had always been a home girl, passionately devoted to her family, putting them before anything else in her life. He had often talked to her about it, warning her that, when it came to her own future, she should consider herself first. But it was true. As much as he loved Lizzie, he was only too aware that she could sometimes be a stubborn girl, and that it was unhealthy for her to be so tied to such rigid ideas.

Rob took a moment to pull on his cigarette. 'I know I'm a bit of a pusher,' he said, 'always trying to get my own way, but I just wish that sometimes – just *sometimes* – she'd listen to me.'

'What's the problem, Rob?'

Frank's sudden question took Rob by surprise. But it came as something of a relief to have the opportunity to talk to the one person whom he knew Lizzie trusted. 'Lizzie says it would be wrong to get married so soon. She says we should wait until things get better for you and the family.' He lowered his eyes awkwardly. 'Until you're able to afford it.'

Frank's expression changed. He sat back in his chair, taking stock of what Rob had just said.

'I told her it wasn't necessary,' said Rob, desperately trying to explain. 'I tried to tell her that I've got enough money saved up to pay for the wedding, as long as it isn't too big. I also told her that my own parents could chip in and help out. But Lizzie said you'd be very upset if you knew that you couldn't pay your share.'

Frank pulled on his cigarette. 'I'm not upset, Rob,' he said, with an understanding smile. He was still a good-looking man, and the fact that a few grey hairs were beginning to sprout in his mop of dark hair only made him look younger than his forty-three years. 'As a matter of fact, I'm very grateful that you've been so thoughtful about – my circumstances. However,' he got up from his chair and went to collect a small glass ashtray from the mantelpiece, 'I want you to know that if you and Lizzie want to get married, then whenever it is, I'll be very happy to pay whatever it costs.'

Susan was stunned when she heard what her father had just said to Rob. Listening from inside her parents' bedroom to everything that had been going on, she gently eased the door open just enough so that she could hear more.

Rob also was clearly taken aback by what Frank had just said to him. Lizzie had gone on for so long now about how destitute her family had become since being bombed out, that hearing her father offering to pay for the wedding was the last thing he had ever contemplated.

'That's ... very generous of you, Mr Angel,' he spluttered. 'But I'm sure my mum and dad would want to contribute at least in some way.'

'The best thing we can do,' said Frank, return-ing with the ashtray, 'is for all of us to meet up, and talk things over. All you and Lizzie have to do is give us some indication of where and when you want the wedding to be.'

Rob was reeling. 'With respect, Mr Angel, I don't think Lizzie will take very kindly to you struggling to find money for this.'

'Who said I'd be struggling?' asked Frank.

In the bedroom, Susan couldn't believe what she'd just heard. What was her father saying? Where had all this money suddenly come from?

'You don't have to worry,' said Frank. 'You can count on me to pay whatever's necessary. And as far as Lizzie's concerned, you can leave her to me.' He grinned. 'I love her dearly, but she can be as stubborn as hell when she digs her heels in. You're going to have quite a fight on your hands to tame her!'

Although Rob laughed, he was still shattered. When he'd asked Lizzie if he could have a chat with her father, this was the last thing he had expected to hear.

'What about your job?' Frank asked. 'Lizzie tells me you're working up the market in Petticoat Lane.'

Again Rob was taken aback. 'Oh – yes, that's right,' he replied falteringly. 'But it's only a temporary job. Just filling in really.'

'Until you find something better?'

Rob hesitated before answering. 'It's not quite as simple as that,' he said. 'You see, I've asked Lizzie to emigrate with me. To Australia.'

In the kitchen, Harriet received the same news from Lizzie. But her reaction was somewhat different from that of her husband. 'Australia?'

168

she asked in horror and disbelief, looking at Lizzie as though she had gone stark raving mad. 'Rob Thompson wants you – to emigrate?'

'I know,' replied Lizzie, drying the dishes her mother was washing up at the kitchen sink. 'That's how I felt when he asked me. I've suspected for some time that he dreamed of doing something like this, but I never thought he'd expect me to take it seriously.'

'I hope you told him not to be so childish?' asked Harriet haughtily.

Lizzie looked up at her with a start. 'No, Mum,' she said, somewhat surprised that her mother had made such a snide remark. 'I don't say things like that to Rob.'

'Then what *did* you say to him?' Harriet asked, almost dreading to hear the answer.

'I told him I'd find it very difficult to leave my family, and go all the way across the world to a place I know nothing about.'

Harriet breathed a sigh of relief, and continued to wash the plate she had in the sink. 'And so I should think!' she muttered with relief.

'But I also said I'd think about it.'

Harriet stopped what she was doing, and swung an anxious look up at Lizzie.

'I've agreed to go to one of the film shows the Australians put on at their High Commission building,' said Lizzie, doing her best to avoid her mother's gaze. 'Rob says there are so many people who want to emigrate, they do this sort of thing all the time. Apparently, they offer a ten-pound assisted passage scheme to help any young couples who want to settle there.'

'You mean ten pounds to split up family life,' retorted Harriet. 'Ten pounds to split up families for the rest of their lives. I always thought Rob was a sensible young man. I never thought he'd be so inconsiderate about how me and your father would feel if you were to do such a thing.'

Although Lizzie had anticipated her mother's adverse reaction to the idea, she was taken aback by the way she was turning it into a personal attack on Rob, whom she had always seemed to like so much. 'Mum, I don't think it's fair to talk about Rob like that. He knows exactly how I feel ... how we all feel.'

Harriet stiffened, and with the back of her wet hand pushed back a lock of hair that had flopped over one of her eyes. 'Then why has he asked you to do this?' she demanded.

Lizzie shrugged. 'Because he's restless,' she said. 'Because he wants to make a better life for us after we're married.'

'After you're married? Ha!' Harriet scoffed, and returned to her washing-up. 'You'll be lucky!'

Lizzie was astonished by her mother's tone. 'What d'you mean, Mum?' she asked.

'I mean,' replied Harriet, turning on her, 'that the way things are going, your father wouldn't be able to pay for your wedding for at least another few years. In case you hadn't noticed, we hardly have enough money to feed this family!'

For a moment, Lizzie felt quite stung and hurt by her mother's outburst. She had always enjoyed such a harmonious relationship with her that hearing her talk like this was really quite upsetting. It unsettled Lizzie to know that her mother was being so insensitive and was not prepared to understand how, like so many other young couples around the country, she and Rob were facing the real predicament of not knowing how to deal with their future. 'I think you should know, Mum,' she said, quietly putting down the drying-up cloth on the draining board, 'that Rob has saved up some money to pay for the wedding. He said that if I agreed to go along with this emigration idea, he has enough to pay for that too.' She went across to sit at the kitchen table. 'He also said that he would never allow Dad to get into financial difficulties just because we want to get married. And in any case, his own father would be only too glad to help out.'

Harriet virtually slammed the plate she was washing back into the bowl. 'What?' she growled, turning with a penetrating glare. 'You'd allow Rob Thompson to humiliate your own father? Have you taken leave of your senses? What do you take this family for?'

Lizzie couldn't believe what she was hearing.

Drying her hands on the drying-up cloth, Harriet strode across to her. 'Strangely enough, Lizzie,' she said cuttingly, 'I've always thought you had more respect for your dad. Do you really expect he'd allow somebody else to pay for his own daughter's wedding?'

'No, Mum,' Lizzie replied calmly, trying to diffuse what was turning into an ugly few moments. 'All I'm saying is that Rob knows how difficult it is for you and Dad at the moment. He doesn't want to lumber you with any more burdens. He just wants us to get married as soon as possible.'

'Why?' snapped Harriet angrily. 'What's all the rush? You're not pregnant, are you?'

'Mum!'

'Well, why can't you wait? Why all this rush into doing things that you might regret for the rest of your life?'

Lizzie was shocked. She had never heard her mother talk in such a way, and she hardly knew how to respond to her. 'Mum,' she said, lowering her voice in case Rob could hear her in the sitting room, 'we haven't actually decided anything yet. That's why Rob wanted to come and talk things over with Dad tonight. He wants to share his thoughts with him.'

'Does he now?'

Harriet's cynical reply disheartened Lizzie. She was beginning to feel that anything she said would make no impact on her mother at all. 'Mum,' she said forlornly, 'I love you and Dad. I would never do anything to hurt you.'

Harriet calmly sat down at the table. 'I know you wouldn't, darling,' she said, with a laboured smile. She gently took hold of Lizzie's hand, and patted it. 'So don't let's hear any more silly talk about Australia. The Angels are a good family, and we all love you too. You do know that, darling – don't you?'

On Monday evening, Frank went straight to see Parfitt in his house overlooking Highbury Fields. It turned out to be one hell of a journey from Billingsgate, for the main roads were now so treacherous because of snow turning to ice that buses and trains were in short supply, and Frank had no choice but to walk for part of the way. When he finally reached the house, he immediately had a strange feeling of *déjà vu*, for in many ways the façade of the building resembled the old Victorian house the Angel family had lived in for so many years before it had been devastated by a bomb towards the end of the war. Set on three floors, number 18 Threshold Avenue was part of a long terrace of houses that in the summer was lined on either side by massive chestnut trees, whose leaves were so green and shiny that they provided the most wonderful shade when the summer temperatures were too high. He was greeted at the door by Parfitt himself, whose heavy-knitted white crew-neck pullover matched the colour of his hair.

'Ah!' he said, beaming. 'Good to see you again, old man!'

Frank was shown into the spacious hall, and the first thing he noticed was how warm it was.

Parfitt's wife, Daisy, was waiting for them in the sitting room. She was an elegantly dressed woman in her early sixties, with a head of thick white hair that was brushed back behind her ears to reveal an ageless fair complexion, and thin tight lips that contained only a faint trace of pale red lipstick, and a small mole on the right-hand side of her chin, which had been delicately picked out with black mascara.

'Come and sit by the fire, Mr Angel,' she said, in a cultured voice that matched her appearance. 'It's such an awful night.'

A few minutes later, Frank found himself sitting on the sofa alongside the redoubtable Daisy Parfitt, sipping a gin and tonic, and wondering what he was doing there with two perfectly charming people who were, in reality, nothing but a couple of crooks. He also found the sheer normality of the room very unsettling, for it could have been the home of any of the down-to-earth people he had known all his life. Ordinary people in an ordinary sitting room, surrounded by ordinary furniture and ordinary everything, including wallpaper with a faded pattern, and framed family portraits scattered all over the place.

'That was a grand job you did at Peckham,' said Parfitt, who had settled down to smoke his pipe in his favourite armchair by the fire. 'It was very able of you to get rid of the stuff – and in so little time. Well done, Angel!'

'Thank you,' replied Frank, who felt like a subaltern talking to his commanding officer. 'And thank you for the bonus. I appreciate it.'

Parfitt smiled back at him, and waved a dismissive hand. 'So what can I do for you?'

'I beg your pardon?' asked Frank.

'Dodger sent a message to say you wanted to talk to me.'

Only then did Frank remember why he had come. He suddenly had a panic attack. 'Oh yes,' he replied. He took a quick gulp of gin, conscious that both Parfitt and his wife were watching him closely. 'I have a situation at home,' he said awkwardly.

'A *situation?*' asked Parfitt warily.

'It's my daughter,' replied Frank, shifting about uneasily on the sofa. 'She wants to get married. I have to find quite a lot of money to pay for the wedding.'

'Ah!' said Parfitt, exchanging a relieved look with his wife.

'When's the happy day, Mr Angel?' Daisy asked.

'Some time in the spring.'

'And who's the lucky man?' asked Parfitt through a cloud of pipe smoke.

Frank felt uneasy talking about Lizzie and Rob to these people. After all, Lizzie knew nothing about the kind of 'extra' work he was doing, and would be horrified if she found out, but if he was to fulfil the wild promise he had made to Rob about paying for the wedding, he had no choice but to play along with Parfitt. 'He's a very nice young chap,' he said. 'He wants the two of them to emigrate to Australia.'

'Australia? Did you hear that, Daisy?' As he spoke, a brown Persian cat suddenly appeared from under Parfitt's chair, and leaped on to his lap. 'It's a small world, isn't it?'

Frank was puzzled.

Daisy explained, 'My son from my first marriage emigrated there before the war. He's doing very well in textiles.'

'There are so many more opportunities out there,' said Parfitt, stroking the cat, who was purring so loudly Frank could hardly hear what was being said. 'I wouldn't blame any young couple who want to get away from this country. If Daisy and I were thirty years younger, we'd do

175

it ourselves.' He turned to her. 'Wouldn't we, dear?'

'I suppose so,' replied Daisy, who gracefully, with one finger, wiped back a couple of strands of hair that had strayed across her forehead. 'But I'd find it difficult to cope with all those horrid insects. And apparently they have crocodiles in some parts of the country.'

'Yes, but not where Johnny boy is,' Parfitt assured her. 'However,' he continued, 'that's another story. What you're looking for is some more money, old chap. So we must find a way to help you. Isn't that right, Shah?'

The cat on his lap responded with even louder purring, and then by rubbing the side of his face sensually against Parfitt's pullover.

Frank thought the whole thing was getting more and more bizarre. It was as though he was attending a social function with a vicar and his wife who were capable of getting them all sent to prison.

'What we need,' said Parfitt, 'is a job – a bigger job – one that will give you a chance to make a more profitable return. But what?' He flicked a look at his wife.

'How about Wethersfield?' asked Daisy.

Parfitt's face lit up. 'Ah!' he replied. 'Now there's a thought.' He turned back to Frank. 'Have you ever heard of a place called Wethersfield, old boy?'

Frank shook his head. 'I don't think so.'

'It's a small village in north Essex,' continued Parfitt. 'It's main claim to fame is an American Air Force base. Those boys did a grand job for us

176

during the war.' He picked up the cat, and stood up. 'Come on, Shah,' he said, gently dropping the creature to the floor. 'I can't sit here nursing you all night.'

Frank watched Parfitt carefully whilst he went across to what looked like a mahogany flip-top portmanteau on the other side of the room.

'We have a couple of very good contacts at Wethersfield,' said Parfitt, checking through some papers he had taken from the drawer of the portmanteau. 'From time to time they cooperate very well with our own people. Yes – here we are.' He found what he was looking for. 'The base PBX stores are expecting a new consignment at the end of the month.'

'That's next week,' said Daisy.

'So it is,' said Parfitt, who knew perfectly well that it was. He came back to his seat with one of the pieces of paper in his hand. 'There's some very good stuff in that load,' he said, sitting down again. 'We need to organise a safe drop.'

Frank looked puzzled. He wasn't familiar with crooks' jargon.

Parfitt grinned. 'Someone to collect the merchandise,' he explained, 'and take it to one of our secure storage units. It's an important job, old man – good quality whisky and vodka, nylon stockings, American cigarettes, chocolates – that sort of stuff. Sell like a bomb on the market.' He paused just long enough to take a puff on his pipe. 'It would be quite an adventure for you, old man. If we give it to you, it would be a sign that we trust you. After Peckham, we're prepared to do just that. What d'you say?'

Frank felt his stomach churn. He was only too aware that 'quite an adventure' really meant that he was being asked to take a risk. Was it worth it, he asked himself. 'What would it involve?' he enquired.

Parfitt looked across at his wife. 'My dear?'

'It's very simple really, Mr Angel,' explained Daisy. 'We'll give you a suitable vehicle to go to Wethersfield. There's a very nice pub there where you could meet our two contacts. They would then tell you how and where they intend to pass the stuff over to you, and fix a time for doing so. It would probably be somewhere in the countryside, away from the base itself.'

Frank felt quite sick. He was getting deeper and deeper into all this, and he knew it.

'You look unsure, old man,' said Parfitt, eyeing Frank guardedly through a cloud of pipe smoke.

'I don't know,' replied Frank. 'I don't know whether I could take on something like that. I'd be quite nervous going all that way.'

Parfitt and his wife chuckled at each other. 'Essex is only a stone's throw from London,' said Daisy. 'And it's a lovely journey through Epping Forest, and some beautiful countryside.'

'Not so beautiful in the middle of winter,' Frank reminded her. 'Not in *this* weather.'

Parfitt sat back in his chair. He was on the verge of being irritated by Frank's reaction. 'Of course, the job carries more money,' he said. 'Much more than you've earned from us so far. If our contacts in Wethersfield report back favourably on their dealings with you, it's possible we could let you do this on a more permanent basis. And

178

that, of course, would mean a considerable increase on what we pay you now.'

When Parfitt talked like this, all Frank could think about was Lizzie. Regular money coming in, *good* money – it would solve so many problems, like winning the football pools.

'I know how you must feel,' said Daisy, who had the sweetest, most sympathetic smile. 'It isn't easy doing things that you've never done before. It's a whole new experience trying to find money to buy the things you so desperately need, things that, before the war, were never considered to be luxuries.' There was a strange yearning in her voice. 'These days, when I look in shop windows, I think of all the beautiful things I used to have, and can't any more. Sometimes I wish they would just jump out of the window and straight into my pocket. We have a right to those things, Mr Angel – no matter *how* we get them.'

'So what do you say, old man?' asked Parfitt impatiently. 'D'you want to have a go at this thing?'

Frank took a moment before answering. The anguish of trying to make a decision was tearing him apart. 'I'd like to,' he said finally. 'But if the law caught up with me, I don't know if I'd be able to cope. To tell you the truth, I'm not sure if it's worth the risk.'

Parfitt sat upright in his chair. *'Risk?'* he asked in disbelief that Frank could even consider such a thing. 'Good God, man. We're not asking you to rob a bank!'

Although it was still very cold, when Lizzie left

179

work that evening she was relieved to see that there was a slight thaw. It was easy to tell, for the heavy falls of snow that had turned to ice were now wet underfoot, and as she walked along the pavement, her feet were crunching in the slush. Once she'd turned the corner into Andover Road, she made straight for old Lil Beasley's ground-floor flat in one of the few houses that hadn't been too badly damaged by bomb blast.

'Who is it?' yelled the old girl through her letter box. 'I don't want no bleedin' visitors after dark.'

'It's me, Mrs Beasley – Lizzie – Lizzie Angel. I've brought your Zubes.'

'Well, why din't yer say so?' bawled Lil, slamming the letter box.

A few minutes later, Lizzie was inside Lil's back parlour, which, although clean and tidy, was dark and dingy, and badly in need of some new wallpaper and a fresh coat of paint. Her old pine dresser was crammed with ornaments of every description, and a set of hairpins that she'd used so many times, most of them were now bent into every shape imaginable. The framed photo of her late husband, Jack, which was the centrepiece, was still draped in black ribbon twenty years after his passing. But at least the place was warm, for Lil was of an age where she felt the cold more than anything else, and a fire in her grate, no matter how small, was an essential part of her life during the long winter months. Unfortunately, however, during the recent very cold weather, Lil had developed a hacking cough, and, much against her will, she had had to rely on her neighbours to do her shopping for her.

180

'Bleedin' fings,' she growled, popping a medicated Zube sweet into her mouth. 'They give me the wind! Good job I don't live wiv no one. They'd 'ave ter open all the windows!'

Lizzie was only glad that she didn't have enough time to hang around and find out what Lil meant, for later that evening she was due to meet Rob, who was going to take her to the pictures. 'Mum says she's going to make you some hot chicken broth for your lunch tomorrow,' said Lizzie, who still had her head covered with her cotton scarf. 'She got some bones from Dorners yesterday afternoon.'

'Don't know wot she wants ter go to *them* fer,' Lil grumbled. 'They're bleedin' huns. It's their lot who got us inter the mess we're in now.'

'That's not quite true, Mrs B,' said Lizzie. 'Mr Dorner and his family have lived in England for years. I doubt they've even been to Germany since the end of the first war. And, in any case, they're one of the best butchers in Holloway – and they've always done their best to get meat in for their regular customers.'

Lil grunted, and sat down at her parlour table. She still wasn't convinced. 'Go an' put the kettle on,' she demanded, sucking on her Zube. 'Let's 'ave a cuppa tea.'

'Thanks a lot, Mrs B,' said Lizzie, 'but I'm afraid I can't. Mum's got her hands full with Benjamin and Cissie recovering from chicken-pox, and I always try to get home to help her out. But I'll make you a cup, if you'd like one?'

'No!' growled Lil, through loud sucking sounds. 'Wot do *I* want wiv a cuppa bleedin' tea?

181

I fawt yer'd come in fer a chat, that's all.'

Lizzie felt quite crushed. She knew how lonely the old girl was, and felt guilty at how insensitive she'd been. 'I always love a chat with you, Mrs B,' she said quickly. 'Perhaps I could come in over the weekend, and I'll tell you about all the things I've been doing over this past week.'

Lil snorted. 'I shouldn't bovver,' she said dismissively. 'I won't be 'ere by then!'

Lizzie did a double take. But then she remembered how for years Lil had been going on about her own passing, so much so that she had been putting away sixpence a week for ages to pay for her 'box'. 'Well, you'd better hang on for Mum's chicken broth,' Lizzie said. 'We can't afford to waste it.'

'Don't talk ter me about your mum,' moaned Lil, sorting through a pack of playing cards she had spread all over the table. 'Always sayin' fings she don't mean.'

Lizzie was a bit put out by that remark. 'In what way?' she asked tersely.

'Like when she was round 'ere this mornin',' said Lil. 'Goin' on as 'ow 'er family don't care a monkey's fer 'er. Reckons yer dad's given 'er so many kids, she's nuffin' more than a skivvy round the place.'

After the way her mother had reacted to the news that Rob wanted to take Lizzie to Australia, Lizzie suddenly felt quite concerned.

'She don't mean it, er course,' said Lil. 'She only says it 'cos she wants ter keep yer all tergevver. If any of 'er kids was ter leave 'ome – 'speshully you – I fink she'd just give up. Yer know

182

wot *I* fink? I fink yer mum's spoiled. She'd soon know it if she 'ad ter spend as many hours on 'er own as I do!'

On her way home, Lizzie thought about what old Lil had told her. Although she had known for some time that her mother was disturbed about something, until that moment she had no idea how serious it was until Harriet's extraordinary outburst when she heard that Rob had asked Lizzie to emigrate to Australia with him. There and then, she made a conscious decision not to bring up the subject again. But the more she thought about it, the more she resented the fact that her mother was trying to interfere in her relationship with the man she loved. After all, Lizzie told herself, she may not be officially old enough to marry without her parents' consent, but she was now old enough to make her own decisions in life. And if she decided not to go to Australia with Rob, then it should be her own choice, and not her mother's.

Lizzie put the key in the front door, and, once inside, she knew immediately that something was wrong. She found her mother slumped in a chair at the sitting room table. 'Mum!' she cried, going straight to her. 'What is it? What's wrong?'

Harriet sat up. She looked exhausted. 'I've had just about all I can take of this,' she said wearily. 'What with your father, then you, and now – *this!*'

Lizzie swung with a start as she heard Susan's voice yelling out hysterically from the bedroom. 'It's not fair!' she screamed. 'I could kill them!'

Lizzie rushed into the bedroom. In the dark,

183

she could just see Susan crouched on the bed, shielding her eyes from the light streaming through the door from the sitting room. 'Susan!' she cried. 'What's going on?'

As Lizzie turned on the light, Susan yelled out. 'No! Turn it off! Turn it off!'

Lizzie went to her. But as she got there, Susan immediately pulled the eiderdown over her head. 'Keep away from me!' she sobbed. 'I hate you! I hate *all* of you!'

'Susan!' cried Lizzie, who thought her sister was having some kind of fit. 'What's the matter with you? Stop this now, d'you hear? Stop it!' Without another word, she grabbed at the eiderdown, and pulled it away.

Susan screamed out hysterically, 'No!' and tried to cover her face.

Lizzie perched on the edge of the bed. 'Susan,' she said, trying to calm her sister, 'what is it, darling? Tell me.'

Susan hesitated a moment, then slowly raised her head. Her face was covered in a deep scarlet rash and spots that turned her milky white skin into a battleground. 'I'll never forgive them for this!' she sobbed. 'Never!'

Chapter 9

The assassination of Mahatma Gandhi on 30 January sent shock waves around the world. Even in Andover Road, where the residents had often referred to the Indian statesman as 'that silly old sod in a loin cloth', the air of disbelief was mixed with outrage that such a monstrous thing could have happened. 'The world's gone bleedin' mad again!' said old Lil Beasley, who had lived through a lifetime of wars and human catastrophes.

However, whilst Gandhi's tiny, frail body was being cremated in the presence of millions of mourners on the other side of the world, life went on for everyone else, including the Angel family.

Lizzie's relationship with her mother was now under strain. Ever since Lizzie had told her about Rob wanting her to emigrate to Australia, Harriet had repeatedly refused even to discuss the matter. It was a difficult dilemma for Lizzie, for, despite Rob's assurances that they would live a better and more fulfilled life in such a young and vital new country, she was still not convinced that it was worth abandoning the life she had always known with her family, and, much to her distress, the whole thing was becoming a constant source of friction with Rob. However, she did eventually make one concession.

A church hall in Baker Street, and in the middle of one of the harshest English winters of the century, seemed an odd place to be watching an Australian promotional film about the wondrous joys and opportunities awaiting those who were seeking a new life 'down under'. To make matters more bizarre, the only heating came from four rather inadequate paraffin oil heaters placed around the hall, which meant that the audience were forced to sit wrapped up in their overcoats, scarves and hats whilst they sampled on film the steaming hot beaches of Queensland, the rounding up and shearing of sheep in the outback, strange wild creatures called kangaroos leaping in and out of the Bush, and cuddly marsupials called koala bears hugging the branches of trees that they were greedily stripping of their leaves.

Lizzie, with Rob at her side, watched it all with a mixture of quiet bewilderment and desperate foreboding. To her, and no doubt to the other prospective emigrants who were sitting all around her, everything in the film seemed so far removed from life in what some of the officials from the Australian High Commission were calling 'the old country', so detached from reality. She was also concerned that Rob watched it all goggle-eyed, and was particularly impressed with the talk by a young Australian couple after the film, in which they painted a rosy picture of opportunity and the advantages of living in a bright, challenging environment. When it was all over, they filed out of the hall armed with colour brochures that gave details not only of how easy it was to apply for the ten-pound assisted passage scheme, but also the type of enriched life they could expect if they decided to abandon the

186

gloomy weather of 'the old country.'

As they made their way in the dark towards the bus stop in Marylebone Road, Rob was talking nonstop about all the things they could do once they had taken the plunge after they were married. 'Just think of it, Liz,' he said. 'With a decent job, we could afford to actually buy our first home, a *real* home – beautiful views, a garden at the front, a garden at the rear, as much food as we can eat, no ration coupons, no rain day after day, and above all – no politicians making a mess of things and breathing down our necks all the time.'

'Don't they *have* politicians in Australia?' Lizzie asked, quite unprovocatively.

For one brief moment, Rob's racing enthusiasm was dented.

Before they reached the bus stop, it started snowing again. 'Let's go and have a drink,' he said.

Lizzie had never cared for pubs, but once they were settled down at a table in the public bar of one of the oldest pubs around, she suddenly developed a fondness for the warm, cosy atmosphere, and the people who were drinking, laughing and joking together. She even enjoyed listening to the cocky banter of the rowdy young men playing darts together on the other side of the room.

'It says here,' she said, browsing through the brochure she had been given at the film show, 'that before you can get into Australia, you have to have a medical.'

'Only when you apply for the assisted passage

scheme,' replied Rob, becoming very animated as he flicked through the brochure with her. 'If we had tons of money, I doubt we'd have to go through all that. But beggars can't be choosers.'

Lizzie didn't reply. She was not impressed.

'Anyway, Liz,' enthused Rob, 'just think of all that sunshine – trips down to the beach for an early morning dip every day. You know I've always loved swimming, especially in the open air. What a difference to our freezing cold indoor pool down at Hornsey Road.'

'Australia's not all about swimming in the open air, Rob,' said Lizzie, flicking through the brochure without actually reading it. 'In any case, I can't swim.'

Rob realised he was flogging a dead horse, and if he was going to revive it, he was going to have to pull out all the stops. 'You don't have to swim to earn money, Liz,' he said, retaliating in as practical a way as he was capable. 'You know as well as I do, I've never been afraid of hard work, but the harder I try, the worse it gets. In this country, nobody cares a brass monkey if you sweat your guts out. There are no rewards, Liz. You're just a number.'

She looked up at him. 'You're a number wherever you go, Rob,' she told him. 'We all know only too well that nothing comes easy in life. It doesn't matter *where* you live, it's how you cope.'

'We can't cope *here*, Liz,' insisted Rob. 'This country's finished. Anyone can see that.'

Lizzie shook her head. 'You keep saying that,' she said, 'but it's not really true. We've had difficult times before but we've always got through them – somehow. This is a wonderful country, Rob. A lot of people have died fighting for it. And that's what we should be doing now, not running away as though we don't care any more.'

Now it was Rob's turn to shake his head. 'I *don't* care any more, Liz,' he said. '*I* fought for this country too, remember, and what have I got in return? Dole queues, and a life of misery.'

In the background, the winner of the darts match was suddenly cheered by a roar from his mates, who then followed it up with a resounding chorus of 'There'll Always Be An England'. For Liz, this was an ironic diversion, but one that seemed to be reinforcing what she was trying to say.

Rob watched her as she continued to flick aimlessly through the brochure. He knew what was going through her mind, but didn't know what more he could say to reassure her. With the rowdy singsong booming out behind them, all he could do was to slip a comforting arm around her shoulders.

When the excitement from the dart players eventually subsided, he leaned in to her and said, 'You know, everything we saw on that screen tonight wouldn't mean a thing to me if I didn't have you by my side. Don't worry, Liz, I'd never make you do *anything* that you wouldn't want to do. You're too precious to me for that.'

Liz looked up suddenly at him and, for the first time, smiled. At last she felt hope.

'But I promise you,' Rob continued, 'you *will*

feel different once we're married. We'll be out there on our own, making our own decisions.' His face was now so close to hers, he could feel the warmth of her breathing. 'Once we've talked things through,' he continued, 'I promise you, you *will* think differently.'

Liz's brief moment of hope immediately returned to despair. She looked back down at the brochure again, and didn't respond when he kissed her fondly on her neck.

On Tuesday, the weather was quite raw, following a night of gusting winds, which had brought heavy drifts of snow, causing havoc in the streets around Woolworths store in Holloway Road. Consequently, some of the shop girls were late getting in for work that morning, especially those who had to travel in from far-off places such as Camden Town, Crouch End and Islington Upper Street. By the afternoon, the real problem was freezing fog, which made getting around even more hazardous. Despite this, however, the store was bristling with customers wrapped up in a variety of heavy clothes as though they had just journeyed across the North Pole.

As there had been very little custom on the gramophone record counter since the New Year, Lizzie had been temporarily transferred to kitchen utensils, which was located in the far part of the L–shaped store, close to the Seven Sisters Road entrance. Fortunately, she and the other shop girls were allowed to keep their topcoats on, for the temperatures in the store didn't seem to be much higher than the street outside, and colds and flu amongst the staff were hazards at the best of times, and more so in a winter that was turning out to be one of the worst on record.

By lunch time, Lizzie was feeling very pleased with herself, for during the morning she had sold several saucepans, a large porcelain mixing bowl, a scrubbing board, a large size metal iron, several kitchen knives and a rolling pin. But whilst all this was going on, she was constantly on the alert, her eyes frequently darting around the counters to see if she could catch a glimpse of the shoplifter who had cost Maple her job. Despite intense vigilance amongst the other girls, the middle-aged woman Maple had described as 'the Tuesday lady' had, for the past two Tuesdays, proved thoroughly elusive.

But soon after Lizzie had returned from an early lunch in the staff canteen, she noticed a woman matching Maple's description, slowly weaving her way in and out of the other shoppers. Dressed in a long black winter coat, and a scarf wrapped around her head so that only part of her face was visible, she was conspicuous only by the length of time she spent at each counter. She seemed to linger most at stationery, where she took ages to pick up and look at different packets of envelopes, writing pads, rubber bands and children's coloured crayons. A thin haze of freezing blue-grey fog had drifted into the store during the afternoon, which, in the poor overhead lighting, made it difficult for Lizzie to see what was going on from where she was working at kitchen utensils. But the moment she saw the woman pick something up, then pop it into the large shopping bag she was carrying, Lizzie moved in a flash, waving frantic signals to the other shop girls as she went. As soon as she got to the stationery counter, she realised that the girl working there hadn't noticed what had been going on. 'She took something!' Lizzie called, quickly checking over the stock on display.

The counter girl looked bewildered, and stared at Lizzie as though she had gone stark raving mad.

'Didn't you see her?' spluttered Lizzie impatiently.

The girl shook her head. 'Who?' she replied, looking at the customers milling around the store.

Lizzie did a quick check of the counter stock, and knew instinctively what had been taken, for the neat display of propelling pencils had been reduced to only two. Without hesitating a moment more, she swung around, just in time to see the other girls pointing to the Tuesday woman, who was briskly making her way through the other shoppers towards the Seven Sisters Road exit.

'Stop that woman!' Lizzie yelled, at the top of her voice.

Galvanised by Lizzie's shouts, everyone came to an abrupt halt, and gazed back at her in shocked astonishment.

Realising that she had been noticed, the Tuesday woman suddenly panicked, quickened her pace, and rushed out through the exit doors as fast as she could.

'Stop – thief!' yelled Lizzie, racing after the

woman, shouting frantically as she went. 'Stop her! Don't let her get away!'

The dense freezing fog had now engulfed Seven Sisters Road, and the moment Lizzie came hurrying out of the store, the only thing she saw was the back of the Tuesday woman merging into the other shoppers, who were all weaving in and out of the fog like mysterious ghostly creatures. Utterly frustrated, she desperately strained to catch a glimpse of the Tuesday woman shoplifter, who seemed to have disappeared without trace. But as Lizzie moved out on to the pavement, and tried to decide which way to search, she suddenly saw that the woman was just stepping off the kerb in an attempt to cross over to the other side of the road.

In a flash, Lizzie went for her. 'Stop!' she yelled boldly.

Horrified to have been caught, the woman froze, but refused to turn round to face Lizzie.

'Give me that bag!' demanded Lizzie, grabbing at the woman's large shopping bag.

The woman turned round, pulling the bag away from Lizzie, and for several moments they both struggled to hold on to it.

'Help!' yelled Lizzie. 'Thief!' But to her frustration, the people in the fog seemed to want no part of what was going on, and merely scuttled off in every direction. To make matters worse, the woman finally regained control of her shopping bag. 'You won't get away with this!' bawled Lizzie. 'You're a wicked woman! You got my friend the sack!'

The woman, who until that moment had

managed to keep her face concealed behind her headscarf, slowly looked up at Lizzie. In the dim muggy blue fog, Lizzie could just make out a face that suggested she could be anywhere in her late fifties or sixties, a fair, almost flawless complexion that was only vaguely tinged with red from the cold, and thin tight lips that contained only a faint trace of pale red lipstick. But for Lizzie, the most distinguishing feature on the woman's face was the small mole on the right-hand side of her chin, which had been delicately picked out with black mascara. The woman's expression was fixed. She remained silent, staring impassively back at Lizzie.

'What kind of a woman *are* you?' asked Lizzie contemptuously.

The woman hesitated, and then gradually held up her shopping bag for Lizzie to take. 'It's a game, my dear,' she replied, in a cultured voice. 'Only a game.'

Puzzled, and wary of the woman's gesture, Lizzie took the bag.

The Tuesday woman stared Lizzie out for a moment, then turned, and disappeared into the murky freezing fog.

Lizzie watched her go without trying to follow. But she called out, 'If I ever see you around here again, we'll get you!'

A moment later, Lizzie returned to the comparative warmth of the Woolworths store. She paused for a moment to check the contents of the bag, which she found empty but for a clutch of propelling pencils, and several children's picture books.

Gran Perkins had never really got on well with her daughter, Harriet. Gran had always been one for a good laugh, as opposed to her daughter, who only ever seemed to smile when she got the better of a conversation. In her young days, Florence Perkins had been considered quite a beauty, and at the time that Albert Perkins had proposed to her, she already had at least half a dozen beaux panting to take her out. Surprisingly, the marriage turned out to be a good one – mainly because Florence and Albert shared only one thing in common – a sense of humour. Neither took the other seriously, and they carefully built their relationship on making fun of each other. They also prided themselves on the fact that in all the years they were married, they never once had a quarrel, and if they disagreed on anything, they spent hours finding a compromise. Florence's relationship, however, was somewhat different with her only child, Harriet, who, although in many ways a kind-hearted and generous woman, had never compromised on anything since the day she had married Frank Angel. And that was never more obvious than now, when she was doing her best to enlist her mother's support in her efforts to deter Lizzie from emigrating with Rob to Australia.

'If it's true,' said Gran, with a certain amount of glee, 'then good luck to her! I tip my hat to any youngster who has the guts to get up and make a go of things.'

Harriet stiffened, and got on with the ironing. 'Making a go of things, Mother,' she replied tersely, 'shouldn't be at the expense of your family and friends.'

'Poppycock!' growled Gran, thumping her fist on the kitchen table of her own house in Tollington Park. 'Life isn't only about family and friends. It's about adventure, and taking care of number one.'

Harriet didn't even bother to look up at her. 'That's a very selfish thing to say, Mother,' she scolded.

Gran merely grunted, and carried on with knitting the same cardigan for Lizzie she had been working on for over a year. She had never liked Harriet doing the washing and ironing for her each week, and only let her do it because her legs were now riddled with rheumatism. 'Is it definite then?' she asked. 'Has Lizzie actually said she's going to emigrate with this boy?'

'Not in so many words,' replied Harriet. 'But I know Lizzie. She's at an impressionable age, and she'll let him force her into it.'

Gran didn't believe that for a moment. What *she* knew of her eldest granddaughter was that she was someone who had a mind of her own, and was not stupid enough to make decisions without first weighing up the pros and cons.

'And in any case,' continued Harriet, 'I don't know where she thinks she and this boy are going to get the money from to go all that way. It's going to cost enough for Frank to pay for the wedding.'

'Wedding?' Gran sat up excitedly in her chair. 'Is there going to be a wedding?'

Harriet sighed impatiently. 'Really, Mother,'

196

she said, irritated, 'd'you think Frank and I would let a daughter of ours travel the world with a man who wasn't even her husband?'

'Why not?' Gran barked. '*I* would!'

Harriet slammed down the hot iron on to the asbestos stand on the kitchen table, which she was using to do the ironing. 'Don't be so foolish, Mother!' she said. 'I hope you don't talk like that in front of Lizzie.'

Gran calmly put down her knitting. 'And why shouldn't I, may I ask?' she replied, squaring up to her. 'You know, Harriet, you should stop being so narrow-minded. These days, a lot of young people sleep together before they get married.'

Harriet ignored her mother's distasteful remark, picked up the iron, and returned it to the oven hob.

'Well, it's true,' insisted Gran. 'You can't ignore it. It's a hard life so why shouldn't people who love each other take what few precious moments of comfort they can? I know I did.'

Harriet, stoking up the oven fire, stopped what she was doing and swung a look of horror at her mother.

'Oh, don't look so shocked!' said Gran, with a mischievous twinkle in her eye. 'I don't regret for one single minute what I did.'

Harriet could bear to hear no more. She turned, and tried to leave the room.

'No, Harriet!' growled Gran. 'Come over here and sit down. This is a talk we should have had a long time ago.'

Harriet was intent on defying her, when she reluctantly changed her mind, and did what

Gran asked her.

Gran settled back in her chair, pulled a small handkerchief from her cardigan pocket, and wiped her nose with it. 'Life was different in those days,' she began. 'We never knew from one day to the next whether we'd still be alive the following morning or not. We had to grab the moment as much as we could. And that's exactly what I did. I *had* to, despite the fact that your grandmother and grandfather were tyrants. They kept me under their thumb twenty-four hours a day. I knew I had to break loose sooner or later. I was already in my twenties, and when I met your father, I had the chance I'd been waiting for. That's where *you* came in.'

Harriet lowered her head. She couldn't bear to look at her mother.

'Stop feeling so sorry for yourself, Harriet!' Gran snapped. 'You've had five kids. I've only had one – thank God!'

Harriet looked up. 'But you weren't even married?' she asked reproachfully, even though she knew the answer.

'That's true,' replied Gran, without any sign of remorse. 'No, I wasn't married at the time. But it didn't matter – I don't know why, but to me it just didn't. Of course, when your grandfather found out, he threw me out of the house. But I didn't care. I went and shared a flat with my Albert. Then you came along.' She could see that Harriet had taken the news badly, and was in the depths of despair. 'It's not as bad as it sounds, Harriet,' she said. 'We set up a good home for all three of us.' She leaned forward in her chair and

198

reached out for Harriet's hand. 'What I'm trying to say,' she continued, 'is that if you try to interfere with your kids, they'll only turn against you, and do their own thing. One day I'll be dead. So will you and Frank. Then what? D'you expect to hold on to your kids until you go? Lizzie needs your understanding, Harriet. She needs your *love*.'

'I love Lizzie just as much as I love *all* my children,' Harriet said firmly, 'but I believe in standards. I believe in showing them what's right and wrong. I don't believe she wants to be bullied into going to Australia – especially before she's married, and had time to think things over.'

Gran's reply was immediate. 'Just how long do we have in life to think things over, Harriet?' she asked wistfully.

'Marriage should be for ever,' replied Harriet. 'It's the most important thing two people will ever do in their two lives. They can't exist without it.'

'Is that so?' asked Gran, who smiled wryly. 'Your father and I existed without it, and it made no difference to us.'

Harriet froze. She was too shocked to say anything.

'Yes, Harriet,' said Gran, sitting back in her chair. 'We were *never* married. Not that we didn't want to, just that – well, we never seemed to get round to it. But we still loved each other. In fact, we still do.'

Chapter 10

Old Lil Beasley hadn't been too well of late. What started as a real snorter of a cold had now turned into a nasty bout of flu, and the doctor had filled her up with so many pills that, in her own words, she was beginning to rattle. Consequently, she had been confined to her bed for almost a week, and she was getting thoroughly fed up with it. Her one consolation was Lizzie, who popped in to see her most evenings on her way home from work, and as the old girl's eyesight wasn't what it used to be, Lizzie either read to her some of the day's news from the *Star* or the *Evening Standard,* or a chapter from Charles Dickens's *The Old Curiosity Shop,* a copy of which, to Lizzie's surprise, was the only book amongst the old girl's collection of penny thrillers and old newspapers. Lizzie was also not to know that it was the only book that Lil had ever read in her entire life, for she never went to school, and earned her living from when her dad had put her out to work in a glass blowing factory when she was just nine years old. But although she had read the book more than a dozen times since she found it on a rubbish tip more than forty years before, this was the first time she had had it read aloud to her, and there was a look of rare pleasure on her face as she lay back in bed, listening to Lizzie's warm and tender voice, relating the story of some of

Dickens's characters, who in many ways were not so dissimilar to those she had met in the early years of her own life.

However, by the time Lizzie had been reading for half an hour or so, the old girl looked exhausted, for she had a hacking cough that had drained her of her energy, and at times she found it difficult to breathe. Lizzie was worried about her, and the moment she saw that the old girl's eyes were drooping, she closed the book quietly, put it down on to the small bedside cabinet, got up, and tiptoed towards the door.

'Is it still snowin'?'

Lil's voice took Lizzie by surprise. But when she turned back to look at her, her head was still resting back on the pillow, eyes closed. 'Why don't you try and get some sleep, Mrs B?' Lizzie called quietly from the door. 'I'll pop in and make you some cocoa a bit later.'

'I like the snow,' said Lil, eyes still closed. 'All that white – it makes the world look so diff'rent. Little Nell liked the snow, din't she? She was always goin' out in it.'

Lizzie turned and went back to her. 'You wouldn't like it tonight, Mrs B,' she said softly. 'It's bitterly cold out there. They say we're going to get a lot more before the week's out.'

'I don't bleedin' care,' replied Lil, with a touch of her old defiance. 'When yer get ter *my* age, yer take everyfin' in yer stride.' As she spoke, she broke into a violent fit of coughing.

Lizzie perched on the edge of the bed for a moment, and waited for the old girl to settle down again.

Her eyes still closed, Lil reached for her handkerchief from beneath the bedclothes, and spat up some phlegm from her chest into it. 'My trouble,' she said, struggling to speak through her breathlessness, 'is that I've made too many bleedin' mistakes in my life. Not gettin' married again after I lost Jack Beasley was one of 'em. Bleedin' 'ell, I was only a young gel at the time. I 'ad all me life ahead er me, and so wot did I do? I shut meself away and cried me bleedin' eyes out till it was too late ter do anyfin' about it.' She was interrupted by another bout of coughing.

During all this, Lizzie watched her carefully, not with pity, but with admiration. Old Lil was part of a generation who had learned to survive in a world that had never done them any favours. As she looked around the old girl's bedroom, it could indeed have come straight out of a Dickens novel, with the dark walls covered with faded patterned wallpaper, a pretty rose motif adorning the border of what had once been a pure white plaster ceiling, heavy lace curtains, which had been patched up so many times, at the windows, a china jug and bowl on a small table in the corner, and gas mantles, which flickered constantly, casting dancing shadows on the wall as though the room was inhabited by scores of previous late departed residents.

'My ol' mum – Gord bless 'er,' continued Lil, wiping her nose on her handkerchief, 'she always used ter say, "Never muck around wiv yer life. Always do somefin' the first time yer fink about it, 'cos if yer don't, yer may never get anuvver chance." That was my trouble, yer see. After I lost

202

Jack, I 'ad plenty er chances, plenty of offers from men who loved me – or at least, they *said* they loved me. But no, I said ter me self, there was only one man in me life, and there always would be. So wot 'appens? I spent the rest of me days locked up all on me own in a dump like this, wiv a landlord just waitin' ter boot me out the moment 'e gets the chance.' Again she coughed.

Lizzie gently eased back Lil's hairnet, and soothed her forehead. 'Try and get some sleep, Mrs B.'

Lil's eyes suddenly sprang open. 'Sleep?' she growled. 'I've got plenty er time fer bleedin' sleep when I'm in me box. That's the only time that bleedin' landlord's goin' ter get me out of this dump!' But as her eyelids flickered, it was easy to see that it would not be long before she did in fact fall asleep.

Lizzie waited a moment or so, and when she was satisfied that Lil was at last drifting off, she quietly got up from the bed, and made her way to the door. But before she could get there, once again the old girl's voice called out.

'If someone'd told me he loved me – *really* loved me – I'd've gone to the ends of the bleedin' earf wiv 'im.'

Lizzie took one last look at the old girl, then quietly slipped out of the room.

The heavy snowfall of the day was now turning to ice, and even though old Lil's place was only a stone's throw away from the Angels' prefab in Andover Road, Lizzie found it hard work trying to get there.

When she did, she found the entire family, with

the exception of her sister Susan, toiling away in the dark with a garden shovel and brooms, all of them desperately trying to remove the massive drift of snow that had blocked the front door. They weren't the only ones, for all along Andover Road the biting night air was echoing to the frenzied sound of shovels scraping on garden paths and the pavement outside. Despite the fact that it wasn't easy to see what they were doing by torchlight, there was laughter too, for in the middle of it all, the local kids were clearly having a whale of a time, snowballing each other with whatever soft snow remained beneath the icy surface. Now that the Angel family had more or less recovered from the chickenpox infection that had kept them confined for the past few weeks, everyone felt much better for being out in the crisp fresh air, despite the fact that they were all wrapped up like Eskimos.

The moment she got there, Lizzie mucked in, and soon she, James, Benjamin, and Cissie were all joining in a rousing chorus of 'Hi-ho, hi-ho, It's off to work we go,' one of their favourite songs from the film *Snow White and the Seven Dwarfs*. Lizzie was particularly glad to see her dad there, for these days he was rarely at home any evening. Even her mother seemed to be in a better mood for once, for she too was joining in the singsong.

'I called in to see Mrs Beasley on my way home,' said Lizzie, struggling to sweep frozen snow from the front doorstep. 'She doesn't look too good to me. She's got a terrible cough.'

'I took her a flask of chicken broth this

morning,' called Harriet, trying to sweep her patch near the garden gate. 'She said she doesn't want to see the doctor again. So there's not much we can do. At least she's got the gas fire in her bedroom to keep her warm.'

'Even so,' said Lizzie, 'I think we should keep an eye on her. Nobody else round here seems to.'

Once the paths were as clear as they could get them, Harriet rounded up the kids, and hustled them back into the house. 'Don't be long,' she called as she went. 'I've got some mutton stew on the stove.'

Lizzie was about to follow them all in, when her father called her. 'Hang on, Liz,' he said, keeping his voice down. 'I want a word with you.' Once the others had disappeared inside, he led Lizzie back to the garden gate. 'I've got a bit of money for you,' he said. 'Ten quid. You can start building up for the wedding.'

Lizzie couldn't believe what he had just said. 'Dad!' she spluttered.

'It's all right,' he said, keeping an eye on the house to make sure no one was there to hear him. 'It's only a start. By the time you get married, I'll have enough to pay for the wedding. You won't have to ask Rob's parents to chip in.'

'But – where did you get so much money?'

'Don't ask questions,' replied Frank. 'Then you won't hear any lies.'

Lizzie faltered for a moment. 'Does Mum know what you're doing?' she asked.

'I'm a grown-up man, Liz,' he replied, scolding her. 'I don't have to tell your mum everything I do.'

Again, Lizzie faltered. 'Dad,' she said anxiously, 'you earn only just enough to make ends meet. You're not doing anything ... illegal, are you?'

Frank stiffened. 'I don't question you how you make *your* money, Liz,' he replied sternly, 'so please don't ask me where I get mine.'

Lizzie suddenly felt quite awful. Although she couldn't really see him in the dark, she was so close to him that, in the cold evening air, she could feel the warmth of his breath. 'Oh, Dad,' she said quickly, desperate not to hurt him, 'I didn't mean to pry. It's just that – well, ten pounds is a lot of money.'

'You're going to need a lot more than that if you're going to Australia,' he said.

Lizzie was taken aback by her father's remark. 'I don't know what you're talking about,' she replied. 'I haven't said I've agreed to go to Australia.'

'But Rob's asked you,' said Frank. 'That's why he came to see me the other week – isn't it?'

Now it was Liz's turn to stiffen. 'He came to ask you if you approve of us getting married.'

'That's a bit old-fashioned, isn't it, Liz?' he teased. 'Even for you.'

To his surprise, Liz was not amused. 'In case you've forgotten, Dad,' she replied curtly, 'I'm not yet twenty-one. The law says I can't get married without your consent.'

'I'm sorry,' said Frank guiltily. 'I shouldn't have said that. All I wanted to say, Liz, is that I would never get in the way of anything you wanted to do. You're the most level-headed person in this family, and I know that you wouldn't do anything

206

without giving it a lot of thought first. But, Liz, there comes a time in everyone's life when you have to think of yourself first. You've got your whole future ahead of you, and if you want to go to Australia with Rob, then you should do it.'

'But I *don't* want to go to Australia – or anywhere else,' said Liz emphatically. 'Why can't you understand that, Dad? Why doesn't *anyone* understand it? This is all Rob's idea – not mine.

'But you love him,' Frank reminded her. 'Otherwise you wouldn't want to get married. You do *want* to marry him, don't you?'

Norman the 'nancy boy', as he was known down Petticoat Lane, had a real struggle to reach his local boozer, the Hen and Chicken in Aldgate High Street. Unlike most days, the heavy falls of snow had settled and, instead of thawing within an hour or so, had turned to ice, making his epic journey there a challenge rather than a pleasant evening stroll. Once he had got there, it took him several minutes to unravel the scarf tied around his head beneath his battered trilby hat. He was quite relieved that there was only a scattering of customers in the private bar, so the first thing he did was to go straight to the counter and order a whisky and ginger ale and a packet of Smith's crisps from Rita the barmaid, who had known him for years. Once he'd passed his usual pleasantries with her, he settled himself down at a small table in front of a vast log fire, and tried to rub some life back into his frozen hands. When he first started coming into the pub, eyes always turned to look him up and down, and crude comments were whispered about whom he'd be taking home that night. But these days, nobody even gave him a passing look; he had practically become part of the furniture. He sipped his whisky, and breathed a sigh of relief and ecstasy. Then he ripped open the top of his crisp bag, took out the small blue packet of salt, and sprinkled it over the crisps. He had only just popped one in his mouth when he realised that he had company.

'Mind if I join you, Norman?'

Norman looked up, totally surprised to find Rob standing over him. 'Hello, duckie,' he said. 'You're a bit off your patch, aren't you?'

Rob drew up a chair and sat with him. He had already bought himself a pint of bitter. 'Charlie Feather told me this was your local,' he said. 'Thought I'd come and look you up.'

Norman looked at him suspiciously. 'Why?' he asked.

'I need a favour.'

Norman grinned. 'With my reputation, you could get stoned for that!'

They shared the joke.

Norman, however, recognised that troubled look in Rob's eyes. 'What's up now?' he asked, taking out his tobacco tin and fag roller from his coat pocket. 'Have you been upsetting that poor girl of yours again?'

Rob took a gulp of his bitter, and drew on the cigarette he had already lit. 'I took your advice,' he said. 'I told her the truth.'

'Oh yes?'

'I told her all about my job with Charlie up the

Lane, and that I wanted her to emigrate with me to Australia.'

'And?'

Rob inhaled deeply on his cigarette, and exhaled the residue. 'She said she didn't like the idea at all, and that she needs time to think about it.'

'Fair enough, I would have thought,' suggested Norman.

'You don't know Liz,' said Rob. 'When she says she wants to think about something, it usually means she wants no part of it.'

Norman frowned. The fag he was rolling was now ready, so he held it together with his fingers whilst he licked the sticky ends of the paper. Over at the bar counter, two heavy-looking labourer types were downing their pints, and flicking the odd glance across at him.

'Has she given a reason why?' Norman asked, sticking the rolled-up fag between his lips.

Rob shrugged. 'She doesn't want to leave her family and her life here – or this country,' he sighed. 'I just don't understand her. Surely anyone in their right mind can see that getting out and having your fare paid to Australia is a golden opportunity. A new start in a new country is what people dream about.'

'Not all people,' said Norman, lighting up his fag in a cloud of smoke. 'There are plenty of people who think that life in this country is perfectly all right as it is. As it so happens, I don't agree with them, but they're entitled to an opinion.'

As Norman spoke, for the first time Rob really

noticed the sibilance in his voice, and for one fleeting moment it unsettled him.

'However...' Norman said, knocking back a swig of his whisky and ginger ale, and gradually feeling the warmth seeping back through his body, 'what happens now?'

'That's what I wanted to talk to you about,' replied Rob. 'You see, the way things are going, I'll never be able to convince Liz that this is the right thing to do. She's as stubborn as hell, and if we wait until after we get married, we'll just get stuck in a rut, and stay in it for the rest of our lives, living from hand to mouth, and getting absolutely nowhere. Let's face it, Norman, it could take this country years to recover from the mess we're in now – if it ever does recover. If we don't grab our chance now, it may never come again.'

'I know all that, Rob,' said Norman, with a deep sigh. 'You've told me this over and over again. But where does it get you? If your girl doesn't want to emigrate, how the hell d'you think you're ever going to persuade her?'

'*I* can't,' said Rob, 'but that's where *you* come in.'

Norman's eyes widened. 'Me?'

'If you talked to her, I'm sure she'd listen.' Rob moved in closer so that he couldn't be overheard. 'You're one of the few people I can really trust, Norman,' he said. 'She'd realise that you have nothing to gain from talking to her, so if I could just bring her round to see you–'

Norman cut straight across him. 'You've chosen the wrong person, duckie,' he said. 'You're sensible

210

enough to know that I'm not exactly the most popular person around Petticoat Lane – or anywhere else, for that matter. You've only got to look at those two over there to see what I mean.'

Rob turned and looked at the two men drinking at the bar. The moment they saw him noticing them, they casually turned their backs.

'The world is full of people who don't know,' said Norman, draining the last of his whisky. 'Poor darlings – why should they?'

Rob glared at them. Although he was puzzled by Norman's remark, he knew only too well that there were plenty of people around – including Charlie Feather – who hated Norman's guts. They saw him as some kind of a freak, not only because he made picture frames, which in their eyes was a poncy thing to do, but because he didn't talk and move and think like them. But Rob was undeterred. 'I'd still like you to talk to Liz,' he said. 'Will you do it for me, Norman? Will you?'

The heavy snowfalls that had started during the early evening were now building in intensity, and by the time people were turning out of the pubs and cinemas, it had become a race against time to get home before the freezing snowdrifts completely blocked the roads. To make matters worse, visibility was appalling, for with the snow came a blinding white mist that turned to ice the moment it came into contact with hats and overcoats and scarves. By eleven o'clock at night, conditions everywhere were utterly atrocious.

Lizzie only just had enough time to deliver a

vacuum flask of cocoa to Lil Beasley before a howling gale added to the misery, and sent snow and mist crashing against her face. Once she'd used Lil's key to let herself in, she went straight up to the old girl's room where she found her fast asleep and snoring loud where she had left her just a few hours before. Once she had made sure that Lil was comfortable, she left the vacuum flask on the bedside table, turned down the gas mantles on the wall as far as they would go without going out, and slipped quietly out of the room.

Although she had been in Lil's place for no more than five minutes, by the time she had reached the front door again, she was horrified to see that the snow had drifted against the door again and formed a solid white wall.

At the Angels' prefab, Harriet did her best to peer out of the window to watch for any sign of Lizzie's return. But the windows were not only frozen over, but sealed with what looked like several inches of snow. However, Harriet's foreboding was not matched by James, Benjamin and Cissie, who were jumping up and down excitedly on the edge of their bed, trying unsuccessfully to open the window to peer out. 'We're in an igloo!' yelled Benjamin. 'We're going to be trapped here all through the winter!'

'Don't be so daft!' chided James. 'We've all got to get to school in the morning.'

'I hope not!' added Cissie longingly.

In Holloway Road, late night buses and trams

either came to a standstill, or were taken out of service. One old chap, coming out of the Marlborough cinema with his missus, slipped in the freshly fallen snow, and came crashing down in agony. In the prevailing weather conditions, it was clearly going to be some time before help could arrive from the nearby Royal Northern Hospital.

Rob Thompson got back to Arthur Road just before eleven o'clock at night. The journey from Aldgate High Street had taken him over an hour on the tube, and by the time he reached Holloway Road tube station, he faced a blizzard that seemed to be getting more out of control each minute. When he did manage to get home, he found the place in darkness but for a light in the front passage. After taking off his snow-covered duffel coat and knitted cap, he went straight up to his bedroom on the top floor, passing his mum and dad's room on the first floor on the way. The sound of his dad's snores assured him that he at least was quite oblivious to what was going on in the street outside. In his bedroom, Rob quickly lit the gas fire and changed into his pyjamas.

Before he got into bed, however, he collected the coloured brochure he had been given at the Australian emigration film show. He felt the warm glow of the sun-drenched beaches as he flicked through page after page for the umpteenth time. He eventually drifted off into sleep, leaving the bedside light on, and the brochure still resting on the bedclothes in front of him. Soon, he was dreaming of Lizzie and himself building a magnificent house with their own bare hands. They were laughing happily, with the Australian sunshine binding them together in marital bliss.

In the real world outside, however, the bliss was remote, and far removed from the difficulties that lay ahead, and the problem of how to get Lizzie to talk to a freak from Petticoat Lane, with whom no one seemed to have anything at all in common.

As usual, Norman was the last customer to leave the Hen and Chicken in Aldgate High Street. By then, the 10.30 closing-time ritual 'Time gentlemen, please!' had been called three times, and if Norman hadn't downed his fourth whisky and ginger ale quickly, he would probably have been physically thrown out of the place.

In the street outside, he was met by a snowstorm that very nearly knocked him over. Undeterred, he waddled his way through the gusting winds, grunting to himself through his drunken haze, whilst using both hands to hold on to his trilby hat, which he had pulled down right over his ears. After a moment or so, he started to giggle to himself, and he was soon singing 'Jingle Bells' out loud, his shrill, high-pitched voice deadened by the relentless anger of the gale that he was now struggling against. It took him more than half an hour to reach Mrs Wiggs's Victorian terraced house just off Aldgate High Street, where he had a top-floor flat. Even when the worse for drink, Norman was always able to do the journey on foot in no more than five or six minutes, but by the time he got there tonight, he was ready to drop. At the front door of the house, he paused in the gale to search his overcoat pockets for the keys, all the while cursing the fact that the stupid things were clearly deliberately trying to avoid him. Whilst he was doing so, however, he became aware of two images that were hovering in the mist and snow to one side of him. Attempting to focus, he shook his head and tried to rub the snow from his eyes with the back of his hand. The two dark images quivered in the unnatural light that was coming from an electric light bulb suspended from the wall high above them. Despite his fuzzy mind, Norman stopped what he was doing, and fixed his gaze on the two sinister dark figures gradually moving towards him in the snow. They came to a halt immediately in front of him.

'Hello,' he said cheerily, wavering from side to side. 'I wondered where you two had gone.'

The first blow he felt was a huge fist to his face, and the crunching sound of his own nose as it cracked wide open. Then a foot landed in his crutch, and a rabbit punch to the back of the neck felled him. A few minutes later, everything was a solid dark void, in complete contrast to the scarlet red blood that trickled down from Norman's nose on to the glaring white snow that was now engulfing him.

Chapter 11

The following morning, the streets of Islington looked like the frozen wastes of the North Pole. The blizzard that had raged all night had still not blown itself out, and by the time alarm clocks everywhere had burst into life at the start of another day, the landscape had changed into a dazzling white blanket of snow. It seemed like the great freeze-up of the previous winter was back again.

The Angel family woke up to find that not only were they virtually prisoners in their own home, but that their water pipes were frozen solid. Although the drama was a huge joke and great excitement for James, Benjamin and Cissie, it was no laughing matter for Harriet, Frank, and Lizzie for it meant that they had to find a way to defrost the pipes without causing them to burst. They finally decided that the only real solution was to heat up the place as much as possible, so they lit the fire, and kept it going all day, whilst at the same time wrapping up any exposed pipes they could find with rags and cloths. Getting out of the house, however, was more of a problem, for when they tried to open the front door, they found it frozen hard, and sealed with a huge drift of snow that had turned into a solid wall of ice. For Cissie, in particular, it was all a godsend, for it meant that there was no way the school was going to be able to open in such weather, and even if it did, the classrooms would be much too cold for both children and staff to sit in.

At about ten o'clock in the morning, the blizzard subsided just enough to allow the front door to be thawed out by the heat from the fire, but even after frenzied efforts from all members of the family, except Susan, who was too ill, it still took another hour to clear a path to the garden gate.

Once this was done, Lizzie decided that her first priority was to make an effort to get to old Lil Beasley's place, before making the perilous journey to work. Despite being well wrapped up against the biting Arctic wind, Lizzie felt as though every vein in her body was frozen stiff, and as she struggled to keep her balance on the icy surfaces, she found it a daunting task to plod in and out of the heavy falls of snow, for she was wearing only rubber galoshes on her feet, and also because roads and pavements were extremely treacherous. All along the way, people were clearing the snow from their doorsteps, and this was increasing Lizzie's anxiety about old Lil. However, the moment she finally managed to reach the end of Sonderburg Road, and turned the corner into Bedford Terrace, she was astonished to see the old girl in the street outside her house, wrapped up like an Eskimo, clearing the snow from her ground-floor windowsills with a hand coal shovel.

'Mrs B!' yelled Lizzie as she approached. 'What on earth d'you think you're doing?'

Lil looked up, and growled back, 'Wot the

bleedin' 'ell d'yer fink I'm doin'?'

'You'll catch your death of cold!' scolded Lizzie, as soon as she reached the old girl.

'I ain't made er bleedin' jelly, yer know!' snapped Lil, who was clearly back to her old self. Reluctantly, she allowed Lizzie to take the shovel from her, and shuffle her back indoors.

Lizzie was horrified to discover that Lil's back parlour was like a block of ice, so she quickly set to and built up the fire in the oven grate. After that, she made her a cup of tea, and when she was satisfied that the old girl was snug and comfortable, she tidied up the place a bit before preparing to leave for work. 'If Mum can get round later,' she said, 'she's going to bring you some of the rabbit stew we had left over from last night. She can always heat it up on your hob.'

'Why's everyone treatin' me as though I'm bleedin' 'elpless?' grumbled Lil. 'I've got some bangers in my scullery. I'm perfectly capable of doin' me own cookin'.'

'You save your sausages for another meal, Mrs B,' said Lizzie. 'They'll come in handy if we get any more snow and you can't get out.'

As Lizzie busied herself doing last-minute chores, Lil watched her carefully, noting her every movement with more than a passing interest. 'It's about time yer married that bloke er yours,' she grunted.

'What did you say, Mrs B?' asked Lizzie, calling from the scullery.

Lil shouted back. 'I said, it's time yer got married and settled down!'

Lizzie came back into the room, carrying a fill-up of tea. 'Now what on earth gives you that idea, Mrs B?' she asked.

''Ow old are yer?' asked Lil.

'You know how old I am, Mrs B,' replied Lizzie, putting the cup and saucer down on the table in front of her. 'It's my twenty-first in a few weeks' time.'

'Ridicoluss!' proclaimed Lil, fiddling around in her apron pocket for her saccharin tablets. 'I'd bin married two years by the time I was your age. Jack Beasley did 'is best ter give me a bun in the oven. Poor bugger. Weren't 'is fault I couldn't oblige. Still – that's life. Not much use moanin' about it.'

Lizzie smiled as she watched the old girl pop two saccharin tablets into her tea. She had always admired the way Lil had coped over the years with being childless, for to Lizzie's way of thinking she would have made a wonderful mum.

'Mind you,' continued Lil, 'I'd've done anyfin' fer that man. Gone to the bleedin' ends of the earth if 'e'd asked me to. As long as I was with 'im, that's all *I* ever cared. Jack Beasley was one of the best. They don't make 'em like 'im these days.' She watched Lizzie carefully as she put on her gloves ready to leave. 'There ain't nuffin' like bein' with the man yer love.' She glanced across the room briefly to look at an old sepia snapshot of herself as a young woman, posing happily with a soldier. 'When yer love someone like I loved Jack, nuffin' else matters.' She turned her look back to Lizzie. 'Not even yer own kiff and kin.'

Lizzie smiled weakly. She knew exactly what the old girl was getting at.

It took Rob almost two hours to get to Petticoat Lane. When he finally got there, he found the place a hive of activity, for, like everywhere else in London, there were drifts of snow from the heavy fall the night before, blocking the roads and making it almost impossible to get around on foot. But, in true wartime spirit, the market traders were out in force, shovelling and chipping away at snow that had turned to ice on their stalls, and exchanging good old cockney banter about how they could turn 'the Lane' into a ski resort.

'I'd like ter see ol' Attlee or Cripps or Morrison doin' this job!' quipped Charlie Feather, the moment he saw Rob, referring to members of the current government, who these days weren't exactly the most popular politicians in office. 'Yer can bet yer life they won't give us a tax cut fer doin' this!'

Rob immediately grabbed a shovel, and started chipping away at the ice on the pavement around Charlie's second-hand stall. 'The papers say it's the worst blizzard since last winter,' he said, above the clatter of shovels and brooms all along the market. 'Our pipes at home are frozen solid.'

'Is that all?' asked Charlie. 'My missus went ter the lav this morning, and found she couldn't pull the bleedin' flush!'

Rob laughed, though it was no laughing matter. Whilst he was working, he paused a moment to look up and down the Lane. Something caught his eye. Norman's picture frame stall was the only one that was deserted, and practically submerged with frozen snow.

'Norman not in yet?' he asked.

Charlie carried on with what he was doing. ''Ardly likely,' he replied, 'under the circumstances.'

Rob turned back to him. 'What d'you mean?'

Charlie looked up. 'Don't tell me yer 'aven't 'eard about our Norman? Everyone else 'as.'

'Heard what?'

'He took a real tumble down the Hen and Chicken last night,' said Charlie, with just a faint suggestion of a smirk. 'Got 'imself a real corker. I'm not surprised. It's bin comin' fer some time, if yer ask me. I mean, let's face it, 'e's the type, in't 'e? Anyway, at least it's got 'im full board down Whitechapel!'

'Norman?' Rob spluttered, shocked. 'Norman's in hospital? But I was only with him last night.'

Charlie gave him an old-fashioned look. 'Were yer now?' he quipped mockingly. 'Well, fancy that!'

Over the years, the London Hospital in Whitechapel Road had dealt with more than its fair share of casualties. During the war, the destruction wrought by the Luftwaffe in the East End had filled the wards to capacity. The ability of both doctors and nursing staff to cope whilst fierce air raids were still raging overhead was little short of a miracle, and had created many unsung heroes. Today, however, the hospital was having to cope with a peacetime crisis brought about by one of the worst winters in living memory. The place was full of elderly people who had either fallen down in the treacherous icy conditions, or had had to be rescued from freezing cold homes for which no fuel was available to keep them warm. To make matters worse, the roads throughout London were so blocked with snow and ice, it was a major task for ambulance drivers to reach the scene of any accident, let alone get the patient back to the hospital.

When Rob made his way through the vast main entrance gates, he found the place in complete chaos, with people milling around the reception hall, children crying, porters struggling to keep up with the influx of patients who needed wheelchairs, and harassed medical staff rushing back and forth along corridors trying to keep up with the mad influx.

'Don't anyone ever try ter sing bleedin' "Jingle Bells" ter me again!' grumbled one old-age pensioner in the emergency outpatients' waiting room, arm in sling, and a nose so bright red it looked like a traffic light.

'Norman?' asked one of three harassed middle-aged women at the reception desk. 'Norman who?'

Rob had never had the faintest idea what Norman's surname was, and now he was being asked for it he was at a loss for words. 'Well...' he spluttered awkwardly, 'he's about five foot four, dark eyes, must be in his fifties or so, oh – and he usually wears a beret or a dark trilby hat.'

The woman looked at him as though he was stark raving mad. 'Oh, it's easy then, isn't it?' she quipped sarcastically. 'Why don't you just go round the wards and yell out his name?'

'But you don't understand,' explained Rob. 'There's nobody quite like him. Norman's ... different. Somebody beat him up at the pub last night.'

The woman had had enough. 'Try Casualty,' she snapped, returning to her paperwork. 'Just follow the signs.'

Realising that he was not going to get any further with the woman, Rob did what he was told, and made his way off down the corridor, following the signs. When he got to Casualty, he found pandemonium. He imagined it must have been like this during the blitz, for the place was overflowing with people of all ages who had either had accidents in the snow, or had been brought in suffering from frostbite or other severe weather-related problems.

'Norman who?'

Rob wished he hadn't asked the question. 'He came in last night,' he said, expecting the nurse he had stopped on her rounds to give the same terse reply that he had received from the woman on the reception desk. 'He got beaten up in a pub.'

To Rob's surprise, he was greeted with a sweet smile, albeit a slightly mocking one. 'Are you a friend?' she asked.

Rob shrugged. 'Sort of,' he replied.

'I think the person you're looking for is in a room upstairs,' said the nurse. 'On the first floor – next to the casualty ward.'

'Room of his own? Blimey!' said Rob. 'Didn't know he was so important. Good old Norman!' He thanked the nurse profusely, unaware that as she hurried off, she had taken a quick look over her shoulder at him, a huge grin on her face.

Although it was not visiting time, there were plenty of people hanging around outside the casualty ward. The place was thick with fag smoke, with anxious relatives waiting for news of loved ones who had come a cropper in the ferocious blizzard of the night before. Rob went straight to the men's ward, but as there were so many people waiting to see any one of the nursing staff, he decided to look around for the single room Norman was supposed to have been put in. He found one of them to the side of the ward, and peered in. The bloke in there certainly wasn't Norman. Too fat and too manly.

'Can I help you?' The male voice next to him turned out to belong to some kind of junior doctor.

'Oh,' Rob replied with a start. 'I was looking for a friend of mine. His name's Norman. He got beaten up at the pub last night.'

The young doctor needed no prompting. 'The room on the other side of the women's ward,' he said tersely. 'You'd better check with Sister first.'

'Why?' asked Rob, but the doctor had already disappeared down the corridor.

Women's ward? He sighed. Typical, he thought. Putting poor old Norman in a women's ward just because he was – well, just because he was like he was. Rob made his way there and soon found a single room alongside. He peered through the window. Although it was light outside, the curtains were drawn. But he could just make out Norman stretched out in bed, his head swathed in bandages and his arm in a sling. Rob hesitated before going in, for there was a large notice on the door making it quite clear that there were to be 'NO VISITORS'.

'So what's all this, then?' he asked, voice low, going inside and closing the door behind him.

The mess that was Norman opened his one good eye. 'Duckie!' he spluttered through swollen lips. 'What a lovely surprise!'

'What the hell have you been up to?' asked Rob. He took a quick look over his shoulder to make quite sure he wasn't being watched from outside, then sat on a chair at the side of Norman's bed. 'Can't leave you for one moment without you getting into trouble. What happened?'

'Nothing happened,' replied Norman. 'Nothing out of the usual.'

'After I left the pub last night, you went home?'

'Yes.'

'So what happened?'

Norman swallowed hard. He was thirsty. 'Could you pour me some water, please, duckie?' he croaked.

Rob obliged, and waited for him to sip it.

'My two friends were waiting for me,' said Norman, handing the glass back to Rob with his one free hand.

'*Friends?*'

Norman tried hard to smile. 'Not *those* kind of friends, duckie! As a matter of fact I've never seen them before in my life. Well – I've never *noticed* them – those two who were in the bar at the same time as us. Actually they were quite good-looking. Both of them.'

'Come off it, Norman!' said Rob impatiently. 'Are you telling me those two thugs beat you up?'

'It would appear so.'

'Why?'

'Do people need a reason to do things like that?'

Rob sighed. It was obvious what had happened. At least, that's what it looked like. 'Well, what about the police?' he asked. 'Have they caught them?'

Norman attempted a chuckle. 'Oh, duckie!' he said, squirming with the sudden pain in his arm. 'The boys in blue have got better things to do with their time. It was a pig of a night last night. For all they care, I could have just been one of the unlucky ones who took a nasty fall in the snow.'

'You mean, you haven't told them?'

'I told them all they need to know. All they *want* to know.'

Rob sighed. He knew it was no use pursuing the subject any further. 'So is that why they put you in a room next to the women's ward?' he asked.

Again Norman tried a smile. 'Women, men...' he said. 'What difference does it make? I mean, in the end we're all human beings, aren't we? Anyway, I'm quite enjoying meself. At least I get three good meals a day, which is more than I get on my ration coupons outside.' He tried to move, but the searing pain was shooting through his arm, and a small patch of blood on his bandaged head seemed to be slowly spreading.

'Listen,' he said, 'I've been thinking.' He

226

motioned for Rob to draw closer. 'If you'd still like me to, you *can* bring that girl of yours round to see me one night. Not just yet, of course, but as soon as I get out. I've had plenty of time to think about it, lying here all night. As a matter of fact, I reckon I could give her a word of friendly advice. Mind you, I'm not going to try and talk her into going off to Australia with you. That's a decision only she can make. But at least I can tell her about some of the decisions I've had to make in my own life.' Once again he tried to chuckle, but it was a real effort.

'Oh, Norman!' said Rob, quite unconsciously giving Norman's good hand a grateful squeeze. 'You're a toff! You're a real toff!'

'A toff!' Norman raised his bandaged head only long enough to flop it down on to the pillow again. 'I've been called a few things in my time, but never that!'

'Excuse me, sir!'

Rob looked up with a start to find the ward sister coming into the room. With her was a police constable. Rob immediately stood up.

'I'm not sure if you can read,' said the sister sternly, 'but there is a "No Visitors" notice on the door. Now will you please leave – immediately?'

Rob exchanged a quick look with Norman. 'Sorry,' he said, with a shrug.

'Do me a favour,' said Norman, with the sister and the constable now hovering over him. 'Could you pop a note through my letter box? Tell my landlady I'll pay the rent as soon as I get home. Her name's Mrs Wiggs. You'll find the address on my stall up the market.'

''Course,' said Rob. 'Take care of yourself.'

'If you please!' demanded the sister, glaring at Rob.

Rob knew he was pushing his luck, so he quickly made for the door. The last thing he heard as he left the room was Norman greeting the constable: 'Now then, duckie. What can I do for *you?*'

The Angels' prefab was in darkness. The power, which had gone off during the night, still hadn't been restored, and the family were now having to make do with a couple of candles that were rapidly flickering dangerously low. 'That's the trouble with this family,' complained Susan, who was having to eat warmed-up rabbit stew at the table in the fading light with her mother, brothers and sisters. 'It's absolutely ridiculous waiting until the last minute before doing things. We should always have a supply of candles to cope with in emergencies like this.'

'If you think that,' said Harriet, 'then you should have bought some yourself.'

Susan wasn't used to being rebuked by her mother in such a way. It was so unlike her. 'Really, Mother!' she replied, the wind taken out of her sails. 'Just where d'you think *I'd* get the money from for things like that? In case you've forgotten, I'm still at the polytechnic.'

'Oh, I've not forgotten,' replied Harriet tersely. 'You'd never let us do that.'

Susan couldn't actually see that her sister Lizzie was grinning at her in the flickering light, but she knew she was doing it all the same.

'I think you've done a marvellous job, Mum,'

Lizzie said. 'I just don't know how you've managed to cook all this food on that paraffin stove.'

'I don't like rabbit stew,' grumbled Benjamin, who was toying with the bones on his plate. 'It's like eating Hoppy.' Benjamin had never got over the death of his pet rabbit, who had been killed when the family had been bombed out.

'Beggars can't be choosers, Benjamin,' said his mother. 'We're lucky to have food in our stomachs. It's only thanks to your dad we've got any meat at all. If he hadn't been given this rabbit as a present from one of his friends at work, we'd have had to make do with vegetables for supper.'

'I'd prefer vegetables to *this!*' moaned Benjamin.

'Oh, stop grumbling, Ben!' chided James. 'If you don't want it, pass it over here.'

'Don't you dare,' said Lizzie. 'Mum's gone to a lot of trouble for us all.'

Benjamin grunted, and continued to toy with his food.

Lizzie had finished eating, so with the candles flickering to their last, she got up from the table and went to the grate to stoke up the fire.

'Well, you can say what you like,' waffled Susan. 'If Dad had got a good job instead of cutting up fish in Billingsgate Market, none of this would have happened.'

'Don't talk about your father like that!' snapped Harriet. 'He's doing his best to keep this family going, and don't you forget it.'

'That's all very well,' continued Susan, totally oblivious to her mother's feelings, 'but Dad never seems to make the effort to get something better.

He shouldn't just be doing a grubby little job like that. He's worth so much more. He should be a manager in a store – like he used to be. And another thing – where does he go to every night? We hardly ever see him.'

'Dad promised to take me to the Arsenal last Saturday – and he didn't!' complained Benjamin.

'Don't be an idiot!' snapped James. 'The game was cancelled 'cos of the weather.'

'Dad told me he'd play snowballs with me on Sunday,' said Cissie, joining in. 'But he didn't.'

'Dad *never* keeps his promises!' insisted Benjamin. 'He always says he's going to do something, then he doesn't!'

'I agree!' said Susan, putting down her knife and fork, and ruffling up her hair. 'He never asks me anything about what I'm doing at the polytechnic. I doubt he even cares.'

'Shut up, Susan!' snapped Harriet. 'All of you, shut up!'

'Yes, Susan,' Lizzie called from the fireplace. 'Mum's got quite enough to cope with without all of you grumbling and complaining.'

'Well, it's true!' insisted Susan, getting up from the table, and flopping down on the sofa on the other side of the room. 'Dad leads a life of his own. He couldn't care less about all of us!'

Lizzie was about to say something when her mother suddenly slammed her fists on the table, and got up. 'Don't you ever say such a thing about your father, d'you hear?' Her voice, firm, loud and shaking with emotion, filled the final few moments of light in the room. 'Your father's a good man. All his life he's worked to keep this family going. Without him, we'd be nothing – absolutely nothing. I'm sick to death of hearing you all running him down. D'you think he *wants* to work in a fish market each day, getting up at the crack of dawn, in all kinds of weather, both hot and bitterly cold? What kind of a family are we that we can't support him, understand him, know that whatever he does is for us – *us* – not for himself, but for us? If I'd known that I was going to bring such an ungrateful bunch of stupid children into this world, I'd have – I'd have...' She suddenly burst into tears, and rushed off towards the bedroom.

Lizzie caught up with her just in time, and tried to comfort her. 'Mum!' she cried, trying to hug her. 'Don't take any notice of them. They didn't mean it. They didn't mean anything. They're just silly and thoughtless.'

'Please leave me alone,' sobbed Harriet, rushing off into her bedroom. 'All of you – just leave me alone!' She slammed the door behind her.

For a few moments there was deadly silence in the room. Turning slowly around to look at her brothers and sisters, Lizzie could see that their mother's outburst had stunned them. She was incensed by their behaviour. They weren't just silly and thoughtless, they were cruel and selfish.

'Well, I hope you're all satisfied with your-selves,' she said calmly. 'What's the matter with you? How can you say such things to Mum when both she and Dad are struggling to keep us all going? I'm ashamed of you, Susan. I'm ashamed of all of you. I never thought my own brothers and sisters could be quite so selfish.'

'It's all very well for you,' said Susan cuttingly. 'You'll soon be getting married. You won't care a damn what happens to all of us!'

Lizzie went straight across to her. 'And you're the worst, Susan,' she said, without raising her voice. 'You of all people. You should be setting an example to us all.'

'Me?' asked Susan, astonished.

'Yes, you, Susan,' said Lizzie, coming straight back at her. 'And d'you know why? Because at the moment, you're the one that's getting the most out of the tiny wages that Dad's getting for what you call "a grubby little job". If there was any justice in this world you would be going out to work to bring some extra cash into the family. But no – you go off to your studies in the morning, and contribute absolutely nothing for your upkeep. Now under normal circumstances, that wouldn't matter a bit. You have a right to get as much out of your education as you can. But you also have a responsibility to know where that hard-earned money is coming from, and what sacrifices have to be made to keep you in your polytechnic.'

Susan, absolutely speechless for once, slumped back sulkily into the sofa.

'And you three.' Lizzie turned to Benjamin, James and Cissie. 'Are you satisfied with yourselves now that you've made Mum cry?'

At the dining table, Cissie and her two brothers cowered.

'What's the matter with you? Why don't you think about helping, rather than criticising all the time? I know it's been difficult for you since we were bombed out – it's been difficult for all of us – especially Mum and Dad. But we all have to help each other, help Mum and Dad to get us through this terrible time.'

At that moment, the last of the two candles went out, and the only light in the room came from the flickering flames of the coal fire.

'Make an effort,' Lizzie said. 'That's all I ask. We've got to make an effort for Mum and Dad – and for ourselves.'

Out of the silence came the sound of Cissie starting to cry.

Lizzie went to her. 'It's all right, Cissie,' she said, putting her arm around her young sister's shoulders. 'But we mustn't upset Mum any more, must we?'

'No...' Cissie said tearfully.

As she did so, the front door opened, and Frank appeared, only just visible in the flickering flames of the fire. 'Hello,' he called brightly. 'What's going on here, then?'

An hour or so later, Lizzie, carrying a bowl of what was left over of the rabbit stew for old Lil Beasley, made her way along Hornsey Road. After a lull of a few hours, it was now snowing again, but as there was no wind, the fall was light and, apart from negotiating the slippery conditions on the pavement, the journey was fairly uneventful. On the way, she thought about the appalling scene that had just taken place back home, and the friction between the younger members of the family and their parents. She felt

233

thoroughly sick at the way Susan in particular had behaved, and at what a selfish, spoiled girl she had turned out to be. She also felt numb about how, during the past few months, the Angel family had changed. What had happened to all the fun they used to have, the way they talked and laughed together, and felt a sense of unity with one another? Why had they been torn apart by criticism and lack of consideration? Even the regular Sunday evening family entertainment had been abandoned, and what had taken its place had been nothing but discontent.

She strolled along streets that were dark with night but coloured white with the relentless march of winter snow. And as she went, she felt nothing but despair. Despair for the changing times, despair for what had once been her loving family, and despair for a future that she just couldn't see.

She turned the corner into Bedford Terrace. Lil Beasley's house was close by. Lizzie felt for Lil's front-door key in her coat pocket. But as she approached the house, she stopped. Something was not quite right. There were lights on in the windows of nearly all the houses in the terrace, all except Lil's. She approached the front door. To her horror, it had not been locked, and was slightly ajar. Alarmed, she went in.

The passage in Lil's house was in darkness. There was no electric light switch because Lil had solidly refused the changeover from gas. Lizzie cursed the fact that she had not brought her torch, and so after putting down her bowl of rabbit stew, she had to pick her way carefully in the dark.

'Mrs B?' she called, surprised that she could see no light coming from beneath the old girl's bedroom door on the first-floor. She eventually found her way to the foot of the stairs, and started to climb. 'Mrs B?' she called. 'Are you all right? It's me – Lizzie. Lizzie Angel...' She had climbed no more than two or three stairs when her foot suddenly knocked against something. Feeling totally helpless in the dark, she panicked, and for a brief moment or so, she stood completely motionless, hardly daring to move. 'Mrs B?' she cried falteringly. She finally plucked up enough courage to stoop down. Her hands reached out. She gasped. 'Oh my God!' she cried out loud. 'Mrs B! Oh my God...!'

Chapter 12

Lil Beasley's sudden death greatly distressed Lizzie. It wasn't just the fact that the old girl had died of a heart attack whilst climbing the stairs, but the thought that her body had been lying there alone all day. Lizzie blamed herself for not taking more notice of the poor old girl. If only she had gone to see her more often; if only she had told someone to look in on her during that morning when Lil had been defying common sense by clearing snow from her windowsills. If only... The more Lizzie thought about it, the more she realised that if Lil had to go, this is the

235

way she would *want* to go – no fuss, quick and into her cherished 'box' that she had so meticulously saved up for for years.

But it didn't help when, later on the same day, Lil's only sister turned up with her son to take over the proceedings, which Lizzie imagined soon meant that they were looking around Lil's rooms for any cash that might be hidden there.

When Ada Sykes and her son, Malcolm, came round to see Lizzie at Woolworths the following morning, Lizzie was suspicious of both of them mainly because, to Lizzie's knowledge, neither Ada nor any of her family had been to see, or had been in contact with, Lil for years.

'Where d'yer dig that pair up from?' asked Potto, as she watched Ada and her son leave the store. 'Looks like they've come straight out the graveyard!'

Lizzie shook her head with a sigh. 'Well,' she said, 'at least they can't hurt Lil any more.'

'Hurt her?'

'Lil once told me how hurt she was that none of her own ever bothered to come and see her,' said Lizzie. 'Apparently, the day their mum died, the relatives went straight into the house, even before the poor woman was cold. They stripped the place of everything – before Lil even had the chance to get there. You know, money does terrible things to people, Potto.'

'You're tellin' me,' agreed Potto. 'Not that *I've* ever 'ad any money ter do fings ter me!'

A few moments later, Lizzie caught an anxious glimpse of Maple, who had been reinstated in her job after some of the other girls had backed up her story about the 'Tuesday lady' shoplifter, and who had now transferred to one of the two hardware counters close to where Lizzie and Potto were selling gramophone records.

'Can you hold for the moment, Potto?' said Lizzie. 'I just want a quick word with Maple.'

Potto gave her a thumbs-up sign, and went on to serve a customer.

As it was only an hour after opening time, the store was not very full, which gave male back-room staff the opportunity to replenish stock on some of the counters. It was still bitterly cold, and a lot of the girls were wearing mittens and scarves, but when Lizzie reached the hardware counter, her anxious, distant view of Maple beneath her layers was confirmed. 'Maple!' she said. 'What's been going on?'

Maple, her right eye and cheek bruised and swollen, was taken by surprise to see Lizzie at her counter, and immediately became self-conscious. 'Oh ... Lizzie,' she said sheepishly, trying to shield the side of her face with her hand. 'How are you?'

'What's happened to you, Maple?' Lizzie asked, ignoring the pleasantries.

Maple, trying to bluff as usual, resumed her pseudo-Canadian accent. 'Oh – *this*, you mean?' she said casually. 'It's nothing – really. I – I walked into an open door last night, that's all.'

'*Another* open door?' asked Lizzie disbelievingly. 'How many more doors d'you have in your house to walk into?'

'It was an accident.'

Lizzie shook her head. 'Pull the other one, Maple,' she said dismissively. 'You've been in a

237

fight, haven't you?'

Maple quickly shook her head. 'No, Lizzie,' she insisted. 'Nothing like that.'

Lizzie took a brief look to make sure that no supervisor was around. 'Come on, Maple,' she said, lowering her voice, and leaning over the counter to her. 'Was it a boy who did this to you? Who is he? Tell me!'

Maple's good eye flickered all round, terrified that someone would overhear them. Fortunately, there were still no customers. 'I can't tell you now,' she said. 'Can we meet some time later – in the canteen?'

Woolworths' staff canteen was practically empty, mainly because most of the girls and backroom staff had finished their lunches, and were gradually making their way back to their respective jobs. The place smelled of boiled cabbage, fried sausages, fish cakes, and baked beans, and whilst Lizzie and Maple were talking together at a table tucked away in the corner, two of the catering staff were busily clearing and cleaning the rest of the tables.

'Your stepfather?' Lizzie asked. 'Your own stepfather beat you up like this?'

Maple felt thoroughly awkward and tongue-tied. 'I shouldn't really be telling you this,' she replied. 'He'd kill me if he found out.'

'Maple!' said Lizzie in disbelief. 'You're telling me that your stepfather's been beating you up, and you're afraid to tell anyone in case he finds out?'

'You don't know him,' said Maple. 'He has a

238

terrible temper.'

'To hell with his temper!' snapped Lizzie. 'Why, Maple? *Why* is he beating you up? This is not the first time. How long has it been going on?'

Maple, elbows leaning on the table, face cupped in her hands, shook her head despairingly. 'Ever since he married my mum,' she said, her voice faint, the Canadian accent discarded. 'Six years ago.'

Lizzie was puzzled. 'Six years ago?' she asked. 'But – you were in Canada.'

Maple slowly looked up at her. She shook her head.

'What d'you mean?'

'I've never been to Canada, Lizzie,' said Maple crushingly.

Astonished, Lizzie stared at her. 'But you were evacuated there?'

Again Maple shook her head. 'I made it all up,' she said, close to tears. 'I never left England. Never. I was here all through the blitz, living with my mum and – and *him*.'

Lizzie could hardly believe what she was hearing. 'Maple,' she said, 'why? Why would you want to make up a story like that? The way you speak, the things you've always talked about over there...'

'I know, I know,' replied Maple, shifting about uneasily on her chair. 'It was a dream really – a dream I always wanted to come true. But it never did. I got the idea from reading an article in *Picture Post*. There were such wonderful pictures – mountains, rivers, beautiful houses. I could imagine myself being there, but the only way I could do it was by telling everyone that I'd been evacuated there. I suppose it was a kind of ... escape.' She looked up at Lizzie with a pleading face. 'I've never ever told anyone about this, Lizzie,' she said. 'You're the first to know. You won't let on, will you?'

Lizzie took a moment to get her breath, then shook her head. 'I won't tell anyone, Maple,' she replied.

Maple breathed a sigh of relief.

'But you *must* tell me about this stepfather of yours,' insisted Lizzie firmly. '*Why* does he beat you up?'

Maple became withdrawn again.

They both sat back in their chairs as one of the catering staff cleared their table. Once she had gone, Lizzie leaned forward again. 'Why, Maple? Tell me.'

Maple hesitated before answering. 'He doesn't love my mother,' she said. 'He never has. He's never liked the fact that she had a child of her own, somebody else's child. Because he couldn't do anything about it, I suppose he just wanted to take it out on me.'

'But what does your mother say about all this?' asked Lizzie anxiously.

Maple's eyes lowered. 'She doesn't say anything,' she replied. 'She still loves him.'

'Even after all he's done to you?'

'She loves him,' was all Maple could reply.

Lizzie found it impossible to comprehend what Maple was telling her. Despite all the worries and concerns that she had with her own family, Lizzie had never experienced anything like this. It was nothing more than mindless brutality. 'Maple,' she said, 'if your mother won't do anything about it, then you *have* to go to the police.'

Maple immediately panicked. 'No!' she cried. 'I can't do that! I'd *never* do that!'

'But this man's dangerous,' said Lizzie, reaching across to cover Maple's hands with her own. 'If he keeps beating you up like this, one day he could kill you.'

'You don't understand,' said Maple, pulling her hands away.

'Maple,' pleaded Lizzie. 'Please listen to me.'

'You don't understand,' repeated Maple. 'There's something more. There's a reason why he beats me.'

Lizzie stared hard at her.

'You see...' Maple looked briefly down at the table, then looked up again. There was pain, anguish and tears in her eyes. 'He – tries to do things to me.'

Despite the bitterly cold dark evening, and the drifts of snow that had now turned to solid ice, Lizzie was only too relieved to get out into the fresh air. Most of all, she was desperate to see Rob, and to feel his comforting arms around her. The last twenty-four hours had been absolute hell. What with arguments and quarrels within the Angel family the evening before, and then finding poor old Lil's body on the stairs, it had all been too much for her, and it had left her absolutely drained. But now, on top of everything else, there was Maple. The more she thought about all Maple had told her, the more she was stunned with disbelief. She was utterly repelled by the idea that a man could try to force sexual advances on his own stepdaughter. But she was even more repelled by the fact that because Maple wouldn't co-operate, he had used violence on her. The man was a brute, an aggressive brute, and he should be locked away. But how could Lizzie help Maple when all the girl wanted to do was to keep the whole thing quiet?

'Not much you can do,' said Rob, after Lizzie had told him about what was happening to Maple. 'The best thing I can think of is to send a couple of heavies around to sort out this character.'

'It's not as easy as that,' sighed Lizzie. 'You don't know Maple. If anything happened to this stepfather, she'd probably blame herself and be riddled with guilt. She's a very mixed-up girl.'

It wasn't the best of evenings to go for a stroll, for, although most of the main roads had been cleared, the gutters were piled high with hills of snow, which had been chipped away from the pavements, and were now solid ice in the below-zero temperatures. But at least it wasn't snowing, and as Lizzie and Rob strolled arm in arm along upper Hornsey Road, their warm breath was darting out in little spurts from their mouths as it clashed with the ice-cold air, which was as fresh as if they were walking along the top of a mountain. For several moments, they walked in silence, their cheeks tingling and blood red in the relentless cold, and above them, trillions of stars were clinging to a clear moonlit sky, like precious stones sparkling from the roof of some vast dark cave. They stopped briefly at the entrance of the old Star cinema, once a much-loved 'fleapit', but closed and boarded up since before the war.

'I have to do something about Maple,' said Lizzie, snuggling up to Rob as they gazed aimlessly through the broken iron gates of the dilapidated foyer. 'If anything happened to her, I'd feel responsible.'

'Don't be silly, Liz,' said Rob, pulling her closer to him. 'You can't take on the problems of the entire world.'

'And you can't turn your back on them either,' replied Lizzie. 'Maple has no love in her life. It's not fair, because she's actually quite a nice girl. I'd like to bring her along to meet you one night. Would you mind?'

'Why should I mind?' replied Rob. 'But if this bloke is the kind of person I think he is, I want you to be careful. You're more precious to me than all our friends.'

Rob's remark sent a warm glow through Lizzie's cold veins. She looked up at him, and he kissed her. 'Last night,' she said, 'Dad asked me if we'd thought any more about getting married.'

'My mother asks me the same question daily,' said Rob. 'Don't you think it's about time we gave it some thought?'

'I never *stop* thinking about it.'

'Then what are we waiting for?'

Lizzie hesitated. 'You,' she replied.

'Me?'

'This emigration thing.'

Rob sighed. 'Oh,' he said.

'If you're still intent on going ahead with it,'

said Lizzie, 'I just don't know where it leaves us.' She eased him round to look at her, and she could just make out his features, which were fluorescent white from a dazzling shaft of moonlight. 'Does it really mean so much to you, Rob?'

For what seemed like an eternity, Rob thought long and hard. Should he lie to her? Or should he just play for time? 'Yes, it does, Liz,' he replied. 'But if you didn't come with me, it wouldn't be the same.'

They walked on in silence. Rob could almost hear Lizzie's mind churning over. Was this crunch time, he wondered. All his fears were now coming to the surface, all his anxieties about persuading Lizzie to leave her family and join him on what for both of them would be the biggest upheaval they would probably ever have in their entire lives.

'If only I knew,' Lizzie said quite suddenly. 'If only there was one little person inside me who could tell me what I should do, tell me that I should forget all the people who have always meant so much to me, and just think of myself.'

'Think of *us*, Liz,' pleaded Rob.

They strolled on at a leisurely pace, heading off up the hill in the direction of Hornsey Rise. Once or twice their feet slipped on the icy pavements, and they had to use all their efforts to prevent themselves from taking a nasty tumble. They passed a pub where the regulars were clearly having a whale of an evening, for the place was echoing to laughter and cheerful banter, and someone thumping out a tuneless song on the old 'joanna'. But Lizzie couldn't really hear them. Her mind was miles away. She wasn't thinking about how disillusioned she was with the state of the country, or how awful England had become since the end of the war. She was thinking about duty. As the eldest child in the Angel family, she asked herself, hadn't she a responsibility to stick by them, and see them through all their hardships? But then she thought about what had happened the night before, the selfishness of her sister Susan, and the petty wrangling that had changed the whole nature of the family she had always loved so much. She thought about her mother, and why she had become so possessive. She thought about her father, who had become so secretive, and not nearly so easy to talk to as he used to be. A few weeks before, she had been adamant that nothing in the world would persuade her to give up the life she had always known in favour of an uncertain future. But now ... now she wasn't so sure. Her mind was racked by indecision. Quite unconsciously, she suddenly brought them both to a halt. 'What if I said that I'll give your idea some thought?' she said.

Rob felt his entire body tingle with excitement. 'Liz!' he cried. 'D'you mean it? D'you really mean it?'

'Give me time, Rob!' she replied. 'That's all I ask.'

'Darling, of course I'll give you time!' said Rob, brimming with new-found optimism. 'Look. I picked up some application forms from the Australian High Commission the other day. Why don't you come over to my place tomorrow and we can go through them together? It'll give you an idea of what we have to–'

'Rob!' Lizzie immediately brought him back to earth. 'All I said was, I'd give it some thought. I think that's the least I owe you.'

'Oh, Lizzie!' Rob said, hugging her as close to him as he could. 'Let's talk about it. Let's talk about it now.'

'No, Rob!' insisted Lizzie. 'I can't think about it today,' she said, impersonating the infamous southern belle Scarlett O'Hara, in the film, *Gone With The Wind*, 'I'll think about it tomorrow!'

Ada Sykes was not at all the sort of person her sister Lil Beasley had talked about. When Lizzie and her mother turned up for the funeral, which was about to set out from Lil's place in Bedford Terrace, what they found was a rather amiable old lady, who in many ways looked very much like her older sister, for she had the same blue eyes, and thin, tight lips that curled up at the edges, straight white hair, and the same habit of sniffing without ever blowing her nose. The only real difference was that, in contrast to Lil, she was pint-sized, so that most people, including Ada's son, Malcolm, towered above her. Malcolm, however, was a different kettle of fish. Lizzie could tell immediately that he had a mean look about him, and was clearly just waiting for the funeral to be over before he stripped the place and sold everything. Apart from Lizzie and Harriet, the only other mourners who had been invited to have a cup of tea before the arrival of the undertaker's men were Martha Cutting, from Andover Road, who was there more out of curiosity than grief, and Fred Barker and his missus, Gert, who ran the local newsagent's shop where old Lil always bought her copy of the *Star* in the morning and the *Evening News* in the evening.

'Salt er the earth,' said Fred, a plump, affable man in his sixties, who was the only one of the mourners who had to brush away an occasional tear from his eye, while sipping tea from one of Lil's chipped cups and saucers. 'They don't make 'em like 'er these days.'

'Never owed us a penny in all the years we knew 'er,' added Gert, whose black coat, dress and hat smelled of mothballs.

'She wasn't the only one,' sniffed Martha, as though the newsagent's wife was getting at her. Sipping her tea, back upright in her chair, she shrugged her shoulders. 'I always pay *my* bills the moment I get them. If yer don't believe me, you can ask my landlord.'

'We believe you, Martha,' said Harriet, after exchanging a quick look with Lizzie.

It was an unreal experience for Lizzie, sitting there in the middle of Lil's back parlour, dressed from head to toe in black, watching this odd collection of people around her, sipping tea, talking as though anything they said could make any difference now to the poor old girl, who was lying prostate in her open 'box' in the next-door front parlour. What did it matter now, Lizzie asked herself. Talking about her couldn't bring her back. In a few hours' time she would be lying in her grave, and the only memories of her would be of a little old lady who lived all on her own for so many years, with hardly anyone ever going to see her.

'I was very fond of 'er, yer know,' said Ada, who rarely raised her eyes to look at anyone. 'I know I 'adn't shown it much over the years, but I thought about 'er an awful lot.' She turned to her son, who was sitting beside her at the kitchen table. 'In't that so, Malcolm?'

Malcolm, who was in his sixties, and unmarried, nodded, and brushed back his greying quiff. 'She was always very fond of Mum,' he said, addressing the others. 'In fact, she idolised 'er.'

'Is that so?' asked Martha, squaring up her shoulders. 'Funny she never talked about 'er. Not ter me anyway.'

''Ow many times did *you* talk ter Lil then, Martha?' asked Fred's missus cattily.

Martha stiffened. 'As a matter of fact, Lil and I always exchanged a few words whenever we met. She used ter tell *me* fings that would curl yer 'air.'

'Really, Martha?' asked Harriet. 'What things?'

'All sorts er fings,' replied Martha. 'About people she couldn't bear. About the way she'd bin ignored over the years.'

'Aunt Lil was *never* ignored,' said Malcolm, chiming in. 'At least, not by my mum she wasn't.'

'Nobody cared about her condition,' said Martha.

'Condition?' asked Ada.

'Legs!'

Ada and Malcolm exchanged a look. 'Legs?'

'They didn't belong to 'er,' said Martha.

'Didn't yer know?'

'Don't talk such rubbish, Marfa!' said Fred Barker. ''Ow come 'er own legs din't belong to 'er?'

'Arthritis!' replied Martha. 'Riddled with it. She was always complainin' about the pain; often used to say how she wished she could just end it all, and jump in the lake up Finsbury Park.'

'What I remember about Lil,' added Harriet, 'is that she endured pain better than anyone I know. She was not only kind, but she was also courageous.'

'When we was young,' said Ada, addressing her remark directly to Lizzie, 'me an' Lil used ter play hop, skip and jump down your road. She always won, though. That's because she had more determination than me. It was the same when she got married. When Jack Beasley was killed in the war, she carried on with 'er life as though nuffin' 'ad 'append. "Yer can't stop bleedin' livin' just 'cos one part of yer ain't there any more," she used ter say.'

'Lil 'ad guts all right,' added Fred. 'We could all take a leaf out of 'er book.'

Lizzie looked at them all, sitting round the room, black coats and dresses, black hats, black ties, black shoes, sipping their tea, recalling someone who meant something different to each one of them. To Lizzie, however, old Lil was more than just a determined woman, or someone who had a lot of guts. She was a woman of her time, a woman who stood out alone against the march of progress, who remained true to herself to her dying day. 'If it's all right with you, Mrs Sykes,' she said, 'I'd like to go and see Mrs Beasley just once more before – *they* arrive.'

'Of course, dear,' said Ada, whose black hat veil had slipped over her forehead.

Everyone took a sneaking look up at Lizzie as she put down her cup and saucer on the table, and quietly slipped out of the room.

Although the curtains were drawn in Lil's front parlour, there was enough light filtering into the room for Lizzie to see old Lil lying in her beloved 'box', waiting for the undertaker to arrive to screw down the lid. Lizzie quietly approached the marble-like figure. There was something unreal about it, as though it wasn't really Lil at all. But as Lizzie drew closer, she recognised that grumpy, stubborn old face, which in death was even more beautiful than in life – cold, smooth – her hair tidy, with no curlers for once, and no longer held in place with a hairnet. Lizzie stretched out her hand, and gently touched the old girl's forehead. Yes, this used to be Lil all right. But not any more. Dear old Lil was somewhere else now, cursing everyone with her 'bleedin' this', and 'bleedin' that', and sweeping the doorstep of her new place just as she had done every day of her earthly life. But one thing Lizzie *was* sure about, and that was that Lil was no longer alone.

'This is for you, dear.'

Lizzie turned with a start to find Ada Sykes standing there. She was holding out something to her.

'I know Lil wanted you to have it,' said Ada, her voice barely audible in the deathly silence of the room, 'because she put your name on the back of it.'

Lizzie took the framed photograph that Ada was offering her. It was the old, faded, sepia one, with Lil as a young girl posing with her soldier husband, Jack Beasley. She turned it over, and looked at the back. There was a piece of envelope stuck there which read, 'This is for Lizzie Angel. She'll know why.'

'She was quite a character, wasn't she?' said Ada softly.

'Oh yes,' replied Lizzie, with a faint, wry smile. 'Oh yes.' But as she stood there, looking down at the ice-cold figure, wearing what was probably the only decent Sunday dress she had ever had, all Lizzie could hear were the final words the old girl had said to her the last time they had talked together: 'There ain't nuffin' like bein' wiv the man yer love.'

Chapter 13

1982

That old sepia photo of Lil Beasley was very much on Lizzie's mind as she and Rob made their way in their Ford station wagon to Brisbane. Although it had been thirty-four years since Lil had died, now that Lizzie was actually on her way to meet her mum at the airport, memories of her early years in the old country were flooding back to her. In fact, ever since her mum had finally agreed to pay Lizzie and Rob her first ever visit to Australia, Lizzie's mind had been consumed with the past, so much so that she had hardly slept a wink since she'd got the letter to say that Harriet had agreed to accept Lizzie's invitation to come.

'I still can't believe it,' she said, as Rob turned the car into the eastern suburbs of Toowoomba, and headed out east towards the Great Dividing Range and the new Warrego Highway. 'I never thought Mum would do it. I'd resigned myself to never seeing her again.'

'Well,' said Rob, 'just shows that all you had to do was to ask her. I reckon it's about time you two got together to get rid of some of the shadows.'

Lizzie thought about that. Rob was right. It *was* time to clear the air. In fact it was long overdue. 'Perhaps,' she said, her mind miles away.

The city's beautiful Queens Park and natural bushlands of Redwood and Jubilee Parks were soon behind them, and as they finally wound their way through the Darling Downs, with a clear view of Drayton town in the distant southern suburbs of the city, Lizzie found her eyes drooping in the full glare of a hot December summer day – and by the time they reached the highway, she was dozing, though not asleep. As her head lay back in the seat, heat turned to intense cold as she recalled that eventful winter of 1947/48. In her mind's eye, she could see the Angel family prefab in Andover Road, entombed in ice and snow, the struggle to dig themselves out, and the effort it took to get to work at

Woolworths in Holloway Road. Most of all, she remembered the family itself – her young sister, Cissie, brothers, Benjamin and James, and her impossible sister, Susan, who always seemed to live in a fantasy world far beyond anything she could expect in life. Where were they all now? They had all married and settled down with families of their own, but rarely did any of them put pen to paper. Out of sight, out of mind. It was the same the world over. She had loved her family, and always would – at least, the happy memories of them, especially those Sunday family entertainment evenings. And she had loved her mum and her dad – especially her dad, because she could talk to him, because he was someone who would always listen to her and discuss her problems. Why then did she leave him, and at a time when he had involved himself in such danger? Why had it taken her mother so long to forgive her – if she *had* actually forgiven her? And what happened after she had left home? Why *had* her dad died so suddenly? Soon she would find out. Soon, all those questions would be answered. They *had* to be answered if she was going to be able to continue her life without the burden of guilt. Or would she?

The sound of Rob's car horn woke her up with a start. Sweat was streaming down her face, her flimsy cotton dress was soaked, and the car was filled with the stifling smell of smoke from Rob's cigarette. 'What was that?' she asked, in a daze.

'Just some bloody joker,' grunted Rob. 'Tried ter cut me up!'

'It's time we got ourselves some aircon in this

thing,' Lizzie said, dabbing her forehead with her handkerchief, and opening her window as far as it would go. 'Surely it wouldn't cost more than fifty dollars for a reconditioned?'

'Look,' said Rob, 'if I've got fifty dollars ter spare, I'm not spending it on bloody air conditioning!'

'You've been promising it to me for the last five years,' replied Lizzie.

'Sure sign you're getting old,' replied Rob mischievously.

Lizzie poked him in the ribs. 'We're *both* getting old!' she jibed. 'And, in any case, you're one year older than me.'

'Ah, but *I* don't look my fifty-five years!' he quipped cheekily.

Lizzie gave him another dig in the ribs. As she did so, a huge airliner swooped low over the road they were travelling on, and made for the runway a couple of miles to the west of them. They were approaching the precincts of Brisbane Airport, and Lizzie suddenly felt a surge of anxiety. Soon it would be over. Soon, thirty-four years would be rolled back to reveal the hidden face of uncertainty.

Harriet Angel was wide awake. She had hardly slept a wink since Singapore, not only because the Aussie girl she had met on the flight out to Sydney had insisted on sitting next to her again on the transit journey to Brisbane, but because she had that sense of anticipation which all travellers feel when they are approaching the end of a long journey. But there was more to it than that. At the end of this journey, she would be seeing her daughter Lizzie for the first time since she set sail from Southampton for Australia thirty-four years before. It was an awesome and, in some ways, nerve-racking thought.

She peered through the window for the umpteenth time in fifteen minutes. The plane was gradually descending, and she could feel a heavy pressure in her ears, which almost cut out the sound of the airliner's engines. Down below, she could see a long stretch of coastline, miles and miles of white sandy beaches, and so many different colours of blue in the water such as she had never seen in her life before, especially on the only holidays she and the Angel family had ever previously had, in Worthing and Bournemouth.

'Can yer see the good ol' Gold Coast?' asked the girl in the next seat.

Harriet turned to her. 'Gold Coast? What's that?'

'That's where you're going, lady,' said the girl, with a huge grin, leaning over her to peer out through the window. 'Good ol' Brisbane – state capital of Queensland – third largest city! Did yer know that?' She didn't wait for a reply. 'Looks exactly the same ter me. At least, I hope it does. I'd hate ter think it's changed.'

'I thought you told me earlier, change is for the best?' said Harriet.

The girl slumped back in her seat again. 'Did I?' she asked. 'Did I really say that?' She didn't wait for an answer. 'Well, maybe it is – *sometimes*. But not always.' She grinned sideways at Harriet. 'Depends how old yer are, I guess.'

255

Harriet turned to gaze out of the window again. As the plane skimmed what appeared to be a very populated coastline, she could now see what looked like a lot of new tower block buildings, all gleaming white, and dazzling windows reflecting the bright rays of a burning sun. So *this* is what Lizzie left home for, she told herself. Is all this *really* so much better than Andover Road, and the old terraced houses in Islington?

'Ladies and gentlemen, we're about to land at Brisbane Airport. Will you please fasten your seat belts.'

The chief steward's voice booming out of the plane's Tannoy system took Harriet by surprise. A little unnerved, she gripped the arms of her seat, and waited for her ears to clear. She looked out of the window again, and her view of the sea and harbour suddenly disappeared, to be replaced by the sight of the plane's wings skimming rooftops and aerial masts. With the plane now on its final approach for landing, the ground was getting closer and closer, but in those few minutes, time for Harriet seemed to be suspended. Airport buildings and cars and other aircraft parked on the tarmac were all blurred, for all she could see in her mind's eye was Lizzie. Not Lizzie, the mature Englishwoman torn between two worlds, but that lovely young girl she remembered so well, laughing and joking, the perfect mimic, the perfect daughter, the solid support her family had come to rely on so much during those dark days during and after the war. She took a deep breath, and sighed. Oh God, what was waiting for her down there, she asked herself. How different would Lizzie be after so long? How would she be able to face Rob after the way she had blamed him for taking her daughter away from her at a time when she needed her most? Her stomach was swollen with mounting anxiety, her mind flooded by painful memories, guilt, and recriminations. When she saw Lizzie waiting at that airport, how would she, Harriet, be able to put into words what she had been churning over in her mind for so many years? What was the *real* reason she had travelled all this way across the world? Was it really to put things right, or was it to satisfy herself that Lizzie had made the wrong decision? Despite the joy and excitement of seeing Lizzie again, something inside told her that what she had to say to her daughter was going to be the most difficult task of her entire life.

Rob was exhausted. Apart from being forced out of bed at dawn, and having driven a hell of a long way from Toowoomba to Brisbane Airport, Lizzie had also dragged him to the Arrivals barrier half an hour before Harriet's plane had even landed. It was inevitable, of course. He knew only too well that Lizzie had been on tenterhooks ever since she'd gone to bed the previous evening – in fact, ever since she'd first got her mum's letter accepting her invitation to come and spend the Christmas holiday with them.

He was also quite edgy himself. After all, Harriet had not been exactly the most endearing future mother-in-law during those last few weeks before they left the old country, so meeting up with her again was going to be, at the very least, interesting.

'I don't understand it,' said Lizzie, pacing up and down the barrier, constantly looking up at the arrivals indicator. 'It says the plane arrived half an hour ago. She should be out by now.'

'Fer Chrissake, cool it, Liz!' said Rob, scolding her, at the same time pulling nervously on his cigarette. 'They've got to get the bloody baggage off the plane first!'

'For God's sake!' insisted Lizzie, getting more agitated by the minute. 'The plane's only come from Sydney. It can't take all that long to get Mum's baggage off. And please don't swear like that in front of her. She'll think Australia's made you common!'

Rob had no answer to that. If Lizzie was determined to work herself up, there was nothing he could do about it. And in any case, if Australia had coarsened him up a bit, he had no regrets. Better than being all churned up in bloody Pomland!

Lizzie took a deep breath, and did her best to keep calm. The airport was brimming with passengers and friends and relatives, a sure indication that air travel was now the most sensible way to get around in this vast, sprawling country. So different from when she and Rob had turned up on the ship at Sydney Harbour all those years ago, eyes agog, apprehensive, just two young people amongst hundreds of hopefuls about to start a new life in a country they had only ever read about. Was it really thirty-four years since they first arrived? Thirty-four years

258

since they got on that train and travelled the long journey in a hot railway carriage all the way up the western coast to Brisbane? It just didn't seem possible that they had surmounted all their fears and doubts and settled down so joyously in dear old Toowoomba.

'Passengers on Qantas flight five-oh-two from Sydney are now in the Baggage Hall.'

'And about bloody time!' Rob shouted impatiently at the Tannoy speakers.

Lizzie glared at him, but was unable to scold him because her heart had just missed a beat. Oh God! Where is she? she asked herself, craning to get a look over the heads of the crowd who were thronged around the arrivals exit. Don't let me miss her! Please God, don't let me miss her? But what if I don't recognise her? What if she doesn't recognise me? Will she have aged so much that she could get lost in the crowd without being noticed?

The first passengers, pushing their luggage on trolleys, appeared at the exit gate, and rushed straight into the joyous arms of their families and friends. They were quickly followed by others – young couples with small children, elderly couples looking around anxiously for whoever was going to meet them, single young and elderly men, single young and elderly women. But so far, still no sign of anyone who looked remotely like Lizzie's mum.

'Oh, where *is* she, Rob?' cried Lizzie, who was now so agitated trying to scan the arriving passengers that she looked fit to drop. 'D'you think she missed the plane?'

'Don't be such a sheila, Liz!' growled Rob, cigarette in lips, also checking the face of every person coming through the arrivals gate.

Lizzie was now so desperate, she was prepared to gate-crash the baggage hall and search the place for her mum. But just as she was on the point of doing so, Rob called to her, 'Liz! Over there!'

Lizzie swung with a start to look where Rob was indicating, just in time to see Harriet, with suitcase and holdall packed on to a baggage trolley, struggling out through the exit gate. Once again, Lizzie's heart missed a beat. 'Mum!' she yelled. Without another word, she ducked under the barrier, and made a wild, frenetic rush through the crowd. 'Mum!'

Harriet stopped, turned and froze. Her face was a picture – first shock, then emotion.

For one fraction of a second, both mother and daughter came to a standstill, just staring at each other. Then Lizzie rushed at Harriet, and engulfed her in her arms. 'Oh, Mum!' she said, hugging her, voice shaking. 'Mum...'

Hesitant at first, Harriet threw her arms around Lizzie, and hugged her back. 'Hello, Lizzie,' she said, her voice also tinged with emotion.

With crowds still pushing and shoving past them, Lizzie, eyes welling up with tears, pulled away from her mother, and took a good look at her. The first thing she noticed was that Harriet's auburn-coloured hair was now completely white, and her face was much more lined than the last time they had been together.

'You look wonderful,' she said, half laughing,

half crying. 'You don't look a day older.'

Harriet smiled awkwardly. Even though her daughter was no longer a young woman, and had filled out somewhat since the days when she lived at home, Lizzie had still retained her lovely, fresh complexion. 'I wish I could say the same about you,' she said jokily. 'But *you* look wonderful too.'

After waiting a moment whilst the two women had their private reunion, Rob eventually joined them. 'G'day, Mrs Angel,' he said awkwardly, stretching out his hand for her to shake.

Harriet smiled at him. 'My name's not Mrs Angel, Rob,' she said. 'It's Mum.' She ignored his hand, and kissed him on both cheeks.

Lizzie's face crumpled up.

On the way back to Toowoomba, Harriet saw little of the passing countryside. She and Lizzie were too busy catching up on what had happened to various members of the family over the years. Lizzie heard an awful lot about her nieces and nephews, and how Harriet absolutely idolised her grandchildren. She heard about Susan and her husband, Don, and how much they had enjoyed their visit to Lizzie and Rob a few years before, and how Susan had turned out to be a loving, caring mother with two girls of her own, who were both now married with children of their own. She also heard about how well Benjamin was doing as a senior aviation designer at the British Aerospace factory in Bristol, and about his wife Ellen, and their two teenage girls and one boy, and Cissie, who had never married, but had dedicated herself to a career in nursing.

However, Harriet's one disappointment seemed to be James, always the one laidback member of the family, who had never married, and who had spent much of his time drifting in and out of jobs over the years. In turn, Harriet heard from Lizzie all about her own two kids, Betty and Lou, and Lizzie and Rob's own grandchildren, during which time Rob smoked the car out with his cigarette, and let the two women get on with it while he drove back west, towards the Warrego Highway.

It was only when they reached the outskirts of Toowoomba that the two women paused for breath long enough to notice the scenery, with Lizzie pointing out some of the highlights.

'That's Drayton down there,' she said, pointing towards the southern suburbs of Toowoomba, as the car climbed the steep slopes of a high ridge. 'It used to be a separate settlement, but it got kind of swallowed up by the big city.'

'Drayton?' remarked Harriet, peering out of the open window, the hot afternoon air rushing against her face. 'Sounds a very English name.'

Rob answered her from the front. 'It is,' he replied. 'Named after some poms back in the old country.'

'Poms?' asked Harriet, puzzled.

'Take no notice,' said Lizzie, giving Rob a scolding slap on his head from the seat behind. 'That's where we live – down there. That's Toowoomba.'

Harriet looked down the ridge to where Lizzie was pointing. What she saw from this high vantage point was a proliferation of parks and gardens, newly constructed office buildings, and what looked like neat single- and double-storey detached houses set on either side of long, tree-lined streets. It seemed a long way from the backstreets of Islington.

A short time later, Harriet found herself standing in the blazing heat with Lizzie outside one of those timber-panelled houses, with its neat, oblong patch of garden in front, and well-stocked flowerbeds, which showed a lot of loving care. The two-storey house itself was box-shaped, with colourful hanging flower baskets draped over the porch and veranda, and pretty shuttered windows all along a wide balcony running right round the house on the upper floor. These reflected the fierce rays of the late afternoon sun. Whilst Rob unloaded her baggage from the car, Harriet couldn't help wondering what her late husband, Frank, would have made of it all. After all, in many ways, he *was* partly responsible for Lizzie being there.

'So, Mum,' asked Lizzie, putting her arm around her mother's waist as she looked up at the house. 'What d'you think?'

Harriet smiled indecisively. 'It's a far cry from Andover Road,' she replied.

'You haven't lived in Andover Road in a long while,' said Lizzie tentatively.

'I know,' said Harriet. 'But I still think about it.'

Fireflies were a totally new experience for Harriet. She had never seen such things before, and as she, Lizzie and Rob sat by the small swimming pool in the back garden, pondering a

vast evening sky crammed with an endless southern constellation of stars, she was entranced by
the tiny flecks of luminescence that fluttered in
and out of the hanging baskets, settling briefly on
the geraniums there, and then disappearing into
a thin shaft of the crescent-shaped moon. Harriet
found it hard to believe that it was only nine
o'clock in the evening, for her inner clock was
telling her that, if she was still in England, she
should have been in bed hours ago. But this
wasn't England, this was Australia, a long way
from the dreary December winter she had left
behind, and despite her jet lag and the vast
difference in time, she still hadn't brought into
focus all she had seen and experienced during
the few hours since she stepped off that airliner
at Brisbane Airport.

One of her first surprises had been how well
Lizzie had learned to cook. To have steak and
mushroom pie in the open air, at the side of a
swimming pool, and ten thousand miles away
from home, just somehow didn't seem real.

'I once wrote to Gran about these fireflies,' said
Lizzie, her voice breaking the near mystical
silence. 'It was just before she died, about the
time I was pregnant with Betty. She wrote back
and said that if you see a firefly, it's probably an
angel come to tell you that everything's all right.
I feel as though I've been flying with the angels
ever since.'

Harriet hesitated. 'Your grandmother had a
way with words,' she said tersely.

Lizzie realised that in talking about her
grandmother she was on thin ice, for it had been

she who had strongly defended Lizzie's decision to get married and leave home.

'I miss her,' reflected Lizzie wistfully. 'I – I've missed you too, *and* all the family.' She was having difficulty finding the words she wanted to say. 'I miss Dad so much.' To Lizzie's disappointment, Harriet didn't respond to what she had just said. 'It wasn't fair what happened. It was so cruel. He was far too young to die.'

'It doesn't matter what age you are,' said Harriet. There was a note of irony in her voice. 'Death doesn't have to give any excuse. It can come at any time.'

There was a brief silence. It was one of many awkward moments between them since Harriet had arrived. The lost years were not breaking down as easily as Lizzie had hoped.

Fortunately, Rob was there to relieve the tension. 'Well, I wish I could say that I miss *my* family,' he said, coughing on his cigarette. 'My ol' woman said she an' Dad'd come out an' visit me twenty years ago, but they never made the effort. God knows, they weren't short of a bob or two. Outer sight, outer mind. They were probably pleased ter see the back of me.'

'That's not true, Rob, you know it isn't,' insisted Lizzie. 'Both your parents had such bad health. You can't blame them. It must've been a daunting thought for them to travel out all this way. Wouldn't you say so, Mum?'

'That's more or less what they told me,' Harriet replied.

Rob sat bolt upright in his lounger chair. 'They did?' he asked eagerly. 'You mean, you were in touch with them?'

'From time to time,' replied Harriet. 'I went over to tea with them a couple of times, and they came to me once or twice after Frank had died, after we'd moved into the new house in Thane Villas.'

Rob turned to look at her. He could see her face quite clearly, reflected in the underwater light from the swimming pool. 'Did they – talk about me much?' he asked tentatively.

'Oh yes,' replied Harriet. 'Frequently. They talked a great deal about when you and Lizzie went away. I got the feeling that they felt quite sad by the thought that they'd probably never see you again. Your father found it very difficult to cope with your mother's death. They seemed very close.'

Lizzie was waiting for Rob's response, but he just went very silent. Lizzie wished her mother hadn't spoken about Rob's parents, for she was beginning to realise that, deep down inside, consciously or unconsciously, Harriet was still harbouring resentment for what Rob had done.

Rob got up, threw his cigarette down on to the paving stones by the pool, and twisted it hard with the sole of his shoe. 'I need another packet of fags,' he said. 'I'll be right back.'

Harriet waited for him to go. 'I hope I didn't say the wrong thing?' she asked.

'What makes you think that, Mum?' asked Lizzie, her reply tinged with criticism. 'You're only telling Rob what he already knew. He's a good, loving man. He missed his folks a great deal. He's always been so sad that they could never make the journey out here. He did so want to show off to them about how well he's done.'

'Have *you* done well, Lizzie?' asked Harriet, subconsciously hoping for an adverse reply.

Lizzie paused a moment. 'Better than I ever dared hope,' she replied. 'But it was a risk – a huge risk. When we first got out here, I spent the first few weeks crying myself to sleep every night. I felt so far away from home, so cut off. If it hadn't been for Rob, I think I'd have got on the first boat straight back home. Trouble was, I hated the people. I hated the way they called us "bloody poms", and the way they treated us, as though they were a breed apart. It was so stupid, especially when you think that so many of them come from the old country anyway.'

'The *old* country,' reflected Harriet, implying disapproval. 'It's such a curious way to talk about your roots. But then, compared to this place, I suppose it is old.'

'It's a term of affection really,' said Lizzie. 'I often think about the good days back home. I even think about dear old Andover Road.' There was another long, awkward pause between them. 'When Susan was out here a few years ago, she told me they'd pulled down our prefab.'

'Long ago,' replied Harriet. 'When I heard they were doing so, I went up there and watched the men dismantling it. It was strange seeing it all go quite so quickly. Our lives had been hanging on a thread there for what seemed like an eternity, and then suddenly – it was gone. I was glad to see the back of the place. I'm sure I must have told you about it in my letters?'

'No, Mother,' said Lizzie reprovingly. 'I've never had many letters from you.'

There was another pause before Harriet replied vaguely, 'I've never been a great one for letter writing. I left all that sort of thing to your father. Anyway,' she said, in an effort to change the subject, 'everything's fine now, is it? You have good neighbours?'

'Oh yes,' replied Lizzie, casually. 'The Aussies are actually very warm-hearted people. It just took us a time to get used to them.'

Harriet yawned. She wasn't really interested in the question she had just asked.

'Why don't you turn in now, Mum?' said Lizzie, beginning to feel the strain. 'It'll take you a while to get over your jet lag and our down-under clock.'

'Perhaps you're right,' said Harriet, getting up from her lounger.

'Betty, Lou and the kids are coming up from Adelaide tomorrow,' said Lizzie. 'They're looking forward to meeting their grandmother.'

'I can't wait to meet them too,' replied Harriet enthusiastically. 'I only wish Frank could have been here to see them.'

There was another of those brief silences, which had so frequently marked the evening. 'We've got a lot to talk about, Mum,' said Lizzie.

Harriet lowered her eyes. 'Yes,' she said.

Above them, a cluster of large moths were fluttering recklessly around a fluorescent pool-side lamp. In the changing-room porch at the far end of the pool, they could just see Rob sitting on his own, deep in thought, smoking his fag.

'Say good night to him for me,' said Harriet.

Lizzie nodded. 'I will.'

Harriet started to go, but then stopped and turned. 'Is it always as hot as this at night?' she asked.

'It's worse now it's summer,' replied Lizzie. 'But you have a fan in your room.'

'Doesn't it ever rain in Toowoomba?'

'Only when we want it to,' replied Lizzie.

'Not like the old country.'

'No,' said Lizzie. 'Not like the old country.'

Harriet went to her and kissed her on the cheek. 'Good night, darling.'

'Good night, Mum,' said Lizzie, giving her only a gentle hug. 'Welcome to the new world.'

Harriet forced a smile. 'Thank you, darling,' she replied. She stood there for only one more brief silence. Then she quietly left, and went back into the house.

Lizzie waited for her to go, then wandered to the end of the pool to join Rob, who was clearly miles away, oblivious to anything around him. Lizzie quietly squatted down beside him, put her arms around his waist, and snuggled up to him. It was a balmy night, no wind, not even a breeze. But the cicadas were out in force all around the tree-lined streets, with their collective high-pitched drone, one of the many kinds of creatures of a tropical night.

'Mum said good night,' said Lizzie, her voice barely audible.

'I'm sorry,' said Rob. 'I shouldn't've left like that.'

'Don't worry,' said Lizzie. She understood –

she understood only too well.

'Is she all right?'

'Fine.'

'Feel better now?'

Lizzie shrugged. She still had a lot on her mind, which wouldn't be cleared until she and her mother had had a chance to talk things through. 'For the moment,' she replied uncertainly.

They sat there for nearly an hour, just gazing up at the sky, trying, like so many before them, to understand the true mysteries of the galaxies, trying within them to piece together the tiny fragments of their lives. But no matter how hard Lizzie tried, the past was there – it just wouldn't go away. She had so much to know, so much to ask. The ghosts of that past would haunt her until she knew the truth about what happened to her father. He was there, he would always be there, and she would feel the guilt of his early passing until she had found out what had really happened after she had left home. So many questions. But would she get the answers? Only time would tell. After so many years, Islington was now that much closer. She suddenly felt cold. She could *feel* the cold of that ghastly winter back home in the 'old country'. Why? Tomorrow, she would get all the answers. Tomorrow, she hoped, the past would become crystal clear. After all, tomorrow, as Scarlett O'Hara would say, is another day.

Chapter 14

Frank Angel parked the truck in some woods less than half a mile away from the perimeter fence at RAF Wethersfield. It hadn't been an easy thing to do, for there was still plenty of snow hanging around from the heavy falls during the previous two weeks. Most of it had frozen solid, and as the woods were hardly the place for anyone to venture out into during such weather conditions, Frank hoped that the pick-up he had come for wouldn't take too long. Whilst he waited, he sat in the dark in the front of the vehicle, smoking a cigarette, and keeping a careful watch on the lights from the base, which had been used by the American Air Force ever since the United States had entered the war in 1942.

Frank wasn't a happy man. He knew what he was doing was wrong, but he also knew that there was no turning back now, and he had to go along with it, for the sake of his family. More especially, he was doing it for Lizzie. If he was going to keep his promise to pay for her wedding to Rob at the beginning of April, then he had to make as much money as he could, and in as little time as possible. But the black market was no petty crime; over the weeks, he had learned that only too well. He knew that, if caught, he could go to prison for years. Then what would the family do without its principal breadwinner? The only consolation he had was that this was the last time – the last job he would do for the redoubtable Mr Parfitt and his smooth but likeable wife, Daisy. He had made up his mind after reading in the newspaper about how the Flying Squad had broken up a black-market gang, who had been tried in the High Court, and given prison sentences of up to five years apiece.

However, there was still this one last job to cope with, which for Frank was the most nerve-racking thing he had ever been asked to do, mainly because on the previous occasion he had been asked to come out to Wethersfield the trip had had to be cancelled at the last minute, due to the consignment in question not being available. Now Frank was ready to launch into the job. He had already carried out instructions, and met his two contacts in The Fox, the pub in a nearby village called Finchingfield, and now he was poised to accept the goods they were bringing over to the specified meeting place. It was not, however, the best of nights to be out, for it was pitch-dark and bitterly cold, and the owls that kept up a chorus of hooting from the trees all around were only heightening the already eerie atmosphere.

After he'd been there for twenty minutes or so, Frank became concerned that there was no sign of his two contacts. Apart from the two huge USAF cargo planes that had landed at the airfield soon after he had got there, the place remained as silent as a graveyard. In desperation, he climbed out of the driver's seat in the truck, and, having got his eyes accustomed to the dark, he tried to see if there was any sign of life anywhere in his vicinity. He could neither see nor hear anything. To his surprise, however, he did smell something that had become familiar to him over the past few weeks or so. It was the smell of pipe tobacco.

'Not the best place to be on a night like this, old chap.'

Parfitt's voice took Frank completely off guard. He swung around and saw the glow from 'the Guv'nor's' pipe. 'Mr Parfitt!' he gasped, his own cigarette falling from his lips to the ground.

'Don't mind me,' came Parfitt's breathless voice out of the dark. 'I like to do this kind of thing from time to time. I like to do a little field-work. Makes such a change from sitting in a boring old living room.'

Although Frank couldn't actually see Parfitt's features, he could feel the proximity of his body, which was dimly outlined in the dark. 'I was getting a bit worried,' he said. 'The two people I met in the pub haven't turned up yet. It's getting late.'

'No need to panic, old boy,' said Parfitt reassuringly. 'Sometimes there are reasons for holding back until the time's right.' It was several minutes before he spoke again, which only unnerved Frank even more. 'Daisy and I are very pleased with you, Frank,' said Parfitt, his voice deadened by the huge snowdrifts all around them. 'You've adapted so well to the work. If you pull off *this* job, I think you'll be in a very good position to pay for your daughter's wedding.'

Frank hated Parfitt knowing why he was

273

desperate for the money. He hated the way anything about his own daughter had to be brought into the conversation.

'When's the big day?' Parfitt asked brightly. 'Have the happy couple set a date yet?'

Frank hesitated. He was reluctant to answer Parfitt's question. 'April,' he replied vaguely.

'Ah!' said Parfitt. 'One way to beat the taxman, eh? Tax rebate, end of the financial year and all that.'

'Something like that,' Frank replied dourly.

They stood there in silence for a moment or two, leaning against the bonnet of the truck, Parfitt puffing away at his pipe, and Frank lighting up another cigarette. In the distance, they could just make out the floodlights on the base perimeter fence lighting up the sky, and beyond that, the lights from the base itself, where there seemed to be very little activity.

Parfitt checked his wristwatch with a pencil torch. It was nearly half-past midnight. 'They should be here any minute now,' he said, his voice soft, but very chesty in the biting cold. 'It's a funny old game this. You spend most of the time hanging around.' He turned to look at the outline of Frank in the dark. 'Have you any idea how much stuff the Yanks have in that PX store over there?' he asked, without expecting an answer. 'I'd say, enough to keep the likes of you and me going for the best part of a year. Lucky sods! They come into the war late, and then live off the fat of the land. You know what they used to say about the GIs? Overrich, overfed, and over here.' He gave an ironic grunt. 'Still, why not?

They're miles away from home, and in any case, why should *they* care if our own people can't run the ruddy country properly...?'

Before he could finish speaking, they heard the quiet chug of a truck engine approaching.

'Someone coming!'

'Keep down!' said Parfitt, with urgency.

Both men hurried to the other side of the truck. After a moment, they could just see the dipped lights of a large USAF service van approaching down the narrow lane, which led into the woods where they were parked.

'It's them all right,' whispered Parfitt. Frank made a move to go to them, but Parfitt immediately restrained him. 'No!' he growled firmly. 'Let them get here first!'

The van slowly wound its way towards them, but then it came to a sudden stop. Although they couldn't see the two men inside the vehicle, a torchlight flashed on and off several times from the front passenger seat.

'That's the signal!' said Parfitt. 'They won't move until we respond. Have you got the torch?'

Frank suddenly realised that he had left the torch on the dashboard of the truck. 'I'll get it!' he whispered.

But before he could even climb back into the vehicle, the air was pierced by the sound of police whistles, and dogs barking.

'Christ!' gasped Parfitt.

Whilst they both looked on helplessly from their concealed position in the woods, the USAF van was suddenly surrounded by American military police, RAF personnel, British civilian police officers, and a posse of Alsatian tracker dogs. With the dark night air now fractured by flashlights and police car siren bells, the two uniformed occupants of the van were un-ceremoniously dragged out of the van, and made to spread-eagle on the ground in the snow.

'It's a bloody trap!' yelled Parfitt, in a strangulated whisper. 'Let's get out of here!'

Frank, heart thumping, made a wild dash back into the truck, but Parfitt quickly pulled him out again.

'Not in *this*, you idiot!' he barked, throwing his pipe as hard as he could into the bushes. 'This way!'

Before the search party had realised that another vehicle was nearby, Parfitt, with Frank at his heels, bid a hasty, silent retreat into the heart of the woods. As they went, they could hear angry shouts from the American military police personnel, but by the time they had managed to battle their way back to the main village road, from the distance it sounded as though the truck that Frank and Parfitt had left behind had been discovered.

'Right!' said Parfitt, pulling up his coat collar, and adjusting his trilby hat. 'This is where we split up.'

'Split up?' spluttered Frank, who was bathed in perspiration and, at the same time, shivering with the cold. 'But–'

'We stand a better chance if we each go it alone,' said Parfitt. 'Make your way on foot to Great Dunmow. It'll take you about an hour to get there. With a bit of luck you might be able to pick up a lift of some sort. Get back to town as soon as you can. Just get away from this area as quickly as possible!'

'But what about you?' asked Frank, absolutely bewildered. 'Which way are *you* going?'

'Don't worry about me, my dear fellow,' Parfitt countered. 'I was in the army myself once, remember. I know how to take care of myself.'

Before Frank could say another word, Parfitt had disappeared into the dark. Frank looked around. Sweat was pouring down his back, and despite the intense cold, he felt as though he was on fire. It was now the early hours of the morning. Ahead of him lay a walk of several miles to the nearest village, and then to Great Dunmow. Following a disastrous night, it was a bleak prospect.

'Shall I be mum?' asked Norman, as he poured tea for Lizzie and Rob in his very cosy sitting room on the second floor of Mrs Wiggs's terraced house just off Aldgate High Street.

Both Lizzie and Rob were very impressed with the flat, which was spread out on the top two floors of the house, because it was very tastefully decorated, with some lovely furniture, which Norman had apparently inherited from his mother when she died a few years before. But the most interesting part for Lizzie were the paintings, all of them framed by Norman, and hung in carefully chosen places. She particularly liked the watercolour landscapes of the Devon countryside, and old photographs of famous music-hall entertainers back in the early part of the century. The only thing that seemed to be missing were any family portraits or photographs.

Norman's excuse for that was that he knew what all his family looked like, so why did he need to have photographs of them?

'I think you've got a lovely place here, Norman,' said Lizzie, who was sitting alongside Rob on the chintz-covered sofa in front of a roaring fire in the grate. 'Have you been here long?'

'*Too* long, if you ask me,' replied Norman, handing her a cup of tea. 'Help yerself to milk and sugar. I've got plenty of ration coupons left, and I can always get some more sugar on the black market.'

'Bad man!' said Rob, scolding him. 'They'll lock you up for dealing in that sort of thing.'

'That's not the only thing they'll lock me up for,' said Norman sniffily.

Lizzie lowered her eyes uneasily.

'And in any case, who cares? Just show me one person in London who hasn't done a bit on the black market at one time or another.'

'The people who nick other people's goods are scum, Norman,' said Rob. 'If they had no one to buy the stuff, they couldn't exist.'

'There'll always be someone to buy the stuff, duckie,' said Norman, whose face was still showing signs of the beating up he had suffered a couple of weeks before. 'And who's to blame for that? The country. Those creatures who run the country, or *think* they run it. They've kept the prices high ever since the war ended. In fact, there was more food around *during* the war. That's why we're all so fed up. That's why we have to make do as best we can.' He carefully observed them both over his cup of tea. 'That's why you want to get out of it all – isn't it?'

Rob immediately swung a look at Lizzie, who was drinking her tea, and trying not to react.

Norman smiled, and put down his cup and saucer. 'So, Lizzie,' he continued, 'how are things going for the wedding?'

Lizzie looked up, and forced a smile. 'Fine – I think,' she replied. 'It's still a long way off.'

'Beginning of April?'

Lizzie nodded.

Norman smiled affably. 'What about your wedding dress, duckie? D'you have anyone to make it for you?'

Lizzie did a double take. 'Make it?' she asked. 'I don't think I've ever met anyone who can actually *make* a wedding dress.'

'*I* can,' said Norman, getting up. 'I make a lot of things. I'm very good with me petit point.'

Rob was now looking decidedly uncomfortable.

'Don't look so nervous, duckie,' Norman said to him. He crossed to an armchair in front of the window on the other side of the room. 'It doesn't matter whether you're a man or a woman: everyone should put their hand to doing something useful. Look at this.' He picked up a colourful headrest tapestry from the armchair. 'I made this for my mum years ago.' He brought it across to Lizzie, who put down her cup and saucer to look at it.

'It's beautiful,' she said.

'Took me weeks to do it,' said Norman, 'but it was worth it. I always get a kick out of doing something different. It's a sense of achievement. Wouldn't you agree, duckie?'

Lizzie nodded at him, and passed the tapestry to Rob, who took it, and gave it straight back to Norman.

'I always say,' said Norman, addressing his remark as much to Lizzie as to Rob, 'it's good to do things that are not expected of you. That way, you can be yourself.' He took the tapestry back, and returned it to the armchair. 'So what happens after the wedding?' he called.

Lizzie resisted the temptation to turn and look at Rob. She was too confused, too unsure of why he had asked this particular person to talk to her. It was true that Rob *had* asked her to come and meet Norman, and despite his oddball manner and appearance, she did like him. He was brave and courageous – for all sorts of reasons. He was clearly a man who stood by his convictions, and refused to be brow-beaten by people with narrow minds. But she still couldn't understand how he could possibly help her to accept what Rob was asking her to do.

'We're not quite sure yet, Norman,' said Rob, breaking the ice. 'Got plenty of plans, but we still have a lot of things to talk about.'

Norman smiled, and went to look at himself in the mirror above the mantelpiece. 'I must tell you a little story,' he said, running his fingers through his shaggy grey hair. 'When I was about your age, my mum left my dad, and took me off to live in a basement flat in Stepney. She didn't have a penny to her name, poor thing, but somehow – she managed. We lived in that terrible hole for nearly six years, till eventually I decided that I wanted to have a life of my own. You see, I'd met someone, someone I liked very much.' He stopped briefly to sneak a look at Lizzie and Rob, who were reflected in the mirror in front of him. 'Unfortunately, my mum didn't feel the same way, and she kicked up a hell of a fuss. She made my life absolute *hell!* Well, I put up with it for as long as I could, until one day this other person and I decided to get married. When I told my mum, she went stark raving mad. She and I had been the best of pals all those years, but then – quite suddenly – I didn't know her any more.

'After that, I didn't sleep at nights. I didn't know *what* to do. After all, didn't I have a duty to Mum, who'd struggled to bring me up and look after me? What could I do? I was only young, but I desperately wanted a life of my own. I kept asking myself, if I leave Mum now, how will she ever survive on her own? I couldn't leave her, I just *couldn't*.' He turned round and looked across at Lizzie. 'But I *did*,' he said. 'I did leave her. And d'you know what? After I'd left, she got on far better without me.' He grinned. 'That's a turn-up for the books, duckie, wouldn't you say? Rather hurtful in a way – but true. When you come to think of it, the human spirit is really quite resourceful. If you *have* to do something, you just get on and do it.' He came back to his chair opposite, and smiled warmly at her. 'None of us is indispensable, duckie,' he said. 'My marriage

281

broke up years ago, but if I was given my chance all over again, I wouldn't't've changed a thing.'

Lizzie and Rob walked hand in hand to the tube station. They moved in silence, along pavements that had only recently been cleared of snow, oblivious to the world, to anyone who happened to pass them by. Lizzie was deep in thought, and Rob didn't want to intrude on the anguish he knew she was suffering within.

'So what do you think of Norman?' he asked eventually.

Lizzie looked up with a start, as though she had just been woken. 'Norman?' she asked. 'Oh – he's special.'

Rob was puzzled. 'Special?'

'There's so much more to him than what you see,' said Lizzie. 'He's very brave.' She turned to look at Rob. 'In so many ways.'

Rob didn't quite know what she meant.

Lizzie smiled inwardly. 'You'd have to be a woman to know what I mean,' she said.

Rob still didn't understand, so he waited a moment before he spoke again. 'Did he help?' he asked.

'Help?' She hesitated. 'Oh – about Australia, you mean?'

Rob hadn't expected her to be quite so blunt, but he took it in his stride. 'Yes,' he replied. 'Has he changed your mind at all? I mean, has he given you something to think about?'

Lizzie brought them to a halt, and looked at him. 'Rob,' she said, 'I haven't stopped thinking about this since you first asked me. In fact, it's been haunting me day and night. I understand what Norman was saying, but I'm not sure. I still can't be sure.'

Rob sighed. He felt despondent.

'It's not you, darling,' said Lizzie, affectionately pulling up the collar of his duffel coat. 'It's me. I'm a mess, a real mess.'

'Is there anything I can do to help?' Rob asked, leaning both his arms across her shoulders and locking his hands behind her neck.

'To persuade me, you mean?'

'Whatever,' he replied.

'Yes, Rob,' she said. 'There *is* a way you can help. Give me time. Give me just a little more time. Things are happening at home, things I don't understand. Soon I'll know what to do. But not now. Not just now. Please, Rob. *Please.*'

They kissed. Behind them, a drayhorse, urged on by his driver, was pulling a fresh cartload of brewery beer towards a pub further down Aldgate High Street. As he passed Lizzie and Rob, who were locked in each other's arms, the horse gave a robust snort, and nodded his head up and down rigorously in approval.

Lizzie spent the following Sunday afternoon talking through her wedding arrangements with her mother and father, discussing mainly who they were going to ask from their side to the reception, which, for financial reasons, was going to be held at a modest banqueting room at the Ancient Order of Foresters Hall in Upper Holloway. Lizzie had already decided that she wanted only Susan and Cissie to be her bridesmaids, and, as the weather at the beginning of April was still likely to be very cold, her wedding dress would be no more than a smart woollen dress, which she had seen in Jones Brothers window, and which she would be able to buy with the extra clothing coupons all brides were allowed to claim.

The idea, however, was not going down well with her mother, for Harriet had not taken too kindly to the fact that once Lizzie had married, Rob Thompson would eventually persuade her to leave the family and go off to Australia. For that reason alone, she had recently taken a dislike to Rob, and would never say anything nice about him. Lizzie's father thought quite differently. It had been almost a week since his narrow escape from the net that had closed in on Parfitt and himself in the Essex countryside, and every knock on the front door unnerved him. As far as he was concerned, the sooner Lizzie married Rob and got away from the shame that could befall the Angel family at any minute, the better it would be for her.

'If I was twenty years younger,' he said, 'I'd be off in a flash.'

'Why d'you keep saying such things, Dad?' asked Lizzie. 'You're just about the most English person I know. You know you don't mean what you say.'

'Oh, but I do,' insisted Frank, who these days was looking decidedly older than his forty-three years. 'I no longer feel a part of this country. It doesn't belong to me or my family any more. It belongs to the politicians.'

'All countries belong to the politicians,' Harriet reminded him. 'Someone has to be in charge.'

'Not when they make such a hash of things that people feel they have to act out of desperation.'

Lizzie swung an anxious look at her mother, whose eyes remained lowered. 'What kind of things, Dad?' she asked gingerly.

Sitting with Lizzie and Harriet at the table, Frank realised he was revealing too much tension. 'It doesn't matter,' he said, getting up from his chair, and going to collect his packet of cigarettes from the mantelpiece. 'In any case, I thought we were supposed to be working on this guest list. What about your Uncle Dennis? Have you put him down? You know he gets very upset if he's ignored.'

'He's already on the list,' replied Lizzie, watching him with some misgivings. 'Is anything wrong, Dad?' she asked tentatively.

'What d'you mean?' snapped Frank. 'Of course there's nothing wrong. What's the matter with everyone in this house? Haven't you all got something better to do with your time than ask such stupid questions?' He grabbed his cigarettes, and rushed off to the bedroom.

James and Benjamin, who were sitting side by side on the sofa, working hard on a giant jigsaw puzzle, hardly looked up when their father slammed the bedroom door behind him. But Cissie, flat on her stomach on the rug in front of the fire, drawing in a picture book with her crayons, jumped with a start.

'What's up with Dad?' she called. 'Has he got the grumps?'

Lizzie abandoned the wedding guest list she had been working on in a notebook at the table, and motioned to her mother to join her in the kitchen. 'What's the matter with him?' she said, once the two of them were alone together. 'Is he ill or something?'

'I have no idea,' replied Harriet coldly. 'Perhaps you should ask yourself that question.'

Lizzie froze. 'Mum! What are you talking about?'

'If you really don't know,' said Harriet, 'then I don't know what's happened to you. Can't you see how upset he is about your wanting to go away?'

'Upset?' said Lizzie. 'But that's ridiculous. I've never said I was going away. All I've ever said is that, after we're married Rob would like us to emigrate. I've never actually said that I would.'

'But you're giving it some thought?'

'Of course I'm giving it some thought,' replied Lizzie. 'It's only right that I should. After all, if I'm to marry Rob then the least I should do is to consider what he's asking me to do.'

'You can't fool *me*, Lizzie,' said Harriet, arms crossed. 'You can't fool me *or* your father. We both know that you've already made up your mind.'

'This is crazy!' said Lizzie. 'I just don't know what you're talking about. You know as well as I do, Dad has always said he wouldn't blame any member of his family if they wanted to emigrate. Only a few minutes ago he was saying that if he was twenty years younger he'd do it himself. He's *always* saying it!'

Harriet was having none of it. 'He may say it,'

286

she growled, 'but he doesn't mean it!'

Lizzie was astonished by her mother's interpretation of how her father felt. She suddenly felt hemmed in by Harriet's attitude, her determination to put all the blame on her for whatever crisis was befalling the Angel family. 'Mum,' she said, calmly trying to reason with her. 'What *is* wrong with Dad? I mean – what's *really* wrong with him? Is he in some kind of trouble?'

Despite the hard exterior she was showing, Harriet's eyes were welling with tears. 'Why don't you go and ask him yourself?' she replied, turning her back on Lizzie, and going to look aimlessly out of the window.

Lizzie was thunderstruck, and didn't know what to do. In a daze, she turned and slowly left the kitchen.

As she came out into the living room, there was a sharp knocking on the front door. Being nearest, she went to open it.

'Evenin', miss!' said the cheery young bloke standing on the doorstep, all wrapped up in a knitted cap, and long fawn duffel coat that was far too big for him. 'Wonder if I could 'ave a word wiv Frank – er – Mr Angel.'

Lizzie was puzzled.

'It's all right,' continued the young bloke, with a broad grin. ''E knows who I am. We work tergevver up Billin'sgate. Tell 'im it's Dodger.'

Lizzie left the door slightly ajar, and went into the bedroom to tell her father.

In the bedroom, Frank was stretched out on his bed, smoking his cigarette. He looked terrible.

'Someone to see you, Dad,' Lizzie said.

Frank sat up with a start. 'Who is it?' he asked nervously.

'It's a young bloke,' said Lizzie. 'Says he works with you at Billingsgate. His name's Dodger.'

Frank sprang up from the bed, and rushed out of the room.

Lizzie followed him out. The first thing she heard him say as he came face to face with the young bloke was, 'I thought I told you never to come here!' Then he closed the door, and Lizzie couldn't hear any more. Intensely curious as to what was going on, she carefully peered out from behind the curtains, just in time to see Frank hurrying to the front gate with the young bloke. She was even more curious when she noticed that a small car was parked nearby, and a tall, well-dressed woman got out of the car to greet him.

Now convinced that Frank had got himself in some kind of trouble, she quickly put on her topcoat, rushed to the back door, and quietly went out into the garden. As soon as she got there, she concealed herself behind the timber work-shed that Frank had installed soon after he was demobbed at the end of the war. There she eased herself into a position where she could get a better, but safe, view of what was going on near the front gate. She couldn't believe what she could now see. She recognised the woman her father was talking to – recognised her instantly. It was the shoplifter who had nearly lost Maple her job at Woolworths.

It was the 'Tuesday lady'.

288

Chapter 15

Frank had a lot of explaining to do. Until that moment when Lizzie had caught him talking to Daisy Parfitt in the street outside the prefab, he had no idea that she was the shoplifter whom Lizzie had confronted in Seven Sisters Road. Suddenly, his whole world was falling apart. As it was, each day he was making more and more excuses about where he had been, and why he was away so much, but now this. The fact that Parfitt's wife was also a compulsive petty thief, whom Lizzie had recognised and identified, was a serious development. It was all Dodger's fault, he told himself. How many times had he warned him not to divulge his address to anyone, let alone bring a woman like that to his own front door?

At least Parfitt, like himself, had managed to escape the trap that had been set by the USAF military police at Wethersfield that night – though only just. However, the incident had now appeared in the daily newspapers, and despite Daisy Parfitt's assurance that their two American airmen contacts would not 'squeal' on them, Frank was convinced that it could only be a matter of time before the Law came looking for him.

'She's a crook, Dad,' said Lizzie, walking back with him from the garden gate. 'She's been shoplifting in Woolworths for months. She nearly got my friend Maple the sack.'

Frank just didn't know what to say to her. Shivering with the cold in his shirtsleeves, all he could do was to make up anything that came into his mind. 'I haven't the faintest idea *who* she is, Lizzie,' he said. 'All I know is that she's a friend of Dodger's.'

'Then why did she want to see you?' asked Lizzie unrelentingly.

Frank hesitated just long enough to work out an answer. 'She needed my help,' he replied.

Lizzie was mystified. 'Your *help?*'

'She's actually – Dodger's aunt,' said Frank falteringly. 'I – knew about – what she'd been doing. Dodger told me about her some time ago. She needs help, and he asked me to talk to her. It's as simple as that.'

Lizzie was having none of it. 'Dad,' she said firmly, '*I* told you about that woman weeks ago. How come you've never mentioned this to me?'

'Because she's desperate!' snapped Frank. They reached the front door of the house, but Frank wanted to end the conversation before they went back inside. 'I feel sorry for the woman.'

'Dad!' insisted Lizzie. 'That woman is a crook! She probably goes around all the shops taking things that don't belong to her. Woolworths have told the police. They're keeping a look out for her everywhere.'

Frank did a double take. It was bad enough that his own daughter had recognised the woman he had been working with, but the fact that she was on a police wanted list was something he hadn't bargained for. Now beside himself with anxiety, he looked up and down the street to see if anyone had seen him talking to the woman.

'Listen to me, Lizzie,' he said, lowering his voice and drawing her closer to him. 'I know shoplifting is a crime – well, a sort of crime – but it's not quite like that, Lizzie. It's compulsive.'

'Compulsive?' asked Lizzie, puzzled.

'She can't help herself. When she sees something in a shop window, she just has to have it. She can't help herself.'

'And what about the people she steals *from?*' asked Lizzie. 'Who helps *them?*'

Frank stared her out for a brief moment, then went inside.

Lizzie watched him go, but instead of following, she turned and strolled off to the garden gate. The way she was feeling, she just wanted to get away for a while from her father, her mother and all the rest of her family. She needed time to breathe, to rid herself of the stifling atmosphere of home.

Once out in Andover Road, she quickly wandered off round the backstreets behind Hornsey Road. Within the hour it would be dark, and although the weak late afternoon sun was still struggling to shine through dismal grey clouds that were bulging with snow, lights were already being switched on in the front parlours of terraced houses all along her route. As she passed one house, in Sonderburg Road, she could hear voices booming out in a happy, late Sunday afternoon singsong, but the sounds of people enjoying themselves only made Lizzie sad, for it recalled for her so many wonderful times when the Angels also enjoyed their Sunday evenings, with her and her brothers and sisters putting on their own regular variety show for all the family. What had happened to them, she asked herself? Why had Susan, James, Benjamin and Cissie become so selfish and uncaring? And why had her mother turned so much against her, just because Lizzie had found someone who loved her, and wanted to take her away to what he believed would be a far better life? What was her mother afraid of? Was it because she wanted to keep a tight hold on Lizzie – or was it because she was jealous? But the most worrying thoughts that now dominated her mind were of her father.

Quite unconsciously, she had reached Bedford Terrace, and was standing outside the front door of what had been, until only a short time before, Lil Beasley's two-floor terraced house. It was in darkness now, with tattered curtains drawn at the windows, and no sign of the colourful old woman who had lived there for so many years. I wonder what she's doing now, thought Lizzie, with a fond, affectionate smile. She could almost hear the old girl's voice scolding her, 'It's time yer got married and settled down!' How right she was, Lizzie now agreed. Until that moment, she had never imagined that she would ever think such a thing. But after the way her family was behaving, Lil's words had suddenly become more prophetic: 'When yer love someone like I loved Jack, nuffin' else matters. Not even yer own kiff and kin.'

Lizzie didn't really know Camden Town too well.

292

The only time she had been there was when Rob had taken her on a couple of occasions to the Gaumont cinema in Parkway, an elegant building built in the grand style of pre-war days, and which often featured some wonderful double-bill programmes, different from those of its sister cinema in Holloway Road. They had also once visited the old Bedford Theatre of Varieties in Camden High Street, one of the great music halls of its time, where great artists such as Charlie Chaplin first appeared in a revue called *Fred Karno's Army*, but which had recently been staging old Victorian melodramas, in which the audience was invited to cheer the hero and hiss the villain: all great fun for Lizzie, except that Rob had shamed her by cheering and hissing louder than anyone else around him. However, her visit this evening had nothing to do with heroes and villains – or at least she hoped it hadn't, for it was Maple she had come to see.

The terraced street she was looking for turned out to be far more presentable than she'd expected. It was situated just off St Pancras Way, far enough away from the sound of trains rumbling across the nearby LNER railway bridge for it to cause little disturbance. The house itself was also a bit of a surprise – probably built during the early part of the century, set on three floors, and with a small front garden that was just big enough to sit in on hot summer nights. But this was no hot summer night, for although the extreme temperatures were now beginning to climb a little, there was still no sign of a real thaw, and once she'd knocked on the front door, Lizzie hoped it wouldn't be too long before someone appeared. She was not disappointed.

'Yes?'

The man who answered the door was not a bit how Lizzie had imagined Maple's stepfather would look. He was in fact well-dressed, in collar and tie, a smart V-neck pullover and neatly pressed black trousers. He was also a handsome-looking man, with dark curly hair, and eyes and complexion that suggested to Lizzie that he was probably only in his early thirties, which again was younger than Maple had indicated.

'I'm a friend of Maple's – I mean Mabel,' said Lizzie, suddenly remembering that Maple was her Woolworths nickname. 'I was wondering if I could–'

'Mabel's out,' replied the man in the doorway. 'She'll be back in ten minutes or so.'

'Oh, I see,' said Lizzie. 'Well – thanks anyway.'

'You can come and wait inside if you like,' said the man. 'You'll freeze to death out there.'

Lizzie was taken aback by the man's thoughtfulness. 'Thank you,' she said, going inside.

'Mabel won't be long,' said the man, closing the door behind her. 'She went round the off-licence for me.'

Lizzie was glad to get out of the mist and cold, and into the warmth of what seemed to be a well-lit and well-heated house. 'Thanks very much,' she said again.

'Come in and meet Mabel's mum,' said the man, leading her into the sitting room. 'Oh, by the way, my name's Desmond, Reg Desmond. Most people call me Des.'

Lizzie followed him into the room.

'Got a visitor, Sal,' he said to the woman who was playing cards on her own there. He turned to Lizzie. 'Sorry. I didn't get your name.'

'Lizzie. Lizzie Angel.'

Mabel's mum, Sally Gosling, looked up. 'Hello, Lizzie,' she said weakly. 'I've heard Mabel talk about you.'

'Hello, Mrs Gosling,' said Lizzie. 'I'm sorry to intrude.'

The answer came from Desmond. 'You're not intruding, Lizzie,' he said. 'Come and sit down till Mabel gets back.'

Lizzie sat in a chair at the card table, facing Sally Gosling. She was completely taken aback by the cordial way in which she had been greeted, especially by Desmond, who seemed the very essence of good manners, and especially after all Mabel had told her about him.

'So you and Mabel work in good old Woolies then, do you?' enquired Desmond, who collected an unfinished cigarette from an ashtray beside the chair he was sitting in by the fireplace. 'Bit hard on the feet, I reckon. Standing on them all day, I mean.'

'Not really,' replied Lizzie. 'You get used to it after a while.' As she watched Desmond, she realised how exceptionally handsome he was, almost like a film star, and that he was very articulate. It had also not escaped her notice how considerably younger he was than his wife, Sally Gosling.

'Funny when you think how many good-looking girls there are working in that place,' said

Desmond, who was doing his best to make eye contact with Lizzie. 'Mabel's the exception, of course,' he added, laughing at his own joke. 'No, not true,' he said quickly. 'Our Mabel's got a lot going for her. She'll find someone one of these days – that's for sure. I've got a lot of time for that girl, a lot of respect for the way she gets on with her own thing.'

Lizzie found it difficult to respond to all the nice things he was saying about Maple. As she watched him pull on his cigarette, and run his fingers through his head of dark, tight curly hair, she couldn't help asking herself if this was the same man who had been regularly beating up his own stepdaughter. Or had he? Could it *really* be true, or was this just some kind of story that Maple had made up in her own mind, perhaps to draw attention to herself? And yet, how could it be? After all, what about all the times Maple had turned up at work with her face covered with cuts and bruises? That was real enough, no one could deny that. But when she looked at Desmond now, absurdly good-looking, perfect manners and utterly charming, she found it difficult to believe that he was the kind of person Maple had talked about. But just as she was questioning in her own mind all the things Maple had told her, there was a moment that unsettled her. It came when Desmond briefly made eye contact with her. It was, to Lizzie's way of thinking, a look that lingered just a little too long.

'Why don't you go and make Lizzie a nice cup of tea?' said Desmond, turning to his wife. 'It'll help to warm her up.'

'Oh – no, thank you,' replied Lizzie. 'I'm fine.'

Desmond smiled. 'Ah!' he said, with just the suggestion of a grin. 'I can see you'd like something a little stronger.'

Lizzie shook her head. 'I don't drink alcohol,' she replied quickly, even though it wasn't entirely true.

'I'll make some tea,' said Sally, getting up from the card table. She had a worn look about her, and what had clearly once been a beautiful face now showed sign of stress. 'I feel like one myself, anyway.' Without saying another word, she quietly slipped out of the room.

Lizzie now felt uncomfortable. She didn't know why, but being left alone in a room with Maple's stepfather made her feel just a little too awkward.

After Sally had gone, Desmond got up from his own chair. 'Poor Sal,' he said, as he slowly ambled across to join Lizzie at the card table. 'She's really not herself these days. She gets so depressed – for no reason at all. Still, that's what you get for marrying someone so much older than yourself. They see things differently.' He sat down opposite Lizzie. 'I suppose I should have found someone more my own age.'

Lizzie averted his gaze, and quickly looked aimlessly around the room at anything that caught her eye. She hardly noticed the décor, even though it was actually quite tasteful, with expensive semi-antique furniture, and an imitation fitted Persian carpet that was now fading in the centre. For a brief moment or so she managed to ignore Desmond's presence, until the smoke from his cigarette came slowly drifting across towards her.

'It's not exactly *my* style,' Desmond said.

Lizzie turned, to find him looking directly at her. 'I beg your pardon?'

'All this,' explained Desmond, indicating the furniture and fittings. 'I prefer the simpler things in life myself. Still, it's what Sal likes, and since she's the one who pays the bills, who am I to complain?'

Lizzie was now feeling decidedly uneasy, and she looked towards the door in the hope that either Sally or Maple would return.

'So what's it like working at dear old Woolies?' asked Desmond, one elbow on the table, cigarette in his lips, but only half turned towards her.

'It's fine,' replied Lizzie casually.

'What's it like working with my stepdaughter?' he asked, with a slight smirk on his face.

Lizzie had no hesitation in her reply. 'I like working with her very much,' she said. 'Mabel's my friend.'

'You don't find her – moody?'

Lizzie shook her head. 'No. Not at all.'

'She *can* be,' said Desmond. 'Takes after her mum there. They're a pretty rum pair at times, I can tell you! They often gang up on me.'

Lizzie looked puzzled.

Desmond smiled. 'I'm afraid I have a bit of a roving eye,' he said, flicking a quick look up at her.

Lizzie waited a moment before replying. 'I thought once people got married they stopped doing that sort of thing?' she asked primly.

'Depends on what kind of a marriage you have,'

replied Desmond guardedly. 'I mean, after all,' he tried to elicit a smile from her, but without success, 'we're all only human – aren't we?'

'Some are more human than others, Mr Desmond,' said Lizzie pointedly.

Desmond's expression hardened.

The door opened, and Maple appeared. 'Lizzie!' she called, astonished.

Lizzie sprang to her feet, and hurried across to meet her. 'Hello, Maple!' she cried, the relief clearly showing.

'What are you doing here?' Maple asked, with a mixture of shock and delight.

'Do I need to have an excuse to call on a best friend?' asked Lizzie, perfectly aware that Desmond was watching them.

Maple's face lit up. She left Lizzie for a moment, and went quickly across to Desmond. 'Here!' she said curtly, plonking down the quart bottle of brown ale she had just collected from the off-licence.

Desmond glared at her as Maple returned to Lizzie.

'Let's go upstairs to my room,' said Maple.

Lizzie followed her to the door.

'Nice meeting you, Lizzie,' called Desmond.

Lizzie stopped only briefly to flick a brief glance at him. Then she left the room with Maple.

James was at one end of the kitchen table doing his geography homework, Benjamin was at the other end counting through his collection of used bus tickets, and in between them, Cissie was hard at work on a crayon drawing of her mother, which she was to hand in to her art teacher the following morning. Whilst all this activity was going on, Harriet was at the kitchen draining board, mincing the remains of the mutton they had had for Sunday lunch, for the next evening's meal. In the next room, Frank was left in peace to read his Sunday newspaper, and ponder on Lizzie's revelation that Daisy Parfitt and the Woolworths shoplifter were one and the same person.

'I don't see why Susan didn't take *us* to the pictures with her,' complained Cissie. 'I like going to the pictures on a Sunday. They have murder ones.'

'Don't be silly, Cissie,' said her mother, struggling with the handle of the mincer. 'You know very well murder films are not a U certificate. And, in any case, you also know that Susan always goes to the cinema on a Sunday with her friend Jane. She certainly doesn't want her whole family tagging on behind.'

'I hate Jane Hetherington!' growled Benjamin, who had just counted twenty-six penny bus tickets, and was now on the penny ha'pennies. 'Every time I see her she turns up her nose at me.'

'I don't blame her,' said James drily, without looking up from his homework.

With his mum's back turned towards him, Benjamin did a rude two fingers to his brother.

'In any case,' said Cissie, admiring her handiwork, 'I don't see why they don't give a U to murder films. I'm fed up with Shirley Temple.'

'Little girls should not be allowed to see

murder films, Cissie,' insisted Harriet.

Cissie swung round and glared at her mother. 'I'm *not* a little girl!' she barked.

'Oh yes, you are!' teased Benjamin. 'You're little and you're stupid!'

'I'm not! I'm not!' spluttered Cissie, throwing one of her pencils at him.

Harriet turned round, and snapped at her. 'Stop that, Cissie! James is trying to do his homework.'

'Fat chance of that in *this* place,' mumbled James, who always tried to keep his distance from his brother and sisters.

'So why do your homework in the kitchen?' asked his mother. 'You've got a perfectly good table in the living room.'

'It's warmer here,' James replied dourly.

'I am *not* little!' Cissie again insisted, refusing to let Benjamin get away with it.

'Course you are!' said Benjamin. 'You're smaller than the Seven Dwarfs!'

'I'm not! I'm not!' yelled Cissie, having a tantrum, and kicking her foot against her chair. 'I'm growing up fast. Susan's boyfriend told me I am!'

Harriet swung round with a start. 'What was that?' she asked. 'Susan's boyfriend? *What* boyfriend?'

'She and Jane Hetherington's got a lot of boyfriends,' mumbled James. 'Who cares?'

'I saw them all smoking fags in Seven Sisters Road the other day,' said Benjamin mischievously, and now fully obsessed with his penny ha'penny tickets. 'They didn't see me, though.'

Harriet wiped her hands on her apron, and came across to them. 'How long has Susan been seeing this boy?' she asked Benjamin.

Benjamin shrugged his shoulders. 'Haven't a clue,' he replied. 'She's had lots of 'em.'

Harriet felt her stomach seize up. Realising that in their present mood, she wasn't going to get much more information out of the three of them, she went straight to the door to find Frank.

James looked up briefly from his homework. 'Big mouths!' he said to his brother and sister.

'Did you know Susan and Jane have been going out with boys?' Harriet asked Frank, the moment she entered the living room.

Frank looked up from his newspaper. 'Oh yes,' he said.

'Is that all you can say?' said Harriet, scolding him.

'Well, what else d'you expect me to say?' he asked. 'What's wrong with Susan having boyfriends?'

'But she's only eighteen years old,' said Harriet. Although he looked tired and on edge, Frank just managed to summon up a smile. 'Harriet,' he said, 'my dear, darling Harriet, come and sit with me for a minute.'

Harriet perched herself unwillingly on the arm of his chair.

'Now listen to me,' he said, taking hold of her hand and gently stroking it with his thumb. 'Our kids are growing up. We won't be able to hold on to them for ever. In a few weeks' time we're going to lose Lizzie. One by one they'll all go. If we try to hold them down they'll bear a grudge against us for the rest of their lives.'

'We can't just ignore what they get up to,' insisted Harriet. 'I mean, just look at Lizzie. It's one thing to get married, but then to be dragged off to the other side of the world against her wishes...'

'Is that what it is?' asked Frank. 'Is it *really* against Lizzie's wishes, going off to start a new life with the man she loves? Shouldn't we be encouraging her to do what she wants, not criticising her?'

Harriet looked at him. She just didn't understand that he could feel this way. After all, wasn't Lizzie their own daughter, and hadn't they a duty to love her, and to protect her? 'If Lizzie goes all that way, don't you realise that we may never see her again?'

Frank's whole expression changed. 'Yes, Harriet,' he said, with obvious anguish. 'I *do* realise that.'

'Won't you miss her?'

Again Frank hesitated. 'You'll never know how much,' he replied.

Although Maple's bedroom was really quite pretty, to Lizzie it was also quite sad. Above Maple's bed the wall was covered in magazine cut-outs of pictures taken in Canada, and on her chest of drawers there were framed photographs of her mother in her far happier, younger days, arm in arm with Maple's father, who had deserted his family before the war by going off with another woman whilst Maple was still only a young child. The room told a story without

303

words, a story of a girl who had suffered a great deal of unhappiness and frustration during her short life. But for these few short moments at least, Maple was sublimely happy. Having Lizzie to talk to, squatting there together on the rug in front of the gas fire, was something she had never dreamed could, or would, ever happen.

'So what do you think of him?' Maple asked.

'Your stepfather?' asked Lizzie. 'Oh, he's quite a character all right.'

'But you liked him?'

Lizzie shrugged.

'Most people do – when they first meet him.'

'He doesn't fool me for one single minute,' Lizzie assured her.

'Really?'

'As a matter of fact, I feel quite uncomfortable in his presence.'

Maple lowered her eyes. 'That's because he's so good-looking,' she said edgily.

'There's quite an age-gap between him and your mother, isn't there?' asked Lizzie. 'D'you think that's why – he's the way he is?'

Maple shrugged. 'All I know is,' she said, 'I can't bear it when he touches me. I'm so scared of him, I keep this door locked at night.'

Lizzie sighed. 'But why doesn't your mother do something about him?' she said. 'You really should tell her, Maple.'

'I don't have to tell her,' replied Maple. 'She doesn't actually say anything, but I've got a good idea she knows what goes on. Don't worry, though. One of these days I'll pluck up enough courage to get out of here.'

For the next half-hour or so, the two girls sat and talked, and even giggled a lot together. Lizzie was amazed how different Maple was once she'd been brought out of her shell. In fact, she was such good company that Lizzie really began to feel that she had made a good new friend. Even so, every time she looked at the remains of the cuts and bruises inflicted by that menace of a man downstairs, she realised only too well that Maple had a long way to go to have her confidence in life restored. However, the one thing Lizzie was determined to do was to ensure that Maple stood up to her stepfather, for which she offered her unqualified support. But there was something that Lizzie needed herself from Maple.

'The Tuesday lady?' said Maple in disbelief. 'She came to your house?'

'She came to see my father,' said Lizzie. 'He went to talk to her outside our house. He found it hard to believe who she was when I told him later.'

'But – why did she come to see him?' asked Maple incredulously. 'She's a thief.'

'I know,' said Lizzie. At that moment, all her fears, all her anxieties about her father's activities, came rushing at her. 'I think he's had some kind of dealings with her. I don't know what, but it's something I've got to find out about.'

'How are you going to do that?' asked Maple, with some trepidation.

'I don't know,' said Lizzie. She got up, went across to Maple's bed, and perched on the edge of it. 'The first thing I intend to do is to find this woman.'

'Find her?' Maple got up from the floor, and joined her on the bed. 'But if you find her,' she asked, 'what can you possibly do? I mean, what d'you expect to get from her?'

For a brief moment, Lizzie thought hard about this. At the back of her mind was the desire to know what this woman was up to, and whether her hunch was true that she was involved in something more than just petty shoplifting. But the situation was far more serious than even that. For some time she had suspected that her father had been in possession of far more money than he could ever earn in his humdrum job at Billingsgate Market. The fact that he had offered to pay for her wedding had worried her right from the moment when he first said he would do it. What with that, and the endless number of times he had come home late at night, a pattern was beginning to emerge that both worried and scared her.

'I want to know who this woman is,' she said.

'But we know who she is,' said Maple. 'She's a petty thief who nearly lost me my job.'

'She's more than that, Maple,' said Lizzie.

'What do you mean?'

'I mean,' said Lizzie, 'that if my father is in some kind of trouble, I want to know what this woman has to do with it. And I won't rest until I find out.'

Chapter 16

February was slowly drawing to a close. It had been an appalling month, with some of the worst snowfalls ever recorded, and temperatures remaining below zero for so long that most people were beginning to think that winter would never end. The heavy grey skies that hung relentlessly over the streets of the capital, were depressing everyone and that, together with the country's dire economic situation, meant more and more people were looking for ways to get away from it all. None more so than Rob Thompson, who was feeling the strain of not getting any kind of decision out of Lizzie about his desperation for them both to emigrate to Australia.

But with the first week of March upon them, and the first signs of a slight thaw, Lizzie and Rob's wedding plans were slowly taking shape. Lizzie's one main problem, however, was her father, and on the day when he paid the two-pound deposit for the hire of the reception hall, she had no alternative but to confess the fears she had about him.

'I'm scared, Rob,' she said, as they sat together in John Essex's men's 'fashion' store in Seven Sisters Road, where Rob was trying to choose the suit he was going to wear for the wedding. 'Dad just doesn't have that sort of money. He must be getting it from somewhere.'

'But I thought you said he's getting some part-time work?' Rob asked.

'That's what he calls it,' said Lizzie. 'But I think it's something more than that.'

Rob looked up with a start from the material of the dark grey three-piece suit he was feeling. 'You think he's been doing something shady?'

Lizzie sighed. 'I don't know, Rob. But this woman I told you about – this shoplifter – how he's mixed up with her, I just don't know.'

'Have you managed to find out any more about her?' Rob asked, returning to the rack of men's suits he was going through.

'Not a thing,' replied Lizzie. 'As far as I can tell, she just turns up one minute, and disappears the next. It terrifies me that Dad's got himself mixed up with someone like that.'

'I wouldn't worry yourself too much, Liz,' said Rob, with little thought. 'Your dad's been around in his time. He can take care of himself.'

Lizzie was hurt that he had treated her concern so lightly. So she just went back to the seat she had been sitting on to wait for him.

Rob immediately went to her. 'I'm sorry, Liz,' he said. 'I didn't mean to sound so disinterested. All I meant was, your dad is probably doing what so many people are having to do these days – make a bit of money on the side, no matter where they get it from.'

'That's all very well,' replied Lizzie. 'I wouldn't mind if that's all there was to it. But this is different. He looks awful. He's only forty-three years old, and he looks worn out.' She sat back in her chair, thoroughly despondent. 'I think the worry of being found out, and the extra worry of trying to find enough money to pay for the wedding is all too much for him.'

'But I've told you, Liz,' insisted Rob. 'There's no need for your dad to pay one brass farthing. Between us, my folks and I can cope with whatever's needed.'

Lizzie looked up at him. 'What do you take us for, Rob?' she asked indignantly. 'I know the Angel family are going through hellish times, but we do still have our dignity.'

As she spoke, an elderly male shop assistant approached them. 'Found anything you like yet, sir?'

'Not yet,' replied Rob. 'Still looking.'

The assistant smiled benevolently. 'Well,' he said, 'if you need any help, just give me a call. Got to make sure we get you kitted out properly for the big day.'

The big day. As Lizzie and Rob watched the assistant move back to his counter, they were feeling more and more as though the only thing big about their forthcoming wedding day was all the problems it was bringing.

'I didn't mean to sound condescending,' said Rob affectionately, putting his hand under Lizzie's chin. 'I'm such an insensitive oaf at times. I can't imagine why you'd want to marry someone like me.'

Lizzie quickly grabbed his hand. 'Oh Rob!' she said, kissing it. 'I'm sorry I'm so grumpy. I wouldn't want to marry anyone else in the whole wide world.'

Nearby, two customers, a middle-aged man and his wife, strolled around the shop behind them, clearly disapproving of the way they were smooching together. Lizzie and Rob were aware of this, quickly got up, and returned to the rack of readymade suits.

Despite the fact that most people had very few clothing coupons to use on anything new, the shop was filling up, but mainly with browsers rather than prospective customers.

'What d'you think about this one?' Rob asked, sorting out a light grey three-piece suit.

'Bit on the pale side, don't you think?' suggested Lizzie, watching Rob as he held the suit up against him. 'Might look out of place in the middle of winter.'

'Ruddy winter should be well and truly over by April!' said Rob. 'Or else!'

'Or else what?' asked Lizzie, grinning.

'Or else I'll go off my rocker!' he snorted. 'Anyway, it could come in handy for Australia.'

Lizzie did not react. She merely went very quiet, and looked at some of the other suits along the rack.

Rob suddenly realised what he had said, and was about to gloss over it. But he changed his mind, and decided to come right out with what he was thinking.

'We can't go on ignoring it, Liz,' he said, returning the grey suit to the rack.

'Ignoring what?'

'You *know* what,' he replied firmly. 'We've got to come to a decision sooner or later. We can't just go on pretending that the subject doesn't even

310

exist. If we're going to go ahead with this thing, I think it's about time we filled in the application forms.'

Lizzie pulled out a navy-blue suit. 'I like this one,' she said, evading everything he was saying. 'It's more suitable for a wedding.

'Liz!' Rob grabbed the suit, and hung it back on the rack. 'If we miss this chance now, there may not be another one. The ten-pound assisted passage scheme won't last for ever. When I went up to the Australian High Commission in the Strand the other day, there were hordes of people queuing outside. The bubble's going to burst soon, Liz. We can't afford to miss it.'

'Who's *we*, Rob?' asked Liz. She was now beginning to feel the pressure that was being put on her. Yes, everything Rob was saying may be true, but she wasn't going to be bullied into doing something without giving it absolute thought. She wasn't going to do something just because Rob *wanted* her to do it. Whilst he was standing there, waving his arms around, scolding, lecturing her, she found herself looking away, watching all the people who were browsing round the shop, thinking to herself that things couldn't really be as bad as Rob was always trying to make out. Why was he such a pessimist, she asked herself. Why couldn't he look on the bright side of life?

But then she thought about her father, and about the despair he was suffering, that same despair that had made him also say on countless occasions that survival of the fittest was the only way to solve problems. Did she agree with such

311

extreme views? Did she really believe that life was only about oneself, to the exclusion of everyone else? Why should she go to the far side of the world to start a new life when she still hadn't lived long enough to experience the life she had now?

'So what are we going to do, Liz?' demanded Rob. 'Just tell me, darling. What are we going to do?'

Billingsgate Market was in chaos. After a period of relative inactivity because of storms, heavy snowfalls, and mountainous waves in the North Sea, fish supplies were gradually improving, and the priority now was to get them out to the customers as quickly as possible. Frank and Dodger were run off their feet. Starting work at the crack of dawn, they found it difficult to keep up with the amount of cod that was coming in by the truckload, waiting to be gutted, packed in ice, and collected by wholesalers, restaurant and fish shop owners, and with the endless queues of housewives who turned up as soon as the first stocks arrived. Although the adverse weather conditions were now tempered by some weak sunshine, it was still bitterly cold, and if Frank hadn't been wearing mittens and gloves, his hands would have been in danger of frostbite. But above it all, the sounds of the market were magnificent. Porters singing 'Here We Go, Here We Go, Here We Go Again!' echoed through the sheds as the men conveyed and trucked the morning's stocks, foremen shouting orders, a medley of tuneless whistling, and jokes and laughter all around – it all blended so naturally. It was impossible for anyone to be lonely in a place like that; there just wasn't the time.

However, things were a bit different this morning, for it was the first time Frank had met up with Dodger since Frank's fatal meeting with Daisy Parfitt outside the prefab on Sunday afternoon. But with Bert Spinks, their foreman, on the prowl, they didn't really get a chance to talk together until the lunch time break. For this, they opted for a different location from usual to eat their sandwiches, which was a pub a short distance away, rarely used by the other market workers.

'So tell me why?' Frank said sharply to Dodger, the moment they had settled down at a table in the corner of the public bar. 'Why did Daisy Parfitt come to see me at my place?'

'It's like she said,' replied Dodger, keeping his chirpy rough voice as low as he was capable. 'After what 'appened out at that air base, we've all got ter lie low fer a bit. Those bloody Yanks got the tip-off from someone all right.'

'To hell with the Yanks!' snapped Frank. 'What about my money?'

Dodger was puzzled. 'Money?' he asked.

'The money I should have got for doing the job!'

'But – yer din't do no job,' replied Dodger. 'The stuff never got fru.'

'That's not my fault!' insisted Frank. 'I still had to risk my neck to go out there. I need that money. I *want* that money. I've got Lizzie's wedding coming up in less than a month, and I can't afford to let her down.'

Dodger sat back in his chair. He hadn't bargained for this. Until now, Frank had toed the line, and if the Guv'nor got wind of what Frank was demanding, then there'd be trouble – plenty of it. Behind him, the pub was crowded with lunch time workers from the offices and warehouses around London Bridge. It made him feel uncomfortable, and he wished he hadn't joined Frank there. Dodger's trouble was that he was in a quandary about who he owed the most allegiance to – the Guv'nor and his missus, or to Frank. 'Don't know what I can do, mate,' he said. 'The Guv'nor finks the world er you. If 'e knows you're playin' up, 'e might – well, I don't know wot 'e might do. 'E could cut you out of the business altergevver.'

Frank put down his sandwich, and looked Dodger straight in the face. 'Frankly, Dodger,' he said, 'I couldn't care a monkey's what Parfitt thinks – or his wife. And you can tell Daisy from me that it's thanks to her we're all in a heap of trouble.'

Again Dodger was puzzled. 'Wot d'yer mean?' he asked falteringly.

Frank leaned towards him. 'Did you know she's a shoplifter?'

Dodger's mouth dropped open. 'A wot?'

'A shoplifter, Dodger,' Frank repeated. 'You know, a petty thief – someone who goes around shops and department stores nicking things and dropping them into their shopping bags. Someone who the Law is always on the look-out for.'

'Blimey!' gasped Dodger.

'Yes – blimey!' said Frank. 'And you may be interested to know that she's been identified by a whole lot of shop girls in Woolworths – including my own daughter.'

Dodger nearly choked on the fag he was smoking, and the mouthful of bitter he had still not fully swallowed.

'So what are we going to do about it, Dodger?' said Frank, pursuing him relentlessly. 'Are we going to just sit around and let our Daisy lead the police straight to us? Because that's what her slippery fingers are going to do. And who's going to suffer, Dodger? No, it won't be our Daisy or the Guv'nor, because by then they'll be miles away, where nobody can find them. It'll be *us*, Dodger – you and me. We'll get five to ten years – and for what? For a few measly pounds of blood money. Are you prepared to go to prison for that, Dodger? Are you?'

Dodger tugged at the collar of his pullover beneath his overalls as though he was choking. The air in the place was now thick with fag smoke, and a game of lunch time darts was just starting up on the other side of the bar. 'I don't know wot ter say,' spluttered Dodger. 'Wot can we do?'

'Well, I know what *I'm* going to do,' said Frank, looking surer of himself than he had ever been before. 'I'm getting out before it's too late.'

'Yer mean – you're quittin'?'

'Yes, Dodger,' said Frank, putting on his trilby. 'But not until I've got what's owing to me.'

Harriet Angel had always liked Arthur Road. She

had often made a short cut through there on her way from Seven Sisters Road to Jones Brothers in Holloway Road, and there was hardly ever a time when she didn't pause for a few minutes to look up longingly at the fine terrace of three-storey houses. Living in a real house again was her dream, and when she was invited by Rob's mother to come and have a cup of tea with her there, she found it difficult to conceal how envious she was.

'I'm sorry there's no butter for the sandwiches,' apologised Sheila Thompson, 'but I'm afraid that between my husband and my son, the family ration doesn't go very far!'

'Please don't apologise,' said Harriet. 'Believe me, I have the same problem with my lot.' Harriet liked Rob's mother. She had always found her to be a very practical and down-to-earth type of woman, who was rarely given much credit by Rob for her wide range of knowledge about what was going on in the world.

The two women sat in front of the fire, sipping tea and eating fishpaste sandwiches, comparing notes about Lizzie and Rob's 'big day'.

'It's coming up so fast,' said Sheila. 'I'm still trying to scrape up enough clothing coupons to buy a new dress from Selby's for the wedding. Thank goodness Graham's sister Gladys has offered me some of hers. Another cup of tea, Harriet dear?'

'Thank you,' said Harriet, handing over her cup and saucer.

'But what about poor Lizzie?' Sheila asked, pouring tea. 'I hear she's not going to be in white.

Won't be the same, will it?'

'Lizzie *will* be in white, Sheila,' replied Harriet firmly. 'What on earth made you think otherwise?'

'Well – Rob,' replied Sheila, a little flustered and embarrassed. 'He said something about how she was going to get married in a woollen dress.'

'A woollen dress!' retorted Harriet, taking the cup from her. 'Oh no. I'm afraid you're mistaken about that, Sheila. I'd never allow a daughter of mine to get married in anything but white. As a matter of fact, we're going off tomorrow to look at a dress she's taken a fancy to – in Jones Brothers.'

'Oh really?' Sheila's face immediately lit up. 'How wonderful!'

'But I have to tell you, Sheila,' said Harriet, putting her cup and saucer down on the small side table. 'I think we have more problems to think about than what Lizzie and Rob are going to wear at their wedding. It's what's going to happen *after* that Lizzie's father and I are worried about.'

Sheila looked a bit taken aback. 'What d'you mean?' she asked.

'Don't you think it odd that the two of them are thinking about this emigration thing?'

Sheila sighed with relief. 'Oh – that,' she replied.

'Well, don't you?' pressed Harriet.

Sheila returned her own cup to the saucer. 'Yes,' she said lightly. 'I suppose when you come to think about it, it *is* a daunting thought. Graham and I have talked about it a lot lately.

But both he and I have had to admit that if that's what Lizzie and Rob want to do, then it wouldn't be right of us to interfere.'

Harriet was taken aback. It wasn't the response she had been expecting – or hoping for. 'But,' she said, leaning forward intensely in her chair, 'Rob is your only child. Has it occurred to you that you may never see him again?'

Sheila hesitated before replying. 'Yes it has, Harriet,' she replied. 'But when you think about what's going on in the country at the moment, the prospects for young people are so bleak.'

At this point, Harriet dropped all pretence at being an understanding mother. 'Oh, I'm so sick of hearing people say that,' she said. 'Things are bad – of course they are – but they'll improve. They always improve. It just takes time, that's all.'

'Young people don't *have* the time,' said Sheila. 'They live for today. They need to move on, to keep on the move, to improve their lot in life. I've heard a lot of wonderful things about Australia. It offers all kinds of challenges to those who want to face up to them. I happen to think that both Rob and Lizzie have the determination to do just that.'

Harriet waited a moment to let Sheila's response sink in. 'I'm sorry, Sheila,' she said calmly. 'I'm afraid you're wrong again. At least in the case of my Lizzie you are. You see, she's not quite the girl you – or even Rob – may think she is.'

Bewildered, Sheila sat up in her chair. 'What do you mean?' she asked.

'Just that...' Harriet faltered, 'well, to tell you the truth, Lizzie's quite a restless girl. I was only talking to her father about it last night. There was a time when I could rely on her to help me look after her brothers and sisters, to keep the family together, and give me the chance to support my husband. Frank has had such a rotten time over these past two years. He gets so depressed. With the tiny wage he earns, he does so need someone to bolster his confidence.'

'But I've always thought what a wonderful support Lizzie is to you and your family,' said Sheila, who was really astounded by what Harriet was saying.

'She used to be,' replied Harriet, 'up until the time when we were bombed out. But after that – well – things seemed to change.'

'Change?' asked Sheila. 'In what way?'

Harriet leaned towards her, and lowered her voice. 'Can I talk to you in confidence, Sheila?' she asked.

'Not a word will go beyond these four walls,' Sheila promised.

'The fact of the matter is that the family can no longer rely on Lizzie any more,' said Harriet. 'And the reason for that is that we hardly ever see her.'

Sheila's eyes widened. 'What?'

'When she's not out with Rob,' continued Harriet, adopting a pained expression, 'she seems to be out an awful lot with her friends at Woolworths. That's all very well, of course, but where they go off to, neither Frank or I would like to say.'

Sheila froze. 'You're not suggesting...'

'It would be no use us trying to deny that Rob is the only boy she has ever been out with,' said Harriet, eyes lowered.

Sheila clasped her hand to her mouth. She was genuinely shocked.

'Please don't get me wrong, Sheila,' insisted Harriet, who was prepared to say anything that might prevent Rob from taking Lizzie away from her and the family. 'Lizzie's a good girl. She's always been a good girl. But just occasionally, she becomes quite irrational. What I'm trying to say is, if she's going to get married, I can only hope that she'll be fair to Rob.'

'Fair?' asked Sheila, sceptically.

'Australia is a long way off, Sheila,' said Harriet. 'It would be so awful to think that, once they're out there, Rob might be – well – disappointed in Lizzie. I mean – it would be very difficult for him, wouldn't it?'

Thursday afternoon was Lizzie's afternoon off from work, and as the sun had at last decided to put in an appearance, she and Rob took the opportunity to get on a Green Line bus and go out for a ride to Windsor. Despite the radiant blue skies, it was still extremely cold, but it was encouraging to see that the endless heaps of dirty frozen snow along the roads were gradually shrinking, and that icicles everywhere were beginning to drip. After the long weeks of being inside their houses, Lizzie and Rob found it lovely to watch the happy, smiling faces of people strolling along the banks of the River Thames, lapping up at last some of the good things in life that nature could offer.

'Isn't it amazing what a little bit of sunshine can do?' remarked Lizzie, as she and Rob wandered hand in hand along a much-used towpath. 'People look so different.'

Rob grunted. 'It may make them look different,' he murmured, 'but it doesn't change the way they feel.'

Lizzie didn't react. They hadn't discussed Australia since they'd nearly quarrelled about it in the men's clothing shop a few days before, and she didn't want to have to deal with it now – not now, when she was having such a wonderful time. Surprisingly, last winter, this stretch of the river had frozen over for the first time in living memory, but with the picture-postcard views of Windsor Castle on the far side in the distance, the river was now shimmering in the weak sunshine. After a while, they came to a huge oak tree around which was wrapped a timber circular seat. As it was completely dry, they sat there, and watched some children feeding the ducks with scraps of bread and cake. It was an idyllic scene, and one that Lizzie wouldn't have missed for the world. 'I wonder if they're sitting down to tea and hot crumpets in front of a big log fire over there,' she said, glancing across at the majestic castle framed against an azure-blue sky.

'Who?' asked Rob, following her eyeline.

'The King and Queen,' replied Lizzie.

'If they've got enough ration coupons,' quipped Rob dourly.

'Don't be so silly!' said Lizzie, chuckling. 'The

King and Queen don't need ration coupons. They're not like us.'

'Why aren't they like us?' asked Rob, only half-seriously.

'Because they're not,' replied Lizzie, scolding him. 'The King is the Head of State. He's entitled to some privileges. So is the Queen – and the two princesses.'

'I don't see why,' said Rob. 'Why shouldn't they suffer like all the rest of their subjects? If they can have as much tea as they like, and log fires to keep them warm, why shouldn't we?'

Lizzie didn't like to hear Rob talk in this way. It was so unlike him, especially as his parents were such ardent supporters of the Royal Family. 'I don't think it's right to be jealous of someone,' said Lizzie. 'The King and Queen are different from the Government. They hold us all together.'

'I'm not jealous of the King and Queen, Liz,' said Rob, taking out a cigarette from a packet in his pocket, and lighting it. 'I'm not jealous of anyone. But if they know what's going on in their country over there, if they know how most of their subjects are going through hell trying to make a decent living, then they should show that they're capable of making sacrifices – just like the rest of us. That's why I want us both to get out of this place – once and for all!'

'Please, Rob,' sighed Lizzie, 'don't let's start that all over again.'

'Why not, Liz?' snapped Rob, turning to face her. 'Why do we have to keep putting off talking about something that could change our whole lives? We can't go on brushing it under the carpet for ever.'

Lizzie got up and wandered to the edge of the river. After a moment Rob joined her. 'Why can't we talk, Liz?' he said softly, slipping his arm around her waist. 'You know how important this is to me.'

'It's important to me too, Rob,' she replied. 'That's why I want to be sure.'

'But what more is there to be sure *about?*' he asked, with great frustration. 'We know that if we stay in this country for the rest of our lives, we're not going to get on any better than we are now.'

'No, Rob,' said Lizzie. 'We *don't* know that. Dad often told me how bad things were after the first war, but they picked up – in time.'

'But things have never been as bad as they are now,' he said. 'Why can't you understand that, Liz? Look at the price of everything. We have to pay two and sixpence more for coal, just to keep warm.'

'They've put up the butter ration by one ounce,' countered Lizzie. 'And Stafford Cripps has frozen food prices.'

'Big deal!' growled Rob, who was getting near the end of his tether with her. 'And what about him increasing the price of petrol for charabancs?'

'How often do you and I go on charabancs?' asked Lizzie, half-jokingly.

'That's not the point, Liz!' he snapped. 'How many times do I have to tell you that this country is in a hell of a state? Everyone says so. Even your own father says so.'

At the mention of her father, Lizzie felt her

stomach churn. 'Dad doesn't know what he's saying these days,' she said.

'Well *I* do!' snapped Rob, swinging her round to face him. 'Listen to me, Liz,' he said. 'You and I are two young people. We're fit and strong, and we can make a go of this if only we stop putting obstacles in the way.'

Lizzie shook her head. 'I don't know, Rob,' she said. 'I still don't know. It's such a huge risk to take.'

'Liz!' he said, clasping hold of her shoulders. 'Everything in life is a risk. Everything we do, every move we make, is a risk. That's life. That's what life is all about. Even this.'

To Lizzie's horror, he suddenly broke loose from her, and walked out on to a small ledge of ice that had formed by the river bank. 'Rob!' she squealed. 'Come back!'

'Life *is* a risk, Liz!' Rob proclaimed. 'It's a challenge! But no more than stepping out on to this river.'

'Please, Rob!' she yelled. 'Please come back! It's dangerous! It's beginning to thaw! Can't you see? Look at the ice around the edge.' She pointed to the pools of water that were now forming alongside the path, ice that was being melted by the faint warmth of the sun. 'Rob!' She looked around desperately to see if anyone was near enough to be able to help, but the children had gone, and only the ducks were watching them.

'It's safe, Liz,' Rob assured her. 'Believe me, it *is* safe. Look at those ducks. They're not scared. They're not scared to take the risk.' He held out his hand to her. 'Come on, Liz,' he pleaded. 'Take the risk with me. We can do it, Liz. As long as we're together, we can do *anything!*'

'No, Rob, no!' Lizzie, frozen with fear, backed away.

'Trust me, Liz!' Rob again pleaded. 'If we're going to spend our life together, then you *must* trust me.' He again held out his hand to her.

Lizzie, close to tears, suddenly felt a surge of warmth flow through her entire body. As she looked at Rob's hand stretched out to her, she gradually decided that what he was saying was true. If they were going to spend their lives together, then she must trust him. After all, they loved each other, and no matter how determined Rob was to get his own way, she knew that he would never let any harm come to her. Yes, life *was* a risk, but it was up to both of them not to be afraid to take that risk.

'*Please*, Liz,' called Rob, hand still outstretched. 'I love you.'

After a moment of complete silence, Liz finally took a few steps forward. Once her feet touched the edge of the towpath, she stretched out her hand to take his. But it was still a few inches away. Slowly, methodically, she stepped out on to the ice.

'Don't look down, Liz,' said Rob, voice calm and caring. 'Trust me.'

Lizzie felt her way precariously. Quite un-expectedly, the ice was firm beneath the thin layer of snow that was settled on the surface. With renewed courage, she moved out further, until their fingers touched. But just as Rob had grabbed hold of her hand, the ice suddenly cracked, and gave way beneath her.

'Rob...!'

'Liz!'

With Rob still clinging to her hand, Lizzie's legs sank down beneath the ice, and into the bitterly cold water beneath. 'Rob!' she yelled hysterically. 'Help me! Please help me!'

'Hold on, Liz!' yelled Rob, struggling frantically to keep the rest of her body on the surface.

Within a few moments, several people appeared, amongst them a group of men who came rushing to Rob's aid.

'Hold on, Liz!' yelled Rob. 'It's all right, darling! It's all right! Hold on!'

After an immense battle, Lizzie was eventually pulled clear of the ice, and dragged back up on to the towpath.

Rob was shaking with fear and apprehension. Kneeling down beside Lizzie, he quickly took off his coat, and wrapped it around her. 'Oh God, Liz,' he cried, desperately trying to rub some life back into her hands. 'I'm sorry, darling! I'm *so* sorry!'

'Somebody call an ambulance!' shouted one of the rescuers.

'Get some blankets!' yelled a woman onlooker.

'You'll be all right, Liz!' Rob said over and over again, his heart racing with alarm and anxiety. But the shock of falling into the sub-zero temperature of the river had caused Lizzie to lose consciousness. 'Oh God, Liz!' Rob gasped, his voice strangulated with desperation and guilt. 'What have I done? Dear God – what have I done!'

Chapter 17

Rob took a solemn oath in his own mind that he would never forgive himself for what he had done to Lizzie. After his crass, self-indulgent act of madness in enticing Lizzie out on to the melting surface of the River Thames, it was a miracle she was still alive. Even now, twenty-four hours after it had all happened down at Windsor, like Lizzie herself, Rob was still in a state of shock. Only the prompt aid of onlookers and an ambulance had saved her life, and even though it had only been necessary for her to remain in hospital overnight, the repercussions and dismay the accident had caused with both the Angel family and his own parents was something Rob was going to have to live with for the rest of his life. He was now prepared for the worst. Although Lizzie had hardly spoken to him since being brought back home in an ambulance the following morning, in his heart of hearts he knew only too well that getting her to emigrate to Australia with him would now be out of the question. Worse than that, however, was the certainty that Lizzie would call off the wedding. And who could blame her? Daring her to take a risk was something he no longer had the right to expect of her.

For Harriet Angel, Lizzie's close encounter with death brought mixed blessings. When Rob's father, Graham, turned up on her doorstep the previous evening, bringing news of what had happened to Lizzie, she nearly hit the roof, and by the time Lizzie arrived home in the ambulance with Rob the following morning, it was only Lizzie's intervention that prevented her from barring Rob from entering the prefab. But her obvious distress about Lizzie's condition was tempered by the fact that she now had a perfect excuse to persuade Lizzie that Rob was hardly the most suitable person with whom to spend the rest of her life.

But Harriet's hopes soon misfired when Rob turned up during the evening carrying a large bunch of daffodils he had bought up Petticoat Lane.

'I can't ask you to forgive me, Liz,' he said, with obvious anguish, 'but the least I can do is say sorry.'

Lizzie, sitting in an armchair opposite her dad in front of the fire, took the daffodils and smelled them. 'Thanks, Rob,' she said. 'They're absolutely beautiful. It just shows you – spring isn't far away now.' She turned to look at Rob. 'Nor is our big day.'

Rob's heart missed a beat. He was so delirious to hear what Lizzie had said, he went to her, and threw his arms around her. But he was suddenly embarrassed, knowing that Frank and Harriet were there. 'Oh – I'm sorry, Dad,' he said.

Frank grinned. 'Oh, don't mind us,' he said admiringly. 'We're only the in-laws!'

Harriet reacted with despair to what Lizzie had said. Without saying a word, she quietly took the daffodils from Lizzie, and retreated with them into the kitchen.

'You two have got a lot to do,' said Frank, after Harriet had gone. 'Just over three weeks now. You'll have to get your skates on.'

'Not *ice* skates though, Dad!' quipped Lizzie, with some irony.

Frank chuckled, and gave Rob a sympathetic look. 'Let's hope there's no ice around by then,' he said. 'It might be a bit cold in that reception hall. Gran won't stop grumbling the whole time.'

Lizzie's expression changed. 'I wanted to talk to you about that, Dad,' she said. 'I've been thinking about this reception, and I don't think it's absolutely necessary.'

'What?' said Frank, surprised. 'The reception?'

'We just don't need it,' insisted Lizzie. 'Why should we pay out all that money just so that a whole lot of people can have a good time? It's far better if we just have a quiet wedding in a registry office, and invite just a few close friends and family, say, no more than a dozen or so.'

'A registry office!' blurted Rob. 'Whatever gave you that idea?'

'Oh, Rob,' said Lizzie, 'does it matter where we get married? Whether it's in a church or a registry office, it all means the same thing. As long as it's all legal, why should we go to all that expense?'

'But–' Rob's protest was interrupted before he had a chance to say another word.

'There'll be no wedding in a registry office,' said Frank, rising from his chair, and reaching for his packet of cigarettes on the mantelpiece. 'It'll be in the Emmanuel Church as you've planned, and the reception will go ahead in the Foresters Hall. As far as your guests are concerned, that's up to you to choose who you want. But if you want to make sure that you don't start a whole lot of rows and quarrels amongst them all, I advise you to ask the whole lot of them – from *both* our families.'

'Hear! Hear!' agreed Rob.

'Dad – we don't need it!' said Lizzie. 'Honestly, we don't!'

'Lizzie,' replied Frank, calm but firm, 'a wedding is the most important day in the life of any man and woman. It's something you'll look back on for the rest of your lives. If you don't make the effort, believe me, you'll always regret it.'

'I agree with Dad!'

Everyone turned to find Susan standing in the open doorway of the bedroom she shared with her brothers and sisters.

'If I'm going to be a bridesmaid, I want it to be in a church, with a lovely dress, and lovely flowers – and everything that goes with it. I don't want to sit in some dreary old town hall with a whole lot of grey-faced grumpies.'

'That's all very well, Susan,' said Lizzie, 'but *you're* not the one that's getting married. And it's all going to cost a hell of a lot of money!'

'How many times do I have to tell you, Lizzie?' snapped Frank. 'Let *me* worry about that – not you!'

Lizzie shook her head. 'That's just what I don't want you to do, Dad,' she said pointedly.

Frank knew what she was getting at, and turned

330

to look down forlornly into the fire.

Lizzie got up, and went to him. 'It doesn't matter, Dad, really it doesn't,' she said, trying to comfort him. 'Rob and I don't need a lot of money to get married. As long as we both have our families around us, that's all we ask.'

In the open bedroom doorway, Susan reacted with shock and disbelief. Although she fostered a quiet jealousy of the affection the family held for her older sister, she found the thought that Lizzie would soon no longer be there for them *or* for her, deeply upsetting.

'Liz's right,' added Rob. 'But I promise you, I won't let her get all her own way. I'll make sure we have a day that we'll all remember.'

Behind them, Harriet quietly slipped back into the room, carrying the daffodils, which she had put into a vase.

'Anyway,' continued Lizzie, 'we've got far more important things to think about. If Rob and I are going off to make our fortune, we shall have to start hatching some plans.'

Rob suddenly went stone-cold. He felt as though a thunderbolt had hit him. 'W-what did you say?' he spluttered.

Lizzie turned and gave him a great big smile.

Rob's eyes widened. 'You – you don't mean...?'

'If this is what you want, Rob,' said Lizzie. 'If you want me to take the risk, then I'm willing to take it – if you are.' She turned and looked back at her father.

Frank gave her a warm, loving and poignant look. He opened his arms, and she went to him. Then Rob joined them, and they all hugged each other.

Behind them, unnoticed by the others, Harriet paused just long enough to place the vase of daffodils on the table, before quietly returning to the kitchen.

Lizzie didn't go into work until after the weekend, but when the other girls there heard about what had happened to her on her afternoon off at Windsor, they were all up in arms.

'Yer must be out of yer mind stickin' to a feller like that!' barked Potto, who, as usual, had put on so much bright red lipstick, she looked as though she'd cut herself. 'If it was me, I'd tie a brick round 'is bleedin' neck an' push 'im off Westminster Bridge!'

'That's a bit drastic, Potto,' suggested Lizzie, as they stacked some of the new week's stock of hit gramophone records on the shelves below their counter. 'In any case, it was my fault for going along with it. When I saw him standing on the ice, I thought I was just being a bit of a coward.'

'A coward?' spluttered Potto indignantly. 'Yer wouldn't've caught me walkin' out on to a bleedin' river. To my knowledge, there's only ever been one person who's done that an' lived ter tell the tale.'

Lizzie was puzzled. 'Who's that?'

Potto pointed up towards the ceiling.

Lizzie pulled a face. 'Potto!' she said, voice low. 'I had no idea you were religious.'

Potto also pulled a face. 'Don't be so ridiculous,' she replied indignantly. 'Of course I'm religious. I often go ter church – well, sometimes. I went ter my cousin Edie's wedding once, *an'* my Uncle Jim's funeral.'

Lizzie chuckled to herself.

'But don't you ever dare try a thing like that again, d'yer 'ear?' said Potto, pausing for just a moment to adjust the large clip that was holding her hair in place on top of her head. 'Next time you could get yerself killed!'

'I won't,' said Lizzie. 'I promise. In any case, I doubt we'll find any frozen rivers where Rob and I are going.'

Lizzie's wistful comment prompted Potto to look up with a start. 'What was that you said?' she asked, rising up from beneath the counter.

Lizzie, still working on the lower counter, looked up at her. 'We're going to Australia, Potto,' she said. 'I've told Rob.'

Potto's shock was put on hold when they were suddenly interrupted by a middle-aged lady, who wanted to buy a record she had heard on *Family Favourites* on the wireless the previous morning. But all she could remember was that it was a song sung by a popular singer of the day called Donald Peers. Fortunately, Potto's photographic knowledge of the top hit tunes of the day soon identified the title as being 'By a Babbling Brook'. The delighted customer paid up, leaving Potto to take in what Lizzie had just told her.

'D'yer mean Rob's persuaded yer?' she gasped. 'You're actually goin' ter do it? You're goin' ter emigrate?'

Lizzie rose up from behind the counter. 'Yes, Potto,' she said. 'I've finally decided that I've at least got to give it a try.'

'*Got* to?' asked Potto. 'You mean – because Rob's bullying you into doing it?'

'Yes, Potto,' replied Lizzie. 'Rob *is* bullying me to do it. But this is *my* decision – not his. I've been churning it round in my mind over and over again. It's kept me awake at nights. I've hardly thought of anything else since he first asked me.'

Potto was flummoxed. 'So what's suddenly made you decide?' she asked.

'Oh – everything really,' replied Lizzie forlornly. 'Well, that's not exactly true. I suppose it's something that all sorts of people have been trying to tell me – that, as much as you love your own family, they have to do without you sooner or later. My mum has been relying on me too much – I can see that now. My being with her all the time only brings out the worst in her.'

'But wot about yer dad?' asked Potto, still reeling from Lizzie's news.

Lizzie's whole expression changed. 'That's another problem,' she said. 'Something's happened to him that's completely changed him. There are times when I look at him that I feel so – guilty. He's in trouble, Potto, I know he is. And it's all because of my blasted wedding, because he wants me to have what he thinks is every daughter's right. But it isn't. All I want is for him and Mum and all the family to be free of worry. The way I feel right now, I'd just like Rob and me to run away and forget all about weddings and receptions and obligations.'

'Well, why don't yer?' asked Potto.

Potto's quite innocent question took Lizzie by surprise, and for some strange reason she felt she had to combat it. 'Because I still have a duty to my family, Potto!' she snapped. 'Apart from the way I feel, I'd never do anything to hurt them.'

'But you're going away,' Potto reminded her. 'Won't *that* hurt them?'

Lizzie was about to reply, when Maple came across in a hurry from her own counter. 'Got to talk to you, Lizzie!' she said, her voice low but urgent. 'Over there!' She nodded her head towards the back door.

Maple was waiting for Lizzie in the ladies' staff lavatory.

'What's up?' asked Lizzie.

'I've seen her again,' said Maple.

'Who?' asked Lizzie, puzzled.

'*Her!*' spluttered Maple, voice lowered, but clearly very worked up. 'The Tuesday lady!'

'You saw her?'

'Just five minutes ago,' said Maple excitedly. 'I slipped out to get Mum's prescription from the chemist down Seven Sisters Road, and I saw her crossing over the road. She went into the store opposite.'

'The North London?' asked Lizzie urgently.

Maple nodded enthusiastically.

Lizzie waited to hear no more. She rushed straight to the door.

'Lizzie!' called Maple, as she rushed after her. 'What are you going to do?'

'What d'you think I'm going to do?' called Lizzie, as she hurried into the staff locker room

335

to collect her coat. 'I'm going after her.' She stopped briefly at the door. 'If the super asks where I've gone, tell her I've taken an early lunch.'

'But it's only eleven o'clock!' called Maple, to no avail.

Lizzie had already disappeared out through the back door of the store.

Once she'd cleared the back entrance in Enkel Road, Lizzie made a wild dash out towards the main road. Monday mornings were always busy along Seven Sisters Road, and this was no exception, for now that a slow thaw had at last set in, the shoppers were out in force. Sainsbury's and Lipton's were particularly busy, with long lines of people queuing up in the hope of using some of their remaining food coupons on some fresh butter, bacon, cheese or sugar, or hoping that the sacks of broken biscuits or dried peas wouldn't be finished before it was their turn. Hicks, the greengrocer's shop, was also filled with customers, desperate to be there when the day's meagre supply of potatoes arrived, all of them still angry with the Chancellor for imposing a ration on even this, the most basic of vegetables.

It took Lizzie some moments to cross the road, and she was so eager to do so, she was nearly knocked down by a number 14 bus that was just pulling to a halt outside the front entrance of the North London Drapery Stores.

Lizzie began her frantic search for 'the Tuesday lady' inside the large grey tiled store, which had been built before the war on the site of the old bug-hutch Holloway Cinematograph Cinema, known affectionately in the neighbourhood as 'Pykes'. She started on the ground floor, rushing from counter to counter, occasionally raising herself up on tiptoe to try to peer over the heads of the mainly women shoppers who were milling around the sparsely stocked cosmetics and linen department counters. It was like trying to find a needle in a haystack, and without even knowing whether the woman was still in the store, or had slipped out through a side entrance.

More or less satisfied that there was no trace of the woman down there, Lizzie quickly moved out on to the stone steps leading up to the first floor. There, amongst the Axminster carpets, rugs and fireplace accessories, she found a few people looking around, but as she moved off into the store's annexe, quite a few customers were browsing around the electrical department, enthusing over the latest range of radiograms, which was the current craze amongst those who liked the idea of having their wireless and gramophone in one stylish cabinet. Still no sign of the elusive 'Tuesday lady', and as today was only Monday, Lizzie was beginning to wonder whether Maple had mistaken someone else for the woman she was looking for. But just as she was wandering into the garden tools department, and pondering on whether to abandon her search so that she could move up to the top floor furnishing and curtains, she caught a passing, distant glimpse of a tall, well-dressed woman, hovering over some trays of hammers, pliers and screwdrivers. Lizzie moved in a flash. Before she had even got there, the woman had picked up a pair of pliers, and dropped them discreetly into her shopping bag. Lizzie shadowed her carefully, allowing her to disappear quickly out through the swing doors on to the first floor landing.

The woman quickly started to pick her way down the stairs, but she had only managed to go a short way, when Lizzie called to her: 'Were you thinking of paying for that – madam?'

Daisy Parfitt swung round, saw Lizzie standing at the top of the stairs above her, then quickly tried to make a dash for the ground floor.

Lizzie rushed after her, watched her disappear through the side exit into Sussex Way, and caught up with her in the street outside. 'Who *are* you?' she asked, darting in front of Daisy so that she blocked her way.

Daisy came to a halt, staring at Lizzie with a look of fire. Then she tried to walk round her.

Again Lizzie prevented her from passing. 'What sort of a person are you?' she asked, challengingly. 'Have you *no* conscience?'

Daisy finally spoke. 'I don't know what you're talking about,' she said sternly. 'Now will you please get out of my way before I call the police?'

Lizzie smiled. 'Go right ahead,' she replied. 'As a matter of fact, Hornsey Road Police Station is just round the corner. Why don't we go there together?' She took a step closer towards Daisy. 'I'm sure they'd be very interested to take a look at that pair of pliers in your bag – the pliers you declined to purchase inside the store.'

Daisy hesitated. She had a look of thunder in her eyes. The fact that she had been caught twice

338

by the same person was not only nerve-racking, but also extremely irritating. 'What do you want me to say to you?' she asked.

'Quite a lot of things,' replied Lizzie. 'You could start by telling me why you do this sort of thing.'

Before replying, Daisy waited for two young women pushing prams to pass. 'I'm not a criminal,' she said haughtily. 'What I do is a kind of hobby – nothing more.'

Lizzie stared at her in disbelief. 'A hobby?'

'I do it because I like things, because I want them, because I *must* have them.'

'Have you ever thought about *paying* for what you take?' asked Lizzie sceptically. 'You hardly seem to me the kind of person who's without money in your pocket.'

The woman smiled wryly. 'Oh, I have money all, right,' she replied. 'But it's not the same. I suppose it's the thrill of taking something that doesn't belong to me. Some people call it compulsive. *I* call it – exciting. To see something that catches my eye in a shop window is quite exhilarating. Nothing expensive. Nothing too grand. Just things – simple things. Things that we use in our everyday life. Nobody misses them. Why should they – they have so many things that are never bought. In a way, I'm doing them a service. I'm helping them to get rid of things that no one wants. Except me.'

Lizzie was almost mesmerised by the woman's explanation. It seemed to have no logic, and yet – in some ways – it did. 'It still doesn't belong to you,' she said. 'None of it belongs to you unless you've paid for it. Whether you like it or not, it's still stealing.'

As if to emphasise Lizzie's point, the sound of a police car siren bell echoed out in the distance.

While they waited for the sound to pass, Daisy stared at Lizzie impassively. 'So what are you going to do?' she asked coldly. 'Are you going to turn me in, or have you finished scolding me and are prepared to let me go?'

Lizzie continued staring hard at her, without saying a word.

Daisy took that as meaning she was free to go. So she turned and slowly started to walk away. But she stopped dead, when Lizzie called to her.

'Why did you come to see my father the other day?'

Daisy hesitated, then turned to face her.

Lizzie approached. 'You came to my house – the prefab in Andover Road. You came to see my father. I want to know why.'

For the first time, Daisy was not only taken off guard, she was clearly shattered. 'Your *father?*'

'Are you teaching him to be a shoplifter too?' asked Lizzie. 'Or are you two working on something more important than just pliers and screwdrivers?'

In those few astonishing moments of revelation, Daisy quickly tried to piece together the connection between this girl, and the 'special' work her father had been doing for Parfitt and herself. The coincidence was terrifying. But how much did the girl know? How much should she be told? As she stood there in a cold backstreet in Holloway, staring into the eyes of a wisp of a girl who had unmasked her, she found herself in a predicament that seemed to have no solution. 'What is your father's name?' she asked, without trying to show panic.

'*I* ask the questions,' said Lizzie. 'Not you.'

Daisy hesitated, then smiled wryly. 'I thought Angels were only God's messengers,' she said, looking up at the sky. 'They usually fly around the heavens.'

'Is he working with you?' asked Lizzie.

'Something like that,' replied Daisy, with a blank expression.

'Black market?'

Daisy did not respond.

'I'm warning you,' said Lizzie. 'If you don't tell me, I shall go straight to the police.'

'As you wish, my dear,' said Daisy. 'But let me tell you something. Your father is quite a special man. He told me that he's been saving up for your wedding. What he's been doing, he's only done for you. Now if you feel you want to go to the police, then you must do so. But it would be a great pity if your father's dream wasn't allowed to come true.' She waited a moment, allowing Lizzie to stare at her in pained silence. With no response, she turned, and slowly walked away.

Lizzie watched her go, but made no attempt to follow her.

Frank Angel left Billingsgate Market soon after five in the evening. It had been a hard day, and by the time he'd washed up, and cleaned off his apron, he was all in. On his way to the bus stop, he made a rare stop at the pub to have a drink.

He felt in his pocket and found some change, which he handed over to the barman. The few coins he had left over set his mind racing. Money. He just couldn't get it out of his mind. With Lizzie's wedding closing in on him, he was now getting desperate. He needed money not only to pay off the balance of what was owing on the reception hall, but the cost of the food and drink. It was true that Rob's father had offered to pay his share, but despite both Rob and Lizzie's pleas, Frank was determined to pay for everything himself. But how? With the collapse of the Wethersfield USAF job, Parfitt had so far paid none of the funds to Frank that were owing to him, and time was running out. As he quietly propped himself up at the bar counter, and drank his half-pint of Guinness, he tried to think of ways of getting his hands on some extra cash. But try as he might, not a single idea came into his head.

Then he thought about Lizzie, and how she had finally made up her mind about emigrating with Rob to Australia. Despite all the support he had given her, and his determination to ensure that she should give herself the chance of a better life, his heart sank at the thought of losing her. For the past two years, Lizzie had been at the centre of his life, always there to cheer him up when the going got rough, always prepared to make him laugh with her impersonations and mimicking, and the way she had constantly helped him to look through the local papers for any job that would give him scope for a decent career. In short, he idolised her, but when she

342

had gone, he had no idea how he would cope without her. Oh yes, he loved Harriet, and always would, but she could never take the place of Lizzie. By the time Frank had finished his drink, and found his way to the bus stop, he had made a conscious decision to go to Parfitt and force him to hand over the money that was owing to him.

It was pitch-dark when he got to Parfitt's house overlooking Highbury Fields and, to make matters worse, the fields themselves were engulfed in a freezing fog, which was always a hazard at this time of year. Owing to the fuel shortage, there were no street lights, and it reminded Frank of what it was like during the war, when he came home on leave and found he had to use a torch to get around. He wished he'd had a torch at that moment, for it was difficult to know where the pavement came to an end, and the fields started. Eventually, he did find his way, and once he'd crossed over to the far side of the fields, he knew he'd find number 18 Threshold Avenue, because he still remembered the huge chestnut tree outside Parfitt's house, which was one of many that lined the street.

By the time he reached the house, his hands were freezing cold, so he blew into them to try to warm them up. The blanket of fog was wrapping itself around everything, including the front gate of the house, and it took him a moment to work the latch so that it would open. He didn't bother to close the gate behind him, for there were hardly going to be any more visitors that evening. He looked up at the windows, but the curtains were drawn, and he couldn't see any lights inside. He knocked on the door. For the best part of a minute he waited on the doorstep. With no reply, he knocked again. But there was still no response. Although he didn't consider that something might be wrong, he had a strange feeling that he had made a foolish decision to come without first checking with Dodger. He knocked again, and this time he bent down, opened the letter box, and called through it, 'Mr Parfitt! Are you there?' Still no reply. He called again, 'Mr Parfitt! Mrs Parfitt! It's me – Frank Angel. Can you hear me? Are you in there?'

'You're wasting your time!'

Frank looked up with a start. The woman's voice he could hear was coming from the front door of the next house. 'I beg your pardon?' he called, without being able to see who was there through the fog.

'If you're looking for the major,' called the elderly woman, 'you're too late. They've gone. They've both gone!'

'Oh – right,' said Frank, who saw nothing wrong with the Parfitts going out for the evening. 'Thank you very much. You wouldn't know what time they'll be back?' he asked.

'They're not coming back!' returned the woman. 'They've left for good!'

Frank's stomach churned. 'Left?' he asked.

'They had the removals van in all day. The whole place was cleared out by four o'clock.'

'But – d'you know where they've moved to?' asked Frank, with more than a little desperation in his voice.

'Haven't the foggiest,' replied the woman. 'They never talked much to me. Always kept themselves to themselves. Some people are like that.'

Before Frank could ask any more questions, he heard the woman close her front door.

For a moment or so, he just stood there, unable to move. Suddenly, his whole world seemed to be falling apart. The Parfitts had given him the slip. They had left him without the money that was rightly his, the money that would have seen him through until after Lizzie's wedding. He held his face in his hands. He had nothing but loathing inside for what the Parfitts had done, but he also hated himself for ever having got mixed up with them in the first place. Worse than that, was the trouble they had left behind. What happens now? he asked himself. What happens when that knock came on his door in the middle of the night, and he was dragged off to Hornsey Road Police Station? He felt crushed, lost. He made his way to the front gate, and slowly ambled out into the street. He didn't bother to close the gate behind him.

Chapter 18

With just over a week to go to their wedding, Lizzie and Rob found themselves heading off to the Australian High Commission in the Strand. After submitting their application form for the ten-pound assisted passage scheme only a week before, they were surprised to receive such a quick response, especially as the number of would-be hopefuls had multiplied considerably over the past few months, and the backlog of applicants waiting for interviews had been quite substantial. However, after supplying routine medical details from their own doctors, the letter to attend for interview at the Immigration Department of the Commission came quite out of the blue. When they got there, the actual time of the interview turned out to be somewhat flexible, for they sat for almost an hour and a half in the waiting room with hordes of other people.

'What do we do if they turn us down?' whispered Lizzie, snuggling up nervously to Rob on a long bench seat just outside the interview room.

'Why should they turn us down?' asked Rob.

'Well,' said Lizzie, 'I did have tonsillitis and chickenpox when I was young. The doctor put it down on the form.'

Rob laughed. 'Don't be ridiculous, Liz!' he said. 'They're not going to turn us down just because you once had tonsillitis and chickenpox! They've got far more important things to check than that.'

'*What* things?' asked Lizzie sceptically.

'Well – whether you're a reputable person to live in Australian society, for instance.'

'Reputable? Me?' Lizzie sat upright, and glared at him. 'If I'm a reputable enough citizen to live in my own country,' she growled indignantly, 'then I'm reputable enough to live in silly old

Australia! Damned cheek!'

'Lizzie,' said Rob, looking around to make sure no one had heard her, 'stop getting on your high horse. I only said that *might* be the kind of question they'll ask. I didn't say they were *going* to ask it.' He lowered his voice still further. 'But if you start calling them names before we even get there, we'll never get through!'

'I don't care!' replied Lizzie indignantly. 'If they don't like me as I am, they can lump it!'

Rob sighed despondently. This was a fine start, he told himself. It had taken long enough to get Lizzie to agree to filling in the application form, but now that she had come this far, it was not going to be easy to get her through the interview.

Lizzie decided it was probably better for her to keep quiet, so she just sat there, constantly looking around her at all the other applicants, observing them carefully, trying to work out in her mind who they were, where they came from, and what it was that was prompting them to take such a giant step into the unknown. What particularly surprised her was that not all the people sitting there were young. The couple that she spent most time observing were probably aged somewhere in their thirties, and they were really quite well-dressed. For some reason, she had always imagined that the type of person who wanted to emigrate was poor, with not much education, and just looking for an easy way to get a free holiday. But these people had good speaking voices, and while the wife bottle-fed the baby girl she was cradling in her arms, her husband read every page of *The Times* from beginning to end. Would these be the kind of people she would be associating with, if and when they ever got to Australia? But most important of all, how would the locals treat her? During the past few weeks she had read stories in the newspapers that some of the old die-hard local-born residents had come to resent the influx of newcomers, and that anyone from the old country who intended to settle down in this far-flung corner of the world would find it difficult to integrate.

For his part, Rob could only sit and ponder about what he wanted to do once he got to Australia. Until he had got through the interview, he had no idea about which part of Australia he would like Lizzie and himself to settle down in, or even if they would be allowed to choose. And what work could he do? Working in Petticoat Lane was hardly a first-class reference for an immigrant's application, and it was going to take quite a bit of explaining as to why he hadn't taken up some kind of training for an occupation or profession. But he had rehearsed many times what he was going to say. He would tell them that he was a fit and able man, physically strong, but that most of all he was willing to learn. This thought filled him with confidence, until he remembered that in their newspaper advertisements, the Australian Government had indicated that they were looking for much more than bluff and bravado from prospective new Australians.

Lizzie, still fascinated by the couple sitting opposite them, finally plucked up enough courage to talk to them. 'I've never been on a boat before – have you?' she asked, directing her question directly to the baby's mother.

The woman looked up and smiled at her. 'Yes, I did once,' she said in a northern-sounding accent. 'When I was young, my mam took me across to France. It was only a cross-Channel ferry boat, but it was quite an experience. I don't know how this one will take to such a long journey, though,' she said, planting a light kiss on her baby's forehead.

'I doubt she'll know much about it,' added the baby's father, who had an impeccably posh London accent, and looked immaculate in a dark overcoat, grey suit, collar and tie. 'But at least she'll be six weeks older by the time we get there.'

'I hear we go through the Suez Canal,' said Rob, leaning forward on the bench to join in.

'Yes – apparently,' replied the baby's father. '*And* the Red Sea. I'm looking forward to that, I must say.'

'I'm not,' said his wife. 'I've got a terrible feeling I'm going to be sick all the way.'

'Me too,' added Lizzie.

'Of course you won't!' insisted Rob. 'Once you're out there on the high seas, you'll have so much to look at, so much to remember.'

'There'll be a lot more to remember than the journey,' said the baby's mother with a wistful sigh.

Lizzie exchanged a brief, questioning look with Rob. 'D'you think we're doing the right thing?' she asked.

The woman looked up from feeding her baby. 'I don't see what else we can do,' she answered, with a shrug. 'Before we put in for this, we kept hoping and praying that something would come along to stop us from doing it. Each day we looked for something – *anything* – that would show us that things were going to get better.'

'But they never have,' said her husband despairingly. 'Not even the weather. Grey skies every day – it just gets you down. It was my wife's idea to do this, not mine,' he added. 'For the past two years, I've been working as a manager in a hardware firm. Five pounds a week, including expenses. That doesn't even leave enough to pay the rent and buy the week's rations. How they expect a family of three to live on that kind of wage, I'll never know.'

There was a moment's silence between them all before Lizzie spoke. 'So do you think we'll be better off – over there?' she asked.

'Can't do any worse,' replied the man.

'But I'm scared,' added the woman. 'It's such a long way.'

Lizzie smiled back at her, acknowledging their mutual feelings. She knew what the two of them meant. She was scared too – scared of what lay ahead, scared of uncharted waters, and, above all, scared of failure. As she looked around the room at the sea of apprehension, faces from different classes and backgrounds, different shapes and sizes, all sitting there and dreaming of a brave new world, a more hopeful new life, she wondered what the future *really* held for them. And she wondered also what it was that had driven her and Rob and so many other people to take such a desperate step. When life had no hope, what could one do but move on, take the risk, as Rob had asked her to do? At that moment, the baby girl cried. When she eventually disembarked from the ship on the other side of the world, would she really have a better future to look forward to?

Harriet Angel could feel no enthusiasm for Lizzie's wedding. Despite the fact that there were now only two weeks to go before 'the big day', she was taking everything in her stride, and leaving all the arrangements to Lizzie and Rob to sort out. She still didn't know how or where Frank thought he was going to find all the money that was needed to pay for the reception hall, the food and drink, and the hire of two wedding cars, but every time she asked him about it, he merely replied, 'Stop worrying, Harriet. Just leave everything to me.' So – that's what she was doing. She was leaving everything to him. And since her mother, Gran Perkins, was paying for Lizzie's wedding dress, she, Harriet, saw no need to be more involved in the whole thing than was absolutely necessary. After all, if Lizzie and Rob's application for the ten-pound assisted passage scheme to Australia was approved, Lizzie would soon be leaving home for good, and so as far as Harriet was concerned, the wedding was nothing more than a means to an end. However, when Harriet said this to her mother, she got the kind of response that she hadn't bargained for.

'I don't know what's happened to you these

days, Harriet,' said Gran, who had only popped in to the prefab to see if she could help her daughter with any preparations that were needed for the wedding. 'If you ask me, this lack of enthusiasm for your own daughter's wedding is pretty shabby.'

'It's not lack of enthusiasm, Mother,' insisted Harriet quite calmly. 'To my way of thinking, if Lizzie's going away, I would have thought the least important thing to worry about is her getting married.'

'That's what I mean!' muttered Gran disapprovingly, as she watched Harriet doing the ironing. 'All you're obsessed with is the fact that Lizzie's leaving home.'

'Well, wouldn't you be?' replied Harriet, turning on her. 'She's my own daughter, and I shall never see her again.'

'Never say never, Harriet,' replied Gran. 'Besides, if emigrating to Australia is going to improve Lizzie's lot in life, then you should go down on bended knees and thank God for it.'

'I'm not going down on bended knees for *anybody*, Mother,' Harriet assured her. 'I just want this whole thing over and done with as soon as possible. I've got quite enough troubles to cope with as it is.'

Gran put down the cup of tea she had half finished, and replaced it on the tea tray on the living-room table. 'So what's wrong with you and Frank?' she asked. 'Is the sex thing over between you?'

Harriet swung round and fixed her with an icy, outraged glare. 'Don't be so disgusting, Mother!'

she snapped angrily.

'Well – is it?' persisted Gran.

'My relationship with Frank is my own private business, Mother!' she growled. 'You have no right to talk about such things.' She returned to her ironing.

Gran waited. She knew Harriet only too well, and that she would eventually respond to a question that was clearly causing her anguish.

'Things have changed between me and Frank,' Harriet finally said. 'It was all right up until a few weeks ago. But now – it's different.'

'Why?'

Her mother's direct way of questioning had always irritated Harriet, but at this precise moment, she was finding it unsettling. The two of them had not been close for years. Harriet had never quite understood why, except that she herself had always been such a secretive person, who never had the capacity to trust anyone except herself. Cosy fireside chats with her own mother had never appealed to Harriet, and that had consequently kept them at arm's length. But even though she was reluctant to admit it, today she was in need of someone to talk to. She stopped ironing. 'Frank,' she replied falteringly, 'is not a well man.'

Gran leaned forward in her chair. 'Not well?' she asked. 'You mean – he's ill?'

'I don't know,' said Harriet. 'The other night when we were lying in bed, he had a pain – in his stomach. I asked him what was wrong, but all he would say was that he often suffers from stomach cramp, and that it was nothing to worry about.

But I happen to think it is.'

'Why d'you say that?' asked Gran.

'Because there's something on his mind that he can't tell me about.'

'You mean, he's in some kind of trouble?'

Harriet nodded. 'I have a feeling he's got himself involved with the wrong kind of people.'

'How d'you know that?'

'Because all he talks about is wanting to give Lizzie the kind of wedding she deserves. Because someone turned up outside the other day – a woman. I saw them through the kitchen window. I've never seen her before, but they seemed to be having a quarrel.' She went to a chair at the table and sat facing Gran. 'I've got a terrible feeling he's got himself mixed up in the black market.'

Gran slumped back in her chair. 'Oh Christ!' she growled. 'How d'you know?'

'Of course I can't be absolutely sure,' continued Harriet. 'I mean, what can I do if he won't even talk to me about it? In the old days, we used to share each other's problems, we used to confide in each other. But now – I sometimes think we're strangers. That's why I'll be glad to get this wedding over with once and for all. It's Frank's obsession. He once said to me that it was his dream to give Lizzie a good send-off.' She looked at Gran. Her face was drained with foreboding. 'But unless I'm very much mistaken, the way things are going, he's going to end up in prison.'

Lizzie and Rob sat very self-consciously side by side. Opposite them behind a desk was a burly-looking man, whose Australian accent was so

354

thick Lizzie had to concentrate very hard to understand him.

'Well, at least your medicals are fine,' said the man, who had told them his name was Mike Curtis. 'Glad to see you got rid of the chickenpox a long time ago,' he quipped to Lizzie.

Lizzie exchanged a nervous smile with Rob.

'However,' continued Mike Curtis, 'that's only the start of the process. Before we go any further, we've got a lot of things to talk over with you.' He looked down to Lizzie and Rob's application forms in front of him. 'The first thing I'd like to know is, what made you decide you want to go and live in Australia?'

Before they had been called into the room, Rob had told Lizzie to say as little as possible, and to leave him to do all the talking. 'Much the same as everyone else, I suppose,' he replied. 'We saw your ad in the newspaper, and went along to one of your film shows.'

'That's not quite what I meant,' said Curtis. 'I want to know why you want to give up your homes here in Britain, to start a new life so far away.'

Rob shrugged. 'We're fed up.'

'Is that all?'

'Isn't that enough?' asked Rob.

'Not really,' said Curtis, whose muscular build suggested that he had once been quite an athlete. 'I reckon the reason people want to leave everything they've ever known should be because they have at least some kind of a vision of what their future should be.' He took off his horn-rimmed spectacles, and leaned back in his chair.

'What sort of place d'you think Australia is, Rob?'

Rob was a bit surprised to be called by his Christian name. 'A place where we can be encouraged to work hard, and reap the rewards,' he replied, without hesitation.

Curtis smiled. 'Good thought,' he replied. 'Bit different from here then, you reckon?'

'Without a doubt,' replied Rob.

Curtis turned to Lizzie. 'And what about you, little lady? What sort of a life would *you* expect to find out there?'

Lizzie had to think for a moment, but eventually she summoned up enough courage to reply, 'I'd hope to find somewhere where I could bring up my kids, and know that they'd have far better prospects than Rob and I have ever had.'

'Is that a fact?' said Curtis. 'Yes.' He leaned forward and put on his spectacles again. 'Prospects are very important, aren't they? Mind you,' he referred to their application forms, 'to have prospects, you have to have some kind of a qualification – wouldn't you say?'

Lizzie shrugged.

'Not much sign of that here, I'm afraid.'

Lizzie exchanged a quick, worried glance with Rob.

'I see you work in Woolworths, Lizzie,' continued Curtis.

'Yes.'

'Not much skill involved there?'

'Somebody has to do it.'

Curtis took a sly look over the top of his spectacles, and grinned. 'Absolutely,' he replied.

'And how about you, Rob? Any qualifications?'

Rob shifted about nervously on his chair. 'I was in the army for the last two years of the war. Royal Engineers. I'm a qualified mechanic.'

'And what have you been doing since you were demobbed?'

'Trying to find a decent job.'

'And if you could find a decent job,' asked Curtis relentlessly, 'what would that job be?'

Rob hesitated. 'I don't really know,' he answered falteringly. 'I'm open to suggestions.'

Curtis took off his spectacles, scratched his head, and leaned back in his chair again. 'I see,' he said blandly. 'So what do you know about Australia?' he asked Lizzie, after a respectable pause.

'Only what I've seen in your film,' replied Lizzie, 'and in magazines.'

'If I was to ask you what state Sydney is in,' asked Curtis, 'would you be able to tell me?'

Lizzie resisted the temptation to sneak a look at Rob. Her heart was beating far too fast for that. 'No,' she replied. 'I'm sorry.'

'How about – Adelaide? Or Brisbane.'

Lizzie, now convinced that she had ruined their chances, shook her head.

'That's a pity,' said Curtis, flicking through some pamphlets on his desk. 'They're all very interesting places. Especially Brisbane. It's on the Gold Coast – on the eastern coast of Australia. I know a great little town not far from there called Toowoomba. Ever heard of it?'

Lizzie exchanged a baffled look with Rob. 'I'm afraid not,' she replied.

'That's a pity,' said Curtis. 'In my opinion, it's a place that's got a lot going for it. How about you, Rob?' Curtis asked.

'Too – what?'

'Toowoomba,' Curtis repeated. 'I only mention it, because it's a thriving community. There are quite a few work opportunities for young people up there. Depends, of course, on what you want to do. But if you don't have any real ideas...'

'I have *plenty* of ideas,' Rob said instantly. 'All I need is the chance to put them into practice. It doesn't have to be engineering. I can do anything I set my heart on. I'm willing to learn. I'm willing to learn *anything!*'

'Good on yer, Rob!' said Curtis, giving him a thumb-up sign with one hand. 'That's the spirit!' He was not unaware of the desperation in Rob's reply. 'Only thing is, how do I know you and Lizzie here could settle down to such a completely new environment, where people talk differently, where culture may not always measure up to what you've been used to in the old country, and where some folk may not take too kindly to newcomers?'

Curtis was raising all the doubts Lizzie had always had in her own mind. After all, she asked herself, what *did* she know about Australia, and the people who lived there? It was true that at school she had read about the English convicts who had been taken to penal settlements there in the early part of the nineteenth century, and that they were regarded as blackguards and scoundrels by their captors, and used to help fight endless conflicts with the indigenous Aborigine tribes. But these days, there were immigrants from countries from all around the world, people with vastly different cultures and languages. So how would she and Rob cope with *them?*

'I've never found it difficult to make friends with new people,' said Lizzie. 'All I can do is to try.'

'All I can do is to try.' It was a simple, direct answer, but one that quietly impressed Curtis. For the next moment or so, he sorted through Lizzie and Rob's application forms, giving them immense thought, trying to work out in his mind if these were really two young people who deserved that special lift up in life, that would give them the confidence to start afresh in a new country.

Lizzie and Rob sat there helpless, watching his every movement, listening to his weary sighs, taking sly glances at each other, their minds racing between hope and uncertainty. But where Lizzie had already convinced herself that their ignorance and naïvety was about to cost them dearly, Rob was determined not to give up. Undeterred, he reached out for Lizzie's hand, and gave it a reassuring squeeze. But he quickly pulled it away the moment Curtis looked up at them.

'Tell you what,' said Curtis, taking off his spectacles yet again. 'Rob, you're interested in engineering – right?'

'Absolutely!' replied Rob enthusiastically.

'OK then,' continued Curtis. 'If I was to give you a list of potential industries – employers, that sort of thing – would you be prepared to sort through them, and pick out those you think might offer you the kind of job you're looking for?'

'Would I!' replied Rob.

'And what about you, Lizzie? Would *you* be looking for some kind of a job over there too?'

Lizzie looked surprised. 'Of course I would,' she replied firmly. 'I don't intend to sit around being a housewife all day.'

'Not until we have kids,' Rob reminded her.

Lizzie was embarrassed.

Curtis smiled. 'Well, I reckon there are plenty of things you could turn your hand to, Lizzie,' he said. 'I think we could find something better than Woolworths for you.'

At this Lizzie bristled. 'I'm not ashamed of working in Woolworths,' she said indignantly.

Again Curtis smiled. 'Good for you,' he replied. 'OK then!' He got up from his seat. 'Just one more question. If we *were* to offer you the passage out to Sydney, are you in a position to raise the ten pounds each?'

'I already have it in my Post Office Savings,' replied Rob immediately.

'Good,' said Curtis. 'That's a good start.' He held out his hand. 'We'll be in touch.'

Lizzie and Rob sprang up from their chairs, both puzzled at the sudden termination of their interview.

'Does that mean–' said Rob, shaking hands with Curtis.

'It doesn't mean anything, old son,' replied Curtis. 'It just means – when we've had a chance to consider your application we'll be in touch with you.' He now offered his hand to Lizzie. 'G'day, Lizzie.'

360

Lizzie took his hand, and shook it. 'Thank you, Mr Curtis.'

As they left the interview room, Lizzie and Rob were met by a sea of anxious, hopeful faces in the waiting room outside. Although no one said a word, it was clear that they all wanted to know what it had been like inside, and how these latest two applicants had got on. But even if they had wanted to, Lizzie and Rob couldn't have told them, for they had absolutely no idea.

Frank Angel got home just before dark. He found that everyone was out, and he had the place to himself, which he was very grateful for in his present mood. The first thing he did was to build up the fire, make himself a cup of tea, then settle down in his armchair with his cigarettes. He leaned his head back, and pondered over all that had happened that day. It had been a terrible day. What with the shock of hearing that Dodger had left Billingsgate Market several days before and hadn't been seen since, and then his meeting with his foreman, Bert Spinks, to see if he could work some overtime to try to make a little extra cash before the wedding – it was all too much. But the worst part had been his visit to the doctor, who told him that the pains he was now getting regularly in his stomach were quite likely to be ulcers, caused by stress, and a condition he could not afford to ignore. Frank, though, had every intention of ignoring it – at least, until the wedding was over.

But first he had to lay his hands on some money that would see him through. Unfortunately he had never had enough money to open a Post Office Savings account, and so there was nothing there to pursue, but it had been on his mind to try his hand at betting on the greyhounds – except even that idea seemed quite pointless, for he had never bet on anything in his entire life. No. As much as he detested the thought, his only course now was to go to a moneylender. After all, he could take out a loan, and pay it back in instalments, even though he had no doubt it would cost him a bit in interest. But who cared? As long as he could meet the bills for Lizzie's wedding, nothing else mattered. But then he remembered that to take out a loan he would need some kind of collateral, and that was something he didn't have, and the way he was going, he would *never* have. But he had to think of something. Time was catching up on him.

Behind him, the front door opened and closed. 'Frank?' It was Harriet. 'You're home early. Is anything wrong?'

'No,' said Frank, leaning up to give her a kiss on the cheek. 'We finished clearing the last supply just after four. There wasn't much doing after that. There's some tea in the pot if you want a cup. I've only just made it.'

'No, thanks,' she said, taking off her hat, and putting it down on the table. 'I've just had one with Mother.' She then took off her coat, left it over the back of a chair, and joined Frank, sitting in an armchair opposite him. 'Did you know Lizzie and Rob went for an interview this afternoon?' she said.

Frank looked up from his tea. 'The High Commission?'

Harriet nodded her head without replying.

'How did they get on?'

'I've no idea,' replied Harriet, picking up the poker in the hearth, and digging some life into the fire. 'They were going back to the Thompsons' place to tell them first.'

'Oh I see,' said Frank, without further comment.

For several minutes, they sat in silence, both of them just staring into the glowing embers, deep in their own thoughts. 'At least once she's gone, there'll be more room for the others,' said Harriet.

'What d'you mean?' asked Frank, who hadn't really been listening.

'Lizzie,' said Harriet. 'After she's gone to Australia, there'll only be the two girls and two boys sharing the bedroom.'

'Oh,' said Frank, at last taking it in. 'That's good.'

'Good that they'll have more room,' asked Harriet, 'or good that Lizzie's going?'

Frank looked up at her with a start. 'That's a pretty stupid thing to say, Harriet,' he said sharply. 'You know as well as I do, I shall miss Lizzie like hell.'

'Then why have you encouraged her over this emigration thing?'

'I haven't encouraged her.'

'Of course you have!' insisted Harriet. 'You've always told her that she has a better chance of prospects out there than she'll ever have here.'

'Well, it's true, isn't it?' asked Frank.

'I fail to see it,' replied Harriet. 'That's the trouble with everyone these days. They're all so impatient. They can't see any light at the end of the tunnel.'

'Well – can you?'

Harriet thought for a moment. 'Not at the moment,' she said. 'But it'll come – sooner or later.'

'It'll be too late for some people.'

Harriet looked at him with a start. 'What d'you mean?' Realising he had sounded more gloomy than he intended, Frank tried to make light of it. 'They won't have any more clothes to change,' he replied.

Harriet dismissed his silly joke with a sigh. The small companion clock on the mantelpiece sounded the hour. 'As a matter of fact,' she said, 'I think it's very selfish of her to go off and leave her family like this.'

'Who?' asked Frank, who again hadn't really taken in what she had said.

'Lizzie!' said Harriet, irritated with him. 'She's changed so much since she met Rob.'

'I don't think that's true,' replied Frank firmly. 'Rob has been very good for Lizzie. I think they'll be good for each other.'

Harriet didn't like this. 'Don't you care that she's just decided to up and leave,' she asked, turning on him, 'without even discussing it with her own father and mother?'

'She *has* discussed it with us.'

'She may have discussed it with you,' snapped Harriet, 'but she certainly hasn't discussed it with me.'

'That's because you never give her the chance. Because you're always so angry with her.'

'That's not true!' insisted Harriet, springing to her feet. 'All I've ever told her is that she's still our daughter, and after all we've done for her the least she can do is to let us know what she's doing with her life.'

'Don't be ridiculous, Harriet!' said Frank, getting back at her. 'We didn't even give the poor girl a decent twenty-first birthday.'

'Whose fault was that?' she countered. 'If you had a decent job, we could have done something. We could do a lot more for *all* our kids!' Suddenly realising what she had said, Harriet stopped dead. 'Oh God, Frank,' she said, crushed with guilt, 'that was an absurd thing to say. I'm sorry. I'm so sorry.'

To her surprise, Frank wasn't angry with her. As she came across to him and kissed him on the cheek, he merely looked up at her and said, 'I know, Harriet, my dear. I know, my darling.'

'I'll go and see about supper,' said Harriet, close to tears. She left him, and made for the kitchen. But on the way, she stopped, and picked up something from the table. 'Did you see this, Frank?' she asked, returning to him briefly, holding a registered letter. 'This came for you this morning.'

Frank took the registered envelope from her. 'Who's it from?' he asked.

'No idea,' said Harriet, leaving him. 'I don't recognise the name.'

As she disappeared into the kitchen, Frank

turned the envelope over, and looked at the name and address of the sender on the back. 'Atkins?' he said to himself, puzzled. The address was also unfamiliar. Curious, he ripped open the envelope. But when he looked inside, he was surprised to find a wad of banknotes there. Hands shaking, he took the money out, and also the brief letter enclosed with it. There was no name, no address, only the words: 'Sometimes dreams *can* come true. Even for an Angel.' He quickly counted out ten five-pound notes. The shock was so immense, he slumped back into his chair, and closed his eyes. The only thing he could see in his mind's eye was Lizzie, Lizzie in her pure white wedding dress and veil. And then he looked down at the letter again and reread the few words that were scrawled there: 'Sometimes dreams *can* come true. Even for an Angel.' He returned the letter and money to the envelope, and sat there clutching it in his hand. He leaned back in his chair again, close to tears.

He was still reeling from the thought that there was, after all, honour amongst thieves – *and* shoplifters.

Chapter 19

'Duckie!' Norman was genuinely pleased to see Rob again. It had been several weeks now since Norman had been beaten up outside the front door of his house, and after a few days in hospital, and some convalescing at home, he was only too thrilled to be back working again at his picture-frame stall in Petticoat Lane. Although he still had a scar on one cheek, he had done his best to disguise it with a little face powder, and what with a brand-new green beret, he was clearly back on form again. 'I gather the sound of wedding bells is fairly imminent?' he chimed excitedly, poking his finger into Rob's chest. 'Don't tell me that that lovely little gel of yours hasn't seen through you yet?'

Rob chuckled. 'Luckiest little girl in the world!' he quipped. 'Can't do without me!'

Norman pulled a face. 'I've got news for you, duckie!' he said, but not really meaning it. 'So when is it?'

'Next Saturday,' replied Rob.

'Next Saturday!' gasped Norman. 'So soon? Why didn't you tell me?'

'I'm telling you now,' said Rob. 'Don't worry. You're invited.' Norman clasped his hands together in ecstasy. 'Bliss!' he exclaimed. 'But where are you going to live?'

'Well,' said Rob, 'once she's got rid of her tenants, Liz's gran is letting us have a room in her place – till we know about Australia.'

'Australia?' cried Norman, eyes bulging out of their sockets with surprise. 'You mean – it's all happening then? You've talked Liz into emigrating?'

'I've talked her into it,' said Rob, 'but there's no certainty they're going to let us in.'

'What d'you mean?' asked Norman.

'We went along and had an interview at the

367

High Commission,' replied Rob gloomily. 'But I don't think much of our chances. The bloke there didn't seem to like us very much.'

'How d'you know that?'

'Oh, I don't know really,' said Rob. 'It's just the way he asked the questions – as though he thought we were a couple of frauds or something. Anyway, he said he'd let us know.'

Norman scratched his chin. 'When was this interview?'

'Just over a week ago.'

'Well, for God's sake, duckie, it's early days yet.'

'Maybe,' said Rob, unconvinced. 'Anyway, we've got plenty of things on our plate with the wedding coming up. Charlie's given me the rest of the week off. I'm spending most of my time round Liz's place, sorting out the arrangements.'

'How exciting!' said Norman deliriously, clasping his hands together in ecstasy again. 'Well, by the looks of things, you won't be missing much. There's not much going on around here.'

They both turned to look around the market. There was only a sprinkling of customers ambling up and down the stalls, and those that were there seemed more interested in looking than buying.

'So life isn't all that bad after all, is it, duckie?' Norman asked, lighting up one of his roller fags. 'I mean, once you get your papers to go to Kangarooland, you'll be laughing.'

'It'll be some time before I start laughing, Norman,' said Rob. 'But at least now that Liz's dad has managed to cough up some cash, things seem a lot happier at home for her. Apart from Liz's wedding dress, he's paying for everything. He even took us out over the weekend and bought us a teaset for our wedding present.'

'Wonderful!' exclaimed Norman. 'But I thought you said the poor man was terribly hard up? Where's all the money come from?'

'He says it was some kind of a bonus pay-out at Billingsgate where he works,' said Rob, not too convincingly. 'Something to do with working right through Sundays and Bank Holidays during the cold weather. Whether it's true or not, I've no idea. But it's certainly cheered him up.'

'What about Liz?' asked Norman. 'She must be over the moon about it all.'

Rob hesitated. 'Up to a point,' he said.

'What d'you mean?'

'Oh, I don't know,' said Rob. 'I suppose she's just got a suspicious mind, that's all. Anyway, Norman, I want to thank you for talking to Liz the way you did. You sure have the gift of the gab. It helped a hell of a lot.'

'A pleasure, duckie,' purred Norman. 'A pleasure! As a matter of fact, I loved talking to the two of you. I don't get the chance to talk to many people these days, especially around here – except old Mother Wiggs, of course, back home. She sometimes comes up for a G and T. We have a good old chinwag. But you two – *you're* so young, and I'm such an old crock!'

'Rubbish!' said Rob. 'Just look at you. You're still a spring chicken!'

'Well, I certainly don't feel it!' said Norman, casually setting out some picture frames while he talked. 'Still, what difference does it make now? I shan't be round this place much longer.'

Rob took a close look at him. 'What d'you mean?' he asked.

'Just that I have no intention of staying where I'm not welcome,' he said. 'Anyway, I don't mind really. I've been working this stall for long enough. It's time I moved on. Actually, if I had a little bit of money, I'd quite like to have a shop of my own. It'd be nice to have a more upmarket clientele.'

'Hang on a minute, Norman,' said Rob, quite concerned about what his friend was telling him. 'Are you telling me that you're being pushed out of the market?'

'Pushed?' asked Norman haughtily. 'Don't be silly, duckie! I'm just being shoved a little, that's all. But it doesn't matter – really it doesn't. After all, who cares what people say about you? It's how you *feel* that counts.'

Behind them, the market was beginning to come to life. As the weak Monday morning sun gradually broke through thick dark clouds, the whole place seemed to be transformed from a dull grey, to all the rich, vibrant colours of the rainbow. It was as though an artist had put his finishing touches to a vast living canvas, capturing in his mind the sights and sounds of a very special London scene that he knew and loved so well. And in the middle of it all, a strange, colourful character – bold, emblazoned with eccentric qualities of his own, but alone in a world that would always find it hard to accept him.

If anyone had been in Woolworths' staff canteen that Monday evening, they would have thought it was Potto that was getting married, not Lizzie, because she was so overcome by the occasion that every time she even looked at Lizzie she burst into tears.

The trouble was, the two shandies Potto had taken had gone straight to her head, so much so that when their shop supervisor, Betty Walker, arrived for the small farewell party the girls were throwing for Lizzie, Potto, for no reason at all, burst out crying even more, yelling, 'Oh, Lizzie! I'm going ter miss you so much!'

'Don't be silly, Potto,' whispered Lizzie, taking her to one side. 'I'm not leaving. I'm only getting married. I'll be back two weeks today.'

'No, yer won't!' insisted Potto, dabbing her eyes with the sleeve of her dress. 'Yer'll go off ter Australia an' forget all about us!'

'I doubt she'll do that, Edith,' said Betty Walker, who was actually quite a pretty woman, in her early forties, and very popular with the shop girls. 'If I know Lizzie, she's not the sort of person to go off and forget all about her friends. We're all too fond of her for that.'

Lizzie beamed.

'So, Lizzie,' asked Betty. 'Where are you off to for your honeymoon? Somewhere exotic, I hope?'

'Not really, Miss Walker,' chuckled Lizzie. 'Unless you call Great Yarmouth exotic?'

'Anywhere sounds pretty exotic to me,' replied Betty. 'I haven't been on holiday since before the war. When you live with an aged mother, it's not easy to get away.' She gave Lizzie a huge, affectionate smile. 'But I'm so pleased for you, Lizzie,' she said, with great warmth. 'Your young man is very lucky to have someone like you. Is it true, though, that you're both thinking of emigrating?'

'Oh no,' Lizzie said guardedly. 'Rob and I have been thinking about it for a while, but we haven't come to any firm decision yet.'

'Well, I wouldn't blame you if you did,' said Betty. 'If I had half a chance, I'd certainly go. I have a dear school friend who lives in South Africa. She's always telling me how wonderful it is down there. Mind you, the state this country is in, *anywhere* has to be better than this place.'

'I suppose so,' said Lizzie. But it hurt her to agree; it distressed her to think that so many people who stuck up for the country during the war were now dismissing it as a spent force. Despite agreeing to go to Australia with Rob, she still had an immense fondness and devotion for the land she was brought up in, and the friends who had meant so much to her over the years. Why had everything gone so terribly wrong? Why was it that no one could see an end in sight to shortages of everything? Why was everyone so depressed, so pessimistic? Was it really possible that the clouds of despondency would never disappear?

With the help of some of Lizzie's other workmates, Potto was finally calmed, and after a while, all the girls got together with her to talk excitedly about her wedding, what she was going to wear, and whether she and Rob were going to try for a baby straight away. Lizzie was a bit embarrassed by all this talk about babies, especially as it was provoking quite a lot of crude jokes from one or two of the girls. Fortunately, Maple was there to help her out.

'Can you spare me a moment, please, Lizzie?' she asked. 'I just want to tell you something.'

Lizzie excused herself from Betty and the other girls, and went to join Maple briefly on the other side of the canteen. 'Why all the mystery?' she asked.

'I'm sorry, Lizzie,' said Maple, 'but I don't think I'm going to be able to come to the wedding on Saturday.'

'Oh Maple!' cried Lizzie despondently. 'Why not? What's the matter?'

'My stepfather,' said Maple. 'He's – forbidden me to come.'

'What?' growled Lizzie incredulously. 'You must be joking.'

Maple shook her head. 'I'm not,' she said. 'I only wish I were. He says you're a troublemaker, and that you're a bad influence on me.'

'Oh, I see,' said Lizzie, who immediately understood what was going through Desmond's mind. 'Well, I shouldn't worry about that if I was you,' she replied. 'I can assure you that I have absolutely no intention of letting your stepfather keep you away from my wedding. You're my friend, Maple. I *want* you there.'

'But there's nothing you can do to stop him, Lizzie,' said Maple, agitated. 'There's nothing anyone can do. He's so determined.'

'So am I!' Lizzie assured her forcefully. 'Tell me, what sort of job does this man do – that is, if he works at all? I mean, is he away from home during the day?'

'Most of the time – yes,' replied Maple. 'He's always told us that he works up in the city somewhere, but I know for a fact that he spends a lot of his time in Soho.'

'Soho?' asked Lizzie innocently. 'What's the attraction there?'

'I'll give you one guess,' replied Maple.

Lizzie sighed. 'But you say your mother knows about all this?' she asked.

'Oh yes,' said Maple. 'She's got used to it over the years.'

'How can a woman ever get used to a man who behaves like a monster?' asked Lizzie, contemptuously. 'A man who beats up her own daughter?'

'Mum gave up on love years ago,' said Maple. 'She's convinced that if she loses Desmond, she'll spend the rest of her life on her own.'

'But that's ridiculous!' insisted Lizzie. 'Your mother's a lovely-looking woman.'

Maple shook her head again. 'She'll never believe that.'

'Why not?'

'Because no one's ever told her so.'

Lizzie steeled herself. Although she had lots to do during this coming week, she was determined to achieve one thing more during her time off. 'Leave it to me, Maple,' she said. 'One way or another, I'm going to deal with this stepfather of yours. But there's something I *will* promise you. You're going to come to my wedding on Saturday

374

if I have to drag you there!'

Later that evening, Lizzie arrived home clutching her wedding present from her workmates at Woolworths, who had all contributed a couple of bob each towards it. There was great excitement at the prefab, as the family gathered round to see what it was, but when the gift was unwrapped to reveal a Kodak 'Brownie' box camera, Benjamin made a grab for it, convinced that it was something meant for him and not for his sister. It took a great deal of scolding from his dad to return the camera to Lizzie, and he only did so with great reluctance, but with a promise that, if he learned how to use it before the wedding, he would be allowed to take the first picture of Lizzie and Rob outside the church.

'What are you going to wear that's borrowed?' Susan asked suddenly.

Lizzie looked at her sister as if she was mad. 'What are you talking about?'

'Haven't you heard the saying?' she asked grandly. '"Something borrowed, something new." A bride always has to borrow something to wear underneath her wedding dress.'

'Go on, Sue!' mocked Benjamin, bursting into laughter. 'Why not lend her a pair of your knickers?'

Cissie joined in, throwing herself on the sofa in fits of laughter.

'That's not nice, Benjamin!' said Harriet, scolding him. 'You mustn't say things like that! It's extremely rude to talk about ladies' underwear like that. It's private.'

'Yes, it is!' growled Susan at him. 'But then you always were an ill-mannered little twerp!'

Benjamin rushed across and whacked his sister across her bottom with his hand. There followed a noisy brawl as Susan rushed after him, grabbed hold of him, and shook him.

'Stop that – both of you!' yelled Harriet. 'Frank! Say something to them!'

'Oi!' he barked. 'Susan! Benjamin! That's enough now!'

'Well, *he* started it!' insisted Susan.

'I didn't! I didn't!' yelled Benjamin.

'*I've* got something.'

The quiet voice calling from the table silenced them.

Everyone turned to look at James, who had been quietly writing an essay for his homework.

'What did you say, James?' asked Lizzie.

James looked up at her. 'I said, I've got something you can wear under your dress.'

Lizzie exchanged a puzzled look with both her mum and dad. 'What is it, James?' she asked.

'I'll go and get it for you.' He quietly got up, and went into the bedroom.

In the few moments that James was out of the room, Lizzie exchanged another questioning look with her parents. This was so typical of James, she thought, just doing his own thing, without any fuss, without any arguments. Always the quiet one of the family, he was showing that being an adolescent meant that he could do exactly what was not expected of him.

James returned and went straight to Lizzie. 'It's supposed to be something blue,' he said. 'I read it somewhere. I don't remember where.' He held it out for her to take.

Lizzie took it. It was a small, blue enamel badge pin, which he had been awarded when he played for his school football team at the age of ten. 'James!' she said, taken aback.

'You don't have to wear it if you don't want to,' he said, staring at the badge he had just handed over to Lizzie. 'But at least it's blue.'

Lizzie suddenly felt quite close to tears. 'Oh, James,' she said, 'I shall be very proud to wear it. Thank you so much!' She threw her arms around him, and hugged him.

'Yuck!' sniffed Benjamin contemptuously.

Both Frank and Harriet were also moved by James's spontaneous gesture. 'You know what,' said Frank. 'This family is getting too gloomy. You'd never think we were having a wedding round the place on Saturday. What say we have all have a bit of a good old Angel singsong?' He looked around the room. 'Any requests?'

'"Boiled Beef and Carrots"!' yelled Cissie, leaping up from the sofa at the very mention of a song.

'That's a good idea, Cissie!' agreed her father. 'What about it, Lizzie?'

Lizzie was absolutely thrilled by this sudden outburst of family togetherness. It was so like the good old days. 'Right!'

Instantly, the entire family burst into action, rushing in and out of the kitchen and bedrooms, fetching props they needed to bring to life the famous Harry Champion song Lizzie was about to perform. Frank brought his topcoat and scarf for Lizzie to put on, and also his trilby, which Lizzie immediately turned into a bowler. Then, whilst her brothers and sisters brought in pots and pans to use as musical instruments, Lizzie gave herself a black moustache by rubbing her top lip with soot from the grate. Meanwhile, even Harriet participated, hurriedly collecting Frank's mouth organ from the bedroom, and a tin whistle she had used for many a Sunday evening family entertainment.

Within moments the fun had begun, with Lizzie belting out the words of the song in a gravel voice, stamping her foot in time to the music, accompanied by drums utilised out of kitchen saucepans, Frank's mouth organ, Harriet's tin whistle, clapping in time from James and Susan, and an attempt at Harry Champion-style foot thumping from both Benjamin and Cissie. It was an absolute riot of shouting and singing and laughter such as the family hadn't experienced for quite a time. And when 'Boiled Beef and Carrots' came to an end, it was followed by another of the Champion songs, 'Any Old Iron'.

The impulsive family get-together came to an end with everybody collapsing in hysterical laughter on to the sofa, chairs and floor.

'God knows what the neighbours think,' called Harriet breathlessly, above the rumpus. Even as she spoke, there was a sharp banging on the front door.

The laughter came to an abrupt end.

'My God!' gasped Lizzie. 'You're right, Mum!'

'It's all right,' said Harriet, quickly adjusting

her hair and calming herself. 'Leave it to me.'

She took a deep breath, and went to the door. When she opened it, she found a police sergeant and a police constable standing there.

'Good evening, madam,' said the rather stern-faced sergeant. 'Is Mr Angel at home? Mr Frank Angel?'

Harriet's face, which only a moment before had been blood red from laughter, suddenly turned ashen white. She said nothing, merely opened the door wider, and turned back to look at Frank.

Frank took a moment to register what was happening, his face also suddenly pale and drawn with shock. Then, after a quick look back at Lizzie, he went to the door. '*I'm* Frank Angel,' he said.

'We'd like a few words with you, please, sir,' said the sergeant.

'Come in, please,' said Frank.

The sergeant took a quick look around at the staring, anxious faces of Harriet and her family. 'Down at the station, if you don't mind, sir.' He flicked a quick look at Harriet. 'Shouldn't take more than a few minutes.'

Frank hesitated. 'I'll get my coat,' he said. He went to Lizzie, and gave her a look which appealed to her for her understanding.

Lizzie was in a state of shock and distress. She took off his topcoat and trilby, and gave it to him.

Frank put on his coat, punched out his trilby into its proper shape, then put that on too. Then he turned to Harriet. 'Won't be long, dear,' he said.

There were tears in Harriet's eyes, as he stopped briefly to kiss her on the cheek.

As Frank left the prefab, accompanied by the two police officers, everyone rushed to the door to see him go. There was a sense of fear and desperation amongst them all, as they watched their husband and father get into the police car waiting outside, and drive off.

Once the car had gone, Lizzie strolled out to the garden gate, and just stood there. After those few brief moments of sublime happiness, quite suddenly, her forthcoming wedding seemed to be the most unimportant thing in her life.

It was almost midnight, but Frank had not yet returned from the police station. Susan and the kids had gone to bed more than an hour before, leaving Lizzie and Harriet alone in front of the fire. For Lizzie, the clock ticking on the mantelpiece was proof that her dad was in real trouble. He had been gone now for over three hours, and the wait was interminable. Lizzie felt stricken with guilt, convinced that if it hadn't been for her getting married, her dad would not have got himself into so much trouble. But how serious is it? she asked herself over and over again. If her suspicions were now confirmed, that her dad had been involved in the black market, what exactly had he done, and just *how* involved was he? She felt awful, drained of any hope whatsoever. In her heart of hearts, she had known for some time how desperate her dad had been to get his hands on some money to pay for the wedding, but not in her worst nightmare had she ever imagined how foolish he would be.

Harriet's eyes were red raw from crying. Lizzie had tried several times to make her a cup of tea, but each time she let it get cold, and Lizzie had to make a fresh one. Harriet blamed herself for what had happened. She had closed her eyes to what Frank had been doing, knowing only too well how his mind had been disturbed ever since he was demobbed, and had been unable to get a decent job.

'It's a cruel thing for a man,' she said, staring down aimlessly at her hands clasped on her lap. 'Take away his dignity and he'll go to endless lengths to prove himself. I should have known. I should have stopped him.'

Lizzie leaned across from her own chair, and tried to comfort her. 'You mustn't blame yourself, Mum,' she said. 'You're not to blame. None of us is to blame. Dad knew what he was doing. He took the chance.'

'Yes,' said Harriet, suddenly looking up at her. 'But he took the chance for *you*. There was no need to have a grand wedding with all the trimmings. You could have stopped him. You could have told him that it was more important to pull himself together than to go putting his entire family at risk.'

'Putting the family at risk?' asked Lizzie, totally nonplussed.

'If your father goes to prison,' said Harriet, 'where d'you think that leaves us? How d'you think we're going to live down the shame, the humiliation of it all?'

For one brief moment, Lizzie hated her

mother. To talk about shaming the family instead of worrying about what might become of her dad himself made her feel sick in her stomach. But, as she had done so often with her mother lately, she just tried to blame her behaviour on the strain she had been under.

'Mum,' she said, 'I think we may be jumping to conclusions. We don't even know if or what Dad has actually done, so why d'you have to keep talking about him going to prison? I mean, I'm pretty sure that any moment now, he's going to walk in through that door, and tell us that the police had made a terrible mistake.'

'If you believe that,' said Harriet, glaring scornfully at her, 'then you're a fool! It's all right for you. It won't be long before you're away from it all, off with your husband to Australia, away from all the trials and tribulations of living from hand to mouth every day of the week, every week of the year.'

Lizzie sat back in her chair. She was deeply offended and hurt. 'That's not fair, Mum,' she said with calm dignity. 'If you don't know me by now, you never will. I would never leave you and Dad and all the family if I knew you were in trouble. And, in any case, it's more than likely that we'll never get permission to emigrate to Australia. There are far too many hurdles in the way.'

They sat in silence, neither uttering a word to each other, the clock ticking away relentlessly on the mantelpiece. Eventually, however, it was Harriet who spoke. 'I suppose you realise this could kill your father?'

Lizzie looked up. 'What d'you mean?' she asked.

'He's not a well man,' replied Harriet. 'In fact, he's very ill.'

Lizzie was shocked. 'Ill?'

'He went to see the doctor the other day,' said Harriet. 'He thinks I don't know, but I do. Martha Cutting was in Dr Martin's surgery when Frank came out. She told me.'

'Mum,' retorted Lizzie, 'Martha Cutting's a nosy old busybody – everyone knows that. And, in any case, what would *she* know about it anyway? Did Dad tell her anything?'

'He didn't have to,' insisted Harriet. 'You only have to look at the man. I've never seen him look so gaunt and strained. If anything were to happen to him, I don't know what I'd do.'

'Don't you think you're jumping to conclusions, Mum?' said Lizzie. 'I'm just as concerned about Dad as you are, but if he's got himself into trouble and made himself ill, you can hardly blame me.'

Harriet looked up at her. 'Then who *should* we blame, Lizzie?' she asked bitterly.

Lizzie was so incensed by her mother's remark, that she got up from her chair, and made her way to the bedroom. Just as she was doing so, however, she heard the key being inserted into the front door lock. She rushed across to open it just as Frank was coming in.

'Dad!' she gasped, hugging him. 'What happened? What's been going on?'

'What's all the fuss?' he asked, calm and without any emotion. Then he saw Harriet getting up from her chair. 'There's nothing wrong. It's exactly what I thought. They wanted someone for an identity parade – not just me, but plenty of men my height and type. Apparently, they've been picking up men at random from the street all day. It was nothing. I went into this parade, and someone – I don't know who it was – well, he just wasn't able to pick out anyone.'

'Oh, Dad!' gasped Lizzie with relief. 'Thank God for that!'

'Is this true?' asked Harriet, as she came across to him. 'They didn't want to question you?'

'Not at all.'

'But when they came to the front door, they said they wanted a few words with you.'

'And so they did,' said Frank, completely unruffled. 'They asked me where I was between two and four yesterday morning. I told them I was in bed with my wife. I *was* – wasn't I, Harriet?'

Harriet was still reeling from Frank's explanation. 'And it's taken all this time for them to ask you just that?' she asked.

'Yes, Harriet,' Frank said unflinching. 'All this time.'

Harriet was so relieved, the only thing she could do was to go to him, and hug him. 'Let's get to bed, Frank,' she said.

'I'll be there in just a moment, dear,' he replied.

Harriet left them, and went off to their bedroom.

Frank went to his armchair, and sat down in front of the fire.

Lizzie followed, and stood in front of him. After

a tense pause, she asked, 'Is it serious?'

Frank waited a moment before looking up at her and answering. 'Yes,' he said, nodding.

A few moments later, Frank went to bed, leaving Lizzie alone in the room to lock up and turn off the lights. Although her own bedroom was in darkness, she could hear the snores of Benjamin and Cissie, James's soft breathing, but no sound coming from Susan. She undressed, and quietly climbed into her own bed. For a few moments, she lay there trying to imagine what the next day or the day after that was going to bring.

'What's going to happen to him?'

Although Susan's soft voice took Lizzie by surprise, she had almost expected it. 'I don't know, Susan,' she whispered, with a sigh. 'I just don't know.'

Chapter 20

Gran Perkins was furious with her former tenants. Not only had the young married couple left their bedsitting room upstairs filthy dirty, but they had also done a moonlight flit without paying the two months' rent they owed her.

'I'm not surprised,' she told Lizzie, when she and Rob turned up to clean the place out before they started moving in some of their own things before the wedding. 'I should never have taken them on in the first place. They've been a pain in the neck since the day they arrived.'

Gran's room was a godsend for Lizzie and Rob. Since the end of the war, there had been so little accommodation around, they would have had a terrible time trying to find somewhere to live after they were married. Fortunately, Gran had been nagging her former tenants constantly over the past few weeks, and now, all that was needed before Lizzie and Rob moved in was for them to scrub the floors, wash the paintwork, crockery and kitchen utensils, and clean the year-long culmination of grime from the windows. But it was a pleasant enough room, on the top floor of the house, with quite a nice view of Tollington Park down below, which, during the summer months was an explosion of elm, chestnut, and silver birch trees. At the moment, the room was quite chilly, for since the former occupants had moved out, Gran had kept the window open from early morning to dusk each day to ventilate the place, and air the mattress on the big iron bedstead.

The only problem for Rob was that they had to share the bathroom with Gran, and as it was on the ground floor, it was quite chilly having to creep down the stairs in the dark, and in the freezing cold. For Lizzie, however, the prospect of having the space to move about in the privacy of a bedroom that she would only share with Rob was a luxury she had not enjoyed since the Angel family had been bombed out of their own former house.

With only four days to go to the wedding, Lizzie and Rob lost no time embarking on spring-cleaning the room, and by lunch time that day they at least had it spick and span. Even so, Rob was still only referring to the place as somewhere temporary to stay until their emigration papers had been approved by the Australian High Commission.

Lizzie, however, was still unconvinced. Despite the fact that it had been such a short time since they had gone through their interview with the evasive Mike Curtis, she had seen their prospects of a new life in Australia gradually fading into a wishful dream. But in some ways she was relieved that they would not be leaving the country, at least for the time being. The dark cloud hanging over her father had devastated her, and it was even more of a strain trying to keep the truth from her mother.

'But they haven't actually charged him with anything, have they?' asked Rob, as he and Lizzie took a break from cleaning, by perching on the edge of the bed.

'Not yet,' replied Lizzie gloomily. 'But the way Dad was talking this morning, it's only a matter of time. He says there's a possibility the police may come and search the prefab, and if he doesn't consent, they'll get a search warrant.'

For the first time, Rob looked worried. 'But what are they accusing him of?'

'Well, they're not actually accusing him of anything at the moment,' said Lizzie. 'They're just asking him lots of questions about if he's ever dealt in stolen goods, and if he knows any of the people on the lists they've shown him.'

'And does he?'

Lizzie sighed, and shook her head. 'I don't know, Rob,' she replied. 'I don't know half of what Dad has been up to these past few weeks. All I do know is that he's only got himself into trouble because of me, so whatever happens, I've got to support him and Mum as much as I can.'

'I know, Liz,' Rob said, putting a comforting arm around her waist. 'But don't worry, I'm with you all the way. You know that, don't you?'

Lizzie turned and smiled at him, and responded to his gentle kiss. 'Rob,' she said softly, 'I want you to do me a favour. It's to do with my friend Maple. You know, the girl I told you about at work?'

A bit surprised by her sudden sense of urgency, he pulled away from her. 'Yes,' he replied. 'What about her?'

'She's having trouble at home,' said Lizzie, 'and she needs my help. Her stepfather–'

'This bloke who's been beating her up?'

'Yes,' said Lizzie. 'Well, he's now trying to stop her coming to the wedding. He's told her that she's to keep away from me, that I'm a bad influence on her.'

'So you want me to go along there and pummel the life out of him – right?'

'No, Rob!' insisted Lizzie emphatically. 'That's the last thing I want you to do. But I do need you for protection. The real problem seems to be her mother. For all sorts of reasons, she seems to be scared of this creature. Either that or she just can't be bothered.'

'Not bothered when her own daughter's being

roughed up?'

'It's far more complicated than that,' said Lizzie. 'But I've got a plan that I think could help both Maple and her mother. Only thing is, I'm a bit nervous about doing it on my own. Will you help me?'

'What d'you want me to do?' asked Rob sceptically.

The sky above Camden Town was a crystal-clear blue. Not since the end of autumn the previous year had the sun shone uninterrupted, so much so that as Lizzie and Rob made their way to Maple's house in St Pancras Way, she could detect the first signs of a few smiles on people's faces. On the other hand, it may also have had something to do with the headlines on the newspaper billboards, which they noticed the moment they got off the bus in Camden Road: 'TORIES WIN CROYDON. MASSIVE TURN-OUT'. Rob was over the moon at the crushing defeat of Labour in the by-election, which had increased the Conservatives' former slender majority by more than eleven thousand votes. In his mind, this proved that the Government's popularity at the previous general election had been overturned by the total mismanagement of the country. But Lizzie challenged him vigorously on this, saying that it was probably only a blip and, in any case, even if the Conservatives were to be voted back into power at the next election, what proof was there that they could do any better than anyone else? After all, the war had cost the country a great deal, and it would take a long time to recover. Rob dismissed her argument, saying that if Churchill could win the war for them, then there was no need to doubt that he could win the peace. By the time they had reached Maple's house, he was just as convinced as ever that their only way forward was to emigrate, for it would be years before the country was going to have a chance to recover.

Maple's mother, Sally Gosling, seemed quite taken aback to see Lizzie and Rob standing on her doorstep. 'Mabel's at work,' she said nervously, looking from one to the other.

'It was you I wanted to see, Mrs Gosling,' said Lizzie, greeting her with a friendly smile. 'Could we come in for a few moments, please?'

Sally looked anxiously at Rob.

'Oh, I'm sorry,' said Lizzie. 'This is my fiancé, Rob Thompson. We're getting married on Saturday.'

Confused, and doing her utmost to be polite, Sally stood back to let them enter. Before she closed the door, however, she took a quick, nervous look down the road.

Lizzie and Rob followed her into the sitting room.

'I'm sorry it's not very tidy,' said Sally. 'I don't usually expect visitors during the week.'

'Do you have many visitors at all?' asked Lizzie, rather forwardly.

Sally shrugged. 'Sometimes,' she replied. She and Lizzie sat in armchairs facing each other, leaving Rob to find a chair, less conspicuously, near the door. 'What's this about?' Sally asked.

'Has Mabel done anything wrong?'

'Not at all, Mrs Gosling,' said Lizzie. 'Quite the reverse.'

'My name isn't Gosling,' said the woman. 'It used to be, when I was married to my first husband. It's now Desmond.'

'What a shame,' said Lizzie. 'I like Gosling much better. It has such a nice sound to it.'

Sally looked embarrassed. 'What is it you wanted, Lizzie, please?' she asked warily.

Lizzie perched on the edge of the chair. 'Mabel tells me that your husband has forbidden her to come to my wedding on Saturday. Can you tell me why?'

Sally immediately looked ill at ease. 'I – I really can't say,' she replied hesitantly. 'I'm afraid I don't know anything about it.'

'You mean, Mabel hasn't told you anything about it?'

Sally merely shrugged her shoulders awkwardly.

'Mrs Gosling,' said Lizzie, intense and businesslike, 'I want you to know that Mabel's my friend – one of my best friends. I'd be so upset if I thought she wasn't going to be there at my wedding on Saturday.' She paused just long enough to ask, 'Why is your husband doing this?'

Sally again shrugged her shoulders. 'I'm sorry,' she said, getting agitated, 'I'm afraid I don't know anything about all this. What goes on between my husband and my daughter is their business, not mine.'

Lizzie looked at her in astonishment. 'But

Mabel is *your* daughter, isn't she, Mrs Gosling? She's not a child any more. She shouldn't be denied friends of her own because your – *new* – husband doesn't approve.'

'Desmond has been very good to Mabel,' replied Sally, offended, and doing everything in her power not to make eye contact with Lizzie. 'He's done everything he can to take the place of her real father.'

Lizzie found it difficult to understand this woman. At first sight, she seemed a weak-willed person, with very little confidence to stand up to anyone. But as Lizzie looked at her large soulful eyes, and frizzy light brown hair, she was gradually coming round to the thought that Maple's mother was more determined than she appeared. But Lizzie was not prepared to leave it there, and after a quick look over her shoulder to Rob, she returned to the reason she had come there.

'Mrs Gosling,' she said, 'I'm very concerned about Mabel. As a matter of fact, everyone at Woolworths is concerned about her.'

Sally finally managed to sneak a wary look at Lizzie.

'We all want to know why she's been turning up at work so many times with her face battered and bruised.'

At the mention of a subject she was clearly desperate to avoid, Sally got up from her chair. 'This is not something I can discuss with you,' she said firmly but defensively. 'This is a domestic matter. It concerns no one else but us.'

'If our supervisor mentions it to the police,' said

Lizzie provocatively, also rising from her chair, 'it could concern them too.'

Sally took a deep, anxious breath. 'I think you should leave,' she replied sharply, turning away and making for the door.

'You can't turn your back on what's going on, Mrs Gosling,' insisted Lizzie, calling to her. 'No matter how fond you are of your husband, you have a greater responsibility towards Mabel. She *is* your daughter, Mrs Gosling. She needs your love and protection.'

Sally swung back to her. 'How dare you?' she snapped, eyes blazing. 'How dare you come here and preach to me about love and protection. How old are you, Lizzie? Have you lived long enough to know about human relationships? Have you lived long enough to know what it's like to bring up a child of your own single-handed, without a husband to watch his child grow up, a child without a father, who didn't care whether she lived or died? Well, that's how I've had to live *my* life, Lizzie, and I've had to do it in the best way I can.'

Lizzie listened in absolute astonishment. This was Maple's mother as she had not seen her before, with a voice of her own, and a determination to defend herself at all costs. But despite the woman's anger, Lizzie admired her much more.

'I'm not criticising you, Mrs Gosling,' she said. 'I know that things can't have been easy for you, and that you've done what you've had to do, but Maple – *your* Mabel – you can't allow her to be treated as though she's an intruder in her own

393

house. She's a special girl, Mrs Gosling. Give her the encouragement she needs, and you'll be very proud of her.'

For one moment, it seemed as though Sally had actually listened to what Lizzie had said. But remarks like that, coming from a girl less than half her own age, confused her. 'I love my daughter *and* my husband, Lizzie. Please leave me to deal with my own problems. Now I'd like you to go.'

Lizzie, still reeling from the woman's extraordinary outburst, watched her turn and make for the door. Rob, who had deliberately remained silent throughout, moved out of the way to let her pass. But just as Sally had reached the door, it suddenly opened, and Desmond came into the room.

'What's going on in here?' he said. He looked around and, without noticing Rob standing behind the door, immediately caught sight of Lizzie. 'I gave instructions you weren't to be allowed into this house again.'

'Oh, I'm sorry,' replied Lizzie. 'I had no idea *you* owned the house.'

Closely watched by Rob, Desmond went across to her. 'What do you want?' he asked angrily, glaring straight at her.

'I want to know what you're frightened of,' replied Lizzie, without showing the faintest sign of fear. 'I want to know why you use your fists on someone who can't fight back. I want to know why you're trying to stop my friend from coming to my wedding.'

There followed a tense silence, during which

394

Desmond never once shifted his glance from her. Finally he spoke, calmly, but with real menace. 'Get out!' he said.

Lizzie stood her ground.

'I'm warning you just once more,' said Desmond. 'Or else.'

'Or else – what?' came the voice from behind.

Desmond swung with a start to find Rob coming towards him.

'Or what?' repeated Rob.

Aware that he was no match for the muscular young man who was confronting him, Desmond threw an angry look at his wife, then swiftly left the room.

Sally waited for him to go, then opened the door for Lizzie and Rob to leave. They did so.

With the front door of the house closed behind them, Lizzie and Rob stepped back into the street outside. 'Well, I'm not sure what you achieved,' said Rob. 'That woman must be round the bend. I hate to have to tell you, Liz, but you made a great mistake coming up here.'

'I wonder,' Lizzie replied, slipping her arm through his. 'I just wonder.'

Slowly, they made their way back to the bus stop.

Later that day, Harriet went with Lizzie to collect her wedding dress from Jones Brothers department store in Holloway Road. Susan and Cissie went along too, for as Lizzie's bridesmaids, they too had to be fitted out for their dresses. These were also being paid for by their grandmother, who had managed to scrape together enough clothing coupons for the two of them from some of her late husband's relatives. Although Lizzie's wedding dress was only a very modest three-quarter-length Utility synthetic satin dress in pure white, once she had added the thin mesh veil, customers and staff couldn't help but stop to admire her as she looked up and down at herself in the full-length mirror.

Susan was also in good form, admiring her own Utility lilac-coloured dress in the mirror, and helping her mother and the shop assistant to adjust the hemline on little Cissie's dress.

Now that she had received assurance from Frank that he was not in any very serious trouble, Harriet had thrown herself into the wedding preparations with a little more enthusiasm than she had shown so far. But until she could be sure that Lizzie was telling the truth about not going off to Australia immediately with Rob, her relationship with Lizzie remained distant.

On the other hand, Lizzie was warming more and more towards Susan, who was beginning to show the most surprising concern and understanding with regard to the trouble she realised their father was in. This was even more evident whilst they were waiting for their dresses to be packed up ready to take home, which left Harriet free to take Cissie off for a quick stroll around the store. It was Susan's first chance to talk over with Lizzie what had happened the night before, and she clearly wanted to show that she was just as concerned about what was going to happen as her sister.

'So it wasn't true?' said Susan, as she and Lizzie

stared aimlessly out through the shop window to Tollington Road outside. 'Dad just made up all that stuff about an identity parade?'

Before answering, Lizzie took a quick look over her shoulder to make sure her mum was nowhere in sight. 'As far as I can tell,' she replied, 'the police spent most of the time trying to find out if he's been involved in selling illegal goods.'

'The black market?'

Lizzie sighed, and nodded.

'What's he been up to, Lizzie?' Susan asked straight out. 'Is this how he's managed to get his hands on money for the wedding?'

'He says not,' replied Lizzie. 'But then he doesn't actually deny it. The trouble is, they haven't finished with him yet. He says they're talking about coming to search the prefab.'

Susan gasped. 'Can they do that?' she asked.

'The police can do anything they want,' replied Lizzie. 'If they think they've got grounds to suspect that Dad's been hiding stuff at home, they can just apply for a search warrant.'

'Oh – how terrible!' said Susan, in utter despair. 'So what can we do about it? I mean, d'you think it's true? D'you think Dad *is* involved in – this black-market thing?'

'I think he was, Susan,' said Lizzie. 'But not any more.'

'What does that mean?'

'It means that he's pulling out of it all. Or at least, that's what he's trying to do.'

The store was quite full, and they had to stop talking every time customers browsed anywhere near them. In the distance, on the other side of the department, they could just see their mother with Cissie in tow, trying on hats.

'Will they charge him?' asked Susan, once the coast was clear again.

'It depends,' said Lizzie, turning to look at her sister. 'They will if they find anything.'

'What if they do? Will Dad go to prison?'

'I don't know, Susan,' replied Lizzie. 'The thing that worries me is how the police found out that Dad was involved in the first place.'

'D'you think it had anything to do with that woman he was talking to outside the prefab that afternoon?'

Lizzie turned with a start. 'You saw her too?'

'Through the bedroom window,' said Susan. 'They looked as though they were having a row.'

'Yes,' sighed Lizzie. 'It could have been something to do with her. I wouldn't trust a woman like that further than I could throw her. She must be ruthless. She can get innocent people into so much trouble.'

There was a moment of anxious silence between them, until Susan spoke. 'Oh, Lizzie,' she sighed, 'what are we going to do?'

Lizzie turned to look at her. 'There's nothing we *can* do,' she said. 'At least, not until after the wedding. But whatever happens, we've got to stand by him. What he's done is only being done all the time by others, hundreds – probably thousands – of people who are so fed up with trying to make ends meet. Sometimes I wonder who won the war – us or Hitler.'

Frank left work just before four in the afternoon.

As he had been given three days off to help the family with the wedding arrangements, he thought he would pop into the men's clothes shop near London Bridge, where they had a modest selection of ties that he could choose from to wear with the navy-blue two-piece suit he had been allocated when he was demobbed. He did eventually manage to pick out a silver-patterned one that caught his eye, and once he'd surrendered one clothing coupon and the one-shilling piece to pay for it, he left the shop and made his way to London Bridge underground station. However, soon after he had passed beneath the old railway bridge and entered the underground area beneath one of the tiled arches, he noticed someone in the darkened entrance making his way towards him.

''Allo, Frank, mate.'

Frank couldn't believe his eyes when he saw Dodger emerging from the dark. 'You!' he growled. 'Where the hell have you been?'

'Not far, mate,' said Dodger, constantly keeping an eye out for any unwelcome passers-by. 'Sorry to bail out on yer like that, but needs must. Anyway, I gather your little problem was taken care of? Sounds like yer got what was owin' to yer – right?'

'How do you know that?' asked Frank suspiciously.

'Before the Guv'nor an' is missus went,' explained Dodger, ''e told me 'e wouldn't let yer down.'

Frank suddenly grabbed hold of Dodger's collar, and pushed him into the shadows beneath the arch. 'Where've they gone?' he demanded. 'I went to the house. The woman next door told me they'd moved out.'

'Gone, mate,' said Dodger. 'Disappeared inter thin air.'

'I asked you, *where?*' Frank demanded again, tightening his grip on Dodger's collar.

'I don't know, Frank!' pleaded Dodger. 'I swear ter God I don't! By now they could be anywhere in the world. For all I know they're out in the wilds er Borneo or somefink!'

Frank reluctantly released him. 'And what happens to us in the meantime?' he asked angrily. 'Us, who have to stay behind to answer all the questions?'

'Say nuffin', Frank!' said Dodger, straightening himself up.

'What d'you mean – say nothing? I spent nearly three hours in Hornsey Road Police Station last night, being cross-examined by two detectives who know more about me than I know myself. They know, Dodger! Don't you understand – they *know!*'

'Yeah,' said Dodger. 'But 'ow much do they know? 'Ave they found anyfin' ter prove that yer've bin 'andlin' 'ot stuff? 'Ave they caught yer red-'anded out on a job?'

'No,' replied Frank, 'but they know damned well I've been mixed up with the Parfitts.'

For the first time, Dodger sounded concerned. ''Ow?' he asked warily. ''Ow der they know that?'

'Because they've been watching the Parfitts' house,' said Frank. 'They've been watching it for weeks. The Parfitts have been on their wanted list for months.'

'But it makes no diff'rence, ol' mate,' Dodger insisted. 'Proof. That's what they need – proof. Wivout it, they can't do nuffin'!'

Frank stood back and allowed him to come out of the shadows. 'So what happens now?' he asked. 'While our dear friends wine and dine on some sunny beach on the other side of the world, what happens to *us?*'

'Nuffin', Frank,' said Dodger calmly. 'Absolutely nuffin'. All yer 'ave ter do is ter keep yer mouf shut. That way, they can't do a damned fing about nuffin'! But don't worry. I'll be finkin' about yer, ol' mate.' He held out his hand for Frank to shake. 'So – be seein' yer!'

Frank hesitated, then reluctantly shook his hand. 'So what does this mean?' he asked acidly. 'Going off to join them in Borneo, are you?'

Dodger grinned. 'Nah, not me,' he replied. 'Far too 'ot fer me out there!' With his parting words, he disappeared into the hordes of commuters crowding down into the tube station.

Lizzie, Harriet, Susan and Cissie struggled home from Jones Brothers with the cardboard boxes containing the bride's and bridesmaids' dresses. The earlier crystal-blue sky had now given way to grey, late afternoon clouds, which, after a slow progress from the east coast, were now drifting in across the irregular rooftops from Finsbury Park. Lizzie carried the largest of the boxes, which contained her wedding dress, leaving Harriet and Susan to carry the bridesmaids' dresses, and Cissie proudly holding on to the carrier bag containing her mother's new hat. As they passed the front gates outside the Emmanuel Parish Church in lower Hornsey Road, Lizzie felt her stomach churn; all of a sudden the reality of what was about to happen to her in a few days' time was there, within the red brick walls of that same hallowed building in which she had been baptised more than twenty years before. Harriet also felt the memories stir, but she did her best to let them pass as quickly as possible, without so much as a glance up at the building, from where they could all hear the sound of the church organ being played to the tune of 'All Things Bright and Beautiful'.

Once they had crossed over Seven Sisters Road and reached the home straights, all of them were feeling pretty exhausted, and more so once the freezing cold drizzle started to flutter down on to their headscarves. With the prefab at last in sight, they had hoped that nothing would now impede their efforts to get home quickly for a cup of hot tea. But they were mistaken.

'Gettin' close now!' yelled a shrill voice from the other side of the road.

Martha Cutting was the last person any of them wanted to see at a time like this.

'Wot's it feel like to spend your last few days as a bachelor gel?' called Martha, as she hurriedly crossed the road to join them. 'From now on, it's slave labour all the way!'

Lizzie tried hard to smile politely, but it wasn't easy. 'I hope not, Mrs Cutting,' she replied wearily.

To their despair, their tiresome neighbour

walked on with them, nattering all the way, hardly pausing for breath.

'Well, we'll all be there with you on Saturday,' she said breathlessly. 'You won't 'ave ter worry about a good send off, 'cos we'll all be there outside yer prefab when yer leave. Wot a pity it couldn't've been from a decent 'ouse. I always say there's nothin' nicer than seeing a lovely young bride leaving the front door of a house in her wedding dress. Yer are gettin' married in white, I 'ope?'

'Yes, Martha,' said Harriet, irritated. 'Lizzie *is* getting married in white. What made you think otherwise?'

'Oh, I don't know,' replied Martha. 'So many of the young girls of today think it's modern ter get married in an everyday dress, but I don't think it's the same, do you? I mean, yer only get married once in yer life, don't yer?'

'Not *everyone*,' murmured Susan, struggling on behind.

'What was that, dear?' asked Martha, completely unaware that she was being got at.

Susan sighed. 'I said not everyone gets married once in their lifetime. I read about a woman in America who got married nine times.'

'Nine!' grunted Martha indignantly. 'I wouldn't ask *her* ter my place fer tea!'

'What makes you think she'd come?' muttered Susan softly.

'Wot was that, dear?' asked Martha.

'I was just saying – it makes you think.'

'It certainly does,' returned Martha, wiping the dewdrop from the end of her nose with her hanky. 'Still, never mind. It takes all sorts ter make a world, don't it? All I 'ope is that scum don't upset your wedding during the march.'

Lizzie came to a halt. 'March!' she exclaimed. 'What march?'

'Who d'yer fink?' returned Martha. 'Bleedin' trade unions again. They're all at it – busmen, dustbin workers, street cleaners, train drivers – the whole bleedin' lot. I 'eard even the clerks up the town 'all are comin' out. They're all 'avin' a go at poor ol' Attlee – they blame 'im an' Labour fer everyfin'!'

Lizzie exchanged a worried look with the others. 'You mean they're going to have a demonstration march down Hornsey Road on Saturday morning?' she asked.

As usual, Martha was thrilled to be the bearer of bad news. 'Right down 'Olloway *and* 'Ornsey Roads,' she said, eyes bulging with excitement. 'Right past your church. I know wot I'd like ter do with 'em all,' she grunted haughtily. 'I'd put 'em all up against a brick wall, and machine-gun the whole bleedin' lot of 'em!'

'That's a bit excessive, Mrs Cutting,' called Susan, from behind. 'Even for you.'

The tiresome neighbour had no chance to reply to Susan's snide remark, because just as they had reached the front gate of the prefab, they suddenly found Rob calling out from the doorstep.

'Liz!'

Lizzie and the others came to an abrupt halt. 'Rob!' she called. 'What are you doing here?'

He rushed up to them, waving something at her

in his hand. 'It's come!' he spluttered breath-lessly.

'What's come?' asked Lizzie, utterly bewil-dered. 'What's the matter?'

'There's nothing the matter, you lovely, wonderful, beautiful girl!' Despite the fact that Lizzie was struggling to hold on to the cardboard box containing her wedding dress, he managed to wrap his arms round her and give her a huge kiss and a hug. 'We're in!' he exclaimed triumph-antly.

'In?' asked Lizzie, thinking he had gone stark staring mad.

'Our application – to Australia,' explained Rob excitedly. 'We're in, Liz! We've done it!' He held up the envelope in his hand. 'They've approved our application – *both* of us! They want us to give them a call. We're on our way, Liz! We're on our way!'

Lizzie froze. She didn't know what to say, how to react. All she could do was to turn and look at her mother.

But Harriet was already on her way up the garden path, where she quickly disappeared without comment, inside the prefab.

Chapter 21

On Saturday morning, 'Maple' Gosling got up at about six o'clock. It was still dark outside, and bitterly cold, so she lit the gas fire in her room, and poured herself a cup of tea from the vacuum flask she had prepared before she went to the bed the night before. The next thing she did was to wrap up the wedding present she had bought for Lizzie and Rob, which was a bedside lamp Lizzie had had her eyes on ever since it first appeared on the electrical counter at Woolworths. Then she checked the Utility dress she was going to wear, which was already hanging on the outside of her wardrobe. Although it wasn't exactly new – her mother had bought it on clothing coupons just after the war started – it was her favourite: azure-blue taffeta, cut just below the knees, with a narrow white ruff, and long sleeves with matching white cuffs. She had also laid out her clean woollen underwear, prepared for what was bound to be a very cold service inside the church. Then she collected her bath towel, and tiptoed down the stairs to the bathroom, which was on the same floor as the bedroom where her mother and Desmond slept.

However, fearing that she might wake them up, she decided not to have a bath, and so, after lighting the paraffin lamp, she stripped off, and had a thoroughly good wash-down. Although the wedding was not until eleven o'clock, she was determined to get out of the house before Desmond created yet another of his ugly scenes, and before he could get the chance to stop her from going to the wedding of the only real friend she had ever had.

After checking herself in the mirror, and making sure that she hadn't used too much make-up, she put on her coat and gloves, and also the hat she had bought in Selby's a few days before, and made her way as quietly as she could in the dark, down the stairs. There was very little time to spare, for now it was already approaching half-past eight, which was the time her mother came down to make tea for herself and Desmond.

Maple's plan seemed to be working, until just as she was making for the front door the hall light was switched on, and Desmond's rasping voice called from the top of the stairs, 'Where d'you think you're going?'

Maple froze. Then, 'It's none of your business,' she called back abruptly, moving swiftly to the front door.

But before she had even got the chance to open it, Desmond came rushing down the stairs to slam it closed. 'You're going nowhere!' he growled menacingly. 'I've told you I don't want you seeing that girl again. She's a troublemaker. I won't have her upsetting your mother. Is that quite clear?'

'The only person *my* friend appears to be upsetting is you!' Maple snapped back. 'Where I go and what I do has absolutely nothing to do with you. You're not my father!'

Before she had even finished speaking, Desmond grabbed hold of her coat and practically ripped it off her. 'As far as I'm concerned,' he returned angrily, 'I'm the only father you'll ever have. Until you come of age, you do what *I* want you to do!'

Maple pulled away from him, and tried to get to the door. But once again, he blocked her way. 'Let me go!' she cried, struggling with him.

During this, he managed to pull off her coat, which dropped to the floor. She let out a howl of desperation, and tried to get away from him. But as she did so, he grabbed at the sleeve of her dress, and ripped a great tear in it.

When she realised what he had done, she burst into tears. 'I hate you!' she screamed. 'I hate you!' She tried to punch him but he grabbed hold of her fist, and slapped her round the face.

'Just remember something, my dear little stepdaughter,' said Desmond, twisting her wrist threateningly. 'I've tolerated you and your tantrums for far too long. You think you're so superior to me – but you're not. You're just a brainless little Woolworths shop girl, who doesn't have the sense to realise that she'll never achieve anything except share a bed with as many men who are prepared to put up with her.'

He was so close to her now that Maple could feel the warmth of his breath. She cowered back as far as she could to the floor.

'You're lucky to have someone like me to protect you from men like that, Mabel,' said Desmond. 'But you've got to learn to appreciate me. You've got to stop disobeying me.'

Repelled by him, in one swift, unexpected movement, Maple punched him. The blow landed straight on his face.

Totally unprepared for what had happened, Desmond flinched, and moved his face out of her reach. In a daze, unable to believe what she had done, he put a finger up to his lips. Blood was trickling down his chin. His eyes darted up at her. 'You little...!' Grabbing her arm, he dragged her up off the floor, and raised his fist to pummel her. 'This is the last time!' he yelled at her. 'The last time!'

But before he could land the blow, his wife's voice boomed out from behind. 'NO!' she yelled.

Desmond swung round to see her standing in her dressing gown at the top of the stairs. 'If you touch that girl,' she called, 'I swear – I'll kill you.'

Desmond's fist was still raised as she hurried down the stairs. But enraged as he was, he made no move. 'Keep out of this, Sal,' he said through clenched teeth. 'I'm warning you.'

Ignoring him, she went straight to Maple, and took hold of her hand.

Maple, tears running down her face, allowed her mother to pull her up to her feet. 'Oh, Mum!' she sobbed profusely.

'It's all right, darling,' said her mother. The sound of Lizzie's voice echoed in her mind: *'You can't turn your back on what's going on, Mrs Gosling ... she needs your love and protection.'* She hugged Maple, kissed her on the forehead, and smiled affectionately at her. 'You're quite safe now,' she said, gently wiping the tears from Maple's eyes with one finger. 'I won't let anything happen to you – ever again.'

'You stupid cow!' barked Desmond, his chin smudged with blood. 'See what trash you've brought into the world? Look what she's done to me! Just look!'

Sally Gosling turned to him. 'Desmond,' she said calmly, without any sign of fear, 'go and wait for me in the sitting room. I want to talk to you.'

'If you think I'm going to let her get away with this–'

'*Please*, Desmond,' said Sally, calm but firm.

Desmond was stung by his wife's response. But, still dabbing his bleeding lip with his fingers, he turned, and moved off to the sitting room. He stopped only briefly to call back to Maple, 'If you think I've finished with *you*, young lady, you're mistaken!'

Sally waited for him to go, then concentrated her attention on her daughter.

'I tried not to upset him, Mum,' sobbed Maple. 'I really tried.'

'I know, darling,' said Sally. 'I know. Now why don't you go back upstairs and get yourself ready? Don't worry about your sleeve. I'll be up in a minute to sew it for you.'

'But–' persisted Maple.

'No buts, darling,' said Sally. 'Now run along. I don't want you to be late for Lizzie's wedding.'

Astounded by her mother's response, Maple picked up her coat from the floor and slowly made her way up the stairs.

Sally waited for her to go, and once she was satisfied that she was safely in her bedroom, she turned, made for the sitting room, went in, and quietly closed the door behind her.

The Emmanuel Parish Church in lower Hornsey Road, nestled majestically between Pakeman Street School on one side and the Vicarage gardens and Pop's sweetshop on the other. It had been built during the more affluent days of the borough of Islington, when weddings, funerals, and baptisms brought passers-by to cheer the bride, doff their hats to the late departed, and put their fingers to their ears when it was impossible to contain the bawling, newly baptised. Although times had now changed, the Emmanuel carried on in much the same way as it had ever done, even during the war, when the Almighty looked down with mercy on the building itself by sparing it from the ravages of the blitz. Not that it had escaped completely unscathed. When the aerial torpedo came down in nearby Seven Sisters Road, demolishing an entire row of shops and tenements, the blast brought down tiles from the church roof, and shattered nearly all the gothic arched windows. And so, over the years, the Emmanuel Church, together with its estimable vicar, the Reverend Frank Wallace, had continued its much-loved place in the community, remaining a haven of peace, tranquillity and prayer for those seeking an escape from the everyday stress of life.

'Disgraceful!' ''Orrible!' 'Awful!' 'Selfish!'

'Greedy sods!' These were just some of the not so holy comments that greeted the Workers' March, as the protesters wound down Hornsey Road from Holloway Road, and along Seven Sisters Road towards their ultimate meeting place in Finsbury Park. The mixture of a brass band, bass drums and the celebratory pealing of church bells for Lizzie and Rob's wedding service was not exactly conducive to harmony, but at least it was an original way to set out on life's long marital path.

Least amused by the fracas outside the church was Rob, looking smarter than he had ever been in his new John Essex three-piece suit, but whose opinion of workers who were marching for a living wage was hardly suitable for such hallowed ground. Fortunately, his best man, older married brother, Joe Thompson, was there to calm his anger, but it didn't help to know that the march would inevitably delay Lizzie's arrival at the church with her dad.

The rest of the congregation, which half-filled the church, were also not amused, but for quite different reasons, mainly because the march had distracted many of Lizzie's female relatives from the most important reason they had turned up, which was to burst into tears the moment they got their first glimpse of her in her wedding dress. However, by ten past eleven, the march had cleared Hornsey Road, leaving the bridal car and bridesmaids free to reach the few stone steps leading up into the church.

The moment Rob caught his first glimpse of Lizzie processing down the aisle on her father's arm, looking radiant in her pure white Utility wedding dress, veil and posy of yellow daffodils and white narcissi, her two bridesmaid sisters trailing on in perfect unison behind, his fury with the Workers' March outside instantly gave way to the exhilaration of actually seeing his future wife for the first time since they had last been together two nights before. Waiting there to greet them both with Bible in hand, was the Reverend Mr Wallace, his bespectacled, pale face beaming with pleasure and satisfaction.

Lizzie arrived. Rob gave her a huge, intimate smile, and stood with her, waiting for the service to begin. Behind them, in the front pews on either side of the central aisle, sat their two families, Frank and Harriet with James, and Gran Perkins, doing her best to stop Benjamin becoming too restless. And sitting behind them were various relations and friends, all of whom were togged out in their Sunday best, which had no doubt been in their wardrobes and bottom drawers since before the war, and positively reeked of mothballs. On the opposite side of the aisle sat the Thompsons, Sheila and Graham, uncles and aunts and cousins, Charlie and Doris Feather from Petticoat Lane, and even Norman, who looked amazingly chic in a three-piece pin-striped suit, white shirt, and pale blue tie, his shaggy hair immaculately greased with Bryl-creem and combed to perfection, and apparently unconcerned by the stir he had caused just before the start of the service by lighting up one of his roller fags, prompting the verger to remind him, 'God's house is no place for smoking.'

Lizzie's joy was complete, tempered only by the fact that, during her procession down the aisle, she had failed to see Maple amongst the guests, and as she and Potto were the only ones who had been given the time off from Woolworths to attend the wedding, she felt truly disappointed, not only because Maple wasn't there, but because it was clear that her repugnant stepfather had succeeded in having his own way.

Apart from the persistent bawling of two babies from different families who seemed to be competing with each other throughout to disrupt the service, the only other problem seemed to be that little Cissie kept whispering to Susan that she wanted a pee, which produced glares from Susan, and a demand that she would have to wait until Lizzie and Rob had gone off to sign the wedding register.

After the service, Lizzie and Rob came back down the aisle, arm in arm, man and wife. But there were mixed feelings as Lizzie acknowledged with a smile both her mum and her dad, because she knew of their sadness and anxiety about her future. But her most radiant smile came when, just as she and Rob were about to leave the church, Lizzie caught a glimpse of Maple sitting in a pew near the back, looking wonderful in her coat and dress, and the small, cheeky hat she had bought especially for the occasion. And when it came to the family and friends group photographs outside the church, Lizzie made quite sure that it was Maple who caught her posy of flowers when she hurled it out into the crowd of guests, before she and Rob were whisked off to the reception hall in Holloway Road.

It was some time before Lizzie had the chance to have a private chat with Maple, but when she did, she was astonished to hear all that had gone on at the house in St Pancras Way that morning.

'Told him to get out?' asked Lizzie, reeling from the news. 'Your mum actually told him?'

'I know,' replied Maple, clearly elated. 'I still can't believe it myself. But that's what she said. She also said, that if *he* didn't pack up and leave, *she* would. What's more, she said we should do what you and Rob are doing – get out altogether, and go and live in Canada.'

'What?' gasped Lizzie in disbelief. 'I can't believe it!'

'Neither can I,' replied Maple, 'but it's true. She said this time Desmond had gone too far, and that she'd only put up with him these last years because she hoped he would change his ways. I told her, there would never be any chance of that; Desmond is his own person. He'll never change *anything* unless there's something in it for him.'

'But what did he say? What did he do when she told him?'

'He said he'd sue her, that he'd fight her in the courts. But Mum told him that before he could do that, he'd have to find her.'

'Crikey!' said Lizzie. 'I never knew your mum had it in her. No – that's not true. I knew she had a lot of things inside her. All she needed was someone to help get it out of her. And that person is you, Maple.'

Maple shook her head. 'Mum told me about

415

you and Rob going to see her the other day,' she said. 'Whatever you said to her made her determined to fight back. That's the one thing she's never done in her entire life. Thank you, Lizzie. Thank you from the bottom of my heart.'

Lizzie gave her a ravishing smile, and they hugged each other.

They were interrupted by Potto, who was brimming with excitement. 'What d'yer fink?' she asked, eyes sparkling with lust. 'I've clicked!'

Lizzie and Maple exchanged a puzzled look. 'What are you talking about, Potto?' asked Lizzie. 'Clicked? Who with?'

'Who d'yer fink!' she replied, diverting their attention to a handsome young bloke who was browsing around the buffet table, watching her every move. ''Im! That gorgeous lump er man over there!'

'*Him?*' cried Lizzie, laughing. 'You've got to be joking. That's my cousin Pete.'

'I don't care who he is!' insisted Potto. ''E makes me go all weak at the knees. *An'* 'e fancies *me* too. 'E's bin watchin' me everywhere I go!'

This sent both Lizzie and Maple into fits of laughter. 'But I thought you already had a boyfriend, Potto?' asked Maple. 'What's happened to him?'

'As far as I'm concerned,' gushed Potto, 'until this moment I've never 'ad a boyfriend in me 'ole life. This bloke can take me any time 'e likes!'

Lizzie and Maple roared with laughter, until they were suddenly interrupted by Rob.

'Come on, you lot!' he said. 'It's time to nosh.

And you don't want to miss my speech, do you, Potto?'

Potto didn't answer. Her eyes were glued to lover-boy on the other side of the room.

'But Joe's the best man,' Lizzie reminded him. 'I thought *he* was supposed to make the big speech?' Lizzie asked Rob.

'Yes,' said Rob. 'But he's been rehearsing it for the past week, and he's now so nervous, I doubt he'll have enough courage left to even start!'

At the buffet table, everyone seemed to get on well with each other. Although there were no more than about thirty guests there, both sides of the family behaved as though they had known each other all their lives. At the top table, Harriet, Frank, Susan, Cissie, James, Benjamin and Gran Perkins sat alongside the bride, whilst Sheila and Graham Thompson, together with Rob's Aunt Gladys, Uncle Louis, and Grandma and Grand-dad Thompson sat alongside the bridegroom. The buffet wedding breakfast, although paid for by Frank, had been put together by both Harriet and Sheila. With the constraints of the food ration, the two women had worked miracles, using whatever Spam, cooked ham, cold chicken and sausages they could get their hands on. But they had made some wonderful salads, and the kids amongst the party seemed quite happy to contend with fishpaste sandwiches, followed by blackberry and apple trifle topped with raspberry jelly and pink blancmange.

During the meal, Harriet kept pretty much to herself, talking mainly to Frank or Susan, and being drawn into the conversation with Lizzie

417

only when it was absolutely necessary. And Sheila had one or two difficulties with Graham, when he insisted on talking politics to his brother Louis, who disagreed with practically everything he said. On one of the other tables, Potto had struck gold, by manoeuvring a seat next to her dream boy, which she had obtained by practically killing Rob's cousin Eunice, who had been trying to take her place in the seat allocated for her. Surprisingly, nobody complained of the cold, for the hall, sparse and adequate as it was, had been heated by paraffin lamps all day. However, just occasionally, Susan shivered beneath the flimsy bridesmaid's dress she was wearing, having ignored Lizzie's advice to wear some woollen underwear, and to bring a cardigan for the reception.

As expected, Rob's brother, Joe, stuttered his way through the shortest best man's speech ever, much to the disapproval of his wife, Janey, who sat on the table immediately facing him. It was therefore left to Rob to do the honours, and he began by thumping on the table so loudly, it scared his grandmother into dropping a dollop of pink blancmange on to her lap.

'Mum and Dad Angel,' he said in a firm and buoyant voice. 'Mum and Dad Thompson, family, relations, friends, and anyone else who's managed to get in under false pretences...' Chuckles from around the tables. 'On behalf of Liz and myself, I'd like to thank you all for coming today. It's made all the difference to have our relatives and friends with us, so that you can all see what a huge mistake Liz's made!'

Most people laughed at his joke, with the exception of Harriet, who sat quite still and motionless, staring down at her plate.

'Joking apart,' continued Rob, 'I want you to know that I consider myself the luckiest bloke in the world to have Liz as my wife – my *wife!*' He shook his head in disbelief, and turned to look at Lizzie. 'I can hardly believe it! Those of you who have known her over the years know just what an exceptional girl she is.'

Amid applause, murmurs of 'Hear! Hear!' from the guests.

'Of course,' he continued, 'it's not really surprising, because she comes from a pretty exceptional family. The Angels are quite a lot. In these last few years, they've gone through hell and back, what with being bombed out of their home and losing most of their possessions, and then having to cope with being accommodated in a prefab in the middle of one of the worst b– one of the worst winters we've ever known, not to mention the same trials and tribulations we've all been going through since the end of the war.' He turned to Frank and Harriet. 'I tip my hat to you, Mum and Dad,' he said. 'Not many people could survive what *you've* had to survive, and still give me a wife that they can be proud of.'

More murmurs of 'Hear! Hear!' from around the tables.

'But,' he continued, 'I don't have to tell you that the hell we've all been going through these last few years, has taken a toll on us, not least, Liz and me. Whatever you do, or try to do, in this country these days always seems to end in disaster. Now, I don't know why that is, but it's become a fact of life, and no encouragement to young people. That's why Liz and I have decided to quit, to try our luck elsewhere.'

Frank turned to look at Harriet, but she deliberately refused to remove her focus from her plate on the table.

'But I'm telling you, everyone,' continued Rob, 'leaving all of you – our families, our friends, all of you – it's been the hardest decision of our lives. But I can assure you it's a decision we've not taken lightly, and when we leave for Australia on that boat in June, we'll be leaving with heavy hearts.' He paused to put a comforting arm around Lizzie's shoulders. 'But Lizzie and I will never forget you,' he continued. 'We'll never forget who we are, and where we came from.' He picked up his glass of white wine from the table, and turned to Harriet and Frank. 'Mum and Dad,' he said, raising his glass. 'I want to thank you for providing us with the best wedding anyone could ever wish to have. But most of all, I want to thank you for giving me my own special Angel.'

As he took a sip of his wine, someone called out, 'Harriet and Frank!' This was immediately picked up by everyone else, who stood up, and joined in the toast. Harriet smiled only weakly enough to acknowledge the tribute, but Frank mouthed the words, 'Thanks, everyone.'

Once Rob had sat down, there was a flurry of activity, most of it centred around Frank, who was being pressed into replying to Rob's toast. Finally, reluctantly, he rose to his feet.

'Lizzie and Rob,' he started falteringly. 'Ladies and gentlemen, all our good friends and relatives, it's not easy to stand here on such a marvellous day for your daughter and son-in-law, knowing that the days are ticking by when they won't be with you any more. But that's in the future, and today is today.' He hesitated briefly, whilst he looked around at the sea of faces hanging on his every word. 'Rob,' he continued, turning to look at him, 'a few minutes ago, you said how lucky you were to have Lizzie as your wife. Well, I'll tell you something. Harriet and I have been the lucky ones. Having Lizzie as our daughter has been the most rewarding experience any parents could ever wish to have. It's hard to say why. Maybe it's because, during these troubled times, she's always been such a support to her family, as stable as a rock, never fussing about anything, never letting anything get her down.'

Whilst Lizzie listened to her father talking so movingly about her, Rob comforted her by holding her hand out of sight.

'Or maybe it's because she can mimic everybody from Groucho Marx to my mother-in-law!'

As the hall rippled with applause and laughter, Gran Perkins jokily shook her fist at him.

When the laughter petered out, Frank continued, 'But most of all, I think it's because Lizzie had never wanted to be anything other than herself. What you see is what you get with her, and what you get is – as you rightly say, Rob – something special, something very special. I could go on until the cows come home, talking about all the memories Harriet and I have of

Lizzie and her brothers and sisters growing up over the years, but I don't have to talk about it. Harriet and I keep those pictures where we can never lose them – right here...' he pointed to his forehead, 'and here.' He pointed to his heart. 'When she and Rob go off together to start their new life,' he continued, 'it's going to leave a huge gap in *both* our lives.'

He turned a brief sidelong glance at Harriet, who solidly refused to react, but whose knuckles were white with tension under the table.

'Anyway,' said Frank, 'one thing I do know is that she's going to be in good hands. I'm pretty sure Rob is not only going to make a good husband, but a fine son-in-law for Harriet and me.'

There were more calls of 'Hear! Hear!' amid the waves of applause.

'You know, the funny thing about life,' Frank continued, 'is that you never quite know what's just around the corner. So one of these days – it may not be for quite a while just yet – who knows, Harriet and I might get a visit from our grandchild. I just hope he – or she – doesn't speak in some wild Australian accent that we won't be able to understand!'

Gentle laughter around the hall.

'But,' he continued, turning to his daughter and son-in-law, 'although we'll miss you two,' he hesitated, 'you'll always be in our thoughts.'

For the first time, Harriet's eyes flickered as she tried hard to conceal tears.

Rob put a comforting arm around Lizzie's shoulders, and squeezed her.

The sound of Potto sobbing, drifted across from the opposite table.

'And so, ladies and gentlemen,' continued Frank, picking up his own glass of wine, 'may I please ask you to raise your glasses to Lizzie and Rob.'

Everyone got to their feet, and raised their glasses.

'May they live a long and happy life,' continued Frank, 'the life they need, the life they deserve. Ladies and gentlemen, I give you Lizzie and Rob.'

Everyone joined in unison: 'Lizzie and Rob.'

A little later, the mood was somewhat lighter. After the tables had been cleared and removed, and the sound of some of Woolworths top-selling records boomed out from a gramophone player, the guests were afforded a perfect opportunity to launch into a jitterbug, the slow waltz, quickstep and foxtrot. The most astonishing moment, however, came when Potto and her newly found dream boy quite literally threw themselves into a frantic version of the jitterbug, which found Potto being tossed up into the air with wild abandon, and finishing up sliding beneath dream boy's legs, before being dragged up on to her feet again. Lizzie found the whole thing exhausting just to watch, until she was suddenly grabbed by Rob's grandfather, and, to the strains of Edmundo Ros and his South American Rhythm Boys, found herself being dragged around almost as energetically in a passionate, searing-hot tango.

During all these wild goings-on, Harriet sat

quietly in the corner, sipping gin and tonics with Rob's mother, Sheila. Up until that moment, Harriet had done her best to avoid talking about Lizzie and Rob's decision to emigrate to Australia, but when Sheila kept returning to the subject, she had no alternative but to respond.

'It's their decision, Sheila,' Harriet said, her eyes constantly flicking across the dance floor to where Lizzie, an incongruous sight in her wedding dress, flowing around recklessly in the tango, was still being pursued by every male guest, young and old, who could get their hands on her. 'If they want to take that kind of risk, then that's up to them. The only thing I can't understand is why they want to do such a thing at all.'

'Well, let's face it,' said Sheila, 'there's not much left for them in *this* country, is there? You read in the newspapers every day about young people who are leaving in their droves.'

'But why?' asked Harriet. 'This is one of the best countries in the world. Why get out just because the going gets tough? It'll recover. We'll all recover. The trouble is, people are so impatient. They just refuse to wait.'

'I know what you mean,' said Sheila. 'But you can't tell the young *anything*. They have to do their own thing. I suppose we were much the same when we were their age. They'll just have to learn by their mistakes.'

'Maybe,' returned Harriet, uncompromising. 'But by then, it could be too late.'

'Well,' suggested Sheila, 'if they get in any trouble, they'll soon find a way to return home.

At least they'll have their families waiting for them. But I can't deny Graham and I are going to miss Rob. You must feel the same way about Lizzie?'

Fortunately, the start of the 'wedding show' saved Harriet from having to answer.

During the following half-hour, it was like Sunday evenings used to be back home with the Angel family. Made up of sketches based on popular radio shows such as *ITMA, Dick Barton – Special Agent, Variety Bandbox*, and 'Dr Morell' in *Monday Night at Eight*. Lizzie, Susan and Cissie joined forces to mime to an Andrews Sisters gramophone record, James and Benjamin performed in high toff voices as the Two Leslies', and Rob's ample Aunty Gladys brought the house down with a positively knee-trembling performance of Ivor Novello's stirring ballad 'Rose of England'. But the highlight of the show was, without a doubt, Lizzie's impersonations of radio and film stars, such as Mrs Mopp, Bette Davis, Donald Duck, James Stewart, and the irresistible Funf from *ITMA*. The show came to an end with a singsong for everyone, led by Lizzie mimicking Gracie Fields singing 'Sally', 'Wish Me Luck as You Wave Me Goodbye', and the inevitable evergreen Vera Lynn classic, 'We'll Meet Again'.

After the show, everyone returned to the buffet table to clear any scraps of food that might have been left over, and to grab a cup of freshly made tea. During this time, Lizzie went around the hall with Rob, thanking everyone for coming, and for bringing gifts. When she came to Harriet, who was now sitting alone in the corner, she bent down and kissed her.

'Thank you, Mum,' she said affectionately, 'for *everything*.'

Harriet looked up at her. There were a million thoughts racing through her mind, but she had no intention of revealing any of them. 'I hope you'll be very happy, Lizzie,' she said coolly, '*wherever* you are.'

Agonising over the distance that clearly now existed between her mother and herself, Lizzie sat down briefly on the chair next to her. 'Mum,' she said sweetly, gently taking hold of Harriet's hands, 'don't let's drift apart. Please let it be like it always used to be.'

'That's something only you can decide, Lizzie,' replied Harriet impassively. 'All I can say is that if you ever return, God willing, we'll still be here. But I wish you well.' She leaned forward and gently pecked Lizzie on the cheek.

Lizzie watched her quietly get up and go. She felt like crying.

A few minutes later, she searched around, but couldn't see her dad anywhere in the hall. Eventually, she tracked him down to the porch outside, where he was sitting on the front doorstep, smoking a cigarette.

'Mind if I join you?' she asked.

Frank smiled. 'You might get a cold bottom in that dress,' he said jokily, moving over so that she could sit next to him.

For the next few moments, they just sat there in silence, watching the late evening traffic wind its way up and down Holloway Road, to and from

426

Highgate and Archway Junction. Just occasionally a rickety old tram would clank along, its bell sounding as it drew to a halt at the tram stop outside the Gaumont cinema down the road. But there were always those few precious moments when, apart from the distant barking of a dog, they could hear no intrusive sound at all.

'It's been a perfect day, Dad,' said Lizzie.

'Despite the Workers' March?'

'Despite the Workers' March,' repeated Lizzie. She slid her arm around his waist. 'I have so much to thank you for. Especially for the things you said about me in there.'

'You paid me to say it, so how could I refuse?'

She laughed gently with him. They said nothing for several moments, until she leaned on his shoulder, and stared aimlessly out at the cold, dark pavements. 'Oh, Dad,' she sighed, 'I'm so worried about you. Every time I go home, I expect to be told something terrible has happened to you.'

'It won't.'

'How can you say that?'

'Because I know.'

Lizzie straightened up and looked at him. 'You've been questioned once,' she said. 'You said yourself they could call on you any time they want.'

'Yes,' said Frank confidently. 'But that was before.'

'Before what?'

'Before I knew that they couldn't do anything without proof. They don't have any proof, Lizzie. Not a scrap. You don't have to worry. I'm going

427

to be all right. Sooner or later this whole thing will blow over. So you must forget about it now. When you go off in June, I don't want you to think about it ever again.'

Lizzie waited a moment before replying. 'I'm not going, Dad.'

Frank swung a shocked look at her. 'Not going?' he asked anxiously. 'What are you talking about?'

'I'm not going,' continued Lizzie, 'because I can't leave you and Mum and all the family while all this uncertainty is hanging over us. I've told you so many times before, if you're in trouble – if *any* of my family are in trouble – my place is right there with you. I couldn't possibly travel to the other side of the world knowing that you were in trouble with the police. It's no good you arguing, because I've made up my mind. I'm going to tell Rob in the next day or so, while we're down in Great Yarmouth.'

'Now listen to me, Lizzie,' Frank said firmly, swinging round to face her, 'I can assure you that there's absolutely no need for you to make any change to your plans whatsoever. By the time you go off to Australia in June, this whole business with the police will be a thing of the past. I appreciate what you feel, my dear one, but it's totally unnecessary.' As he looked through the shadows at her lovely, anxious face, with her slight smattering of make-up just beginning to fade, he knew only too well how much he cared for her, had *always* cared for her, and how much she had always meant to him. His heart was full of her, full of the joy and happiness she had given him since the day she was born. But he was not prepared to let her sacrifice her life with Rob, the new life that she had earned so much. Now it was time to cut the cord that had bound her to her mother, to him, and to their family for so long. Now was the time to let his angel fly off with the man she loved, and to start a family of her own.

'You know, Lizzie,' he said, gently raising her chin with the tip of his fingers, and staring into her eyes. 'The Angels can't be greedy any longer. We've had our share. Now it's time for somebody else to get a look in.'

'I'm not going, Dad,' vowed Lizzie defiantly, close to tears. 'I *won't* go. I just *can't*.'

'You *will* go, Lizzie,' insisted Frank firmly, but soft and gentle. 'You'll go, and you'll make us all very proud of you. And in any case, who knows, perhaps one day we'll come over there and visit you and Rob. He can treat me to a glass of their famous ice-cold beer that they keep going on about.'

Lizzie shook her head. She was now crying on his shoulder.

Frank held on to her, and stared out at the night, the cold, relentless night that would soon herald the start of a new day, the coming of spring. 'Times change, Lizzie,' he said, looking up at the moon trying desperately hard to break through dark, grey clouds. 'And *we* must change with them.'

His voice sounded confident and full of hope. But inside, he was torn apart by the certainty that he would never again be able to share a moment like this with the angel he loved so much.

Chapter 22

It was so hot, Gran Perkins had told Lizzie and Rob that if there was a nudist camp nearby, she'd move into it right away. Fortunately, for her family at least, such a place did not exist anywhere near Tollington Park, so her radical ideas were not put to the test. Nonetheless, during the current heatwave, she did have to resort to wearing as few clothes as possible, which meant that her summer dresses were very flimsy, much to the disapproval of Harriet, who had still not got over the shock of seeing both Lizzie and Susan going around in trousers, which these days seemed to be all the rage amongst young girls. In contrast to the worst winter that anyone could remember, this month was really living up to its reputation as 'Flaming June', where temperatures had been soaring for almost a week. However, after a most delightful spring, summer was certainly putting a smile back on people's faces, and also causing second thoughts amongst those would-be emigrants who were deserting 'the old country' for a more temperate climate.

Lizzie was still reluctant to go, but as it had now been nearly two and a half months since her father had been questioned by the police she was only now feeling confident enough that what he had told her after her wedding was true – that any suspicions the police were harbouring against him, were not being followed through. But as each day passed, the more she dreaded the thought of setting sail on that boat at Southampton. Before then, however, Lizzie had the emotionally draining task of visiting all her friends and relatives to say goodbye. Two weeks before, she and Rob had been up to Sunderland to see Rob's Aunt Gladys and Uncle Louis, and his cousins, Eunice, Pat and Roger, then they embarked on visits to say farewell to his grandparents on both sides of his family, who lived in Kent and Walthamstow. For her part, Lizzie had to go up to Sheffield to take her leave of Auntie Mary and her son, Pete, whom Potto had fancied so much at the wedding, but when it came to more distant relatives, she decided that as none of them had ever helped her family in their struggles to survive, there was not much point in going to wish them a fond farewell.

But the feelings were somewhat different when they went to pay their final respects to 'the gang' up at Petticoat Lane.

'Well, I can't deny it,' said Charlie Feathers, who was already a little the worse for the tipple he'd got through in the past hour or so. 'Fings won't be the same round the Lane wivout yer, Rob ol' mate. You're goin' ter be missed, that's fer sure.'

'Wot 'e really means,' added Doris, his missus, 'is that 'e'll 'ave ter get up off 'is arse an' do a bit er work fer 'imself, instead of leavin' it ter you!'

There was gentle, ribbing laughter from the back courtyard of the Pork Pie pub, which was pretty well jammed with stallholders from Petticoat Lane, all gathered there during the evening to give Rob and Lizzie a good send-off.

'It's not true, Doris,' insisted Rob, who was also getting a bit bleary-eyed with the endless round of drinks he'd been bought. 'Charlie's one of the best bosses you could ever work for. He's about the only employer I've ever known who really takes care of you.'

'Oh yes?' retorted Doris sceptically. 'And 'ow much 'as 'e paid yer ter say that?'

There followed jeers and laughter from the others, and shouts of 'Good ol' Charlie!' Charlie did two fingers at them all.

'An' wot about *this* poor gel?' said Doris, sitting next to Lizzie at a courtyard table, pink gin in her hand, the ash from her fag threatening to fall at any moment. 'Wot der *you* fink about all this?'

'About what, Doris?' Lizzie asked.

'About being dragged off ter Aussieland? Are yer sure it's wot yer want ter do?'

Lizzie had to think about this for a moment. *Was* it what she wanted to do? Or was she still pretending, forcing herself into believing that whatever Rob wanted, *she* was prepared to go along with? Fortunately, she didn't have to answer the question, because someone answered it for her.

''Er course it's wot she wants ter do, Doris!' called Fred Turret, one of the pearly kings who worked down the Lane. 'Yer can bet yer life she an' 'er ol' man 'ere'll make a bomb when they get out there. Just fink of all them kangaroos they can catch. Luvely wiv chips and pease puddin'!'

432

More boozy laughter all round.

'I 'eard them Aussies've got sharks and crocodiles,' said Ethel Turret, who, as her husband's pearly queen, was all togged up in her buttons. 'Yer wouldn't get me puttin' a toe in the bleedin' water out there!'

'You just stick ter sewin' on me buttons, mate!' retorted Fred. 'Leave Rob to cope wiv the crocodiles.'

Lizzie laughed along with Rob and the others, but although the lively banter was certainly helping to raise her spirits, it was also giving her even more misgivings than she already had.

'Wot I don't like,' said one of the other stallholders, 'is the way the Aussies call us poms.'

'If any of 'em called me that,' added a young hothead barrow boy named Eddie, 'I'd smash their face in!'

'Charming!' said one of the elderly women.

'That's not nice, Eddie,' said Audrey, his girlfriend. 'We call the Frenchies frogs, don't we?'

'An' the Yanks call us limeys,' added one of the other barrow boys.

'Precisely!' said Ethel. 'So wot diff'rence does it make? Why get all worked up just 'cos someone's teasin' yer? It don't make bleedin' sense ter me.'

By now Rob's group of friends from the Lane had been joined by some of the other customers, all of them interested in joining the chinwag about emigrating to Australia.

It was an odd mixture of people, with barrow boys and stallholders sweating in the evening sun in working clothes and flat caps, and office types stripped down to striped shirts and braces, all of them downing pints of bitter or brown ale to quench their thirst.

'So tell me, Rob,' asked Eddie, the barrow boy, 'why *did* yer suddenly decide to get on the bandwagon and ditch Blighty?'

'I didn't get on any bandwagon, Ed,' he replied. 'In fact, Liz and I have weighed up everything very carefully. With respect to Charlie here,' he put a friendly arm around Charlie's shoulder, 'there's no way I could survive here much longer on the wages we all have to live on. It's the same as Liz here.' He cast a quick smile at her. 'She's been on her feet six days a week at Woolworths for the past two years, but what has she got to show for it, except her friendship with all the other girls who work there?'

'So 'ow much d'yer fink yer goin' ter make out in Aussieland, then?' asked Fred Turret. 'Is it all that much more than yer'd get 'ere?'

'I would hope so, Fred,' replied Rob. 'But it's not just about cash or the weather. It's about – opportunity. We only live once. We have to go wherever we can make a go of things.'

'I agree with Rob,' said Charlie. 'I mean, you take ol' nancy boy Norman. *'E* couldn't make a go of fings 'ere, so wot did 'e do? Chucks in 'is lot an' buggers off ter where 'is own sort 'ang out.'

At the mention of Norman's name, Rob exchanged a quick, anxious glance with Lizzie. 'Where's that, Charlie?' he asked. 'Where did you say Norman's gone?'

'Where d'yer fink?' replied Charlie dismissively. 'Bleedin' 'Ampstead – where all the pansies 'ang out.'

Rob went quite taut to hear Norman being rubbished in such an ugly way. It just made him feel resentment towards Charlie, who had in so many other ways been good to him. Inside, he could feel himself saying, 'You know nothing, Charlie, absolutely nothing!' He steeled himself and asked, 'D'you have his address, Charlie?'

Charlie did a double take. 'Address?'

'Lizzie and I would like to go and say goodbye to him.'

Charlie looked at him in disbelief. His face was a picture. He turned to Lizzie. 'Yer'd better watch this one, Liz, gel,' he quipped. 'If 'e goes up ter nancyland, yer might 'ave ter go off ter Orstralia on yer own!'

'Where, Charlie?' persisted Rob, stony-faced. 'Where can I reach Norman?'

Utterly taken aback, Charlie shrugged his shoulders, and left it to one of the other stallholders to answer Rob's question.

'I 'eard 'e's got a shop of 'is own, Rob,' said the middle-aged man who seemed much more understanding than Charlie. 'Still doin' 'is pitture frames. Some little back alley place up near the tube station. I reckon anyone'd know Norman by now. Yer can't exactly miss 'im.'

Aware of Rob's feelings, the others chuckled, but not unkindly.

Once they had got off the subject of Norman, Rob stayed chatting for about an hour with his mates from Petticoat Lane. While he was doing so, Lizzie got into conversation with an elderly woman who had been sitting alone with a glass of stout at a table beneath a tatty sunshade,

435

listening to everything that had been going on.

'Nervous, luv?' she asked, constantly wiping away the sweat streaking down her cheeks.

Lizzie sighed. 'Terrified.'

'Don't blame yer,' said the old girl, whose name was Rose. 'It's a long way ter go when yer don't know wot's at the uvver end.'

Lizzie nodded.

'But yer know,' continued Rose, 'nobody *really* knows wot's at the uvver end of anyfin', do they? I mean, take me. I got married ter my 'ubby when I was eighteen. Eighteen! In those days it was un'eard of – especially wiv *my* ol' mum an' dad. They said they'd cut off from me fer the rest of their days if I did wot I said I'd do – run away wiv my 'Arry. Well, I thought about it, I thought about it 'ard an' long. But in the end, I said ter meself, "Rose gel, if yer don't do wot yer 'eart tells yer ter do, then yer may not get anuvver chance." So I did it. I ran away wiv 'im. It was a risk – oh, I knew that all right. But something inside told me that 'Arry was right fer me, and yer know what? We lived tergevver until we was both old enuff ter get married.' She took a long gulp of her stout, which left her lips covered in white foam. ''Arry died only last year. We was tergevver fer just comin' up ter fifty-six years. I'm glad I took the risk.' She leaned forward, breathing stout fumes straight into Lizzie's face. 'An' as fer me mum an' dad,' she chuckled, 'the moment I took my first baby along ter see 'em, they welcomed me back wiv open arms. It's a funny ol' world – ain't it?'

On the top of the bus with Rob on the way back

436

home, Lizzie thought a lot about what Rose had said. It reminded her so much of old Lil Beasley, who had offered her similar advice: *'When yer love someone ... nuffin' else matters. Not even yer own kiff an' kin.'*

Billingsgate Market was glistening in the early morning sun. Everywhere you looked, porters were rushing around in their traditional white coats and distinctive leather hats, pulling wooden carts of freshly caught fish, loading and unloading them on to lorries and vans, on-site traders buying and selling, supervisors doing spot checks on hauls, and cutters working at fever pitch, gutting and boxing large and small fish, and doing their best to swish away the blood from them with frequent buckets of water.

The smell was atrocious, for the warmer the sun got the more stifling were the working conditions. Frank Angel was in the middle of it all, toiling away at topping and tailing the latest batch of cod, ready for distribution to a chain of wet fish shops, stopping only occasionally to wipe the sweat from his forehead with the back of his hand, or to fan himself with his trilby hat, which was about the only breeze that managed to filter through into the wide open hall. He was only too grateful when it was time to take his midday break, even if the Spam and pickle sandwiches Harriet made him each day were not exactly fresh by the time he came to eat them.

Now that Dodger had gone, Frank was very much on his own down at Billingsgate. His fellow workers still didn't take much of a shine to having a well-spoken bloke in their midst, and when they saw him sitting with a cup of tea and a paperback book during the morning and afternoon breaks, they all said he was a 'square peg in a round hole'.

Midday was Frank's favourite break, for not only did it give him a whole hour to get away from the stench of gutted fish, but the chance to be on his own in an atmosphere that he cherished most of all. This was inevitably the river, and each working day during the hot weather, he would hurry down to London Bridge and find a favourite spot to pitch for half an hour or so, to eat his sandwiches, and to gaze out in awe at the magnificent panorama of ancient buildings stretched out before him.

But today was different. Even on the brisk walk from the market, he felt that something was not quite right. For a time, he couldn't put his finger on what it was exactly that was disturbing him, but by the time he had reached the approaches to the bridge itself, he suddenly became aware that during the previous ten minutes or so he had glanced over his shoulder several times. He tried to fathom out why. On each occasion, he had seen nothing unusual. The lunch-time City workers streamed out of their offices in shirt-sleeves, ties loosened, and small groups of office girls lounged around together in whatever nook or cranny they could find, sapping up the hot rays of the midday sun. Dismissing his concerns, he continued on to his favourite spot on the bridge, squatting down on a stone step beneath one of the old wrought-iron lamps. Through the metal grille of the bridge he could just see the river traffic below: coal barges conveying their valuable cargo to the next fortunate customer; a sightseeing cruiser – one of the few that were still able to operate under the Government's tight restrictions on fuel; and in the distance, the majestic Tower Bridge, slowly opening up to allow the passage of a large cargo vessel, heading for a nearby berth. It was an idyllic scene, and one that Frank had seen a hundred times before. But again, today was different. He still couldn't understand why. It was a feeling, just a feeling.

'Hello, Frank.'

He looked up. A man in a navy-blue suit, trilby hat and collar and tie was standing over him. He seemed an incongruous sight in the searing heat of the day. But then Frank had seen him before, and the sight of him immediately put him off his food.

'I was right,' he said. 'You've been following me.'

The man, Detective Inspector Vic Meadows, the police officer who had interviewed Frank at Hornsey Road Police Station, took off his trilby, and squatted down beside him. 'I didn't think you'd feel like talking to me back in the market,' he said. 'Don't want everyone to know your business, eh, Frank?'

Frank took a brief moment to let that remark sink in. Then he offered Meadows one of his sandwiches.

Meadows shook his head politely. 'Never eat when I'm on duty, old son,' he said.

'What's this all about?' asked Frank.

439

'Just a little follow-up,' returned Meadows, aimlessly watching the river traffic below, whilst fanning himself with his trilby. 'We've picked up a few friends of yours. Thought you might be able to tell us what you know about them.'

Frank avoided his look, and took a passive bite of his sandwich.

'A certain Major Parfitt,' continued Meadows. '*And* his good lady. I think she said her name was – Daisy?'

'Look, Meadows,' said Frank, 'I don't know what you want. I've told you everything I know.'

Meadows ignored what he had said. 'How many times did you go to their house in Highbury, Frank?' he asked.

'I don't know any house in Highbury,' insisted Frank, getting up angrily, 'and I don't know anybody by the name of– whoever you said.' He threw the rest of his sandwiches into the river.

Whilst Frank looked out over the river, Meadows got up, and joined him. 'Looks like the fish are going to have a good meal today,' he quipped.

Frank didn't respond.

Meadows waited a moment before saying anything. When he did speak again, it was more official. 'You've been identified, Frank.'

Frank swung a shocked look at him.

'You and Parfitt were seen together by someone in the village, the night of the Wethersfield job. They identified you from your photo we took when you were questioned at the station.'

Frank was too stunned to reply. He turned to look out at the river again. But he was too distressed to see anything.

Meadows waited for two people to pass by before speaking again. When they were eventually out of the way, he asked, 'D'you have anything to say, Frank?'

'Are you charging me?'

'It *had* occurred to me.'

For Frank, Meadows' flippant reply was chilling. In the depths of despair, he asked, 'What d'you want me to do?'

'Names, places, pick-ups, money exchanged – all the usual things.'

Frank was now in a quandary. How could he go back on everything he had told the police during questioning, he asked himself. Worst of all was naming names, and confirming whom he had done business with. 'What happens if I don't tell you?' he asked gingerly.

'Trade secret,' replied Meadows.

'And if I do?'

Meadows turned to look at him. 'I can be very generous, Frank,' he replied. 'And so can the courts.'

In those few moments, there on London Bridge, Frank's whole life seemed to have come to an end. Time seemed to have been suspended. Across the river, a Union Jack flag was fluttering on the roof of a building that he couldn't identify, in what appeared to be the first slight breeze of the day. But as his eyes aimlessly scanned the river he loved so much, all he could see were the faces of his family – all watching him, anxiously, eagerly, with wave upon wave of hope. He couldn't bear it. He couldn't bear to think what they would do when they heard the worst. How could the children live with the shame of their own father going to prison? How would Harriet feel about having a husband who had descended to what he still considered to be petty crimes? Most of all, he could see Lizzie's face – watching him, caring for him, praying that the trouble he was in would just go away.

'I want a deal,' he said, quite suddenly.

'No deals, Frank.'

'One small condition then?'

'Don't play games with me, please, Frank,' retorted Meadows icily. 'You're in no position to ask for deals or conditions. You're in trouble, Frank, and the only way you can make it easier for yourself is to co-operate.'

'Two weeks,' said Frank.

'I said–'

'Two weeks!' pleaded Frank. 'That's all I ask.'

Meadows, curious, hesitated. 'Why?'

'My daughter,' replied Frank. 'In two weeks' time, she's emigrating to Australia with her husband. If she knew about this, if she knew what was going on...' He clutched his forehead, and wiped the sweat from it. 'I don't want her to start a new life knowing that I–'

'She'll know sooner or later,' said Meadows.

'The least I can do is to make sure it's later,' replied Frank desperately. 'Two weeks, Meadows?'

Meadows stared at him for a moment, then looked down at the river again. The tide was going out, gradually leaving just a sliver of muddy, pebbled shoreline down below.

Frank leaned closer to him. 'Two weeks,

Meadows,' he pleaded again. 'That's all I ask – just two weeks.'

Since her marriage at the beginning of April, Lizzie had called in regularly at the prefab to see how the family were getting on. With most of her few possessions now moved over to Gran Perkins's place, there was nothing more for her to do but make as much of the time she had left as she could with her mum and dad, and brothers and sisters. It wasn't easy for her. Each day that passed, each hour, each minute, it seemed like a countdown to heartbreak. She was dreading the day when she had to say goodbye to them. They had all been such a part of her life for so long, that she couldn't imagine how she would exist without them.

When she arrived at the prefab, Cissie and Benjamin were helping their mother to do the mangling in the back garden, whilst James, stripped off to the waist, was lying flat on his stomach on the small patch of lawn, reading a book. Although it was late in the afternoon, the sun was still burning a hole in the dazzling blue sky, and Harriet, struggling to put the washing through the two rollers, looked as though all the energy had been sapped out of her.

'Why don't you let me do that for you, Mum?' Lizzie asked, only to have her offer politely declined.

'I have to do it when you're not here,' replied Harriet.

Lizzie knew there was no use going through all that again. But she was surprised when Cissie suddenly burst into song, singing perfectly the words of 'Waltzing Matilda'.

When Cissie had finished the song, Lizzie applauded her. 'That was lovely, Cissie,' she said. 'Where did you learn that?'

'At school,' replied Cissie, who had her time cut out preventing Benjamin from drawing her fingers through the mangle. 'I asked Miss Jessop if she could tell me about Australia, and she gave me some books to look at. And she taught me this song too.' She stopped what she was doing for a moment whilst one of her dad's shirts was being drained through the rollers. 'Will you send me a postcard of a kangaroo?' she asked.

Lizzie beamed. 'Of course I will, Cissie,' she replied. 'Lots of them. And when you come out to visit me, Rob and I will take you to see some of them.'

'That's a lot of rubbish,' said Benjamin, struggling to turn the mangle wheel. 'Everyone knows you can only find kangaroos in a zoo.'

'Well, they have to come from somewhere, stupid!' said Cissie.

'You don't know nothing about them!' Benjamin barked. 'You don't know nothing about *anything!*'

'I do! I do!' Cissie roared back at him defiantly.

'That's enough now, you two!' said Harriet, wiping her forehead with the back of her arm. 'Benjamin, go inside and tell Susan to put on the kettle for a cup of tea.'

Benjamin groaned, and reluctantly did as he was told. As he went, Cissie put her tongue out at him, then followed him into the house.

Harriet took one pile of mangled washing to the clothes line, and started hanging them out. 'I do wish you wouldn't make rash promises like that to Cissie,' she said, as Lizzie joined her. 'She's young enough to believe everything.'

'It wasn't a rash promise, Mum,' Lizzie said, helping her with the washing. 'I mean every word I say. As soon as Rob and I have got settled, the first thing we're going to do is to save up enough to bring you all over.'

'Stop talking such nonsense, Lizzie,' said Harriet. 'You know as well as I do, it could take a lifetime to save up that kind of money. And, in any case, I don't have any great desire to go to Australia.'

Although Lizzie was hurt by her mother's constant negative comments about Australia, she refused to let it show. 'It's a beautiful place,' she replied.

'So is *this* country,' insisted Harriet. 'Things are going to be so different when we move into a new house. We'll have a much bigger garden than this. Once your father has found a decent job, we shall probably move out of London. I've always loved the English countryside.' She finished what she was doing, and picked up her empty bowl. 'Oh yes,' she said, 'it'll be so lovely.' She turned, and started to move back into the prefab. But she stopped at the back door, and called, 'Just think what it would be like on a day like this.' With that, she disappeared inside.

Lizzie watched her go with a heavy heart. She knew only too well that there was no way that her mother was going to help her get through these

445

last two weeks without making her feel absolutely wretched.

She strolled across to James, who was engrossed in his book. 'I didn't know you were such a swot, James,' she said. 'You're taking after Dad. He loves reading.'

'I don't have much reading to do,' he said. 'This book is full of pictures.'

Lizzie crouched down beside him. 'What's it about?' she asked, peering over his shoulder.

'The war,' he replied.

'The war?' She was curious. 'I would've thought you'd had enough of the war. We all have – after being bombed out, and all we went through.'

'That's why I want to read about it,' replied James. 'I want to know.'

'About what?'

'About why it started. About how everything can change so quickly.' He turned a couple of the pages. 'There's a picture here of the soldiers landing in France on D-Day. Here.'

Lizzie looked at the stark horror of the black-and-white photograph he was showing to her. It was of a beach covered with hundreds of dead bodies. 'Oh, James,' she said gently, 'd'you really think this is something you should be dwelling on? I mean, the war's over now. Isn't it time we moved on?'

He looked up at her. 'I just want to know what it'll look like the next time.'

'The next time?'

'The next war,' he replied. 'There's bound to be one.'

Lizzie always knew that James was the most complicated member of the family, but she was shocked by his profound assessment of the future.

A few minutes later, Susan came out, and they both strolled up to the front gate to have a chat.

'I wish you weren't going,' said Susan. 'But I'm glad you are.'

Lizzie was puzzled. 'What makes you say that?' she asked.

'Because you and Rob have got the right idea,' replied Susan. 'There's nothing much here to stay for. Not yet, anyway.'

Lizzie's relationship with Susan had changed quite a lot during the past few weeks. Whereas Susan had always been the 'madam' of the family, she had recently shown signs of becoming much mellower and softer, and she was certainly much warmer towards Lizzie herself.

'I'm still not sure, you know,' Lizzie said. 'Every time I think about what it's going to feel like saying goodbye to all of you in two weeks' time, I ask myself if I know what I'm doing.' She turned to look at Susan. 'D'you know what I mean?' she asked.

Susan gave her a reassuring smile. 'You're doing the right thing,' she replied. 'Don't ask me why, but I know you are. I only wish I had the guts to leave home.'

Lizzie was shocked. 'Susan!'

'Oh, don't worry,' she said calmly. 'I've thought about it – lots of times. In fact, a few months ago, Jane and I talked about doing it together – you know, running off and finding a place on our own somewhere.'

'Susan,' asked Lizzie, in disbelief, 'are you telling me you'd leave home, leave Mum and Dad, James and Benjamin and Cissie?'

'Of course,' said Susan. 'That's what you're doing, isn't it?'

'That's different. Rob and I are married.'

'I want to get married one day too,' said Susan. 'But to do that, I've got to feel free. It's not just living in a terrible hole like this – it's much more. It's about freedom, about learning to stand up on your own two feet.'

Lizzie thought about this for a moment. As she stood there at the garden gate watching the residents of Andover Road ambling along lethargically in the stifling heat of a summer afternoon, she suddenly realised that, until this moment, she had never really known her sister. 'Things will change, you know, Susan,' she said, putting her arm around her. 'There's a lot of love in this family. I'm going to miss it. And so would you.'

'Yes, I know,' said Susan. 'The Angels are a funny lot. We know how to act and play the fool, but we never know how to show what we feel.' She turned to look at Lizzie. 'That's the trouble with Mum, you know. She's going to miss you like hell, but she hasn't the courage to let you know it.'

Lizzie shook her head slowly. 'I find that hard to believe, Susan.'

'Oh, but it's true,' said Susan. 'I *know* it is. I can see it in her eyes every time she looks at you, the fear, the dread that you won't be around any

448

more. The other day, I saw her in the kitchen, looking at a snapshot of you at school – you know, the one taken on sports day. She didn't know I was watching her, but she was crying. There were tears streaming down her face. And I also heard her talking to Dad about you, about how things are never going to be the same without you. Whatever you may think, Lizzie, Mum is going to feel lost without you. When you go, I don't think her life will ever be the same again.'

Chapter 23

Saying goodbye to Maple was something that Lizzie was not looking forward to. Although she had spent her last working day at Woolworths almost two weeks before, she had promised Maple that the two of them would spend just one last evening together before the boat sailed at the end of the week. In the short time that Lizzie had got to know her, Maple had proved herself to be a very different person to the silly little girl Lizzie had first taken her for, with her phoney Canadian accent, and her hoity-toity ways. But most extraordinary of all was the way the two girls had become such good friends, growing fonder of one another as each day passed. Lizzie didn't altogether understand why. Was it, she wondered, because they had both suffered so much trauma and suffering over the years, Maple enduring a living nightmare with Desmond, her domineering, aggressive stepfather, or was it simply because they shared a mutual respect for each other, two girls bonding in a relationship that time and distance would never suppress? Neither of them knew the answer. All they did know was that they were going to miss each other.

Their final get-together took place as they strolled along the banks of the canal in Regent's Park, which was only a short walk from where Maple was now living alone with her mother in St Pancras Way. It was a beautiful June evening, with the sun gradually changing from gold to a deep crimson, and as a flight of seagulls skimmed the surface of the water, the blood-red sky was turning their flapping white wings the colour of fire.

'"Red sky at night, shepherd's delight",' said Lizzie, as she and Maple ambled along, quietly taking in the peaceful magic of the moment.

'"Red sky in the morning, shepherd's warning",' returned Maple. She turned a brief, meaningful look at Lizzie. 'Silly old shepherd. I don't need him to remind me about Friday.' They reached a bench, and sat there. 'When I was little,' said Maple, 'my mum used to bring me down here in my pram. There are always lots of kids playing along this path. The ducks keep a watch on them – just in case there's a chance of some titbits. I used to love it here – I still do, especially now Mum's got rid of Desmond.'

'Your mum's quite a woman,' said Lizzie.

'She said the same about you,' replied Maple. 'She said, you don't find many friends like you

450

around. I think you're the first person she's ever listened to.'

'But what about Desmond?'

Maple chuckled. 'He's gone,' she said. 'And good riddance too.'

'Just like that?'

'Well – not exactly just like that. Mum gave him some money. I don't know how much. He's probably shacking up with some girl down in Soho.'

'I hope she has better luck next time,' said Lizzie.

'What d'you mean?'

'If she marries again. D'you think she will?'

'I hope so,' said Maple. 'The trouble is, she needs a man in her life, someone who can actually love her. No man ever has – so far.'

'I hope you'll find someone like that too, Maple,' said Lizzie, 'one of these days.'

Maple chuckled again. 'Perhaps,' she said. 'I'm going to keep my eyes open for a nice, *rich* Canadian businessman.'

'Ah!' said Lizzie, beaming. 'So you and your mum *are* going out there?'

'So she says,' replied Maple, brightly. 'Apparently she has an old school friend and her husband, who live in Toronto. Mum says they've got a big place, and that they'd be only too happy to put us up for a while – just until we sort ourselves out.'

'Oh, that's marvellous, Maple!' said Lizzie, taking her hand and squeezing it affectionately. 'So the dream's coming true after all.'

'Yes – and no,' replied Maple. 'Looks like I'll be further away from you than ever.'

As they sat there, a young couple, hand in hand, strolled past with eyes for no one but each other. Lizzie and Maple watched them until they disappeared across the bridge near the zoo.

'D'you know it's nearly Midsummer Night?' said Maple.

'The shortest night of the year,' said Lizzie. 'We'd better be on our way.' For a brief moment or two there was a sad silence between them.

'Desmond used to say,' Maple said quite suddenly, 'that when I cried, I was just feeling sorry for myself. D'you think that's true, Lizzie?'

Lizzie shook her head. 'There's nothing wrong with feeling sorry for yourself, Maple,' she replied, 'as long as you know the reason why. That's the trouble with people these days. They're so afraid of showing how they feel, so afraid of what other people might think of them. I'm warning you, when I leave you tonight, I intend to bawl my eyes out!'

They both laughed, and stared at each other for a moment. 'Before you go,' said Maple, 'I want to give you something.' She felt into her dress pocket, brought out a tiny packet, and gave it to Lizzie.

Puzzled, she took it. 'What is it?'

'Just something for you to remember me by,' said Maple.

Lizzie opened the packet. Inside was a small silver pendant and fine chain. As she held it up to look at, she found that the pendant was made in the shape of a maple leaf. 'Oh, Maple!' she cried. 'It's beautiful! Thank you *so* much.' She threw her arms around Maple, and hugged her tight.

'But I won't need anything to remind me of you,' she assured her. She looked at her, determined to hold back the tears that were waiting to flow. 'Let's face it,' she said, with great warmth and affection, 'how could I ever forget you?'

A few minutes later, they left the park and made their way back to the bus stop. But the sun still held on for a few more minutes, until it finally sank behind the giant chestnut trees in the distance, abandoning the rich foliage of the park to the calm of a short summer night.

Harriet Angel was up bright and early. She'd decided that she had a lot to do, such as cleaning the kitchen sink properly, polishing the taps in the bathroom, and sweeping down some of the soot that had gathered up the lower chimney. Then there was the lino in the kitchen that needed washing, and the big rug in the sitting room that was full of dust – all jobs that were long overdue, and had to be done if she was going to keep the prefab spick and span. But the moment she set about tackling all these chores, she was suddenly hit by a wave of uncertainty. Why? she asked herself. What was so important about giving the place such a clean-up, and especially now, when Lizzie wouldn't be around to see it anyway. Lizzie? On her hands and knees at the kitchen grate, her hands black with soot, she paused a moment, and sat back on her haunches. Was this what all this frantic activity was about? Was this her way of trying to hide from the reality of what was about to happen, to escape from the fact that Lizzie, *her* Lizzie, would soon no longer be there, no longer rushing around in the mornings so that she wouldn't be late for work, no longer there where Harriet always knew where to find her? Ever since she had known that Lizzie was actually going, she had run through the gamut of emotions, from anger to resentment, from scathing criticism to abject despair. She had tried crying, but that was only temporary relief. She had tried going to sleep at night in the hope that by the time she woke up the following morning, everything she had been dreading would have turned out to be no more than a terrible nightmare. But it wasn't a nightmare. What was happening was real: Lizzie was going away, and she would never see her again. So what could she do to relieve the great pain in her stomach, the pain of guilt – guilt that she had done nothing to make Lizzie's last weeks at home some of the happiest of her life. But there was still time. There was still forty-eight hours left to put things right, to let Lizzie know that when she set off on that boat to the other side of the world, she would carry the love and devotion of a mother who had always adored her. So – why couldn't she do it?

'I think you've done enough work for one day, my dear.'

Harriet was woken from her troubled thoughts by Frank, who was standing over her.

She took hold of his outstretched hand, and let him help her up. 'I've got a lot to do, Frank,' she said. 'The place is filthy.'

She tried to move on, but he gently held her back. 'The place isn't filthy, Harriet,' he said.

With one finger he carefully shifted a lock of stray hair that had flopped across her right eye. 'You've always kept it spotless.'

'Let me go, please, Frank,' she pleaded. 'I've got so much to do before–' She stopped.

'Before what, Harriet?' he asked.

For one brief moment they just stood there, staring into each other's eyes. Then she put her arms around him. They stood like that for several minutes, no words spoken, just a mutual understanding between them.

'We've got to be strong, my dear,' he said quietly into her ear. 'Strong for Lizzie, and strong for us. It's the last positive thing we can do for her.'

She eased herself away and faced him. 'It's too late, Frank,' she said. 'We've already lost her.'

'Lost her to a most wonderful man, Harriet,' he replied. 'Isn't that what we want? Isn't that we want more than anything else in the world?'

Harriet quietly left him, and went into the kitchen.

Frank followed her. He waited whilst she filled the kettle and put it on the stove.

'It's not easy, Harriet,' he said. 'We *all* know that – even the kids. But we can't hold on to Lizzie for the rest of our lives. She has a life of her own to live now, whether it's here, or on the other side of the world. We made a lot of decisions when we were her age, so we mustn't blame her for doing the same thing.' He watched her light a gas ring under the kettle, then go to the kitchen table to sit down. 'It's hard saying goodbye, Harriet,' he said, his tone revealing far more than Harriet realised. 'I don't know how I'm going to cope when I see Lizzie get on that boat on Friday.' He paused, struggling to hold back the sense of loss he was always feeling. 'But it must be like that all over the country, thousands of people just like us, mums and dads and brothers and sisters, all of them feeling as though a part of their own bodies is being taken away for ever.'

'What are you trying to tell me, Frank?' asked Harriet.

Frank sat down at the table with her. 'I'm not trying to tell you anything, my dear,' he replied quietly but resolutely. 'But I'm pleading with you to help make these last few days as bearable for Lizzie as you possibly can.' His voice was beginning to crack with emotion. 'I'm pleading with you to help Lizzie go on her way with the memory of a family who love her, and who are going to miss her like hell.'

Finally unable to contain his feelings, he covered his face with his hands.

For one brief moment, Harriet watched him impassively. Then she reached across and took hold of his hands. 'I'll try, Frank,' she said, her eyes welling with tears. 'I promise you – I'll try.'

Hampstead was not a part of London that Lizzie and Rob knew very well. Although it was mainly known for its artistic community of writers, musicians, journalists, painters and the like, Hampstead Heath was still a great place for everybody, especially on bank holidays when the funfairs, pubs and cafés were full of visitors from all parts of London. Lizzie had only ever been there once before, and that was before the war, when her dad had taken all the Angel family for a Sunday picnic in the grounds of Kenwood House. With the abundance of beautiful old houses, it was a glorious place to live and work, and over the years it had built up a reputation for being one of the most desirable places to live, not only for the cosmopolitan atmosphere, but also for the magnificent views of London that could be seen from the top of the Heath, and Parliament Hill.

It didn't take Lizzie and Rob long to find Norman's new shop. After getting out of Hampstead tube station, all they had to do was to ask the newsvendor sitting on the corner just outside, and he directed them to a narrow winding lane called Flask Walk, which was blessed with a pub, a small café, a boutique that contained some expensive fashionable clothes that needed far too many clothing coupons, and a tiny picture framing shop, intriguingly called Monsieur Norman, that was squeezed between the lot of them.

'Duckies!'

The greeting Lizzie and Rob got the moment they walked through the front door of Monsieur Norman was little short of ecstatic, with kisses and hugs all round, and an immediate invitation to follow the proprietor into his back-parlour workshop.

'This is wonderful, duckies – superb, absolutely superb!' Once he'd got them settled comfortably into two red velvet armchairs, Norman showed that he was clearly quite overwhelmed to receive two of his most favourite people, or so he told them.

'If that's the case,' said Rob, scolding him, 'why didn't you tell us where you were moving to? We haven't seen or heard anything from you since the wedding.'

'Ah!' replied Norman sheepishly. 'I'm sorry about that. But you see, there was a method in my madness. As you know, my colleagues up the Lane didn't exactly approve of me, so I thought the best thing to do was to just melt away into the night.'

'Well, you clearly didn't melt away enough,' quipped Rob, 'because that's how we found out where to find you.'

'Really?' said Norman, not altogether surprised. 'Well, I suppose when you run your own establishment, it isn't always easy to remain incognito. Anyway, what d'you think of it, duckies?' Flouncing about the place like mad, he looked around the cramped back room, proudly exclaiming, 'For me, it's like a dream come true. Just look at it, duckies – my own, my *very* own shop. If anyone had told me years ago that I'd end up with something like this, I'd've thought they were stark raving bonkers. And I can't tell you how many customers I've got! Up here, they really appreciate me.'

'It's lovely, Norman,' said Lizzie, looking round admiringly, 'truly lovely. We're so happy for you – aren't we, Rob?'

'Oh, er – yes,' Rob replied, somewhat less impressed.

'Oh, but I can't tell you what a gorgeous surprise it is to have you here,' said Norman, bustling around excitedly. 'This definitely calls for a celebration. What about a nice G and T, or if you absolutely insist, Rob, I've got an awful bottle of brown ale for you.'

Reluctantly, Lizzie had to interrupt him. 'I'm sorry, Norman,' she said, after exchanging a quick, worried look with Rob. 'I'm afraid we can't stay much longer. We've still got some packing to do.'

Norman immediately stopped what he was doing, and turned with a start. 'Packing?' he asked.

'We've come to say goodbye, Norman,' said Rob.

'Goodbye?' Norman asked, stunned. 'Oh God!' he gasped, clasping his hand in horror to his mouth. 'It's June, isn't it? This is the month!'

Rob nodded. 'We're leaving on Friday morning.'

'Oh ... duckies!' gasped Norman, flopping down into a chair beside them. 'So soon?'

Lizzie nodded. 'I'm afraid so, Norman.'

'If you'd kept in touch, you old reprobate,' said Rob, 'you'd have remembered!'

'There was so much we wanted to tell you,' added Lizzie, 'so many things we wanted to share with you, like where exactly we're heading for, and what Rob's going to do when we get out there.'

Norman was still too stunned and guilty to take it all in. 'Friday morning,' he said gloomily. 'I can hardly believe it.'

'As a matter of fact, Norman,' said Lizzie, 'neither can we.'

During their final few moments together, they sat chatting about Lizzie and Rob's plans for their future in Australia. Norman listened to them both with a mixture of awed fascination and sadness. All around them, his workshop was cluttered with bits and pieces of picture frames that he was working on for his customers, and the place smelled not only of sawdust and carpentry tools, but also of sweet sandalwood joss sticks wafting in from the shop out front. After a while, however, both Lizzie and Rob became aware that Norman's usual *joie de vivre* was beginning to look more superficial than he was prepared to admit. His face suddenly looked more lined than they had remembered, and his whole expression seemed to collapse and become more jaded.

'Oh, by the way,' said Lizzie, 'all sorts of people who were at the wedding want to be remembered to you. My grandmother especially. She took a real shine to you. She said you're one of the wittiest people she's ever met, and that when you danced with her in the evening, you moved like a dream.'

'I never knew you had such a pull with the ladies, Norman,' added Rob flippantly.

Norman forced a smile. 'That's nice,' was all he could say.

Lizzie and Rob exchanged a worried look. Something was wrong. 'Are you all right, Norman?' asked Lizzie, concerned.

'Pardon?' Norman seemed to be miles away. But he suddenly brightened up. 'Oh – yes,' he said. 'I'm fine, just fine. I was just thinking about your gran, Lizzie. She was such good fun. We had a lot in common.' His expression then became quite serious again. 'Actually,' he said, getting up from his chair, 'I'm glad you came, because there's something I've been wanting to tell you two before you go.'

Lizzie and Rob were intrigued to know what was going on, as they watched him go to an old chest of drawers by the back window, and take out a large photograph album.

'Here,' said Norman, offering the album to Lizzie.

Lizzie took it. 'What is it?' she asked anxiously.

'A few snapshots of me,' he replied. 'I thought you'd like to see what I looked like in the old days.'

Rob peered over Lizzie's shoulder as she opened the album. After she had scanned the first page, she looked up and asked, 'Who are all these people, Norman? Your family?'

'Yes,' replied Norman blandly.

Lizzie turned to the next page. Rob was bored already. 'Is this your mother?' asked Lizzie, studying a snapshot of a middle-aged woman on a beach somewhere. 'And I bet this is your father. I can see the resemblance. Who's the little girl?'

'It was taken at Eastbourne,' replied Norman sombrely.

For the next few minutes, Lizzie flicked through the pages, until she came to what appeared to be more recent photographs, featuring mostly a handsome-looking man in a naval petty officer's uniform, followed by several other snapshots of the same man in various poses with an attractive woman. 'Norman, you're keeping me in suspense,' said Lizzie. 'Who *are* all these lovely people? Who's this gorgeous man?' Both she and Rob looked up and waited for a reply.

Norman hesitated, then answered. 'He's my husband.'

Both Lizzie and Rob froze.

'Actually he's my *ex*-husband. We divorced twenty years ago.'

Lizzie and Rob stared at him in disbelief. 'Norman,' Rob asked firmly, 'just *what* are you talking about?'

'You can see the photo, Rob,' Norman replied. 'The man in the uniform is the man I married twenty-five years ago. His name is Malcolm Jordan. I was Norma Jordan. But after we were divorced, I reverted back to my maiden name – Pringle.'

Rob clutched his head in utter bewilderment. 'This is crazy!' he spluttered.

Lizzie restrained him by squeezing his arm.

'It's ridiculous – impossible!' insisted Rob. 'You're telling us that – you're not a man?'

Norman smiled mischievously. 'That's a matter of opinion,' he suggested.

'And the woman in the photograph–' Rob pointed to the page in the album – '*this* woman is *you?*'

Norman's expression became serious again. 'Unfortunately, duckie,' he said, 'none of us can change the way we were born. Not yet anyway. For the first years of my life, I hated what I was, and what I never wanted to be.'

'And yet – you married?' said Rob accusingly.

'I met Malcolm, and fell in love,' Norman replied. 'It was a great mistake, and I've always deeply regretted it. The only good thing I ever did in my marriage was to let him go.'

Rob flopped back in his chair, unable to take in everything he had been told.

'I'm sorry, duckie,' Norman said to him. Then he turned to Lizzie. 'I'm sorry if it makes a difference to the way you feel. I never wanted to deceive either of you. You're two lovely people who've accepted me for what I am, despite the way things were up at the Lane. But it's not easy living with people who take you at face value.'

Lizzie got up from her chair and put her arm around Norman's waist. 'It makes no difference to me, Norman,' she said warmly. 'Nor to Rob. Whatever you are, you are. As long as it's what you want, and what makes you happy in life.' She turned to Rob, and nodded to him.

To Norman's delight, Rob got up, and offered his hand to shake. Norman looked at him and shook hands. His face crumpled. 'You know, if you carry on like this, you two duckies,' he said, his voice cracking with emotion, 'I shall kidnap the pair of you!'

'I wish you were coming with us, Norman,' said Lizzie. 'You'd be a wow in Australia!'

'*Me?*' replied Norman. 'Oh no, duckie! I could never cope with all those rough men cutting sheep's fur. I've got a nice little pub up the road. They know how to look after weird folk like me!'

They all laughed together.

'Just one question,' asked Rob. 'Are you going

to be a man for the rest of your life?'

'Well, now,' said Norman. 'That's a very interesting question. As a matter of fact, I think I will. After all, what you see is what you get.' He gave them a mischievous wink. 'But then it takes all sorts to make a world – doesn't it, duckies?'

Liz and Rob made their way back to the tube station in a daze. Their visit to Norman had turned out to be the most extraordinary experience they had ever known. As they strolled together hand in hand along Hampstead High Street in the afternoon sun, all they could talk about was this funny little creature with the olive complexion and puffed, rouged cheeks, a woman in body, but a man in spirit. It was more difficult for Rob to grasp than Lizzie, for, ever since he had known Norman, he had consistently taken his part against the hostile jibes of the boys up the Lane, who never once stopped to consider what lay beneath the surface of that 'nancy boy' image. He questioned himself how any of them could have known about the struggle Norman had been up against all his life, the struggle to understand who and what he was. But even if they *had* known, would they have treated him any differently? A freak of nature? A self-indulgent whim? Whatever it was, Norman had the right to be treated as a human being.

By the time they had reached the tube station, the early-evening commuters were already racing to take their places in the lift for the start of their stifling journey home. Lizzie and Rob were quite happy to let them get in front, for with the closing of yet another day came the reality that this would probably be the last time they would be part of the busy life of London. When they finally got into the lift, and started the long descent to the platforms, which seemed to be in the bowels of the earth below, Rob put his arm around Lizzie's waist, and between them they scanned the dated adverts in panels on the wall of the lift. Amongst them was a picture of the famous actress Gertrude Lawrence in a scene from a new London stage play, resplendent in a long evening gown, feathered headdress, and a long cigarette holder.

'I must say,' Rob said, 'I'd never have guessed.'

'What?' asked Lizzie.

'Norman,' said Rob. 'What about you?'

Lizzie also looked at the glamorous Gertrude Lawrence advert. 'Oh, I knew,' she replied, with a slight, knowing smile.

Rob turned to look at her. 'You did? How come?'

Lizzie turned and smiled at him. 'Oh – a woman's instinct,' she replied.

Chapter 24

On Friday morning, the wind was blowing hard. In Tollington Park, the tall elm trees were bending so low, some of the upper branches had already snapped off, shedding the midsummer leaves all over the pavements. It was clear that the recent hot spell had at last come to an end, to be replaced by the good old predictable grey skies, thunderstorms and heavy rain. For Lizzie, the weather was shattering her last-minute nerves, and ever since she had got up at the crack of dawn, she had regretted the day she had ever agreed to go to Australia. With her stomach churned up at the thought of her impending departure, she harassed Rob by telling him, 'I'm going to be as sick as a dog, I know I am!'

Rob did his best to ignore her nerves, as she sat on a huge suitcase while he tried to fasten the locks. 'Just keep still, Liz!' he grumbled. 'If these things burst open before we get to the ship, we'll be in real trouble!'

'Come on, you two!' called Gran, marching straight into their upstairs bedroom un-announced. 'Your dad'll be here soon with the taxi. If you miss that boat train, you'll be in big trouble!'

'Oh, please, Gran!' pleaded Lizzie. 'Don't go on! I'm nervous enough as it is. Nobody told me leaving home was going to be as horrible as this.'

'What's horrible about it?' retorted Gran. 'I'll be glad to get rid of the pair of you. At least I can now get some decent tenants!' By making light of the occasion, Gran was deliberately trying to cheer up not only Lizzie, but herself too.

Rob finished fastening the locks on the last of the four suitcases. 'Right!' he said, triumphantly. 'That's it! Liz, you and Gran get downstairs. I'll wait till Dad gets here to help me with this lot.'

'But I haven't made the bed!' gasped Lizzie, buzzing around, trying to collect last-minute things she was taking with her.

'Oh, for God's sake, Liz!' barked Rob, irritated by her panic. 'You can do all that when you get back!'

Both of them suddenly realised the pointlessness of his remark. Consumed with guilt, Rob went across to Lizzie, and gave her a quick, apologetic, comforting hug. 'Sorry, darling,' he said.

Gran shook her head. 'Leave the damn bed!' she barked. 'I've got all day to sort that out!' She quickly left the room and went downstairs.

After Gran had gone, Lizzie picked up her handbag, and looked around. 'This was our first home together,' she said. 'It's not much, but it gave us a start.' Being so het up had left her absolutely drained, so she took a moment to rest on the edge of the bed. 'I can't believe this is happening,' she said.

Rob joined her. They shared a moment's silence, looking around the room for the last time. 'There'll be plenty of good things to look forward to, Liz,' he said. 'You *do* believe me, don't you?'

Lizzie smiled. 'Of course I do, darling,' she replied. 'I wouldn't be doing this unless I did. I'll be all right once we're on our way. But right now, what we're doing seems to be so unreal.' She turned to him, and leaned her head on his shoulder. 'It was a lovely evening our two families had at your parents' home last night,' she said. 'I know you're going to miss them. You'd never admit it, but I *do* know.'

Rob put his arm around her waist, 'Nothing's

ever going to be quite the same again,' he said. 'You know that, don't you?'

Lizzie nodded.

'But I want you to promise me something,' he continued. 'If you ever feel I've let you down, you'll tell me. Will you do that for me, Liz? Will you?'

'Only if you'll do the same for me.'

He was about to answer, but they were distracted by the sound of the taxi arriving in the street down below.

'You'd better get going,' he said, kissing her gently on the forehead.

Lizzie nodded, got up from the bed, and collected the rest of her things. She stopped at the door just long enough to take one last look back at him.

'Good on yer, Mrs Thompson,' said Rob, in a soft, mock Australian accent.

'Good on yer, Mr Thompson,' said Lizzie, returning his comforting jibe. With those parting words, she left the room.

With Rob and her dad having already gone ahead with the luggage to the railway station, Lizzie bid a tearful farewell to her grandmother, and made her way on foot back to the Angels' prefab. On the way down Hornsey Road, she found it difficult to take anything in, because she knew that if she did it would upset her. But as she passed what used to be the old Star cinema on the opposite side of the road, she couldn't help feeling a wave of nostalgia, with abiding memories of when she was young – Saturday morning flicks with Susan, James and Benjamin, all of them lined up in the front row, craning their heads to look up at the week's Tom Mix cowboys and Indians serial, *Adventures on Planet-X*, the Laurel and Hardy two-reelers, and all those cartoon classics such as Felix the Cat, and Mickey Mouse. As she walked briskly past, those days all seemed like a hundred million years away. In fact, this walk along Hornsey Road had a strange air of finality about it, for it was more than likely that she would never do this walk home again. It had been the same when, the previous evening, she and Rob had taken a few minutes off from their packing to stroll round to Bedford Terrace, where they stopped briefly outside old Lil Beasley's place, now boarded up by the landlord, who had already received his first compensation from the local council for the future demolition of the entire terrace of houses. Lizzie had had to smile. *'Bleedin' landlord… Says 'e can't afford ter let people like me 'ang on in 'igh-class property like mine. 'Igh class – ha!'* She could still hear the old girl's anger ringing through her ears.

She reached the corner of Andover Road. There were plenty of people around, because it was rush hour, with commuters hurrying to catch the number 14 bus, which was always packed at this time of morning, children going to school for the last few weeks before they broke up for their long summer break, and housewives already setting out to join the queues for any new supplies of potatoes that may have just arrived at Hicks the greengrocers in Seven Sisters Road, some pig's trotters from Stevens and Steeds, broken biscuits from Lipton's, or some fresh Cheddar cheese, wire cut on the marbled slab at Sainsbury's. All this raced through Lizzie's mind as she hurriedly turned the corner, only to bump straight into someone coming in the opposite direction.

'Oi! Can't yer look where yer– Oh, it's you, Lizzie.'

The one person Lizzie would have preferred not to see at that precise moment was Martha Cutting. 'I'm sorry, Martha,' she said.

'It's all right, love,' replied Martha. 'I know 'ow yer must be feelin'. It's goin' ter feel funny ter fink yer won't be skippin' down every so often ter see the family. Still – yer must be excited, ain't yer?'

'Something like that, Martha,' replied Lizzie.

'Never mind, it's all fer the best, I always say,' said Martha, who was being no help at all to the way Lizzie was feeling. 'Er course, I'd never do such a fing meself. I love my country too much fer that. Anyway, I trust Attlee ter get us out of this mess. You mark my words, 'e'll soon get us back on our feet again.'

'Goodbye, Martha,' said Lizzie, straining to get on her way.

'Goodbye, Lizzie dear,' replied Martha. 'Don't do anyfin' *I* wouldn't do!' Laughing her head off, she went. But before she had gone more than a few yards, she turned once more and called back, 'Oh, by the way, I 'ope there was nuffin' wrong last night – wiv yer dad, I mean?'

Lizzie turned with a start. 'What's that, Martha?' she returned.

'That flatfoot that come ter see 'im.'

Lizzie's stomach turned over. 'The police?' she asked. 'They came to see Dad?'

'Oh, 'e wasn't there long,' said Martha. 'I only noticed 'cos I just 'appened ter be lookin' out of my bedroom window at the time. I wouldn't worry, luv,' she said, moving off. 'Bleedin' flatfoots are always pokin' their noses in fings that don't concern 'em!'

Having done her worst to upset Lizzie in her final moments, Martha scuttled off quite obliviously down Hornsey Road.

For a brief moment or so, Lizzie was transfixed to the spot where she had come to a halt. Her mind was racing again. Could this be it? she asked herself. Could this be what she had feared most of all? Had the police finally caught up with her dad? Had he lied to her about the whole black market thing having blown over, that the police were no longer interested in him? It was this one grim thought that had plagued her nights ever since she had agreed to go to Australia with Rob. But how could she go now, she asked herself. How could she just go off for the rest of her life, knowing that her family were going to have to face up to such a major crisis in their lives? She moved on.

She reached the front gate of the prefab to find Andy Willets waiting there. 'Wotcha, Liz,' he said chirpily as she approached. 'All ready fer the big cruise, are yer?'

'It's hardly a cruise, Andy,' she replied. But it wasn't a brush-off. She had known that Andy, who lived just down the road, fancied her right from the days when they were at school together, and she was very touched that he had come to see her off.

'Well,' said Andy, 'yer know wot I mean. There's an awful lot er water between 'ere an' Aussieland. *I* wouldn't say no if someone offered me the fare ter go out there. Yer never know, yer may find me knockin' on yer front door down there one of these days.'

'I hope so, Andy,' replied Lizzie. 'Rob and I would always make you very welcome.'

'Oh – yeah,' said Andy, with a forced smile. 'Gotcha!' He stretched out his hand. 'So – look after yerself, Liz. Don't ferget yer ol' mates, will ya?'

Lizzie took his hand; shook it. 'I don't think that's ever likely to happen, Andy,' she replied. To his astonishment, she leaned forward, and gently kissed him on the cheek. 'Goodbye, Andy,' she said uncertainly.

Shaken, but trying to bluff through what he was feeling, he smiled. ''Bye, mate!' he said. Then he rushed off, pulling his flat cap tightly on to his head, hands in pockets.

Lizzie watched him go, until she suddenly remembered what Martha had just told her about her dad. She rushed into the house, to find Benjamin and Cissie bursting out through the front door to greet her.

'We're coming too!' yelled Cissie, shaking with excitement.

'We're *all* coming!' exploded Benjamin simultaneously.

Lizzie was taken aback. 'What are you talking

about?' she asked, puzzled. 'Why aren't you at school?'

'We've got the day off,' said Cissie.

'Mum wrote a note to the head teacher,' said Benjamin breathlessly. 'He said he quite understood. He said it'll be quite all right for us to come down to Southampton to see you off.'

'What?' Lizzie panicked. How was she going to cope with *this*? 'You can't! You just can't!'

'It's all right, Lizzie,' said Susan, who was there waiting, as Lizzie, Benjamin and Cissie went into the prefab. 'We all discussed it the other night. We wanted it to be a surprise for you. Dad went down to the station last night and bought tickets for us all on the boat train.'

Aghast, Lizzie tried to speak.

'It's no use trying to object,' said Susan. 'We've made up our minds. We want to be there when you go. After all, we may never...' She broke away, showing clear signs of being overwhelmed with anguish.

'Oh Susan!' Lizzie said. 'I think it's wonderful. I think it's wonderful of you all. But I'm not sure I'm going to be able to cope with it. If I go, I just want to be able to get away as quietly as possible.'

Susan, dabbing her eyes with her handkerchief, looked up with a start. '*If* you go?' she asked falteringly.

Harriet came out of her bedroom. Like all the others, she was already in her Sunday best dress and hat, and ready to go.

'Mum!' said Lizzie urgently, going straight to her. 'What's this about Dad last night?'

Harriet was puzzled. 'What d'you mean?'

'I met Martha Cutting,' Lizzie said. 'She told me the police came to see Dad last night. What was it about?'

Harriet smiled. 'Oh, *that*,' she said dismissively. 'It was nothing, Lizzie – absolutely nothing at all. They came to tell your dad that they've caught the person they were looking for.'

'*Which* person?' she asked sceptically.

'The man they were after when they called your dad in for questioning a few months ago.' Harriet showed no concern at all. 'Don't you remember?' she asked. 'He had to go on an identity parade made up of people they'd picked up at random in the streets, people of the same height and type as this man they were looking for. Well, now they've found him.'

For one brief moment, Lizzie stared at her mum. Something told her that she was not telling her the truth. 'And that's all?' she asked. 'That's the only reason they came here?'

Harriet was puzzled. 'That's all, Lizzie,' she said. 'Don't you believe me?'

Lizzie was so on edge about everything that she just didn't know *what* to believe any more. She smiled back weakly, and nodded.

'Come into the kitchen for a moment, Lizzie,' Harriet said. 'I want to talk to you.'

'The taxi will be here any moment, Mum,' said Susan.

'We shan't be long,' called Harriet, as Lizzie followed her into the kitchen. 'Make sure all the windows are closed before we go. Sit down for a moment, Lizzie,' said Harriet, as they came into

474

the kitchen.

'Mum, I'm much too nervous.'

'*Please*,' pleaded Harriet. 'Just for a moment.'

Reluctantly, Lizzie did what her mother had asked.

Her mother sat opposite her at the kitchen table, and took something out of her handbag there. It was an envelope. 'Take this,' she said, handing it over to Lizzie.

'What is it?'

'It's a little something to help you on your way,' replied Harriet. 'It's not very much, but it'll give you a bit of a start – at least, for the time being.' Lizzie started to open the envelope. 'No – not now,' said Harriet. 'Wait until you're on the boat. It's not much. Just a little I've been putting aside for the past few weeks. There's also a note inside. Once you've read it, you can throw it away.'

'I can't take money from you, Mum,' said Lizzie, putting the envelope on the table in front of Harriet. 'You've got far too many expenses. What with the family, and now Dad paying for all of you to come down to Southampton.'

'Let us worry about the expenses, Lizzie,' said Harriet. 'We've managed so far, and we'll continue to do so.' She slowly pushed the envelope back to Lizzie. 'But before you go, there's something I have to say to you.' She paused. 'This is probably the last chance I shall have to talk to you.'

'Mum...'

Harriet held up her hand to silence her. 'I said "probably",' she insisted. 'No one really knows

475

what the future holds for any of us. But I don't want you to go away without my saying what I've tried saying to you so many times over these past few months.' She stretched out, and covered Lizzie's hand with her own. 'Thank you, Lizzie,' she said. 'Thank you for all the good times, and thank you for helping me and your dad to get through all the bad times. I don't think I could have done it without you.'

Lizzie's face crumpled up. 'Oh – Mum!' she stuttered, her voice cracking. Fighting back tears, she got up, stood behind her mum, leaned her head on her head, and hugged her. 'Am I doing the right thing? Am I?'

Harriet lowered her eyes. 'That's something you're going to have to find out for yourself, Lizzie,' she replied. 'From now on, it's just you – and Rob. We can't shield you any longer.'

Lizzie turned her round, and kneeled in front of her. 'Listen to me, Mum – *please!*' she pleaded. 'If ever you're in trouble, if there's ever a time that you need me, and you can't cope with something, you've got to let me know. D'you understand? *Do* you?'

Harriet smiled at her with some irony. 'Australia's a very long way from Andover Road, Lizzie,' she said.

'I'll get back,' insisted Lizzie. 'Somehow, I'll get back. I won't let you down. I would never let you or Dad down – nor *any* of the family.'

'The Angel family are a pretty hardy lot, Lizzie,' said Harriet. 'I may have made plenty of mistakes in my time, but if there's one thing I *have* learned, it's how to survive.'

For the next moment or so, the two of them remained where they were, holding on to each other in silence. Memories of a lifetime of being a member of the Angel family were whirling around Lizzie's mind, from the horrors of being bombed out to the smell of her mum's cooking from the night before, years of so many things that were such a part of her normal everyday existence, things that she had taken for granted, but which would no longer be there for her when she woke up every morning beneath a different roof, a different sky. And for Harriet it was like cutting an umbilical cord that had always been there, linking her with her daughter as a baby, a child, and now a young woman, a young woman who was about to go out into a world on her own, a world full of mystery, danger and wonderment. In some ways, losing Lizzie like this was worse than if she was about to die. There was a finality about death; nothing could be done about it; there was no turning back. But this was different. Lizzie wasn't going to die – not for a long time she hoped – she was going to be out there somewhere, some place where their hands were never going to be able to reach out to each other again.

'If anything should happen to Dad,' said Lizzie, too distressed to raise her head from her mother's lap, 'you *will* let me know, won't you?' She looked up. Tears were streaming down her cheeks. 'Promise me, Mum – please!'

Neither reacted immediately to the sound of the taxi arriving outside.

Harriet put her hand under Lizzie's chin, and

477

gently raised it. 'Time to go, Lizzie,' she said quietly. 'Time to go.'

The Customs and Excise hall at Southampton Docks was jammed to capacity. Ever since early morning, crowds of passengers, mainly emigrants, had been arriving from different parts of the country, most of them with relatives and friends there to see them off on their long journey to the other side of the world. Just outside, on Pier 16, the huge jaws of the massive ocean liner, the SS *Mauretania*, was waiting patiently to devour passengers and baggage, the thick black smoke from its furnaces already beginning to climb up a thin funnel and into the dazzling June sky.

Despite the sadness of the occasion, the Angel family, together with Rob's mother and father, and his brother, Joe, had enjoyed a good journey down on the boat train from Waterloo. They had all sat in a compartment together. Benjamin and Cissie didn't know whether they were more excited by being on a train for only the second time in their lives, or because they had got a day off from school; James spent the entire journey in what seemed to be a long daydream, staring out of the window in awed fascination as the train, thick engine smoke billowing past, sped its way through green summer fields, lush forests, past lakes and ponds, and myriads of fine English towns and villages. But the rest of the two families had travelled mostly in silence, Lizzie nestled between her mum and dad, Susan occasionally talking to Rob's brother, Joe, and

Rob himself holding his mum's hand whilst his dad, who, with his mind miles away in Australia, puffed on his pipe in a corner seat by the corridor window. When anyone did actually say a few words, it was all fairly innocuous stuff, mainly about how filthy the train carriages were, or how beautiful the countryside was looking at this time of the year.

It was a different story when they arrived at Southampton. Benjamin and Cissie were the same, of course, delirious with excitement to be up close to a huge ocean liner on the quayside just outside the Customs hall, without it ever sinking into their young minds that within a short time they might be seeing their big sister for the very last time.

Once both families had cleared through Customs, Rob spent a lot of his time talking with his mother, who was now becoming very tearful, and his dad, who, despite his bravado act of appearing to take Rob's departure in his stride, was, deep down inside, desperately upset. Oddly enough, it was James who appeared to be the most affected by the occasion: for much of the time he seemed to wrap his arms around his mother, whilst watching every move that Lizzie made.

When passengers and their relatives and friends were finally allowed on to the quayside, they still had a long wait before they could board the boat, so they spent most of the time eating the sandwiches that both mums had made prior to the journey. However, it also gave Lizzie and her dad the opportunity to have one last talk before departure. Surrounded by a sea of distressed faces, Frank kept as close to his daughter as he could, just in case there was suddenly a human tidal wave sweeping them into the sea water alongside.

'Reminds me a bit of D-Day,' said Frank, his arm holding on defiantly around Lizzie's waist. 'There were so many troops crushed together like this, I thought the boat would sink.'

Lizzie knew he was only making small talk in order to distract her from the ordeal they were all going through. 'Please don't talk to me about boats sinking, Dad!' she pleaded. 'I'm scared out of my mind as it is.'

'Don't worry, dear,' he said reassuringly. 'This journey's going to be smooth sailing. You'll have a whale of a time. Just think of it as a luxury cruise, the first real holiday you've ever had – more than *I've* ever been able to give you.'

'You've always given me so much more than holidays, Dad,' she replied. 'I'm the luckiest girl in the world to have had you around all my life.'

Frank smiled warmly, concealing what he was determined she shouldn't know. However, despite the fact that he had made a conscious decision not to show his true feelings when they parted, the strain was clearly visible on his face. 'Well, now I'm getting you off my hands, I can concentrate on the rest of the clan!'

Lizzie gave him a friendly dig in the ribs. She didn't believe a word he had said. The constant buzz of people all around them saying their last farewells was making it necessary for both of them to raise their voices, so she drew closer, and

480

whispered into his ear, 'I want to ask you some-thing, Dad.' Her stomach constantly churned as the minutes ticked away. 'Is this problem with the police *really* over?"

He turned to look at her. 'What problem?' he asked, fully prepared for the question.

Lizzie looked at him. She still didn't know how serious he was. 'Promise?'

'Listen to me, dear Lizzie,' he replied. 'All I want you to do is to get on that boat, and forget about all the problems, all the misery the Angels have had to face over these past few years. You're going into a bright new future now. So enjoy it!'

Her dad's answer was not good enough for Lizzie. 'Promise?' she insisted.

Knowing only too well what the consequences would be if he said otherwise, he answered with a smile, 'Promise.'

Behind them, a few irritated passengers and friends started singing, 'Why are we waiting?', which was immediately picked up by the rest of the crowds waiting to file on board the ship. Soon, the air was echoing to the sound of impatient, nervous voices. But within moments, a voice on the ocean Tannoy system boomed out along the quayside, 'Passengers may now board the ship!'

The irritated singing was immediately replaced by a loud cheer, but that soon changed when the Tannoy voice added, 'Passengers on board only. No visitors, please!'

The cheering ceased, to be replaced by groans of disappointment, especially from Benjamin and Cissie.

481

As the Angel and Thompson families were near the back of the crowd, it took them all of forty minutes to make their way to the gangway. On the way, Lizzie held her dad's hand so tight, their knuckles went white. Harriet followed on immediately behind with Susan, James, Benjamin and Cissie, and behind them came Rob, whose mother, tears streaming down her cheeks, was clinging on to him for all she was worth, whilst his dad and Joe shuffled grim-faced along with them as best they could. Finally, Lizzie reached the foot of the gangway, and waited for Rob to join her. Once they were together, like so many other passengers in front who were saying goodbye to their loved ones, Lizzie hesitated just long enough to hug Benjamin and Cissie. 'Behave yourselves now, you two!' she said, tears cascading down her cheeks. 'Or else!' She kissed them, then turned to her eldest brother. 'Goodbye, James,' she said, almost unable to speak. 'I'll send you some postcards for your collection.'

James's face was absolutely drained white, and impassive. 'I'll miss you, Lizzie,' he said. It was the first time he had ever shown any emotion to Lizzie, or anyone else. She leaned forward, hugged and kissed him on the forehead. 'I'll miss you too, James.'

Susan, tears also streaming down her cheeks, was waiting for Lizzie.

'Oh, Susan!' cried Lizzie. 'Dear, dear Susan.' She hugged her. 'Take care of them for me,' she said softly, into Susan's ear. 'If anything happens … *please* … take care of them!'

'Goodbye, Lizzie,' said Susan, kissing her sister

quickly on the cheek.

Lizzie turned next to her mother. 'Mum...' She could hardly speak.

'Goodbye, Lizzie,' said Harriet, her face drawn with emotion that she was struggling to contain. They embraced for several moments. 'Only remember the good times,' she said quietly into Lizzie's ear.

Reluctantly, Lizzie turned last of all to her father. In that one brief moment, she could see his taut face, and the look in his eyes that had been disturbing her for so long. It was a look that revealed so much, a look that told her she would never see him again. 'Dad!' she said, throwing her arms around him, and hugging him for as long as she possibly could. 'I don't know what to say to you.' Her voice was now practically inaudible.

'You don't have to say *anything*, my dear one,' he said softly into her ear. 'I *know*.'

Behind them, Rob had taken an emotional farewell of his own mother, father and brother, and was now joining Lizzie at the foot of the gangplank. With one last tearful wave, the two of them joined the queue of other distressed passengers filing up the gangplank on to the ship.

Some time later, Lizzie and Rob appeared on one of the lower decks on the starboard side of the huge vessel, surrounded by hundreds of other weeping passengers, all craning their necks to get a final glimpse of their loved ones. Lizzie desperately scanned the hordes of relatives and friends who were waving frantically from the dockside below. It was an incredible sight, a seething mass of faces, shouting, sobbing, waving hats and anything else they could get their hands on.

'There they are!' yelled Lizzie, the moment she spotted the Angel and Thompson families on the quayside below.

Rob looked down to where she was pointing, and yelled out, 'Goodbye!'

Lizzie also yelled at the top of her voice, 'Mum! Dad!'

The calls were returned immediately, but could only just be heard above the chorus of farewells.

'Susan!' shouted Lizzie. 'James! Benjamin! Cissie!' Her voice was now so cracked with emotion, she could hardly get the words out at all.

The chaotic scene was finally eclipsed by the sound of the ship's bell and horn, as the ropes securing the vessel were finally released and wound back on board, leaving the ship to pull slowly away from the quayside.

The ship took quite some time to navigate the delicate waters of the Solent, but even by the time it was practically out of view, the Angel family remained on the quayside watching it go, until it finally disappeared into the murky waters of the English Channel. As they turned to go, Cissie, taking hold of her dad's hand, asked, 'When are they coming home again?'

Lizzie and Rob went up to the top deck to watch the English coastline gradually fade into the horizon. They stood there for what seemed to be an eternity, alone with their thoughts, their

484

memories and their fears.

The ship's horn boomed out across the gradually swelling waves. By then the first gentle breeze hinted the start of a long voyage. Lizzie and Rob held each other tight.

Despite the trauma of those last few rushed moments with their families, they were now ready for whatever lay ahead.

Chapter 25

1982

Picnic Point Lookout was bathed in hot summer sunshine, and hordes of people in shorts and bathing costumes had gathered up there in a desperate attempt to get away from the stifling humidity of the city. Harriet found it an odd experience to think that this was January, when back home the long dark days were probably bringing nothing but rain, wind, frost and snow. But this was not England. It wasn't Islington. She was on the other side of the world, in the middle of a ravishing Australian summer, where she had just spent the most extraordinary Christmas of her life, complete with a rotund, ebullient Father Christmas handing out toys to children in a Toowoomba department store, cotton wool snow adorning shop windows, and pine Christmas trees with all the traditional coloured lights and decorations in every home she had visited.

Harriet had adored every moment of her

month-long visit to Lizzie and Rob, not only because she had been taken on wonderful sightseeing trips everywhere, from the rising skyscrapers in Brisbane, to the beautiful Botanical Gardens in Toowoomba, but because she had met so many of the newest members of her family. She was particularly thrilled to have been able to spend Christmas with Lizzie and Rob's daughter, Betty, and her husband, Mike, and their two kids, Sally and Peter; and Lizzie and Rob's son, Lou, and his wife, Kate, and their three kids, all of whom had come down specially from Adelaide for the unique family reunion. Harriet felt so proud to have five grandchildren, even if they did all have funny Australian accents, which at times she couldn't understand; every one of them was absolutely adorable, except that, like all her other grandchildren back home, they were all utterly spoiled!

Yes, despite her many misgivings, every moment of her visit had been an exhilarating experience for Harriet. She had learned so much, not only about how people lived on the other side of the world, but also about her own extended family, whom she had never expected to meet. As she looked out at the magnificent distant view of the Lockyer Valley, and Tabletop Mountain, she was already dreading the thought that in a couple of days, she would be stepping back on board that airliner for the long flight back to England.

'It's hard to believe you have all this right on your own doorstep,' she said to Lizzie, who was crouched alongside her and Rob on a picnic rug.

'Finsbury Park was never like this!'

Lizzie and Rob laughed. 'Oh, I don't know, Mum,' said Rob in his cutting adopted accent. 'I wouldn't mind betting you that the Finsbury Park ducks have got quite a few relatives of their own out here in Toowoomba!'

They all laughed, a sound that was suddenly dwarfed by the screech of a hawk high up overhead, searching for prey in the valley below.

'Your dad would've loved this place so much,' said Harriet. 'I remember soon after you came out here, he kept trying to imagine the kind of place you lived in, what it looked like, and how you spent your spare time. In fact that's all he ever spoke about for months on end.'

During Harriet's visit, Lizzie had at no time pressured her mother into talking about what happened to her dad and the family after she had left home. Despite the fact that it was something that had been lodged in her mind for thirty-four years, Lizzie knew that her mother would only be able to tell her in her own time.

'At least he had the postcards we sent to James,' Lizzie reminded her.

'Oh yes,' replied Harriet. 'He mulled over them constantly. But it wasn't the same. It was you yourself that he dreamed of. When you went it left such a huge hole in his heart.'

Lizzie sensed that Harriet was in the mood to tell her what she needed to know so badly. With just one look, she signalled discreetly to Rob.

'Reckon I'll go an' have a quiet fag out on the Lookout,' he said, getting up. 'My ol' legs could do with a bit of exercise.'

Lizzie and Harriet watched him go, wandering off towards the edge of the escarpment, hands in his shorts pockets, his old bush hat pushed casually to the back of his head.

'He's a good man,' said Harriet.

'Oh yes,' said Lizzie, with affection. 'He doesn't do too bad for an old codger!'

For the next moment or so, they relaxed in the hot sunshine, both of them wearing identical huge, wide straw hats, brought from a market trader in Toowoomba. Near by, a group of day-trippers from Brisbane were taking more photographs of themselves than of the surrounding scenery, and further down the path back towards the Warrego Highway, an ice-cream seller was doing a roaring trade from the side of his van.

'What happened, Mum?' Lizzie asked, breaking the silence between them.

They turned to look at one another.

'In thirty-four years,' Lizzie continued, 'you never once wrote to tell me what happened to Dad after we left. The only thing I've ever been told is when Susan and Don came out here a few years ago. They told me about how ill Dad had got, and how, just before he died, he'd had an operation for stomach cancer.'

'And that's *all* they told you?' asked Harriet, looking away.

'Yes,' replied Lizzie. 'They kept pretty cagey about everything. Is that what you wanted, Mum? Is that why you wrote me hardly any letters all these years? Is that why you wouldn't answer any of the questions I asked you?' She was determined to press her. 'Why did Dad die, Mum?' she asked bluntly. 'He was a young man. He was far too young to die.'

'He was heartbroken when you left,' said Harriet obtusely. 'He never really got over it.'

'You're blaming *me*?' asked Lizzie tersely.

Harriet hesitated, then slowly shook her head. 'No, I'm not blaming you, Lizzie. In fact, in those final years, you were the only one who gave him the will to live. No, what happened was far more unfortunate than that.'

'Unfortunate?'

'Your father got himself into trouble,' said Harriet, 'and he just didn't know how to get out of it.'

'But that black-market thing blew over?' said Lizzie. 'He told me that himself. He said the police weren't going to do anything about it. He said the whole thing had blown over. I'd never have left if it hadn't.' She was disturbed by her mother's reluctance to answer her. 'Tell me, Mum – please! I've lived with this for long enough. I *must* know what happened.'

Again Harriet hesitated. Then she got up and, with arms crossed, looked out at the views. 'He went to prison for eighteen months,' she said. 'That's why we all agreed to keep it from you.'

Lizzie was so shocked, it took a moment for what she had just heard to sink in. She got up and stood beside her mother.

'I didn't find out until after Frank had died,' said Harriet, 'but apparently, before you left, he did a deal with the man who charged him. He promised to co-operate as long as he delayed the

489

charge until after you'd gone.'

Lizzie screwed up her face in horror. 'Oh God!' she gasped.

'He knew you'd try to cancel coming out here,' continued Harriet, 'but he was determined he wasn't going to allow you and Rob to jeopardise your entire future because of him.'

'Oh God!' Lizzie said again. 'I should have known! I should have known all along that he was lying to me.'

'Not lying, Lizzie,' said Harriet, putting her arm around her waist. 'He was trying to protect you. After all, what good could you have done by not carrying on with your life? It was bad enough that the rest of us had to cope with everything that happened to him.'

'That's what I mean!' insisted Lizzie. 'I *should* have been there.'

'You couldn't have done *anything*, darling, I promise you,' Harriet assured her. 'We were all helpless. He was eventually sentenced to eighteen months for handling stolen goods. It would have been longer, but he co-operated with the police by telling them everything he knew about all the other people involved. Some of them got far longer sentences. Frank hated himself for what he'd done. It was that that killed him.'

'What d'you mean?' asked Lizzie.

'Whilst he was in Pentonville Prison, his stomach condition deteriorated. He was given remission because it was diagnosed as a particularly virulent form of cancer.' She faltered, finding it difficult to go on. 'He'd only been out for two months...' That was as far as she could go.

Lizzie turned and held on to her. 'Oh Mum,' she said softly. 'Why didn't you tell me? Why did you have to keep it from me all these years? Couldn't you trust me enough to know that I would never have been ashamed of Dad – whatever he'd done. I loved him far too much for that. I loved you *both*. If only you'd told me. I'd have been there – as I always had been. I'd never have let us drift apart for so long.'

Harriet shook her head. 'I know, Lizzie,' she said. 'I've always regretted the way I treated you so badly.' She sighed. 'Anyway, we coped as best we could,' she continued. 'After Frank died, my mother helped us to find a rented flat in Thane Villas. It wasn't much, but once Susan, James and Benjamin were old enough to get jobs of their own, we managed to get a mortgage on the whole house and – well, that's where I've been ever since. I think Frank would have approved. He never wanted to hurt me. He never wanted to hurt *any* of us – especially you. You meant everything to him. What he did was not for himself. Nothing he ever did was for himself. It was for his family – "my very own Guardian Angels", he always used to say. I never really had the time to thank him. I never really took the time to – understand him. But he was a good man, and I'll always be grateful that he was my husband, and the father of our children.'

Lizzie pulled her close, and embraced her. A group of young children playing tag nearby giggled when they saw two silly old ladies hugging each other. But it was a moment – a special moment – between the two of them that

491

had been long overdue. There, against the spectacular backdrop of a lush green valley, and the distant view of the magnificent bare Tabletop Mountain, after thirty-four years, Lizzie and her mum had come full circle. But although the memory of that tiny prefab in Andover Road was gradually fading into no more than a hazy dream, the effect it had on the lives of one group of Angels would remain for a very long time.

'Hey, you two!'

Lizzie and Harriet turned, to find Rob, hands on hips, shaking his head. 'Is this some kind of a hen party?' he asked. 'Or can anyone join?'

As always happens, the return journey to an airport is never as inviting as the trip out on arrival. But when Harriet took her leave of Lizzie and Rob's house in the sun-drenched street in Toowoomba, there was a glow inside that told her only good things. It told her that it wouldn't be the last time she would see her daughter, that same daughter she had treated with such callous misunderstanding all those years ago.

For Lizzie, the past month had been illuminating, as though a great burden had been lifted from her shoulders. Although she would never forget the sacrifices her dad had made for both her and their family, she was grateful that over these past few months the world had suddenly become a much smaller place.

Harriet took her leave of Lizzie and Rob at the airport, without tears and without regret, and when they hugged for one last time it was in the knowledge that it wouldn't *be* the last time.

'We'll see you again, Mum,' promised Lizzie. 'Things are going to be different from now on. Nobody's going to be able to keep the Angels apart ever again.'

On the way back home, Lizzie and Rob drove along the same route that they had come when they first met Harriet at the airport. At Lizzie's request, Rob stopped the car for a few minutes so that they could look out at Lockyer Valley, which was now bathed in a deep red sunset. Whilst they were doing so, Lizzie felt into her dress pocket for a piece of paper that she had deliberately sorted out from her box of old photographs and letters back home, and which she had meant to show to her mother some time whilst she was staying with them. She opened it up. It was the note that had accompanied the thirty pounds Harriet had thrust into her hand on the morning Lizzie and Rob had left for Australia. She read it again, as she had done so many times over the years:

Dearest Lizzie,
   You will always be in our thoughts. We shall miss you, but never forget you.
   Fond love always,
   Your mum, your dad, and all the other Angels.

Lizzie smiled, gently kissed the note, folded it up, and put it back in her pocket. She was so glad she had never taken her mum's advice to destroy it.

The publishers hope that this book has given you enjoyable reading. Large Print Books are especially designed to be as easy to see and hold as possible. If you wish a complete list of our books please ask at your local library or write directly to:

Magna Large Print Books
Magna House, Long Preston,
Skipton, North Yorkshire.
BD23 4ND

This Large Print Book for the partially sighted, who cannot read normal print, is published under the auspices of

THE ULVERSCROFT FOUNDATION